GABE OWENS

C. J. PETIT

Printed in the United States of America

First Printing, 2018

ISBN: 9781092972192

TABLE OF CONTENTS

GABE OWENS 1
PROLOGUE 2
CHAPTER 1 6
CHAPTER 2 36
CHAPTER 3 86
CHAPTER 4 160
CHAPTER 5 201
CHAPTER 6 255
CHAPTER 7 286
CHAPTER 8 312
CHAPTER 9 368
CHAPTER 10 396
EPILOGUE 412

PROLOGUE

July 18, 1884
Northeast of Missoula
Montana Territory

Frank Stanford stepped down from his chestnut gelding, tied him to the hitchrail and then climbed the six steps to the boss' large porch. The large number of steps were necessary because of the slope, but still added to the effect of importance.

He crossed the wide porch then knocked loudly on the door as he removed his hat.

Thirty seconds later, the door swung wide, and a tall, dark-haired young woman asked harshly, "What do you want, Frank?"

"Why good mornin' to you too, Becky," he said with a smile, "I need to see the boss."

She turned began walking away and said over her shoulder, "He's in his office meeting with Sheriff Reinhold."

Frank stepped into the house watched Becky appreciatively as she crossed the front room before he crossed the expansive floor and headed for the office door. That Becky was worth watching, he thought.

Frank stood before the closed doors and heard the muffled discussion just beyond but couldn't quite get the gist of the conversation.

After listening for another two minutes, he finally summoned the courage to rap on the door. The conversation died, and he heard Bob Johnson say, “Come in, Frank!”

Frank had no idea how the boss knew it was him, but opened the door, entered and left it open.

Sheriff Jack Reinhold was already standing with his hat in his hands when Frank walked in. The sheriff looked at Frank, nodded then turned and left.

“What do you need, boss?” Frank asked.

“Frank, I think we have a problem. The sheriff tells me that one of the high climbers has been meeting with the railroad’s station manager.”

“I’ll take care of him.”

“It’s not that simple. We need to take care of both ends of the problem before Wheatley sends anything out. You go handle the high climber and when it’s done, let me know and I’ll go into Missoula and take care of the station manager.”

“Okay, boss. Which one of them is it?”

“That new guy, Willie something-or-other.”

Frank asked “Willie Bernstadt?”

Bob replied, “That’s the boy. I want his body brought back here, too.”

“Yes, sir,” Frank said then turned passed through the doorway, crossed the main room taking one more leering glance at Becky before he exited the house to find Red and Tanner.

Two hours later, the tall timber high climber Willie Bernstadt was near the top of an eighty-foot tall pine sawing through the trunk when he felt the tree wobble more than it should in the low wind. He didn't pay any attention at first, but when the wobble became a more pronounced sway, he finally looked down to the base of the tree and knew he was a dead man.

Two cutters had their axes flying as they hammered chunks out of the tree trunk below him. Willie knew he had less than a minute before he fell and began looking for nearby trees that might provide a possible avenue of escape, but he never even removed his climbing belt before he heard a loud crack from below and the pine began its own death fall. He simply closed his eyes as the tree crashed to the ground and fortunately didn't have to feel the massive trunk crush his chest.

Hack Tanner and Red O'Rourke had to cut the trunk away before dragging Willie's body free then carrying it back to Frank for disposal or whatever other plans he had for it.

Three hours after Willie's demise, Mike Wheatley entered his home just before sunset. It had been a long day, and he was glad it was over.

"Angie, I'm home!" he shouted.

He then hung his hat on the rack near the front door and automatically unbuttoned his jacket as he walked past the parlor and down the hallway toward the kitchen.

"Angie?" he shouted, but again didn't hear a reply.

He entered the kitchen, turned, then froze in his tracks as his mouth dropped open before he asked, “What…”

His query was interrupted by a sharp crack and a cloud of gunsmoke as he clutched at his chest, his eyes confused and stunned by what he was seeing before they closed, and he fell face-first to the floor with his life’s blood pouring across the polished wooden surface.

CHAPTER 1

The westbound train was still an hour out of Moorhead having departed from Minneapolis early that morning.

Gabe Owens sat on the outside of the second row of seats in first class and had struck up a lively conversation with two sisters who were enroute to Bismarck where the older of the pair was to marry a man she'd never met. She was decidedly nervous, especially after having met the very handsome young gentleman who had kept them entertained since boarding the train at Wadena two hours earlier.

Gabe thought it was at least a measure of thoughtfulness that Elsa Sorenson's future husband had anted up for first class tickets for his fiancée rather than letting her ride in one of the less comfortable second-class coaches.

Gabe was dressed in a very stylish, well-tailored dark gray wool suit with a vest, gold watch chain and had what appeared to be a modified bowler hat on the seat next to him. He had the look and manners of a well-bred gentleman.

"So, Mister Owens, will you be staying long in Bismarck?" Anna Sorenson asked.

"Not that long, I'm afraid. I'll just stay long enough to conclude some business that required my personal attention before returning to Minneapolis."

Elsa asked, "What do you do for a living, Mister Owens?"

"I own and operate several haberdasheries throughout the West. Perhaps you've heard of G.R. Owens Haberdashery?"

"I'm sorry, but neither I nor Anna have been very far from Wadena," Elsa replied.

"If I may be so bold as to ask why such a handsome young woman is traveling all the way to Bismarck to marry an unknown suitor when I'm sure that there were many anxious young men in Wadena that would have begged for your hand?"

Elsa sighed and said, "Our father has a good friend in Bismarck who fought with him in the war and he was recently widowed. After my father received his letter, he sent his friend my photograph and offered my hand in marriage. He's very well propertied, and my father assured me that I would be living a comfortable life, so I agreed to the marriage."

"Yet, you have never seen your fiancé?" he asked with raised eyebrows.

"Alas, I have not. But my father assures me that he is quite pleasant-looking."

Gabe imagined that pleasant-looking twenty years ago didn't necessarily equate to pleasant-looking today, but it wasn't his business.

"Are you married?" asked Anna with a smile.

"No, Miss Sorenson."

"Without appearing to be too forward, Mister Owens, pray tell why a gentleman with your means, charm and, if you'll pardon me, rather handsome and very masculine appearance, never married?" asked a surprised Anna.

"I was close once, but when I was off on a business trip, the woman married another and was soon out of my life."

Both Sorenson sisters gaped for a moment before Elsa asked in astonishment, “Was she blind or just insane?”

Gabe smiled and replied, “Angela was neither, but I was apparently too busy to pay her enough attention and she found someone who did. It was much more my fault than hers.”

Before either sister could ask another question, the car suddenly jerked as the other cars began to slam into each other when the locomotive’s drive wheels reversed, creating loud squeals and a display of sparks as they slowed the train. Everyone lurched forward and hung onto the nearest seat.

Everyone knew that something was terribly wrong as they were halfway between stops. As the train began to slow, the passengers craned their eyes out the windows to discover the cause for the emergency delay when a passenger in the front row suddenly stood, turned, faced the others and pulled his Colt.

“Get those hands in the air! Now!” he shouted, almost unnecessarily as most passengers already had done just that.

“Now you folks just behave yourselves and you’ll all be able to get to where you wanna go nice and safe. You just won’t have anything worth keepin’ when you get there,” he said loudly with a grin.

He then turned the pistol to Gabe and said, “You! Stand up and toss your wallet to me.”

As Gabe stared at the cocked pistol with frightened eyes, he slipped his trembling fingers inside his jacket and slid the wallet from the inside left jacket pocket and attempted to flip it to the outlaw, but it just fell straight to the floor in front of him.

His eyes followed it to the floor then he jerked his head back to the outlaw as his eyes went wide and he put his palms out in front of him.

"I'm…I'm…sorry, mister. I…I didn't mean to drop it. Please don't shoot me! Can't I just give it to you?"

The bad man snickered before he snarled, "Now ain't you a real brave boy? Did your mama give you a big, wet kiss and pat your behind before you got on the noisy, scary train? You pick up that wallet and throw it over here or I'll put a .44 through your belly!"

Gabe nodded his head vigorously as he bent at the knees and said, "Yes, sir! Yes, sir!"

The Sorenson sisters were both appalled at his cowardly behavior and momentarily forgot about the danger that the outlaw still presented to them and the other passengers as they watched Gabe Owens pick up his wallet from the floor, then faced the man and tossed it to the center of the aisle.

He then said, "May I return to my seat now? Please? I won't cause you any trouble, sir. I promise."

The outlaw spotted the heavy gold chain crossing his vest and said, "Not till you give me the watch and chain."

Gabe slid the gold watch from the vest, held it reverently in his hand then said, "Please, sir. Let me keep the watch. It's…it's so very special to me. M-m-my m-m-mother gave me the watch for my sixteenth birthday."

The bad man was thoroughly disgusted as he said, "You're gonna give it to me or I'll rip it off your dead body and then go back and have my way with your precious mama!"

"If I throw it to the floor, it will break. It's delicate."

The outlaw rolled his eyes and snarled, "So are you, girly boy. Just step out into the aisle and get on your hands and knees. Then you keep your head down and hold it up for me. If you so much as twitch, you get a .44 in the back of your head."

Gabe removed the watch and slowly edged his way out of his seat into the aisle. He then dropped to the floor onto his knees and began crawling to the thief as all of the other passengers watched, most with looks of disgust at the display.

When he reached just two feet from the man's boots, he stopped and began to sob as he held the watch and chain over his head with his left hand while he kept his head down as instructed.

Joe Hill snatched the watch from his shaking hand and wanted to shoot the big sissy, but then he made a mistake when he popped open the watch to see how fancy it was. He had already dismissed the coward on the floor as a danger. What real man would suffer that kind of humiliation just to protect a stupid watch?

As soon as his left hand was hard on the floor again, Gabe suddenly lunged with his right hand, wrapped it behind Joe's left boot at the ankle and yanked as hard as he could.

Joe Hill caught the quick movement but was too late to avoid being thrown off balance and falling backwards to the floor, sending the watch flying, but the Colt remained in his grip as he crashed into the aisle.

Before the outlaw even hit the floor, Gabe's right arm, which was already extended backwards after he had yanked Joe Hill's foot out from under him, came shooting back at the robber with a closed fist and slammed a crushing blow into Joe's crotch.

Joe was just about to pull his trigger at the suddenly attacking coward when the shock of falling was replaced with an incredibly intense pain making him scream in agony, then drop his pistol as he grabbed his nether regions.

Gabe then scrambled over the shrieking outlaw chief, grabbed his still-cocked Colt and then as soon as he could get past the rolling man, stood and smashed the top of his skull with the Colt's barrel. The screaming stopped, and Gabe took a few moments to retrieve both his watch and wallet. He slipped the wallet back into his jacket pocket but slid the watch into his pants pocket. His job wasn't done by a long measure.

He finally looked at the startled passengers and turned his jacket open, exposing a badge and a pistol in a shoulder holster.

"I'm Northern Pacific Special Agent Gabe Owens. This man is one of the Dakota Gang that has been plaguing our railroad for the past year. Now I need to go and get the other five. I don't believe that any more will be coming into this car, so I need everyone to remain in your seats and stay calm."

They were all still staring as the fastidious gentlemen began pulling pigging strings out of his pocket to bind the outlaw, then stopped after he checked the man's pulse and found them unnecessary.

He then ripped off the man's gunbelt and strapped it around his waist before taking off his jacket and remarkably, took time to fold it neatly before setting it on the seat next to his hat.

Then he smiled at Anna Sorenson and said, "Would you mind watching my things, Miss Sorenson? I'd be forever grateful."

Then everyone's mesmerized eyes followed him as he trotted down the aisle to the back of the car, opened the door and after closing it again, simply disappeared.

After he'd gone, Anna Sorenson reached across the aisle, picked up his coat and hat then set them on her lap.

Gabe crossed over the gap between cars easily and when he stared into the first of the two other passenger cars, he stopped and blew out his breath. There was no one in the aisle, but he took a few seconds to step down from the car's steel platform to the ground, looked left and then right. There were no obstructions on the tracks, which he hadn't expected to find in the first place because he suspected the engineer and fireman were in on the robbery.

If the Dakota Gang was following its usual method, the car he'd just found empty had already been robbed by two of the gang members who had taken all the valuables and firearms and exited the back of the car where they joined the last two, who had just robbed the last passenger car. All of them should now be heading for the baggage car which also acted as the mail car and held the safe and the expressman.

He knew that the others would be expecting Joe Hill, the recently deceased leader of the gang, to return from the first-class passenger coach soon. Joe always robbed the first-class passengers, so he could keep all of the good jewelry himself to distribute to the ladies he would try to impress later. He also knew from previous reports that Joe spent longer in the car than the others did because he also searched the women for jewelry they might be hiding, which gave him an extra minute or two before the others would start wondering what happened to their boss.

Gabe then began walking slowly along the outside of the second passenger car not bothering to look into the car itself. He then heard the sound of hooves on the other side of the train and knew the last member of the band had arrived with their getaway horses.

He then climbed onto the second car's platform, glanced into the last passenger car to make sure none of the gang was there, saw only frightened passengers then took one step to the other side of the car's platform and heard the hooves drawing closer. He didn't stick his head out enough to look down the other side of the train because he didn't want to be spotted yet.

He just brought the cocked Colt level, aimed it at the spot where the rider would soon pass and waited. Without those horses, the gang couldn't escape. Everything now depended on the intelligence he'd already gathered about the consistent plan the gang followed when they robbed the trains and hoped that the engineer and fireman would try and play the innocent victims and stay out of it.

Gabe listened as the hooves grew louder and when they were about twenty yards out, he finally stepped forward exposing himself to the other side of the train, glanced quickly to his left, saw four men trying to break into the baggage car then turned back to his right just as the rider spotted him and began to pull his pistol.

The oncoming rider should have shouted a warning to his partners just two hundred feet away, but he must have been too anxious to avoid being shot as his pistol cleared leather a second too late.

Gabe's borrowed Colt spat smoke and fire along with a .44 caliber missile that quickly covered the eighty-seven feet and drilled through the rider's chest on the left side, mangling his heart into so much meat. The rider dropped to the horse's neck then tumbled off to the side.

He hadn't hit the dirt before Gabe was already leaping to the ground from the platform with the Colt in his right hand and racing toward the baggage car. There were four thieves left and he only had four live rounds in the Colt, assuming Joe Hill didn't load all six cylinders but if he had, he could miss once, but wasn't counting on it.

The other four outlaws were all startled by the sudden change in their situation and none had their hammer loops off. The job had been going smoothly, they had all of the passengers' guns and knew that shortly they'd get the expressman to open the doors. But now they suddenly had a gunfight on their hands, and each turned and reached for their pistols.

Gabe was within a hundred feet when he suddenly dropped down to a knee, let everything steady and aimed at the tight group standing before the baggage car door. He fired just a second later, his shot smashing into the shoulder of the outlaw on the far right, dropping him to the ground.

By then the other three had their pistols free and were bringing them to bear, the man on Gabe's far left firing first. The ground about four feet away at his eleven o'clock position exploded when the man's shot hit the ground just as Gabe unleashed his next round, hitting the man last man standing on the right. The bullet tore through the man's gut, making him drop his pistol as he fell to the ground face forward.

Gabe then felt a .44 rip at his right shirt sleeve but didn't catch any skin as he fired at the first shooter, but his shot was high as the man had just dropped to the ground as he fired.

He knew he probably had only one shot left and had to make it count as he took that extra fraction of a second to let his barrel and sights steady before he fired the fifth time at the only standing bandit. But after his partner had dropped to safety, he decided to follow suit but hadn't made that decision soon enough, when Gabe's .44 ripped a large chunk of tissue from the right side of his neck and blood exploded from his severed carotid artery as he fell flat on his face and the last of his life's blood squirted into the face of the lone surviving gang member who was about to fire at Gabe.

The sensation of being soaked by the hot blood of his partner unnerved Carl Jensen more than anything else could have, so any thought of pulling the trigger evaporated as he buried his face into the dirt, tossed his pistol away and put his palms out in front of him.

"Don't shoot, mister! I give up!" he shouted.

Gabe already dropped the Colt and had his hand heading for his Webley when he had seen the pistol fly, making the man's shout unnecessary. So, he stood, picked up the Colt and walked toward the robber keeping him under the muzzle of what he assumed was an empty pistol.

He reached the man, picked up his pistol then exchanged it for the empty pistol, which he shoved into his waist. He did a quick check of the others and found one still alive; the one who'd taken the shot to his shoulder. He was bleeding extensively, and Gabe wasn't sure if he'd survive much longer, but the robbery had been thwarted and the Dakota Gang was no more.

He'd done the hard part of the job, now came the far less exciting but just as necessary, after-shootout cleanup.

He stepped over to the healthy gang member and told him to stay put, asked him a couple of questions about how the train was stopped then turned to the baggage car.

He shouted, "Okay, Harry, you can come out now! We need to clean this up!"

The baggage car door slowly opened and the expressman's face peeked out. After hearing all the gunfire, he wasn't sure what had happened but when he heard someone shout his name, he figured it had to be a man who worked for the Northern Pacific.

"Who are you?" he asked as he looked at Gabe.

"Gabe Owens. Go and get the conductor and brakeman and we'll start cleaning up my mess. I've got to go and talk to the engineer and fireman. Keep an eye on this one with your shotgun."

"*You're Gabe Owens?*" the expressman asked in apparent surprise.

"I was the last time I checked," Gabe replied before he turned and began walking toward the smoking locomotive three hundred feet away.

He still had the second outlaw's Colt in his right hand as he strode past the passenger cars, aware of the faces that were all watching him from the other side of the windows. Their property would have to be returned before the train began rolling again, but that would come after he had his chat with the fireman and engineer.

Carl Jensen, the only surviving gang member had just confirmed his suspicion that the engineer and fireman were both being paid by Joe Hill to stop the train.

He could probably drive the train to its next stop at Hawley, but he'd let the engineer and fireman take the train as far as Bismarck where he'd have them arrested.

He reached the coal car and the fireman, Jack Wheeler, stuck his head out and asked, "What the hell happened?"

"They were going to rob the train. Can you hold it here for another few minutes while we get everything cleared up?"

The engineer, Jimmy Norquist, asked, "Who are you?"

"Gabe Owens. I was heading to Billings to check on suspected theft of railroad property when one of them tried to rob the first-class passengers. I took him down and was lucky enough to get the rest. I'm glad that you saw what was happening and stopped the train."

The engineer said, "I kinda had to because that last one was holding the horses on the tracks."

As the fireman nodded to back his story, the engineer then asked, "You kill 'em all?"

"Yes, sir. They're all dead. So, if you could hold the train here for another fifteen minutes or so, I'll let you know when it's done by firing a single shot."

"Thanks, Mister Owens," the engineer said after letting loose a long breath of relief believing they were all dead and no one was left to tell of his and Jack's complicity.

Gabe gave him a short wave then turned and began walking back to the carnage.

It took closer to twenty minutes for him, the expressman, brakeman and the conductor to get the bodies loaded into the stock car with their horses. The shoulder wounded outlaw had died from blood loss, leaving only one surviving member of the Dakota Gang. They bound him in cord from the baggage car and left him with Harry Bishop, the expressman, to watch over with the car's shotgun and left all of their weapons with him as well.

The conductor, Ed Felton, said he'd handle returning the stolen valuables and weapons to the passengers after Gabe told him that nothing had been stolen from the first-class travelers. Before returning to the first-class car, he told the four men that if anyone asked, Carl Jensen was dead, and all three of them readily agreed to keep it quiet, suspecting what Gabe already knew about the engineer and fireman.

Finally, Gabe took the first Colt he had relieved from Joe Hill, pointed it into the air and pulled the trigger, not expecting it to fire, but more out of curiosity. The Colt bucked in his hand and sent its last .44 skyward. Gabe smiled, shook his head and reinserted the pistol into his waist. He hadn't had to fire a single round from the Webley. It was a very good pistol, but the shorter barrel lowered its accuracy compared to the Colt, and he appreciated the added accuracy in this situation.

The train began rolling westward again as Gabe walked back down the aisle of the first-class coach as the passengers gawked. He removed the Colt from his waist, and as he glanced for his jacket, he found the seat empty then turned to a smiling Anna Sorenson who had the jacket and hat on her lap.

She handed him the hat, which he popped onto his head, then surprised him when she stood, unfolded the jacket and held it out shoulder high. Gabe smiled, slipped his left arm through the sleeve, took the Colt into his left hand and then slid his right arm down the sleeve as Anna stood close behind him and then ran her hand down his arm, pretending to brush it free.

He turned and smiled at Anna and said, "I'll take care of the buttons, Miss Sorenson, and thank you for your help."

Anna smiled back and all but curtsied as she said, "You're welcome, Mister Owens," before returning to her seat.

He was putting his gold watch back into his vest when Anna asked, "Mister Owens, did you know that the train was going to be robbed?"

Gabe sat down and replied, "I had rumors that the Dakota Gang might try and rob one of the Northern Pacific's trains soon, so I did some checking and concluded that this train would be a likely candidate for their attention. But it was just an educated guess, and I wasn't about to alarm anyone."

Elsa then asked, "So, all of that acting was all planned? How did you know he'd ask for your watch?"

"The gang followed the same pattern in each of their previous robberies. They'd get the train stopped then the gang leader, Joe Hill, would rob the first-class passengers while four other members of his gang robbed the other passenger cars, taking any guns that anyone had on them.

"Once the cars were robbed, they'd go back to the baggage car, steal the mail and any money from the car and then have the gang's last member bring their horses to the baggage car for their getaway. Joe Hill always seemed to have an eye for nice jewelry, although he preferred women's trinkets. I thought he'd really be impressed with the heavy gold chain and watch, then I'd be able to get close to him."

Anna smiled and said, "That was a very brave thing to do, Mister Owens. You had my heart beating like a hummingbird."

"I hope I didn't cause you or your sister too much distress," Gabe said as he smiled.

"Oh, no. We were both thrilled to have witnessed such an extraordinary display of courage and skill," replied Elsa.

Then Anna asked, "Are you still going to Bismarck now?"

"No, miss. I'll be getting off at Moorhead and sending some telegrams before returning to the main offices of the Northern Pacific in Minneapolis to fill out my reports."

She then asked, "Was that true about the woman not marrying you, or was that just a story and you really are married?"

"No, that was true. It's better to use the truth whenever possible if one takes on a second persona."

"Do you ever go to Wadena?" Anna asked.

"Sometimes. I go wherever the Northern Pacific sends me."

She smiled and said, "If you do, just ask anyone where the Sorenson farm is, and they'll tell you."

"I'll do that, Miss Sorenson," Gabe replied.

"Please call me Anna," she said with a hopeful smile then added, "I wouldn't be as silly as that other girl."

Gabe smiled back but knew he would probably never stop in Wadena.

After all of the outlaws' bodies, horses, and weapons had been taken off the train at Moorhead, Gabe waved goodbye to the Sorenson sisters and received return waves from everyone in the first-class passenger car as he stood on the platform.

After the train pulled away, he entered the baggage area where they had stored the only surviving gang member waiting for the sheriff. Gabe had ensured that his exit from the train wasn't noticed by the engineer or fireman.

"Am I gonna hang?" asked a dejected Carl Jensen.

Gabe looked at him and replied, "I'm not even sure what they'll charge you with. What's your name, anyway?"

"Carl Jensen. I didn't shoot anybody. Really. None of us ever did, except for Joe. He shot a conductor once."

"The conductor's name was Jeff Powers. He had a wife and three children. I wish I could have seen him hang."

"Did you kill him?"

"Not intentionally. I hit him pretty hard with his pistol, though. I needed him down and out of the way for a while."

"The engineer and fireman were in on it, too. You ain't gonna let 'em go, are you?"

"Nope. I'll send a telegram back to my boss in Minneapolis and I'll have them arrested in Bismarck and sent back."

"Did you know that they were helping us?"

"I was pretty sure. When I reviewed how you did the jobs, two things stuck out. Jimmy Norquist and Jack Wheeler were running the locomotive on each of the robberies, which was a highly unlikely coincidence, and none of the passengers that I talked to ever saw any obstruction on the tracks."

"Is that why you were on the train?"

"Yup."

"How come there weren't more of ya?"

"It was just a hunch and there aren't a lot of us. This was the second time I've taken this train. Your gang was remarkably consistent in your timing, too. I'm guessing that you waited until there was a new moon, so a posse would have to wait until the next day to track you. Is that right?"

"I don't know, Joe decided all that."

"Well, Mister Jensen, I'll tell you what. When we get you to the jail, if you'll write out a statement saying how Jimmy Norquist and Jack Wheeler helped the gang rob the trains, I'll see if I can get them to just send you to prison rather than hang you."

Carl quickly replied, "I'll do it! Do you figure that they'll let that happen?"

"I think we can work it out."

Clay County Sheriff John Collins arrived five minutes later and as his deputies handled the bodies, horses and weapons, he and Gabe escorted the prisoner back to the jail.

As they walked, Gabe gave a verbal report to the sheriff about the robbery and the gunfight. He hadn't quite finished by the time Carl was in his cell and his wrists free from the binding cords.

When Gabe finished his narrative, Sheriff Collins said, "I'll need your statement, Mister Owens. Can you hang around for the trial? It'll be in two or three days."

"I need to talk to you about that, Sheriff. I've talked with Mister Jensen and he'll agree to plead guilty to robbery. As the representative of the Northern Pacific, I'd agree to a plea bargain after he writes a statement about the complicity of the engineer and fireman. I think a ten year sentence would be acceptable."

The sheriff shrugged and said, "If you can come back in a couple of hours, I'll go and talk to the prosecutor."

Gabe pulled out his gold watch, checked the time, then wound it as he said, "I have another five hours before the eastbound train comes through, so I'll just head over to the diner, and get something to eat. I'll see you at three o'clock to write my statement."

"Good enough."

Gabe stood, put on his modified bowler and left the jail. When he reached the boardwalk, he turned left and headed for Madeline's Diner. He'd been there a few times before and liked the food but had to remind himself to pick up his travel bag in the claim area before he headed back. He'd forgotten to do that twice before and it was downright embarrassing to have them send it back after he'd gone.

———

After he finished eating and left the diner, he stopped at the Western Union office and sent telegrams back to his boss, Herb Erikson, giving him the basics of the operation. When he returned to the jail, the sheriff was still meeting with the prosecutor, but the deputy said he should be back soon, so Gabe spent the time writing his statement.

He had just finished when Sheriff Collins returned, told him that the prosecutor had agreed to the plea and sent over the agreement. Carl Jensen wrote out the statement for Gabe about Jimmy Norquist and Jack Wheeler then he signed the plea agreement and Gabe's work was done, at least in Moorhead.

He then walked back to the depot, remembered to pick up his travel bag then had to talk to the ticket master, station manager and baggage handler about the robbery and the gang's demise while he waited for his train. He left out the involvement of the engineer and fireman, though. Gabe preferred not to talk about his cases, but usually did when asked by fellow employees of the railroad. He wanted them to know that men like him and the other special agents of the Northern Pacific would do what they could to keep them safe.

By nine o'clock, he was in the caboose of the eastbound train and after playing a few hands of poker with the brakeman and having told him the story, minus the actions of the engineer and fireman, he removed his jacket, hung his shoulder holster and set aside Joe Hill's still empty Colt before removing his shoes and just stretching out on one of the bunks. He was sound asleep just fifteen minutes later.

Gabe's eyes popped open when they came to a stop at Elk River, fifteen miles north of Minneapolis. He didn't know how his brain knew where the train was or even what time it was when he slid his feet from the cot, set them on the floor of the caboose and began pulling on his shoes. He felt the stubble on his face, knew he needed a bath and a shave, but that would have to wait. He hurriedly donned his vest, put the watch in place before putting on his shoulder holster and jacket. He pulled on his hat, left the caboose and trotted over to the station. After he used the rest facilities, he quickly returned to the caboose, knowing this was just a watering stop and the train would be moving soon.

Forty minutes later, the train hissed to a loud stop at the expansive passenger station in Minneapolis and home of the eastern headquarters and the largest repair shop and storage facility for the Northern Pacific Railroad.

He grabbed his travel bag, left the empty caboose, stepped down onto the platform and was only mildly surprised to see his boss waiting for him.

“Howdy, Herb,” Gabe said with a smile.

Herb Erikson wasn’t smiling as he stepped closer, and Gabe assumed that meant he had a job for him already and he’d probably be leaving in a day or two. It was he nature of the business, he told himself.

“Welcome back, Gabe,” Herb said, “Great job stopping that bunch. You can fill me in back at my office.”

He turned, and Gabe got in step with him as they crossed the large platform, maneuvering around the passengers and families.

“Can’t I even go back to the house to clean up and get changed, Herb?”

"Not this time, Gabe. I need to talk to you. Tell me what happened on the way."

"I wrote my report on the way back, and I have the only surviving gang member's statement about Jack Wheeler and Jimmy Norquist who stopped the train to let them do the robbery."

Herb looked over at him as they walked to the offices and said, "You were right, then. It still makes me sick that two of our own were involved."

Then Gabe asked, "You have another job for me?"

"Maybe. Do you remember the Stevens fiasco in Oregon about a dozen years ago?"

"It was before my time, but I heard enough about it."

"Well, we think we've found the same problem only closer to home."

They turned into the company offices building as Gabe asked, "Timber poaching?"

"Yup, but with a twist that made it a job for you that might make you want to turn it down."

Gabe wondered what differences were involved as he recalled the big lumber poaching scandal that had almost scuttled the Northern Pacific Railroad in the early '70s.

The railroad's surveyed route took it through some heavily forested areas in Oregon and the land granted to the railroad was then harvested for making ties for the hundreds of miles of tracks that they would be laying. It required a massive amount of trees and soon, poachers began arriving on the railroad's land to cut down the trees and use the lumber for themselves.

The railroad had sent Stevens to solve the problem, but he made it worse instead. He not only didn't fix the issue, but had profited from it and when caught, exposed the fact that the railroad itself was poaching timber from government-owned land.

It was a nasty business and the railroad was only saved when Congress failed to fund the prosecution of the case, probably for political rather than fiscal reasons. The NP had realized how close it had been to bankruptcy, and the poaching of timber had become a delicate subject and the harvesting of the forests was watched much more closely, but obviously, they must not have watched closely enough. Although, to be fair, there were thousands of square miles of trees that could be poached and keeping an eye on all of them would be difficult.

They turned into Herb's offices, passed his secretary, and entered his private office then Gabe closed the door behind them as he always did when they were discussing a case.

After he took his seat behind the desk, Herb opened his center drawer and pulled out some papers as Gabe sat down. Gabe set his travel bag on the floor put his hat on top then pulled his report and Jensen's statement from his jacket's inside pocket and slid them onto Herb's desk.

"So, Herb, who has been stealing trees?" he asked.

Herb didn't answer immediately but glanced down at the various-sized papers in his hands. After a few seconds, he looked up at Gabe with a decidedly somber face.

“A few months ago, we received hints of a possible poaching operation in western Montana, so I sent a man out there to check on the situation.”

“Who did you send?” Gabe asked.

“You wouldn’t know him. I sent a man named Willie Bernstadt to investigate the stories.”

“Who is he? He’s not a special agent.”

“He was sworn in before he left, so technically, he was. But I needed a lumberjack to go there and get a job, so he could blend in and find out the facts of the matter.”

“Hell, Herb, I probably know more about trees than I do about locomotives. Why didn’t you ask me to go?”

Herb put up his hand and said, “I know, I know, but I needed to send someone that no one knew. Your name is pretty well known in railroad circles, even if most of them don’t know what you look like. Besides, there was another reason I couldn’t send you, Gabe. I sent Willie to Missoula.”

Gabe sighed then said, “I understand your concern, Herb, but that was in the past. Angela married Mike Wheatley and that was the end of it. Anyway, is that what this job is? You need me to go and clean up what Willie discovered?”

“I need you to go and handle that problem, but things have gotten much more serious. I received just a single report from Willie, and he outlined the basics of the poaching operation. A big-time logging company owner named Bob Johnson built a large logging camp outside of the land grant and started harvesting timber on his land six years ago. When he had almost stripped his land bare, he just shifted his loggers onto Northern Pacific land and government land rather than move his big logging camp. He was doing it for almost a year before Mike Wheatley got wind of it. That's when we sent Willie."

Gabe asked, "So, how did it get worse?"

"I just received a long telegram from the Missoula County Sheriff. He reported that Mike Wheatley was found shot in the kitchen of his house and a second man's body was found with a knife in his gut, too. That man was later identified as Willie Bernstadt."

The news rocked Gabe, but after a few seconds he asked softly, "What happened to Angela?"

"I have no idea. Her name wasn't mentioned in the telegram."

"Did Mike Wheatley know that Willie was a special agent?"

Herb nodded and replied, "He was the only contact Willie had and there's one more thing that you need to know, Gabe. The same day that Willie and Mike died, I received a telegram from Willie, which he was only supposed to use in an emergency. All it said was 'Wheatley part of it'."

Gabe sat back and asked, "As much as I thought that Angela made a poor choice, I never would have thought that Mike Wheatley would do anything like that, Herb. He sure didn't need the money, either. Did it sound right to you?"

"No, that surprised me quite a bit. That's why I'm sending you, aside from the obvious fact that you're the best we've got."

Even as they were talking, Gabe's analytic mind was working on the double homicide.

"Herb, did you issue Willie a pistol?"

"No, but he might have bought one when he suspected that Mike was involved."

Gabe nodded and said, "Okay, I'll take the next train to Missoula after I read those reports."

"Do you need anything else, Gabe?"

"When will they be sending a replacement station manager?"

"They're promoting Joe Lofton, the yard manager, and sending a new yard manager in the next few days," Herb said as he slid the papers across the desk before adding, "This is all I have right now."

Gabe nodded, said, "Joe's a good man," and then accepted the papers from Herb and read them carefully, looking for any new information. He was especially interested in why Willie might have suspected that Mike was involved in the poaching operation.

But the evidence was scant, and Willie's report was too short of details and grammatically so bad that it was difficult to understand and almost appeared to be written in some form of code.

Gabe slid the papers back to Herb, who was reading his report, stood, picked up his hat and travel bag then said, "I'll let you know what I find," then turned, opened the door and left the office.

As he walked through the building toward the exit, he was trying to think more about the double homicide but found that memories of Angela were pushing it to the back of his mind.

Angela was one of those girls who drew attention as she walked by, and Gabe had been smitten immediately. He'd known her for less than a month when he'd proposed, but she had surprised him when she demurred. Then he had to go out west to Billings and when he returned three weeks later, she told him that she was marrying Mike Wheatley, which did far more than just disappoint him.

He didn't attend the wedding and didn't see her again after Mike had been given the position of station manager in Missoula. Now he wondered if she had any children from the union.

Gabe was curious to know what she was doing after the twin killings in her home. *What if she had been the one to discover Mike's body? How would she deal with that?* She would have to be the one responsible for arranging for his burial and all of the other things necessary after someone died, too. She may have broken his heart, but he still didn't want anything bad to happen to Angela.

It would take him three days to make the trip to Missoula and was already planning his logistics for the trip and what he would need once he arrived. He certainly wouldn't be going as a haberdasher. For this job, he'd be going as Gabe Owens, Northern Pacific special agent.

After he got to his house, the one he had purchased when he thought he was going to marry Angela, he took a quick bath, shaved, changed into much more comfortable clothing and began packing for the trip.

He had some extra-large saddlebags that he'd use, and packed two changes of clothing, his toiletry items, a sewing kit, not reserved for fixing torn britches, a small bottle of alcohol, not for imbibing, and his spare ammunition. He had to carry two different size cartridges and packed four boxes of the common .44 cartridges for his Remington Model 1875 and his two Webleys, and four boxes of large .50-95 Express cartridges for his Winchester '76. He glanced at his Sharps but decided that he'd stick with the Winchester for this trip.

Since acquiring the big bore Winchester, he'd found that the only real advantage to the Sharps was the added range. Granted, it was a hell of a lot of range, but he hadn't had to fire it on a job in over two years now. All he used it for was target practice, but Gabe practiced a lot with his weapons.

With the saddlebags packed, he left them by the door and walked to Martin's Livery a block away and picked up his Morgan gelding, Dancer. He had two saddles at the livery, depending on whether he thought most of the work would be done in or near a town or if it would take him out into the wilds, and took the heavier saddle with the bedroll and slicker.

After saddling Dancer, he rode back to the house and brought his Winchester out to Dancer then returned and lugged his heavy saddlebags to his horse before riding him to the stock corral at the depot. Once there, he left him with Charlie Adams, the stock manager, then walked to the station and awaited the 1:10 train.

Less than an hour later, Gabe was rolling out of Minneapolis just a few hours after having returned.

He knew that the train would be taking on coal and water at Brainard, so he'd have enough time to go and visit his parents, who lived just two blocks from the train station. He visited whenever he could, but most of them were just like this one where he'd pass a couple of stories then say his goodbyes and head off to another job. He knew his father understood but felt as if he was cheating his mother.

He was still thinking about the two murders that the sheriff had reported in the lengthy telegram. *Somehow, Willie had shot Mike as he was plunging a knife into him?* Maybe Willie was threatening him with exposure in the kitchen and Mike had grabbed a kitchen knife, taken the bullet and then killed Willie. Usually, someone with a pistol in his hand never lets anyone with a knife get close enough to make use of the blade, so it sounded odd.

Gabe spent the entire trip going through different scenarios to make it work, and he found a couple that might be plausible, but even they were unlikely. Still, what bothered him the most was wondering where Angela was when all this was happening.

By the time the train slowed to enter Brainard, the only thing Gabe was close to discovering was a headache. He knew from experience that many crimes didn't seem to make any sense at first glance and could only be understood after talking to witnesses and examining the evidence. He hoped that the sheriff had done a proper investigation, but he doubted it.

Most lawmen out West were usually overworked and didn't have the time to conduct a full examination of the evidence, especially if it was an open and shut as this one had been described. But then again, he couldn't imagine a double homicide inside the city limits as being that routine in a town the size of Missoula.

Gabe stepped down on the platform, leaving his saddlebags on the train, walked quickly across to the boardwalk and headed west down the main thoroughfare. He then turned left on Fourth Avenue and spotted his parents' house two hundred yards ahead. There was light coming from the first floor's windows, so he knew his mother was home, which wasn't a surprise, but he hoped his father was there.

He turned down the long, bricked walkway and trotted up the stairs,then opened the door and walked inside, inhaling the immediate aroma of baking chicken. After he hung his hat on one of the brass hooks on the wall near the door, he headed for the kitchen.

"Mom, it's Gabe!" he said loudly as he walked down the hallway.

He was greeted by a much deeper voice when his father shouted, "Gabe! It's about time you stopped by!"

Gabe entered the kitchen, saw his mother at the cookstove smiling at him and then was bear hugged by his father.

"So, what have you been up to that's kept you away for so long?" he asked as he grinned at his son.

"Just work, Dad," he answered as he stepped to the cookstove and kissed his mother on the cheek.

"You're just in time for supper," she said as she began setting another place at the table.

"Mom, no food for me. My train is leaving in a few minutes," he replied and almost grimaced when he saw the disappointment in her eyes.

Gabe told them where he was going and that he'd tell them about it on his return trip and promised he'd stay longer.

"Is it going to be dangerous for you, Gabe?" his father asked.

"I'd be surprised if it wasn't. There were some shenanigans going on up there that involved possible timber poaching and it sounds as if someone is getting nervous."

His mother then asked, “What about Angela? What do you know about Angela?”

Gabe shook his head and replied, “Not a word, Mom. There wasn’t anything about her in any of the telegrams or reports. I’ll find out when I get there.”

His mother then wagged her finger at him as she said, “Well, Gabriel, you had better stay a day or two on your return trip if you know what’s good for you!”

Gabe nodded then kissed his mother on the cheek again before he turned, left the kitchen and headed out the front door.

He made it back to the train in plenty of time and aimed for the caboose, so he’d be able to get some sleep on the long, two-day trip. The other advantage of staying in the caboose was the availability of coffee.

By midnight, he was passing out of Minnesota and into Dakota Territory.

CHAPTER 2

Joe Lofton looked curiously at the telegram that had just arrived from the company, then left the office of the station manager that he'd been using since Mike Wheatley's death. He hunted down Jim Clover, the stock manager, and when he found him on the far side of the corral, waved him over.

"What do you need, Joe?" Jim asked when he was close.

"I just got a wire from Minneapolis about our new station manager."

"Who is it? I hope he's not one of the boss' snooty kids."

Joe grinned before he said, "You're looking at him. They gave me the job and will be sending a new yard manager in a week or so."

Jim slowly shook his head before replying, "Well, I guess I'll just go ahead and pack my bags, 'cause I sure couldn't work for an ornery cuss like you."

Joe laughed before Jim broke into a big grin and smacked Joe on the shoulder.

"Well, it's about time, Joe! They shoulda gave it to you last time. Maybe you would have been the one to get shot."

Joe lost his grin then paused and said, "I'm going to go and tell Ella. I hope she's not worried, not after what happened to Mike."

"Aw, don't worry, Joe. There was somethin' goin' on that we didn't know about and you'll be okay."

"I don't know, Jim. But I guess Ella will be happy about the extra fifty dollars a month, so it'll be okay."

"What wife wouldn't be happy about that?" Jim asked, wishing he hadn't brought up Mike's death.

"Well, I'm heading to the house for a little bit and give her the news. The kids will be happy, too."

Jim waved to Joe as he trotted away and hoped that he'd be okay. Deep down, he thought that being station manager was like a death sentence with Wheatley's and the stranger's death in his kitchen. He knew that there was something else going on and it wasn't some lover's quarrel like most folks thought.

But one thing that all of the Northern Pacific employees knew was that the railroad would be sending a special agent to do a real investigation and they all hoped that they'd send Gabe Owens. He was the best they had.

The trip along the northern plains wasn't inspirational but wasn't meant to be. After stopping in Bismarck, the crew was changed, and Gabe had a new poker partner for the rest of the trip. He checked on Dancer whenever the train was stopped to take on coal and brought him oats and some apples when they were available, brushed him down and talked to him, apologizing for the long train ride.

Dancer was short by some standards but was typical of the breed. He was also extremely nimble and would have made a perfect cow horse if he'd been bought by some rancher or cowhand. But Gabe had found Dancer when he was just a yearling in a stock corral outside of Minneapolis and bought him on sight. He was a deep black with four white stockings and a four-point star on his forehead. Gabe had spent two years just befriending Dancer before he rode him. He was now Gabe's only mount and he would trust Dancer with his life and had already done so twice.

———

The train entered Montana Territory early Saturday night on the twenty-first of July, and Gabe still marveled at the rapid change technology was bringing to the world. Just two days earlier, he'd left Moorhead, returned to Minneapolis and was already leaving Dakota Territory going the other way. Fifteen years ago, it would have taken him more than two weeks to go this far, and that was if he'd only taken a horse. If he'd been driving a covered wagon, it would have taken him almost a month.

He pulled out his ever-present Webley and examined the small pistol. Fifteen years ago, there weren't any cartridge revolvers. He slid the pistol back into his shoulder holster and shook his head, wondering what other new marvels would be created in the next fifteen years. Who knew what was on the horizon? Maybe they'd even invent a flying machine.

He'd tried not to think too much about what he would be facing in Missoula because after his initial befuddlement over the possible reasons for the murders, he knew that if he spent more time trying to resolve the issue before he had had more facts, it would only make him even more confused. But he did grow more concerned about Angela as the train rolled west.

———

Frank Stanford waited for Bob Johnson to arrive at his house as he did every morning, even on Sundays. He'd been working as his camp foreman since they'd started and ran a tight, if not heavy-handed operation. He also oversaw the other side of the business, the one that Bob pretended he didn't know anything about but directed in detail.

There were sixty-four workers on the expansive camp, from the lumberjacks, sawmill operators, and laborers to the cooks. It was as complete as most small towns with a smithy and even a bakery. Bob Johnson was the only one in the camp with a live-in woman, but now that Wheatley's wife was in his house, Frank couldn't see it staying that way much longer. He was hoping that Bob would keep the new blond, then toss Becky out and send her his way. She was a real handful, that one, and he liked a fighter.

Bob arrived at precisely nine o'clock, entering the cabin without knocking. Frank had coffee waiting in the kitchen area and poured a cup when he heard the door open.

"Mornin', boss," he said as he sat down at the table.

"Morning. Any news?" Bob asked as he took a seat across from his foreman.

"They got a telegram late yesterday and promoted the yard manager to station manager, which is good 'cause we know him and he's not a problem. They said they'll be sendin' a new yard manager though."

"The burials all done, and the sheriff's reports written and approved?"

"Yes, sir. Read 'em myself. They murdered each other. Case closed."

Bob smiled, took a sip of the too-strong coffee, and asked, "So, how are we doing on the NP section?"

"We've cut about half of it, but I've already sent some crews over to the government section because of the road. It's closer to the sawmill and all downhill."

"Okay. Keep up the good work, Frank," Bob said as he stood, leaving the almost full cup of coffee on the table before walking away.

———

It was wasn't quite sunset at this time of the year at this latitude, despite the hour, as the train pulled out of Bears Mouth, the last stop before Missoula. Gabe was already preparing for his arrival in Missoula and was in the stock car with Dancer and one other horse. He'd cleaned and oiled his weapons and was only wearing one of his Webleys as he began saddling his Morgan.

He was reasonably well-rested, at least as much as anyone could be after riding in trains almost continuously for four days now. He'd shaved and eaten at Helena while they took on more coal and water. Gabe liked Helena and knew that it had better facilities than one would expect in a city in the middle of Montana. With as many gold-created millionaires that still called it home, it provided luxuries that were rarely found West of the Missouri until one reached San Francisco.

Now that he was close to Missoula, he spent some more time reviewing the situation. As Mike was a railroad employee, he was sure the sheriff would expect an NP special agent to investigate his death as it was criminal in nature, but would anyone else be anticipating his arrival? All of the railroad workers probably expected him to show up to investigate the station manager's death, but his real problem was that he was totally in the dark about the overall situation. He'd been in similar circumstances before and he knew the first thing he'd have to do is gather information if he wanted to stay alive long enough to get to the truth, and his best source of information in this case would be Joe Lofton.

———

The train pulled into Missoula a little later than scheduled at 9:50. Gabe slid open the doors to the stock car as the train slowed then waited for the train to stop near the stock corral before he dropped down onto the shorter stock platform and led Dancer into the corral.

Jim Clover saw him, noticed that the man had that look about him then grinned as he asked, "You wouldn't be Gabe Owens, would you?"

"I am, but before I even get some food, I need information. Where can I find Joe Lofton?"

"Well, it's kinda late, but his house is on the corner of Higgins and Pine. Just follow that road there, that's Higgins. Pine is three blocks south. His house is the white one with red shutters on the right side of the street."

"I appreciate it. What's your name?" Gabe asked as he offered his hand.

Jim gave him an appropriately manly handshake and replied, "Jim Clover. Glad to meet ya."

"Good to meet you, Jim."

"I feel a lot better now that you're here."

Gabe smiled, mounted Dancer then waved before he trotted into town. He knew he might be waking Joe, but he knew he had to see him before anyone else knew he was in town and was sure the news was already starting to race around Missoula but wondered why even the stock manager seemed happy to see him.

Joe Lofton was about to turn in when there was a knock at the door. He looked at his wife, Ella, put a finger to his lips then walked barefoot to the parlor, picked up the Colt he had near the door and cocked the hammer.

He unlocked the door and opened it a crack, peered out and then stared at the late visitor, unsure of his identity in the low light.

Gabe said, “Sorry to bother you so late, Joe, but I had to see you right away.”

“Gabe?” he asked in surprise then swung the door open, let him inside and closed the door behind him.

Gabe saw the cocked pistol and was somewhat taken aback.

Joe quickly released the hammer set the pistol back on the sideboard and exhaled.

“Is it that bad, Joe?” Gabe asked.

“I don’t know what’s going on, Gabe. All I know is that after Mike was killed, I’ve been walking on eggshells and now I’m the new station manager.”

Gabe nodded and said, “Listen, Joe, I’m here to investigate Mike’s death and the poaching, but I had to talk to you before I did anything. I’m going to head back to the station and move into the sleeping quarters there until I find out more; if that’s all right with you. Come and see me in the morning and we can have a long talk. Okay?”

Joe nodded and said, “I’m sure glad you’re here, Gabe.”

Gabe smiled turned to leave then stopped and asked, “Is Mike’s wife, Angela, at home right now?”

“Nope. The house is empty as far as I know. Angela, well, she isn’t there. She just disappeared after the shooting.”

Gabe stood in stunned silence for almost thirty seconds before he sighed then said, “Okay, Joe. I’ll head back to the station. Be sure to see me first thing in the morning. Okay?”

“Will do, Gabe.”

Gabe finally left the house having learned much more already and none of it was good.

After he’d gone, Joe returned to the bedroom and Ella asked, “Who was it, dear?”

“Gabe Owens, the railroad special agent.”

“The man who stopped that robbery?”

“He’s done a lot more than that, Ella, and if anybody can clean up this mess, it’s Gabe. Now let’s get some sleep. I’m going to have a meeting with him in the morning and see if I can help him out.”

After leaving Dancer at the station's barn, Gabe carried his Winchester into the sleeping quarters in the station manager's office then closed the door, leaned the rifle against the wall, lowered his saddlebags to the floor and began to disrobe without thinking about it.

The tense, almost morbid atmosphere in Missoula made him seriously start thinking about requesting that Herb send a backup agent but that didn't last long knowing that it would only compound his problems when he had to start worrying about the new man. He knew that few of the agents had his experience and that meant they were more likely to make a critical mistake when he couldn't afford it.

He'd be able to rely on Joe and whoever else he said was trustworthy for logistical support but other than that, he was on his own.

The disappearance of Angela really troubled him. *Where in tarnation could she go?* If she had taken a train back to Minneapolis, surely Joe Lofton would have known about it. So, that meant she had to be Missoula. Maybe she was so spooked by the double murder that she was staying with a friend.

It was after one o'clock before Gabe finally nodded off to sleep with his head still filled with mysteries and questions that needed answers.

———

Gabe had spent a restless few hours of sleep punctuated by strange nightmares that had no relation to anything, so he was already awake before sunrise which was just around five o'clock. After visiting the privy, he cleaned and shaved at the wash basin and donned his shoulder holster before he pulled on his light jacket. He left his gunbelt in the sleeping room because today was just about gathering information.

After putting on his hat, he headed out the door and almost bumped into the ticket master, Al Springer.

“Oh, excuse me,” Al said, “You must be Gabe Owens.”

Gabe offered him his hand and said, “That’s me. Pleased to meet you.”

Al smiled back and said, “Al Springer. Glad you’re here.”

“Joe told me last night that he didn’t know where Mike Wheatley’s wife was. She didn’t leave on a train, did she?”

“No, sir. We haven’t seen her at all since that day.”

As Gabe nodded, Al said, “Well, I’ve got to get my window open. The 7:10 will be here before I know it,” then he smiled, tipped his hat, unlocked the ticket window door and entered the small office.

Gabe left the station, walked to the railroad barn, checked on Dancer then left and continued walking to Parker’s Diner for breakfast. He could have walked another block to the International Restaurant, but he needed to get back quickly and thought the service would be faster.

As he was returning, he heard the whistle of the incoming train, pulled out his plain pocket watch and checked the time as most railroad men did without realizing it. The train was on time and by the time he reached the station, he could see the locomotive already slowing down as it approached the town.

Passengers were waiting on the platform saying their goodbyes to relatives as he passed by and walked to the station manager's office opened the door and wasn't surprised to find Joe Lofton already waiting for him.

He took off his hat, hung it on a wooden wall peg and said, "Good morning, Joe," then closed the door.

"Morning, Gabe," he said from behind the desk, looking decidedly uncomfortable in his new assignment.

Gabe took a seat on a chair before the desk, unbuttoned his jacket and leaned back.

"Okay, Joe. First, tell me about Bob Johnson. He seems to be the central figure in this drama."

"He showed up about six years ago, near as I can figure. It was before I got here. He set up a big logging camp about eight miles northwest of town and began cutting timber. He lives out there and has more than sixty employees. He's got kind of a monopoly on the lumber business in the area and his only competitor is Eli Ulrich, who owns a lumber mill west of town."

"We've gotten rumors that he was poaching NP land. Have you heard that?"

"Just whispers, but it's not unusual. When somebody gets rich, folks always think they're up to no good. In this case, though, I wouldn't be surprised. He's a good-looking feller but seems, I don't know, too slippery to suit me."

"Tell me about the murders. All I saw was the sheriff's telegram."

"I don't know too much more than what's been going around. Mike walked into his house, met the man and they had a fight and the other guy shot Mike and Mike grabbed a knife and stabbed the shooter before he died."

"No one other than the sheriff saw the murder scene? Was Mike's wife in the house at the time?"

"We figured she was there when the killings happened, but we don't know what happened to her after that. The only person to see the inside of the house was the sheriff."

"Do you think the sheriff's crooked?"

Joe laughed and replied, "Crooked ain't close to describing Jack Reinhold. I swear that man's more of a crook than the ones he throws into his jail cells."

Gabe nodded then said, "Okay. Then before I go and see him, I'm going to want to go to Mike's house and examine the kitchen where the murders took place. I need to do my own inspection of the evidence before I get the sheriff's version."

"Gabe, the biggest question we all have about all this is who the other feller was and why he'd be in the house. The rumor going around was that he was visiting Mike's wife."

"Squash that talk, Joe. His name was Willie Bernstadt. He'd been hired by the NP to come here, get hired by Johnson as a logger and then to investigate those stories about possible poaching. He only reported to Mike which makes it very suspicious that they'd kill each other. I'm going to head over there and take a look. I don't have the address, though."

"The address is 112 Washington Street. It's only three blocks south and there's a key in the top drawer somewhere," he said before he pulled open the drawer, rummaged around, found a key ring and held it out to Gabe.

Gabe took the key ring and asked, "One more thing. How secure is the telegraph here?"

"I'm not very sure I'd trust the two operators."

"That's what I thought. I'll assume that Bob Johnson can read anything I send or receive and act accordingly. Maybe I can use that to my advantage," he said then stood and took his hat from the peg.

Joe stood as well, opened the door and said, "Good luck, Gabe," then left the station manager's office to go out to the railyard where he was more comfortable.

Gabe followed him out the door and waved as he headed to Washington Street, leaving Dancer at the station as he wanted the extra time to think. He'd asked the question about the telegraphers because of the last telegram that had been sent the day of the murders. *Why would Willie send a telegram if he was that worried then go to Mike's house?* Even if he brought a pistol, he'd still be putting himself at risk. It was yet another question that needed to be resolved.

It was only a five-minute walk before he turned down the graveled walkway and up the brick steps to a nice house, crossed the porch, unlocked the door and closed it behind him after entering.

Just to be sure it was empty, he shouted, "Angela?"

His voice echoed through the vacant house as he began to explore, starting with the parlor. He wasn't surprised to find nothing of significance in the outer room but before he walked down the hallway to return to the kitchen, he turned and climbed the staircase to the second floor, unsure of where Mike and Angela shared their bedroom. Even after all these years, the image of Angela with Mike let the green-eyed monster loose, if only for a short stroll.

He found the four bedrooms on the second floor all to be unused and was curious why Mike would buy such a large house. It was much larger than a young couple would need and this was much larger than his house in Minneapolis; the one he intended to share with Angela. Gabe assumed that Mike's father bought the house for them and Mike took advantage of his father's generosity.

Gabe returned to the first floor and when he entered the first bedroom, he finally found evidence that someone had lived in the house. The bed was unmade, so he walked past the bed to the closet, opened the door and found only men's clothes. Then he turned to the large dresser on the far wall and as he pulled open the drawers, no longer surprised when he found all of Angela's clothes gone. Either she'd been taken against her will by some very thoughtful kidnappers or she'd gone to a friend's house and sought refuge.

He left the bedroom checked the other two bedrooms on the first floor found them unused then passed by the large dining room and reached the kitchen. He stopped before stepping into the room and did a slow scan of the kitchen and was immediately puzzled by what he saw.

He saw one pool of blood still on the varnished floor on the left side of the kitchen near the table but there was no splatter at all on the walls. There should be a wide splash of blood and tissue on the wall or floor from the exit wound but there wasn't a drop. If the pool of dried blood wasn't there, he could guess that it had been cleaned but the room looked untouched.

Then he slowly stepped into the room, being careful where he put his feet as he examined the floor in greater detail. *Where was the second pool of blood?*

The lack of a cleanup gave him even more disturbing clues.

There was only the one place where there was blood, and it wasn't very large. He was pretty sure that it was Mike's blood as a gunshot to the chest at close range wouldn't bleed as much as most folks thought. He would have died quickly then the blood pressure would be gone and most of the blood would have stayed inside his body. But the telegram from the sheriff said that the second man had been stabbed in the gut and there should be a much larger pool on the right side of the floor, but there was nothing.

He looked back at the far wall and then stepped around the blood even though it was dry. He started with the wall behind the kitchen table and had to pull the table out a bit to be sure. Then he studied the back wall near the hall before examining the other side. When he finished his minute investigation of each of the walls, he finally walked back to the kitchen table, pulled out a chair and sat down.

The missing blood and tissue were bad enough, but there was no bullet hole either. He had hoped to find the slug that had killed Mike after it passed through his chest and buried itself in a wall but there were no holes anywhere. The room was large but even if someone was standing at the far end of the room and Mike was near the other end, almost any revolver would have sent its deadly missile easily through his chest and then into a wall.

He looked down at the blood once again and was sure that it had been a bullet wound because of the size of the pool, but that would mean it would have to be a smaller caliber pistol with much less penetrating power. He ran through the common pistols that met those criteria and the most obvious conclusion was a Remington derringer. It fired a .41 caliber round and was deadly at close distances, but it didn't have a lot of powder or muzzle velocity, so most likely the bullet wouldn't have passed through his chest. It was also very popular which wouldn't help his investigation.

He sat for a few more minutes trying to come up with another conclusion but the only one that fit was that Mike Wheatley had been shot with a Remington derringer, or a similar low velocity weapon and that Willie was either dead before Mike's murder or was killed later and somewhere else.

Either way, he now wanted to go and visit the sheriff and read the official report to see how many lies it contained. Sometimes lies can be a good way to discover the truth.

Gabe finally blew out his breath stood, then walked around the blood and headed back for the parlor. He was getting ready to leave the house when he stopped and looked at the back of the parlor and saw another door. He felt like an idiot as he crossed the parlor and swung open the door to the office and library.

As soon as he opened the door, he knew there was nothing here for him to find. The desk drawers were all open and papers were strewn everywhere. Nonetheless, Gabe entered the room and walked behind the desk. He began examining the open drawers then looking at the papers and not finding anything of interest.

He leaned back in the chair, locked his fingers behind his neck and stared at the ceiling. He had one murder that he was sure had happened in the kitchen. Another murder that could have happened anywhere and now, he had someone who had been searching for information, probably about the poaching.

He finally stood and walked out of the office, crossed the parlor then left the house, locking the door behind him. He walked rapidly down Washington to the center of Missoula to visit the sheriff.

Sheriff Reinhold was in a good mood, all things considered. The two bodies were buried, and no one was the wiser. He'd even gotten it past the prosecutor with minimal fuss and been given a nice bonus from Bob Johnson too.

He had just filled his coffee cup and was returning to his office when the door opened, and he turned as Gabe walked through the door then stopped. Strangers in town normally didn't cause him any concern but this wasn't a good time to ignore one.

Deputy Rafe Collier had the desk and asked, "Can I help you?"

"Good morning," Gabe replied as he showed the young deputy his badge fully aware that the sheriff was standing less than ten feet away, "I'm Gabe Owens and I was sent by the Northern Pacific to investigate the recent murder of our station manager, Mike Wheatley. I was wondering if I might be able to talk to the sheriff."

Deputy Collier turned, looked at his boss who nodded then said, "Mister Owens, I'm Sheriff Jack Reinhold, why don't we talk in my office."

"Thank you, Sheriff," Gabe replied with a smile as the sheriff began walking down a short hall to his office.

Gabe removed his dark gray Stetson, stepped in behind the sheriff and followed him into his office closing the door behind him.

The sheriff set down his coffee, and Gabe shook his hand before taking a seat.

“So, Mister Owens, what do you need to know about this tragic event?”

“As much as you do, Sheriff. I’d like to just write my report and head back to Minneapolis,” Gabe replied as he pulled a small pad and pencil from his pocket.

“Well, it was a grisly scene, I’ve got to tell you. I was told about a gunshot in the house and went there myself where I found two bodies in the kitchen. One was the station manager, Mister Wheatley, and I didn’t know the second man, but he was dressed in lumberjack clothes, so I sent a deputy to Bob Johnson’s lumber camp with his description. Mister Wheatley was shot once through the chest and the second man had a knife stickin’ outta his gut. I got no idea what had caused the feud or the fight. We had the bodies brought to the mortician and were buried the next mornin’.”

Gabe was writing as he asked, “What kind of gun was used in the murder?”

“It was a Colt, Model 1873.”

“Do you still have the pistol?”

“No, I gave it back to Mister Johnson. The shooter took it from the loggin’ camp.”

“Do you recall what cartridge it fired? Was it a .44 or a .45?”

“No. I don’t. It was a pretty open and shut case,” he replied as he licked his upper lip.

“Where was Mrs. Wheatley while the double homicide was happening in the kitchen?”

“I have no idea. No one has seen her since it happened.”

Gabe glanced at the sheriff and asked, “No one?”

The sheriff swallowed before he shook his head and said, “No, sir. Not a soul.”

Gabe grunted and continued to write, then he asked, “Could I read your report of the killings, Sheriff?”

“I haven’t gotten around to writin’ it yet. I’ve been pretty busy.”

“I’m sure. Now I’ll need to go and examine the house. Do you have the keys?”

“No, I’m sorry. I locked the doors after I left, and I assume that Mrs. Wheatley has the only set.”

“Mike Wheatley didn’t have any on him and she’s nowhere to be found,” Gabe said as he finished writing.

“That’s right.”

“Have you checked with her friends to see if she was staying with one of them?”

“Not yet. I figured she’d show up at the burial, but she didn’t, so I guessed that she didn’t want to be found.”

Gabe stared into the sheriff’s eyes and asked, “Doesn’t that bother you, Sheriff? What if she’s been kidnapped or even murdered and her body hidden somewhere?”

“I hadn’t thought of that. I just figured she was too afraid to be seen anywhere.”

“Well, I can’t finish my report until I can find her and get the keys. She may have more information that could explain why this man killed her husband, too," Gabe said as he slipped the pencil and pad into his jacket pocket and stood.

"I'll be back this afternoon to read your report, if that's acceptable."

The sheriff swallowed again then replied, "I should have it done by then."

Gabe smiled back as he said, "I'll see you this afternoon," then turned left the office and then the jail pulling on his hat as he left.

The sheriff sat in his chair for another five minutes until he was sure that Gabe was long gone then snatched his own hat from its peg and rushed out of the office past Deputy Collier without a word, turned left outside the office and headed for the livery to get his horse saddled. Bob Johnson had to know about this development.

———

Gabe had barely cleared the jail's threshold when he began adding up the lies. There were so many that it almost was difficult to separate them. Someone reported a shot to the sheriff who was probably at home after normal hours rather than the deputy who was probably on duty, ran to the house himself, found two bodies then sent a deputy to the logging camp at night to ask for identification of the unknown body.

Then he buries them both the next morning, doesn't find the widow anywhere and returns the murder weapon to Bob Johnson. The fact that he said it was a Colt was the biggest lie of many. *And after all that, he didn't have time to write a report?*

Gabe had traveled over fifteen hundred miles since the murder *and the sheriff couldn't spend thirty minutes writing a report of a double homicide?* He began to wonder about the county prosecutor, too. He should have been on the sheriff's case about the murders unless he did write a report and the prosecutor was satisfied. But he knew he'd never be able to read it because, if it existed, it was already in the sheriff's files and probably would already be lost by this afternoon.

The question now was what the sheriff would do before he returned for the report.

He reached the station and thought his Webley wasn't going to be enough firepower anymore, so he went into the station manager's office and found it empty then passed through to the sleeping quarters, wrapped his gunbelt around his waist then put his saddlebags over his shoulder, picked up his Winchester and left the office leaving none of his property inside.

Once outside, he headed for the barn, saddled Dancer, slipped the Winchester into its scabbard then hung the heavy saddlebags behind the saddle and tied them down. Once everything was secure, he mounted and walked Dancer out of the barn and headed for Ulrich's Lumber Yard and Sawmill. He was Bob Johnson's only competitor and if anyone could give him a real picture of the man, it would be Mister Ulrich.

Sheriff Reinhold rode the eight miles to Bob Johnson's logging camp at a canter. This was a very bad situation and he needed to let Bob know about Owens. He was sure the railroad agent hadn't accepted the story he'd been given and knew that if he wrote another report that was closer to what he'd just told him, it would have all sorts of holes.

He'd already burned the report he'd given to Jerome Williams, the prosecutor. He'd asked questions, mostly about the disappearance of Angela Wheatley, but had finally agreed she probably just left Missoula altogether as the sheriff had written in his report assuming that the sheriff had searched the town for her.

He pulled his tired horse to a stop outside of Bob Johnson's house, quickly dismounted then tossed the reins over the hitchrail and bounded up the six stairs to the porch, knocked quickly on the door and waited anxiously for it to open.

The door swung open and Becky said curtly, "He's busy in back. Is it important?"

"Yes, ma'am. Very important."

Becky stepped aside to let him enter then closed the door after he'd walked past.

Then she shouted, "Bob, the sheriff's here!" before taking a seat in the corner of the large main room.

Two minutes later, a disheveled Bob Johnson exited a bedroom in the back and was stuffing his shirt into his pants when he saw the sheriff standing in the room wringing his hat.

He didn't pay any attention to Becky sitting in the corner as he angrily snapped, "What the hell do you want?"

"Sorry to bother you, Bob, but a railroad special agent just showed up and he's askin' all sorts of questions about the murders and I don't think he's buyin' the stories."

Bob's anger faded before he said, "I figured they'd send one. What's his name?"

“Um...Owens, Gabe Owens.”

Bob surprised the sheriff when he smiled and replied, “Perfect. Okay, I’ll handle this.”

“But he’s comin’ back this afternoon to read a report that I’m supposed to be writin’.”

“Don’t worry about it. Just stall if he does. I already have a plan for Mister Owens, and I’ll make sure that he’s handled.”

Sheriff Reinhold exhaled in relief and said, “Thanks, Bob.”

“Yeah, sure. Now head on back to town and let me start working on fixing this.”

The sheriff smiled then gave a short wave to Becky before leaving the house.

Becky just watched him exit as Bob returned to the bedroom. She knew that things couldn’t last like this for very long and was convinced that she’d be the one who would be paying the price for having the blonde in the house.

Gabe had found the E.L. Ulrich Lumber Yard and Sawmill easily enough but then had to spend another five minutes finding Mister Ulrich as he didn’t seem to spend a lot of time in his small office.

When he finally found him, he was in the main cutting room stripping some bark from a log with two other men. Gabe was smiling as he watched Eli Ulrich do what he probably enjoyed doing rather than sitting behind a desk. His father was the same way, in pretty much the same business. The difference was that his father was strictly into logging and let others cut the timber into useful products.

When a sweating Eli Ulrich finally spotted the well-armed young man standing by the doorway to the large cutting room, he set his double-edged axe down, pulled out a handkerchief from his coveralls and walked toward the stranger.

"Howdy. What can I do for you?" he asked.

Gabe shook his hand and said, "Mister Ulrich, my name is Gabe Owens and I'm a special agent for the Northern Pacific Railroad and I'm here investigating the death of the station manager, Mike Wheatley."

"Well, son, you've got your work cut out for you. Let's go to my office if I can remember where it is."

Gabe laughed but wasn't sure if he was joking or not.

Once inside the small, disorganized office, Eli closed the door and gestured for Gabe to sit while he sat down in another chair.

"My wife, Sarah, does all of the bookkeeping at home in case you're wondering."

Gabe smiled and said, "It did have me a bit curious. Mister Ulrich, I'm already uncovering a lot of problems surrounding the murder and they all seem to point to Bob Johnson. I visited the sheriff a little while ago and had my ears filled with horse manure, so I thought as Mister Johnson's only competitor in the business, you'd be able to push some of that dung out of the way for me."

"Call me Eli, Mister Owens. Now about Bob Johnson, I'm going to have to be honest with you right off and tell you that I hate the man with every bone in my body, and it's not just because he's a competitor. I'm sure that he's poaching timber from Northern Pacific land and government land, too. I told Mister Wheatley about it and he began to do his own checking around, so I wasn't all that surprised to learn that he'd been killed. But the other reason I want him stopped is personal."

"May I ask what it is?"

"You'll find out soon enough anyway. About a year ago, my daughter, Rebecca, left Missoula and went to live with Bob Johnson. He didn't steal her away, though. She ran off with him on her own. She's a rebellious, angry girl and for a long time before she went away, all we've done is fight. She wasn't always like this, but when her mother, Rachel, died giving birth, she was devastated and blamed me for causing it. She was twelve at the time.

"Then six months later, I married Rachel's sister, Sarah and that made it worse somehow. She made it sound as if I murdered Rachel to marry Sarah because Sarah was six years younger. When Sarah gave birth to our son, Aaron a year later, she didn't talk to me for two months. We had a little girl we named Rachel three years ago and that seemed to push her over the edge and turned her into a demon.

"She hated our house and everyone in it. Sarah blamed herself for causing Rebecca's problems, and I haven't been able to change her mind. So, having Rebecca at the logging camp is a touchy subject, as Rebecca is herself. We haven't seen her since she left either. She could have a baby by now for all I know."

"She hasn't even come into Missoula to buy clothes or anything?" Gabe asked with raised eyebrows.

"She might have, but we've never seen her. I thought when she became more of an adult, she'd at least see how misspent all of her anger was, but we never got a chance before she left. I swear Bob Johnson intentionally tried to lure her to his camp just to get at me to add insult to injury."

"Where do you do your logging?"

"I have two sections under contract southwest of Missoula but right now, I can't keep any men working because Bob Johnson hires them all out from under me. I have six men that work the sawmill, and we have enough timber stored to keep us cutting boards and beams for another three months, but I'd really like to get more timber cut."

"That's what I aim to do, Eli. I need to put a stop to his poaching. Tell me about his logging camp."

"It's a really big operation about eight miles northwest of Missoula. There's a logging road that leads to it from the main road about a mile north of town. Bob Johnson lives there in a big house he had built and his foreman, Frank Stanford, who is also his biggest thug, lives in another, much smaller house nearby."

"How many of the workers are shooters and how many are just jacks?"

"I'd guess that he's got four or five rough boys to do his dirty jobs, but they're still lumberjacks. They just get paid extra to let Bob get his way, but he spreads money around town too."

"Like to the sheriff and the telegraphers?"

"You know about those two, do you?" he asked.

"I thought as much when we received a telegram in Minneapolis that didn't sound right to me. How about the deputies?"

Eli shook his head and said, "I'm not sure. I think they're okay, but don't take my word for it."

"Eli, no one seems to know where Mike Wheatley's wife is. Have you heard anything?"

"Nope. I didn't even know she was missing. I hope they didn't kill her, too. She seemed like a nice young lady."

"She was. I asked her to marry me in Minneapolis a few years ago but had to come out to Montana on a job and by the time I returned, she had accepted Mike Wheatley's proposal and moved out here."

"Now there's a coincidence. That's got to be hard for you."

"Not as much as you might think. She made her decision but now, I'm just worried that something bad has happened to her."

"I'll tell you what, Gabe, why don't you come home with me to my house and meet the missus and our children. She might have more information. You know that women usually know more about what's going on than us menfolk."

Gabe smiled and replied, "That's the truth."

"Our house is just a block away, so it's a quick walk," he said as he stood.

Gabe followed him out the door and once outside, he took Dancer's reins and walked alongside Eli.

They arrived at his house just two minutes later. It was about the same size as his house in Minneapolis, and Gabe wasn't surprised at all. If Eli had a house the size of Mike Wheatley's, then he'd be surprised. Eli Ulrich seemed like a down-to-earth type that probably had a lot more money than most down-to-earth types who didn't have the choice of living any differently.

After Gabe tied off Dancer, they walked onto the porch, Eli opened the door and said loudly, "Sarah, I brought a guest."

Before Sarah could reply, a black-haired boy with a big grin on his face bounced out of one of the rooms, ran into the parlor, and leapt at his father with his arms out. Eli caught the boy, who looked at Gabe.

"Hello. I'm Aaron."

Gabe smiled and said, "Well, howdy, Aaron. I'm Gabe."

Aaron put out his small hand, and after Gabe shook it, Eli set him back down then took his hand then father and son began walking to the kitchen.

Aaron looked up at Gabe as they walked then when they reached the kitchen, Gabe saw Sarah helping a young girl eat her lunch.

She paused, looked at Gabe smiled and said, "Rachel eats as if she's starving."

Eli said, "Sarah, this is Gabe Owens. He's a special agent sent by the railroad to stop Bob Johnson and his poaching."

Sarah gave Rachel a big bite of carrots then said, "I hope so. That man deserves to hang for some of the things he's done."

Eli said, “Now, Sarah, you know you’re just trying to act like a hard woman to impress Gabe here, but I know that you’d be happy with a few decades in prison.”

“I suppose,” Sarah said while she wiped Rachel’s face with a wet towel before setting her down on the floor.

Gabe said, “I may not be able to do much more than shut him down, but if I can wrangle a prison sentence out of it, I’ll be sure it’s a long one. And please call me Gabe.”

Sarah laughed and said, “Thank you, Gabe. Please have a seat and I’ll get you some coffee while you tell me why you’re here.”

While Eli washed in the sink, Gabe said, “As I told Eli, I’m a special agent with the railroad and I’m investigating Mike Wheatley’s death. What inspired your husband to bring me here was that I asked about Mike’s wife, Angela. No one seems to know where she could be, but he thought that you might have an idea.”

She was pouring two cups of coffee as she asked, “How much gossip do you wish to hear or are you limiting your scope to just hard facts?”

“Gossip would probably be a lot closer to the truth than the hogwash the sheriff gave me.”

Sarah laughed as set the two cups of coffee on the table then sat down. Eli and Gabe took seats as Aaron just stood next to Eli staring at Gabe.

Sarah said, “I don’t know how much store I put into this because part of me wants it to be true just to make Rebecca’s departure hurt less. Did my husband tell you about Rebecca?”

“Yes, ma’am.”

“Well, I heard rumors that Bob Johnson was paying attention to Mrs. Wheatley while her husband was at work and on more than one occasion was seen entering the back door of their house.”

Gabe took a sip of coffee before asking, “Do you think that there’s a chance she could be out at the logging camp?”

“If no one can find her, it’s as good a possibility as anything else.”

Eli took a sip of his coffee and just shrugged. This was news to him.

Gabe then said, “There was a good chance that I would be paying a visit to the logging camp before but now I’ll probably have to go sooner than I expected. Are there many women out there? I know in my father’s logging camp in Minnesota, the foreman and a couple of the other supervisors have wives but there are a few loose women that stay out there as well and I mean ‘loose women’ in its most common context.”

Eli replied, “Rebecca was living with Bob Johnson, but I don’t think Frank had a permanent woman. There are a few women there that provide services, though. I think he even runs his own bordello.”

Then Eli asked, “How big is your father’s operation?”

“He’s running three different camps now and has about forty thousand acres under contract.”

Eli whistled and asked, “Can I ask why you’re doing this, then? Surely, you don’t need the money.”

“No, sir. It’s never been about money. It’s about doing something that lets me believe I can make a difference.”

“Did you spend much time working the timber?”

“Yes, sir. I started in the summer when I was twelve and enjoyed the work, just like you obviously still do. But I wanted to try something different and hired on with the Northern Pacific as a surveyor, a skill I picked up when working for my father as you might imagine. He probably pulled a few strings to get me the job, too. After a couple of years spent surveying routes across the Plains, I switched over to this job and I’ve been doing it for six years now.”

“You any good at it?” Eli asked.

“I’m the best they’ve got, Eli.”

Eli grinned and said, “I hate all that fake humility. If you’re good at something, you should be able to be proud of it unless you’re just fooling yourself. Just like Sarah here can fly her broomstick better than any other woman in Montana Territory.”

Sarah giggled slightly as her eyes laughed at her husband.

Gabe hated to change the mood but said, “As much as I’ll try to avoid it, there may be gunfire if I go there, and I’d hate to even hit your daughter by accident. What does Rebecca look like?”

Sarah said, “She’s tall, about five feet and eight inches with long black hair and she’s very pretty.”

Gabe asked, “Did you want me to get her out of there?”

Eli answered, “Only if she wants to leave but be ready to have your head handed to you if she wants to stay, too.”

“Then I’ll play it by ear after I get there.”

Then Sarah looked at Gabe and said, “If you do find her, Gabe, could you tell her that we all still love her and hope that she comes home?’

“Yes, ma’am. I’ll do that. Do you think she would?”

“No, but there’s always that hope.”

Eli then said, “Tell her that I’m sorry that I drove her to run away with Bob Johnson.”

“Eli, I doubt if you drove her anywhere, but I’ll see if I can talk some sense into her if I can find her and get her out of there.”

“We’d be happy just to know she was safe, Gabe,” Sarah said.

Aaron had been studying Gabe since he’d been there then, when there was finally a pause, he looked up at Gabe and said, “We’re Jewish.”

Gabe smiled down at Aaron then said, “I kind of figured that out for myself, Aaron.”

“How? Did Papa tell you?”

“I’m kind of a detective and seeing the menorah in the parlor was a hint.”

“Are you Jewish, too?”

“No, sir, just a regular Christian.”

“Do you hate Jews?” he asked.

Gabe smiled at the youngster's blunt question and asked, "Now why would I do that? Personally, I think you're lucky to be a Jew."

"I am? Why?"

"Have you ever tried to spell Episcopalian?"

Aaron laughed as he looked up at his father who was laughing as well.

———

As Gabe was making Aaron laugh, a buggy left Bob Johnson's house and headed for Missoula.

———

It was too early to return to the sheriff's office, so after he left the Ulrich home, Gabe mounted Dancer and headed for downtown Missoula. There was a shop he wanted to visit, but not for the usual reason.

Five minutes later, he was pulling in front of A.J. Staus Gunsmith & Machinist. He stepped down, tied off Dancer and entered the shop, soon inhaling the distinct and much-appreciated odors of gun cleaning fluid, oil and gunpowder.

He walked to the long counter of the well-stocked shop and approached a middle-aged man that he assumed was Mister Staus himself.

"Good afternoon, sir. What can I do for you?" he asked.

"Good afternoon, my name is Gabe Owens, and I'm a special agent for the Northern Pacific Railroad. I'm investigating the death of Mike Wheatley and I was hoping you could answer a question I had that is relevant to that investigation."

"Why certainly, Mister Owens. I read about your exploits in stopping the Dakota Gang. May I ask what weapons were involved?"

"Well, sir. I had my Webley but never even took a shot with it as I disarmed the gang leader in the first car and used his Colt '73 to finish off the others. They were all armed with similar models, and all were chambered for the .44 cartridge."

The gunsmith smiled then said, "Thank you for not calling that pistol the Peacemaker. I abhor that name. I notice that you're wearing a Remington '75."

"Yes, sir. I prefer the Remington. I believe it's more robustly built than the Colt."

"As do I. Now, Mister Owens, how can I help you?"

"How many Remington .41 caliber derringers have you sold in the past year, if you could hazard a guess?"

"Oh, I'd say about thirty or so. They're very popular with the ladies, but they're usually bought by their husbands. They keep them in their handbags and perhaps other, more unconventional locations."

"Have you sold any to Bob Johnson?"

"I may have, but it would have been a few years ago, so I can't be sure."

"Can you think of any other pistol that could be shot at ten feet and not pass through the victim's chest?"

"There's always the possibility that it was a light load, but even that would be unlikely. We don't carry any of the other derringers or those unusual pepperboxes. I do have a few of the old pocket pistols but at ten feet, I would think that even their .32 caliber rounds would pass though."

"That's what I thought, too," he replied as he did a quick scan of the store and said, "You have quite a selection."

"We pride ourselves on always having the latest in quality firearms."

"I'll be sure to visit again before I leave," Gabe said then added, "Thank you for your help."

"I hope I provided the information you needed."

"It was a great help."

Gabe then left the shop, boarded Dancer and sat in the saddle as he pondered his next stop then figured he'd given the sheriff enough time to phony up a new report and wheeled Dancer west for the short ride to the sheriff's office.

He pulled up two minutes later, dismounted, tied off Dancer and stepped onto the boardwalk. He had barely opened the door when he froze as he saw two blue eyes staring at him.

"Gabe!" Angela cried as she popped up from the chair next to the desk and raced across the room.

She threw her arms around him as he entered the office then buried her head into his chest and began sobbing.

Gabe put his arms around her and let her cry as he looked at the deputy who was just staring at them and shrugged with just his eyes as his shoulders were full of Angela.

She shook for almost a minute before she finally stepped back, wiped the tears from her eyes and said, “The sheriff told me you were here, Gabe, but I couldn’t believe it. I’ve been so terrified for days now and almost didn’t come back at all, but I had no more money.”

Gabe then took Angela by the hand led her outside and closed the door behind them, so the deputy couldn’t hear.

He then looked into her sad eyes and asked, “Angela, where have you been? I’ve been looking for you since I arrived, and no one seemed to know where you were.”

She said, “Can we talk someplace private, Gabe? I’m so afraid of being out here in the open like this. Can you take me to my house?”

“Sure. Do you have your house keys?”

“Yes. Let’s go to the house. I have the buggy right there.”

Gabe led Angela to the buggy, helped her inside and then climbed aboard and took the reins, gave them a quick snap and headed for the house. Angela slid close, and Gabe had to admit to being seriously affected by having her pressed against him again after all those years.

“Where did you go, Angela?” he asked.

“I was terrified with what happened that night. I heard shouting from the kitchen then a gunshot, so I ran outside, found that the buggy was already harnessed because Mike had just driven it somewhere. I climbed in and drove like a madwoman until I was out of Missoula and eventually made it to Bears Mouth and stayed there until I was almost out of money.

"When I returned just a little while ago, the sheriff told me that Mike was dead, and they had buried him already. I wasn't even there, Gabe!" she said as she began to cry again then leaning her head on his shoulder.

Gabe turned the buggy into the house's long drive then around the back, stopped the buggy and set the handbrake. After he stepped out, he walked to the other side and helped a still distraught Angela out of the buggy.

"Do you have your keys, Angela?" Gabe asked.

"Oh. I'm sorry," she replied as she opened her purse, reached inside, pulled out a key ring much like the one in Gabe's pocket and handed it to him.

He took the keys and with Angela gripping his arm, stepped up the three stairs to the back porch, opened the door and led her inside, closing the door behind them.

After three steps, Angela glanced down and screamed, "That's his blood!" then collapsed in a faint.

Gabe caught her, slid his arms behind her then carried her down the hallway and laid her gently on one of the unused beds. He took off his hat then his gunbelt, his jacket and his shoulder harness before he sat on the bed next to her.

"Angela?" he asked softly, "Are you here?"

Angela moaned slightly then her blue eyes were slowly revealed as her eyelids opened before she whispered, "I'm sorry, Gabe. I was just so shocked seeing that blood."

"It's all dry now, Angela. I can go clean it up now if you'd like."

She quickly sat up, put her arms around him and said, "Please, don't leave me, Gabe. Please?"

He pulled her close and said, "Don't worry, Angela. You're safe now."

She whispered in his ear, "I was so stupid not to marry you, Gabe. It was such a terrible mistake. You were so special, and I still dream of those two wonderful nights we spent together."

"Why was it a mistake, Angela?"

"Mike wasn't nearly the man you were. You were always so nice to me and made me happy. Then you left, and I was so lonely that I let Mike convince me that he loved me, but I don't think he did. You loved me, didn't you, Gabe?"

"Of course, I loved you, Angela. You're a very easy woman to love."

"See? Things like that. You always said things to make me feel like a desirable woman. Mike just took me like a rutting cow."

"Did he hurt you, Angela?" Gabe asked softly, having already seen two bruises on her neck now that he was close.

Angela nodded then let her arms release him and after she was laying on the bed, she began unbuttoning her blouse, and when she opened the top, he could see more bruising.

"He beat me, Gabe," she said softly, "but never on the face. He hit me here, on my behind, and on my legs."

She then quickly pulled her skirts up to her hips, exposing her thighs. There were bruises everywhere, but her legs were already having an effect on him, an effect he couldn't afford.

He tugged her skirts down somewhat as he asked, “Angela, why didn’t you ever tell me what he was doing to you? I could have helped.”

She replied quietly, “He was my husband, Gabe. If he wanted to beat me, he could and there was nothing you could do about it.”

He then asked quietly, “Angela, did you shoot Mike?”

She didn’t act surprised at all before taking his hand, then replying, “I’m sorry, Gabe. I should have told you right away, but I was still so afraid, and I’m sorry for that, too. I should have trusted you. Now, I’m not afraid anymore. If you want to arrest me and send me to hang, it’s alright. But all I ask is that you make love to me once more before you take me to jail.”

Gabe slowly pulled his hand back as he said, “No, Angela, I’m not going to arrest you. I understand why you did it. Was he going to beat you again?”

Angela visibly relaxed before she answered, “It was much worse that night. He had a knife and was going to cut me, Gabe. I had to shoot him. I had to!”

He kissed her forehead as she began to cry then he said softly, “It’s alright now, Angela. But why did the sheriff lie about the second man in the room?”

She shook her head slowly then replied, “He didn’t lie, Gabe. I did, though. I didn’t go to Bears Mouth after I shot him. I drove the buggy to Bob Johnson’s logging camp and stayed there. Bob knew that Mike was beating me and came over a couple of times and threatened him to leave me alone, so I knew I’d be safe there. When I got there after I’d shot Mike, he came to Missoula and told the sheriff what had happened, and they made up the story about a second man being there to protect me. The man had died in a logging accident that day, so he was able to use the body to support the story.

"Bob sent me here to see you again when he found out you were here and said to tell you the truth, but I was still afraid because I thought you might arrest me, and I'd be hanged. But I could still see there was some love for me when I looked into your eyes."

"Does Bob know that I had asked you to marry me?"

"Yes. He even thought I might run away with you if you didn't arrest me. I think he just wants me to be happy. He's a very nice man, Gabe, and I think he can make me happy, too."

Gabe looked at those incredible blue eyes and said, "You deserve to be happy, Angela."

"Gabe, what are you going to do now?" she asked as she held his hands.

"I was going to do some more investigating about a possible poaching operation, but if you vouch for Bob Johnson then I guess I'll write my report and head back to Minneapolis. Did you want to come with me?"

She sighed before she answered, "Would you be horribly jealous if I married Bob Johnson and stayed here?"

He shook his head slowly before replying, "Of course, I'll be jealous, Angela, but at least he won't hurt you."

She smiled and said, "Thank you for everything, Gabe. You'll never know how happy you made me."

"I'm just glad that you're all right and I know that you'll be cared for now. Are you going to stay in the house?"

"Heavens, no. You can stay here until you leave. I'm going to go back to Bob. I know he won't be as good as you in bed because I don't think that's possible, but I know he loves me."

"That's what really matters," Gabe said as he stood and began to put his shoulder holster back on.

She patted his butt, giggled then said, "Not always."

He leaned over, kissed her softly on her lips before he finished securing his shoulder holster then donned his gunbelt and jacket, pulled on his hat and left the house to walk to the sheriff's office to retrieve Dancer.

He was glad he didn't have to get in the saddle right now and even walking was painful. He knew that Angela really wanted him to make love to her and it was the only honest thing she'd said since he'd walked into the sheriff's office.

For almost three minutes, Angela sat on the bed with her eyes closed as she imagined what had almost been. Just as Gabe had been, she was incredibly frustrated by his refusal to take her up on her offer and knew why he had. It was his deeply held belief that he could only bed a woman that he loved, but she thought that his memories would overcome that fault. When Bob had suggested that she use all of her womanly skills to convince her ex-boyfriend of the story, she had been anxiously anticipating getting him into her bed.

She shuddered once more at the memories of those two glorious nights with Gabe then opened her eyes, stood, buttoned her blouse and straightened her skirts then left the bedroom and the house, locking the door behind her. She walked out to the buggy, climbed aboard and snapped the reins.

She turned the buggy onto the cobbled street heading west back to Bob Johnson's lumber camp and her new life.

As Gabe walked along, he heard the buggy approaching then turned and waved at Angela as she passed, and she smiled and waved in return. He watched the buggy shrink as it rolled away and wondered what was wrong with him.

He knew the moment she had suggested that they go to the house she would probably want him to take her and had already convinced himself that he could. He remembered those two wild times with Angela and thought that would be enough to allow him to do it, but it wasn't. He just didn't love her anymore, but it still had been a serious temptation.

He knew that much of what Angela had said to him was nothing more than a continuing trail of falsehoods. He'd let her keep spinning her web of lies and learned a lot in the process. *Why had she confessed so readily to killing Mike?*

He was sure that Mike had been beating her, though. The bruises were all much too old to be just done for his benefit. She may have even told Bob Johnson about the beatings, but only after he'd seen her naked. He didn't doubt for a moment, even before he'd seen her in the sheriff's office that what Sarah Ulrich had told him was true. Angela was many things, and probably the most honest was that she was a lusty young woman.

He suspected that she might have really killed Mike but probably not in fear of her life. She probably wanted to be free of him, so she could marry Bob Johnson. There was also the equally likely possibility that Bob Johnson committed the murder himself.

He knew that even if he convinced Angela to confess that it had been Bob Johnson who had pulled the trigger, he couldn't believe her after listening to her lies. The weakest part of her story was her apparent complete fear when she first saw him. *Fear from what?*

He had found her in the sheriff's office and the only man who had hurt her was dead, *so what in creation did she have to fear?* She made Bob Johnson out to be a saint among sinners, so she obviously wasn't worried about him either.

Then there was the silly notion of her taking a nighttime ride in a buggy to Bears Mouth. The tracks between Missoula and Bears Mouth were twenty-four miles, but the road was another eighteen because it had to wind so far north. He couldn't imagine her even attempting that drive during a pleasant late spring day.

Now he had to figure out how to take advantage of the extra two or three days he'd just bought by apparently agreeing to drop his investigation.

He finally reached the sheriff's office having already forgotten about asking for the report as he untied Dancer, patted the gelding on the neck and apologized for leaving him there. Gabe then mounted and headed back to the house to plan his new strategy.

He was almost there, still reviewing the last two hours with Angela when he realized that there would soon be a problem at the Johnson logging camp. Eli said that Rebecca was living in Bob Johnson's house and he'd just sent Angela to live with Bob Johnson. Granted, she was probably servicing him already but now, they would see it as a more permanent arrangement and that made Rebecca superfluous. Despite Eli's assertion that she was a raging witch, he thought he owed her at least a chance of redemption just to help Sarah and Eli, if nothing else.

He turned Dancer back to the house and twenty minutes later, the gelding was happily grazing on a big bag of oats and Gabe had moved his things inside.

Angela had driven away from the house in a good mood after having pulled off the impossible. She had confessed to killing Mike and nothing was going to happen to her just as Bob had predicted. She was almost glad that her bastard husband who had beaten her so often and given her all of those sympathetic bruises was dead and the investigation was now over.

She was still in a state of enhanced excitement after being so close to Gabe when Bob's big house appeared as the buggy cleared the trees on both sides of the logging road. He was already on the front porch and waved to her when he saw the buggy approaching. She smiled and waved back hoping that Bob would soon do what Gabe wouldn't. She knew that it wouldn't be nearly as spectacular as they had been with Gabe but right now, she'd settle for anything.

Angela pulled the buggy to the front of the house and Bob trotted down the stairs to take the reins.

As she stepped out, he asked, "How did it go? Did you tell him that you killed your husband?"

Angela grinned and replied, "I did, and he even knew that I was going to come back here to you, but he understood and was glad that I would be happy. He's heading back to Minneapolis soon and not even going to investigate the poaching because I vouched for you."

"Wonderful! I can't believe that you pulled it off!" he exclaimed as he dropped the reins, pulled her into his arms then kissed her hard as he grabbed her behind.

She let her hands wander over him to let him know that she wanted him as much, if not more than he wanted her.

"Well, you seem ready, Angie," Bob said when he let her go.

"I'll always be ready for you, Bob. Let's go inside quickly."

Bob then turned looked back at the front door and shouted, "Becky, take the buggy to the barn and get the harness removed. Then don't come back for at least twenty minutes. I want some time with a real woman."

Becky glared at Bob as she left the house, stepped down the stairs and snatched the reins from Bob's hand before leading the horse and buggy to the barn.

"Let's go inside, Angie, and I'll see how ready you are," Bob said as he took Angela by the hand and walked up the stairs as she smiled.

Rebecca stalked sullenly across the yard leading the horse and buggy to the barn, but it wasn't out of jealousy. She had a deep fear of what she was sure would soon happen to her as she glanced quickly to her left and saw Frank watching her from his house's porch.

Frank had seen and heard the whole show and smiled when he realized he now had a good chance of getting Bob's castoff, meaning Becky. He just sat and admired her as she walked to the barn, knowing he'd soon have her in his bed, and she would have to learn all sorts of new tricks.

Gabe wouldn't need a map to find the logging camp after talking to Eli. With the logging road turning off the main road west of town, as soon as he made that turn, sooner or later, he'd ride into the big camp.

Tomorrow, he planned on going to the area early in the morning on Dancer with enough supplies to last him two days. He'd have his compass and field glasses in addition to his weapons. He'd need some food and eating utensils, so he decided to explore the kitchen and see what he could find, so he could avoid any unnecessary shopping.

After he watched Becky reenter the house twenty minutes later, Frank still waited another ten minutes to make sure Bob was done and dressed again. He still wasn't sure how Bob would react to his request and didn't want to irritate him if it could be avoided.

He was getting antsy by the time he bounced off his porch then tried to slow his walk to the boss' house. He had to play this right. He really wanted Becky, even if Bob didn't.

Frank climbed the steps to the porch, took a deep breath and then knocked on the door. He was bouncing on his toes when the door opened, and Becky gave him one of her 'oh, it's you' looks then asked, "What do you want, Frank?"

He grinned, leaned forward slightly and said in low voice, "You, Becky," then pushed past her into the main room where he spotted Bob and Angela talking on the left side near the fireplace.

"What do you want, Frank?" Bob asked cheerfully after having his needs satisfied by Angela.

Frank took his hat off and stepped closer, not noticing Becky who had walked behind him to argue against what she knew he would be asking.

"Boss, I was just wonderin'. Seein' as how Angela is gonna stay now and, well, Becky is kinda in the way. Well…I was just wonderin'…"

Bob laughed and said, "Go ahead and take the bitch! She's been pissed off at me even before Angela came here."

Becky shouted, "You can't give me away like some damned slave! You don't own me! I'll leave and go back to Missoula before I let that bastard put a finger on me!"

Before Bob could tell her otherwise, Frank suddenly whirled and whipped his open hand across her face, knocking her to the floor.

Bob laughed and said, "Whooeee, Frank! That'll teach her who's boss! Go ahead and drag her out of here and if she tries to leave, make her understand that this is where she's going to stay."

Frank grinned and said, "I'll teach her good, boss!"

Then as Becky began to stand, he took a fistful of her long black hair and began walking to the door as she fell again and struggled to get to her feet.

He opened the door and half-dragged and half-walked her out across the threshold, closed the door and then let her walk down the steps before he marched her to his house, opened the door and threw her inside.

He was still grinning as he followed her into the room and closed the door.

Angela was shocked as much by Bob's reaction as by Frank's violent treatment of Becky. He'd always been so kind to her, and she chastised herself for not noticing how poorly he had treated Becky since she'd been at the house. He had acted as if she was an old servant woman or a piece of furniture even though Angela knew that Becky had shared his bed for almost a year.

Now she knew that not only was Becky a prisoner, but she was too. *How had it come to this?* When she thought about meeting Gabe in Missoula just a short time ago, she realized that she had made the same bad decision yet again and doubted if she'd get another opportunity.

She just hoped now that Becky wasn't going to be covered in as many bruises as she was, although she doubted if Frank would avoid hitting her face because he already had so before he had dragged her from the room.

Gabe had packed his big saddlebags and couldn't think of anything else he needed. He had enough food for two or three days and a small steel frypan to cook in. He'd have to go without coffee but wished he'd bought a pie or cake. Going without coffee was bad enough.

He checked the time and then wound his watch. He would leave early and follow the closest railroad land grants to where he expected to find the poachers. Once he knew they were there, he'd be within his rights to force them off the railroad property under all sorts of threats. If they were on government property, he'd just let the Federal bureaucrats know and leave it to them to stop the poachers. But he had other, higher priorities now.

He still needed to get to the full truth behind the murders of Mike Wheatley and Willie Bernstadt. Angela had just given him her confession and he hadn't placed much stock in it its accuracy but the fact she had so readily confessed meant she knew what had happened, and he wanted evidence of at least Bob Johnson's complicity in the murders, if not his commission of the crime.

He was in bed by nine o'clock, having never used a lamp just in case anyone wanted to visit him that night, although he doubted if anyone would. The doors were locked, and he had the only two sets of keys. As he drifted off, he still had visions of Angela's legs. Bruises aside, it was a pleasant way to fall asleep but there was still that twinge of jealousy knowing that she was warming Bob's bed.

Angela was in fact warming Bob's bed but that was all she was doing. All that was happening now was that Bob was snoring beside her as she lay in her nightdress wondering how Becky was doing.

A few hundred feet away, Becky wasn't crying despite her many new bruises and welts. Frank hadn't been joking when he had said he'd teach her some new tricks and when she had objected, he showed her just how mean he could be. She never cried anymore. Hate and anger served her much better than tears.

Rebecca was furious at the entire world but mostly at herself. She'd defied her father and Sarah, gone off with Bob and for a few months, she had been treated reasonably well. Then things began to go downhill for a reason she refused to think about. But even she hadn't realized just how cruel Frank was. He made Bob Johnson seem like a true gentleman if there was such a thing.

She was doomed to a life here and understood that the monster laying on the outside of the bed next to her would beat her to death one day, and it probably wouldn't be too much longer. She felt that in many ways, she deserved it for what she had done and that terrifying memory still chilled her to the depths of her soul until she could push it back into the darkest corners of her mind.

It was the image of that horrible day coupled with the realization of her imminent death that finally broke through Rebecca's thick crust and she began to quietly weep.

CHAPTER 3

Gabe was up shortly after dawn and soon had Dancer saddled, walked him out of the small barn then west down the street until he left Missoula, knowing that he'd only have a couple of miles before he entered the trees.

He'd eaten breakfast of sorts but had his coffee and then filled one of his canteens with the rest, so he wouldn't be totally coffee-less.

When he turned north on the road, he began looking for the cutoff to the logging camp. It was on the railroad's land, but it had been there before the right of way had been established, so it was a legal easement. It was what he expected to find four or five miles into the trees that wasn't legal.

He passed the cutoff and rode another half a mile or so before he turned into the trees. He didn't want to run into any traffic that might be leaving the logging camp.

As Gabe walked his gelding in his winding path through the pines, he couldn't help but contrast it to the path he'd taken to get here. It had begun among the massive forests of tall pines in Minnesota, before he'd shifted to the open plains of the Dakota Territory as he surveyed for the Northern Pacific and now, he was back among the pines.

It was when he was on the Great Plains that his life had made the dramatic shift from surveying to special agent. He was on a crew that had been surveying land in the western Dakota Territory and had been attacked by a group of twenty-four Lakota Sioux. He was one of only three survivors from the attack and the only one who hadn't been wounded, primarily because of his skill with his Winchester '66 and his Colt New Army pistol. It had been that incident that had made him apply for a special agent job and ensured his acceptance.

He was a bit ambivalent when it had come to fighting the Indians on the Plains. He knew they were crossing Sioux land but was well aware that the Sioux were the big bullies among the Plains Indians, pushing many smaller tribes off their hunting grounds. After having to engage them more than once, both before and after that one incident, he could understand how they did it, too. There were other, fiercer tribes, but he always thought the Sioux were the best organized of the ones he'd met.

So once again, he had Dancer walking among the pines and as usual, enjoyed the smell as the Morgan meandered through the trees. He hadn't gone a mile when he heard the sound of axes in the distance and then a minute later, the sound of a tree crashing to the ground, so he angled due south until he crossed the road and then turned west again. He wanted to get closer to the mining camp without being seen and still be able to see where the loggers were.

Gabe heard the sound of logging operations to his right front much more clearly now and estimated he was only a half a mile from the work.

He was three miles in now and was on the government section of the land grant. On the other side of the road, about a quarter of a mile, the railroad's land began. Now it was just a question of where they were cutting timber today, and it didn't take much longer for him to find his answer.

He saw the trees already thinning which was still on government land and then he was stunned when he pulled Dancer to a stop at the edge of the tree line and saw nothing but stumps and smaller trees until he spotted the lumber camp about a mile away. He then looked to his right and saw that the lumberjacks were working about a third of the way into the railroad land. He felt anger and disgust fill him. They weren't harvesting the forest; they were stripping it naked.

In all of his years in working with his father, the one thing he stressed was to thin the trees, not cut them all. The forests were thick enough that there were still plenty of good, straight pines, but by leaving many behind, the forest would continue to thrive and by the time they reached the end of their contracted land, they could return to the beginning and start over.

Bob Johnson was cutting down every tree in the area leaving a stump-filled wasteland. There were saplings and smaller pines, but it would be decades before the forest returned to a semblance of what it was. It wouldn't be so stupid if there weren't so many trees in the region.

He backed Dancer into the trees again, turned him north and after crossing the road again, entered the railroad section that the lumberjacks were cutting. He was able to curve around the active cutting because they hadn't gotten that deep into this section, so he'd be able to get closer to the camp.

He didn't blame the loggers, although he was sure that many of them, if not all, knew that they were cutting trees that didn't belong to Bob Johnson. They understood that if they objected, there would be others to take their place and make the money that they should be earning. But it still made him angry that Bob Johnson was so arrogant that he thought he could get away with it.

Gabe was sure of two things now: he'd get Rebecca out of there if he could and he'd either haul Bob Johnson into court or shoot him. Personally, he'd rather shoot him.

Becky thought that she'd just be able to cook breakfast and then do something normal, like clean the filthy house that Frank Stanford called home, but Frank wanted to play with his new toy, and that meant more pain.

She thought that she would just unleash her formidable temper on him but had learned quickly that it only seemed to make him more excited and angrier. A submissive, quiet Rebecca may have irritated him, but a few slaps were more tolerable than what happened if she defied him as she had the first two times.

It wasn't until almost nine o'clock that Frank finally left the house to do some real work. Bob had told him to meet him at his house rather than Frank's place and have to deal with Becky any longer.

Becky hoped that Angela was as miserable as she was as she watched Frank leave the house with her one functional eye.

Angela may not have Becky's new bruises, but she wasn't exactly happy either. She thought that she'd be able to disguise her loathing over Frank's treatment of Becky, and she had for a couple of hours, but Bob eventually detected a change in Angela's demeanor and had casually mentioned that he might take Becky back and send her to Frank if she didn't get over it.

Gabe had found a good spot in the trees that was less than a mile from the camp and had hitched Dancer to a branch, then walked a couple of hundred yards and now stood back from the tree line examining the large site with his field glasses. He spotted the tents and cabin for the workers, the chow hall, a smithy, a large barn and corral, and a couple of other buildings that he couldn't identify. But he did notice the two houses that Eli had mentioned, one of them larger than the other with a lot of steps to handle the steep slope. He knew he was looking at Bob Johnson's house and that Angela was inside and maybe Rebecca was too.

Then he spotted a man leave the smaller house and head for the bigger one. He was pretty sure that it was Frank Stanford going to visit his boss, so he kept his glasses trained on the door.

The man climbed the stairs to the larger house then after knocking on the door, it opened, and he caught a glimpse of blond hair before the door closed. Angela was there, but she was too far away for him to see her face, yet just seeing her there made his stomach queasy.

He then swung his glasses to the smaller house about eight hundred yards from his current position. He knew it was outside the range of his Winchester, but it really didn't matter. This shouldn't be a shooting issue, not yet anyway.

Gabe was still estimating ranges when he felt like an idiot, which had happened too often lately. This may be his only chance to see if he could get Rebecca out of the camp, having made the logical assumption that both young women wouldn't be in Bob's house. At least he'd find out if she would hand him his head or not. He put down his field glasses, grabbed his Winchester and began walking quickly toward the second house. He had his badge displayed but didn't think it really mattered anyway.

He was stupidly counting the steps as he crossed the open ground, weaving his way through the stumps. He knew that it was possible that Rebecca wasn't even in the smaller house and she might even scream when he knocked, but he figured he may as well start the show now rather than later.

He kept his eyes shifting back and forth between the two front doors as he passed the four hundred step mark. He estimated he was under four hundred yards away, so at least he had been pretty accurate in his range estimate. He wanted to run or at least trot but kept the slower, less noticeable pace. Someone might be watching him from the trees, one of the houses or other buildings, but he hadn't been challenged yet.

Two minutes later, he calmly stepped onto the porch of the smaller house, walked to the door and knocked loudly.

Becky heard the rapping at the door and thought about ignoring it but knew it would only lead to more problems, so she walked to the door and swung it open then stood there blinking.

Gabe was stunned when he looked at Rebecca. Her left eye was heavily bruised and swollen shut, her mouth was cut and swollen, and the left side of her face was bruised. Even her dress was ripped in places, showing more skin than what was socially acceptable. She looked as if she had been in a bare-knuckle brawl...and lost.

"What happened to you?" he asked, forgetting the criticality of the time.

"Frank happened. Who are you?" she asked, her speech somewhat slurred by her swollen lips.

Her closed left eye had limited her vision and she hadn't spotted his badge.

Gabe regained his sense of urgency and said quickly, “Rebecca? If you want to stay here, fine. If you’d rather come with me, let’s go right now. Do not run, just walk with me.”

Rebecca didn’t care if he was Mary Shelley’s Frankenstein monster once he made the offer. She didn’t hesitate but stepped onto the porch as he turned to leave then quickly walked beside him as they stepped off the porch and began to retrace his footprints to the trees.

“Who are you?” she asked again as she almost had to jog to keep up with his long strides.

“My name is Gabe Owens, I’m a special agent sent by the Northern Pacific to investigate the murder of our station manager and possible poaching of timber.”

“You’re Gabe Owens?” she asked as she glanced over at Gabe, “Bob sent Angela to see you yesterday.”

“I know.”

They continued to walk quickly as each of them glanced to the sides and behind them and not finding anyone watching.

Rebecca said, “How did you know I was there and what possessed you to just walk into camp and ask me to leave? You could have been shot.”

“I’m well aware of that, ma’am. I took the chance because I promised Eli and Sarah when I talked to them yesterday.”

“I’m not going back there, if that’s what you think,” she said as her breathing grew deeper.

"What you do after we're in the trees is up to you, ma'am. You're an adult and as far as I'm concerned, you can turn right around and go back to Frank Stanford."

"You're a real cold-hearted bastard, aren't you, Mister Owens?" she spat as they neared the tree line.

"No, ma'am. I'm sure I'm not a bastard. I know both of my parents, but if you meant to imply that I'm a cold-hearted realist then you'd be wrong about that, too. If anything, I'm at the other end of the spectrum, but that doesn't matter. What I'm telling you is that you need to make your own choices, good or bad.

"Going back to the man who inflicted those wounds would be a really bad choice just as I believe that Angela made one in returning to Bob Johnson yesterday. But it was her choice to make, not mine. Now it's your turn and you can make a bad choice, which is to return to the logging camp, or you can come with me."

They crossed into the trees then stopped and turned to look back, each of them breathing heavily.

Rebecca then turned to Gabe, looked at him and said, "I'll come with you, but not to my father's house."

"Fair enough. Where do you want to go? We need to leave soon before Frank finds that you're missing. I already have the information I need about their setup."

"Let's start back and I can decide that as we go."

Gabe nodded then started walking back to Dancer. When he got to his gelding, he slid his Winchester into its scabbard then turned to Rebecca who had followed.

"You're in pretty bad shape, ma'am. Do you think you can ride?"

"It won't be very comfortable, but I think I can manage."

"I'll tell you what I'll do. I'll make you a pillow of sorts out of my bedroll, and you can sit on it rather than trying to straddle the horse."

"Okay. We can try that."

Gabe pulled his bedroll down, unraveled it then folded it twice and handed it to Rebecca.

"Hold onto this until I'm in the saddle."

She took the bedroll pillow as he mounted then gave it back to him. He set it across the front of his saddle then put his hand out to her.

"Put your foot on top of my boot and then I'll hoist you onto the bedroll."

"Okay."

Rebecca took his hand, put her left foot on his then stood up. He put his other hand around her waist and lifted her gently onto the bedroll. She wiggled herself onto the bedroll, then put her left arm around his waist.

"Okay, Miss Ulrich, let's get the hell out of here," he said as he wheeled Dancer back east then added, "You can keep an eye on our backtrail a lot better than I can. If you see any movement at all, let me know and be prepared to slide down to the ground. If they come, I want you flat on your stomach. I'll have to wait until it looks like they're going to fire before I can start shooting."

"Okay," she answered as she took her first look behind them.

Once they were underway, Gabe began to think about where he could put Rebecca and the only answer he could come up with was Angela's house. The question was the length of her stay and what she could tell him.

"Ma'am, I think I know where you can stay. After Angela and I talked yesterday, she said I could use her house until I left. I have the only sets of keys, so you can stay there until you decide where you want to go permanently."

She looked at him with fire in her gray eyes as she asked, "And I suppose you'll be the perfect gentleman and let me sleep by myself, won't you?"

"Yes, ma'am. I will. You'll have your privacy while I'm there."

"Why? Don't you like women?"

"Some women," he replied.

"You know what I meant," she snapped back.

"Yes, ma'am, I knew exactly what you meant, and believe me, my reply was completely honest. I find women fascinating, but not very many. You have to take my word for it that while you are in the house, and it can't be very long, that I won't touch you."

She glared at him with her one good eye, and said, "Why? Is it because I'm just some tawdry woman who gives herself away like a generous whore? Do you think you're too good for the likes of me, Mister Owens?"

Gabe looked at her angry, damaged face just inches from his and replied, “What I think doesn’t matter, Miss Ulrich. It’s what you think of yourself that’s important. But what I need to have you do right now is stop trying to fight with me. You seem to hate the entire world, which is a waste of time, but I do need to talk to you. Aside from my promise to your parents that I’d try to bring you out of the camp if I could, I need as much information that I can get about Bob Walker.”

“She’s not my mother!”

“I know that. Eli explained your family situation, but it’s easier to say parents rather than your father and Sarah. Now will you please stop trying to argue and just talk to me about Bob Johnson? If you don’t want to because you love him and want to protect him like Angela did then don’t say anything. I’ll do what I have to do without your help.”

Rebecca asked in an almost normal tone, “What are you going to do?”

“I’m going to find the murderers of Mike Wheatley and Willie Bernstadt, and I’m already pretty sure that it was Bob Johnson and probably Frank Stanford. If you want to protect them, I’ll just drop you at the house and continue as best I can.”

“Do you think I’d really protect the bastard who did this to me?” she asked as she pointed at her face.

“I’ve seen women in worse shape than you fight to defend the men who’d injured them, Miss Ulrich.”

“Well, I’m not one of them. What do you want to know?”

“First, I want to know if you heard either of them talk about the murders.”

"On the day that they were killed, Bob learned that Willie had been talking to Mister Wheatley and he told Frank to kill Willie and bring his body back to the camp. Frank sent Red O'Rourke and Hack Tanner out to kill Willie, and Bob told Frank that he'd take care of the problem in Missoula. After Willie was killed, Frank said that they dropped a tree on him, then Bob went into Missoula."

Gabe was more than just surprised as he asked, "They said that in front of you?"

"They said a lot of things in front of me. I was just like a piece of furniture."

Then Gabe said, "You do know how much danger you're in now, don't you?"

"Of course, I do. I'm not stupid!" she snapped.

Gabe sighed. It was almost a normal conversation for a short while, too.

"I didn't say you were, ma'am, but you didn't let me finish. You're not just in danger because they'll want you back. Until you told me what you just did, I hadn't realized that they essentially gave you the power to have them hanged. Now I'll probably have to get you out of Missoula altogether."

"Do you expect me to just get on a train looking like this?"

"No, ma'am. I'll give you money and see if I can't get you some clothes, too. The next eastbound passenger train leaves this evening, so I should be able to get it all set up by then."

"Where will you send me?"

"Wherever you'd like to go. You can go to Helena or anywhere else."

"And what am I supposed to do?" she asked harshly, "Do you think I can just show up in some town, smile sweetly, find a wonderful husband and live happily ever after?"

"You know, ma'am, you're making this a lot harder than it has to be. Eli warned me that you might hand my head to me, and I'm beginning to think that will be the second part of my anatomy that you'll cut off. Now if you'll please let me finish before emasculating me, I'll tell you where you can go."

She wasn't apologetic when she said, "Go ahead."

"You are now a critical witness to the prosecution of Bob Johnson, Frank Stanford and others, so I need to keep you safe. Wherever you decide to go, you'll only have to stay there for a few days while I finish this job. If I'm able to get Bob and Frank into a jail cell, I'll have you returned for the trial, but I don't think that there's going to be a trial. Men who are facing hanging never willingly surrender, especially if they're in a protected location like that camp. So, after they're dead, you can return to Missoula."

"Do you think I want to live here?"

Gabe closed his eyes for a couple of seconds then answered, "You are trying my patience, Miss Ulrich. You hated my idea about moving you away from Missoula, and you're angry about staying here. Now that doesn't leave many places available for you to stay. Do you have any place that you'd like to go?"

Rebecca wanted to scream at him again but realized that as desperately as she wanted to get out of the camp, she really had no place she could go.

After that stark revelation, she said, “Just take me to the house and let me think.”

“Fine. You know, even though you were being snotty about smiling at some man and getting married and having a happy life, I’m sure that if you ever did smile at some man, he’d be smitten, and you could make whatever you wanted out of the rest of your life. I’m just not sure that you’re capable of smiling.”

She glared at him with her one open eye and just snorted in derision.

They both fell into blessed silence as they crossed onto the road and still hadn’t seen any followers, which made no sense at all to Gabe. He’d kept Dancer to a fast walk because of the weight and he didn’t want Rebecca to feel any more pain than she obviously was experiencing. He wondered if her disposition would get any better when she wasn’t hurting but doubted that it would. She was overflowing with hate and most of it was of her own making, at least until she entered the logging camp.

Gabe was wrong in that it made no sense that no one was following if he’d understood Frank Stanford.

He’d spent a longer time than usual with Bob after leaving his house then after their routine review of the current status of the timber operation and future harvesting, he and Bob had spent another twenty minutes engaged in a ribald comparison of the nights spent with Angela and Becky.

Bob, having just fallen asleep with Angela that night, had to substitute his afternoon tryst for his version and even exaggerated that.

Angela had been sitting just twelve feet away, ignored by both of them as they laughed uproariously while she grew more furious with each word. Those pigs! It was as she listened that she began to realize how Becky felt as they acted as if she was a piece of furniture. Even worse was how Frank described how he had hurt Becky. The things he had done to Becky made her sick, and the threat of being turned over to that monster became much more fearsome.

When Frank finally left the house, still chuckling as he crossed the porch, it was more than thirty minutes since he'd entered, and Becky was already sitting on her bedroll pillow three miles away.

He trotted up the steps to his house already excited by the descriptive talks he'd had with Bob and decided that he wanted Becky again.

He threw open the door, didn't see her waiting in the front room then closed the door and shouted, "Becky! Get your butt over here now!"

After hearing no reply, his anger exploded as he swore under his breath then stomped across the room toward the kitchen.

"You're gonna be sorry, you bitch!" he screamed in the short hallway then when he didn't find her in the kitchen, he grew even angrier as he searched the rest of the small house.

Finally, after not finding her anywhere, he suspected she was in the privy. Women were like that. They took longer in there than men did, so rather than continue his search, he poured himself a cup of coffee and sat down at the table waiting for her to return, not once giving even a passing thought that she might have run off. She wouldn't dare.

With the camp only eight miles from town that should have been the most obvious conclusion, but not for Frank. He was so convinced that he had her terrified so badly, Becky wouldn't stray a hundred feet from his house.

He finished his coffee, swore yet again, angrily slammed the cup on the table shattering the heavy porcelain then stood and walked out the back door striding toward the privy with his eyes almost burning a hole through the closed door.

Frank reached the outhouse and snarled, "You're done here, you…" then yanked open the door and found it just as Becky-less as the house.

Then forty-four minutes after Gabe had opened his front door to take Rebecca away, Frank at long last realized that Becky had run.

Now came the dilemma that not Gabe or even Rebecca could have foreseen as Frank panicked. He wasn't concerned about her testimony that could get him hanged because he wasn't thinking that far ahead and really hadn't even noticed that she had been present for most of their conversations. Frank was monumentally afraid of telling Bob Johnson she was gone.

It wasn't that he was physically afraid so much although there was some of that present in his panic. Frank Stanford, although he was only four years younger than Bob Johnson, regarded him almost as a father figure. He was smarter, better educated, and he was the boss. Bob was so much more refined than he was too.

Frank always wanted to be like Bob and never wanted to disappoint him. Now he'd somehow allowed Rebecca to escape and the last person he wanted to tell was Bob Johnson. If he had, then they might have been able to catch up with her and Gabe before they reached the main road as Dancer was still just plodding along, but he didn't even think of telling Bob. In his panicked state, he began to search the camp willy-nilly rather than methodically. He didn't look for her footprints in the heavily traveled main yard but instead began hurriedly going from building to building, his panic and anger both rising with each negative result.

He finally gave up his search and convinced himself she'd return later once she realized she had no money and no place to go. He'd make her pay for leaving, too.

He then went about his normal work as foreman and headed out to where the trees were coming down.

———

Gabe walked Dancer carefully over the tracks and looked down at his hooves as they stepped past the rails and crossties. Once they were on the other side, he set him off at a slow trot, expecting Rebecca to blast him for the added discomfort, but she didn't. She just continued to stare at the road behind them waiting for Bob and Frank to come racing down the gravel surface in a big cloud of dust.

———

Gabe turned east down the alley that ran behind Angela's house. Surprisingly, few people had seen him and Rebecca ride through town and aside from the looks of curiosity, he didn't spot any who might go running to the sheriff which was all that mattered.

Rebecca had been remarkably silent, and he assumed it was because she simply didn't want to talk to him at all. Either that or she was falling asleep and imagined she hadn't gotten much sleep since being moved to Frank's house. Despite the obvious signs of Frank's viciousness, even he couldn't have imagined how she had been dragged to the house and the horrors she had experienced last night.

Nonetheless, Gabe felt a great deal of sympathy for Rebecca even as she treated him like the bastard who had abused her. She may have been an ungrateful, rebellious daughter at home before she left, but she didn't deserve this treatment. No woman, and few men did, but two of them who did deserve it and much more lived in the logging camp.

Rebecca wasn't sleeping, nor was she not talking because of anything she'd already said. She was simply mad at the whole world, even Gabe Owens. He may have brought her from the very jaws of hell, *but why?* He only needed her as a witness. He didn't care about her at all. No one cared about her.

Her father cared about her aunt and their two children, but he had been responsible for her mother's death even though she knew he didn't do it intentionally. Then he married Sarah, her mother's own sister! He took her to the same bed that he'd shared with her mother and made love to her. She had heard them in the next room, and it disgusted her. Sarah had tried to be nice to her, but Rebecca knew it was just because she wanted to please her traitorous father.

She had run off with Bob because it was her chance to really hurt her father and Sarah. She knew what he was, and that had excited her at first. But it hadn't lasted long when she realized what a cold, cruel man he was under that polished exterior. She's stayed and kept his bed warm, but whenever he took her all she did was lay there and let him have his way, and he never even noticed that either, or just didn't care.

Then there was the that long horror that had pushed her even deeper into her hate-filled world. She thought she'd never hate anyone as much as she hated Bob Johnson until last night. Even then, Frank didn't move to the top position, but simply stood beside his boss and mentor. If she had a gun, she'd shoot the pair of them.

Now she was free from that life and sitting on a horse with her arm around a man who actually claimed that he wasn't going to do what Bob had done. He must believe she was as big a fool as Angela was. Angela had fallen for every lie that Bob Johnson had fed her and even now thought he was a thoughtful, considerate man who had saved her from her abusive husband.

But after having watched Frank hit her and drag her out of the house by her hair even Angela had to have been shocked when she heard her beloved Bob laugh rather than stop Frank. All men must believe women are nothing more than vacuous cows that only serve to satisfy their lust before being put out to pasture in favor of a young heifer. She didn't doubt for a moment that Owens was the same beast inside but wore even a better disguise than Bob Johnson.

Now she knew that if he tried to get into her bed tonight, he'd find out just how much fight she had in her. She wasn't going to be a piece of furniture or a mattress ever again. Gabe Owens was nothing more than another pig of a man and she'd be ready.

Gabe turned Dancer into the back yard of Angela's house and pulled him to a stop.

"Okay, ma'am, let's get you down. Take my hand and I'll lower you down. Just slide off when you're ready."

She didn't reply but took her arm from around his waist, took his hand in hers, felt the strength in his arm giving her support then straightened her legs and began to slide. He then lowered her to the ground gently and once she was standing, Gabe turned Dancer toward the small barn and walked him inside.

Rebecca remained standing in place as she watched Gabe dismount, remove his rifle then begin to unsaddle his small black gelding. She may not like Gabe, but she had to admire his Morgan. He was such a handsome animal with his white stockings and the pronounced white star on his forehead. Unlike the men who rode them, horses could be trusted.

Once the tack was all stored, he put his saddlebags over his right shoulder removed the two canteens then hung them over his left shoulder, picked up his Winchester and began walking towards her.

She thought he was just going to walk past her into the house, expecting her to follow, but he didn't.

Gabe stopped next to Rebecca, offered her his left arm then simply said, "Miss Ulrich?"

She ignored his arm, so Gabe shrugged, walked up the four steps, crossed the back porch then reached into his jacket pocket took out a small key ring, unlocked the door and swung it wide to allow Rebecca to walk inside.

Rebecca glanced at Gabe wondering how far she'd get into the house before he grabbed her but entered anyway.

Gabe followed then closed and locked the door again before setting his Winchester against the wall, removing his hat and gunbelt and hanging both on pegs. He then set his saddlebags down, walked to the sink and dumped out the contents of both canteens.

Without turning, he asked, "I was thinking about just reheating the coffee but decided to make some fresh. Would you like something to eat, ma'am? I didn't have much of a breakfast myself."

Rebecca blinked twice and said, "No. Where am I going to sleep?"

Gabe was pumping water into the now empty canteens when he replied, "Just take whichever bedroom you'd like. I'll be sleeping on the first floor, so I think you'd feel safer upstairs. I don't expect any visitors tonight, but if we do, I'll be able to stop them before they get to the stairs."

Rebecca was a bit surprised, but still thought this was a ploy to make her less wary of his planned visit.

"I'll go upstairs and pick one out. Do they have locks on the doors?"

"I wasn't here long enough to notice but go ahead and check them all. If one does, they probably all do. I can't see them just putting locks on some of the rooms."

"Alright," she said as she quickly walked down the long hallway.

She looked around with her good eye as she passed through the big house and was impressed with everything she saw. She reached the large staircase and climbed the steps to the second floor. The first bedroom she checked did have a lock on the door, but she still examined all four of the bedroom doors on the floor and found they all had locks. She knew her dress was in tatters from Frank's unrestrained grabbing but her other clothes were still in her room in Bob's house, so she began searching for a bedroom with women's clothes but didn't find any.

After her fruitless search for something else to wear, she walked back downstairs and began inspecting the downstairs bedrooms for clothes, but only found men's clothing in the bedroom with an unmade bed. The house was empty of women's clothing.

She knew that Angela had brought a lot of clothes with her, and obviously had emptied out her closet and dresser. This presented another problem, and she hated to admit she'd have to ask Gabe Owens for help in improving her wardrobe. Worse yet was she had no money which meant he'd have to spend his own and would undoubtedly expect her to pay him back in services. The idea that she was becoming a whore in all but name made her angrier than she had been when they started and that was already impressive.

She then left the bedroom and walked to the kitchen where Gabe was already pouring some beans into a skillet on the large cookstove.

He turned when he heard her enter and asked, “Did you find a bedroom with locks?”

“They all have locks,” she answered curtly then said, “I don't have any clothes.”

“As I told you before, ma'am, I'll see about getting you some clothes in a little while.”

She knew she should have said ‘thank you', but she believed she was already giving him a price for bedding her by asking for more clothes and the best she could do was to say nothing.

Rebecca then sat at the table and watched as Gabe cooked.

He didn't even look at her when he said, "Ma'am, while I'm gone, I'd feel better if you were armed. If you look in the saddlebag facing you, you'll find a holster and a pistol. Go ahead and take it out of there and I'll tell you how to use it."

Rebecca was a bit startled that he would offer her a pistol, but stood and walked across the kitchen, bent at the knees flipped open the saddlebag's flap and easily found a pistol in a holster, but it wasn't attached to a gunbelt. It was something different.

"What's this?" she asked as she stood holding the shoulder holster and Webley.

Again, without turning from the stove Gabe replied, "That's a Webley Bulldog and I wear it in a shoulder holster, so no one can see it. I'm wearing one right now. The one you're holding is my spare."

She looked at him trying to see the pistol he was wearing but couldn't.

"You want me to keep this with me?" she asked.

"Yes, ma'am, even when I'm here. Maybe you'll sleep better behind a locked door with a loaded pistol nearby because you obviously still believe I'm a cold-hearted bastard. It's fully loaded with five cartridges, so be careful. The Webley uses the same cartridges as my Remington or most Winchesters, so it's a powerful gun.

"The short barrel just means it's not as accurate as a normal pistol, but for close range, it'll do the job. It's a double action pistol, so all you have to do is point it at your target and squeeze the trigger. Don't yank it, or you'll miss even at close range. If you have to protect yourself, just point the gun at the man who's threatening you as if you were pointing your finger at him and squeeze the trigger. You shouldn't need a second shot, but if you do, just squeeze the trigger again. You'll get five shots to stop the man."

"And you want me to keep this?"

"That's what I said, ma'am. Like I just told you, I'll be leaving shortly, and I want to make sure you're safe."

"Because you need me to be a witness. Right?"

"Honestly, Miss Ulrich? Just as I said earlier, and you must not have paid attention, I don't believe this will ever come to trial. Bob Johnson knows he's guilty of poaching and probably a lot worse. Men like him don't just hold out their wrists and wait for me to handcuff them. They'll try and kill me first, and I'll have to stop them. I'm giving you the gun to keep you safe. It's that simple."

"Do you really expect me to believe you?" she asked harshly.

"You can believe what you wish, ma'am," Gabe replied as he stirred the beef and bean mix.

He rarely cooked and when he did, it was usually a disaster, but he thought he'd be safe with this. He'd been annoyed by Rebecca's apparent view of him as a worthless excuse for a man, and was almost willing to let it go, considering the men she'd been living with for the past year. But she'd also spent most of her life with a good man, her father, so she should know the difference.

Eli had warned him how Rebecca seemed to blame him for her mother's death, and she'd begun to hate not only him, but the entire world around her. He had found it hard to believe, but now thought Eli had understated just how belligerent she was and began to have second thoughts about arming her. But he knew that she would never trust him unless he gave her some measure of self-protection.

Rebecca carried the Webley to the table sat down and slid it out of its holster. She felt the steel in her hand, and it felt right. She knew she had large hands for a woman and could probably handle a normal pistol, but this one almost felt like it was part of her hand.

She was still looking at the Bulldog when Gabe put two bowls of the mix on the table then two cups of coffee and two spoons.

"Do you want some cream with your coffee, ma'am?"

"If you have some."

"I'm not sure, but I'll check the cold room."

He left and a few seconds later, returned with a small glass bottle and set it on the table before sitting down. He began to eat without any announcement or conversation, so Rebecca did the same.

She was still silently eating when Gabe finished, stood and stepped to the sink, pumped some water into his empty bowl then washed it and set it in the drying rack.

Gabe turned to Rebecca and said, "Ma'am, I'll be back in a couple of hours or so. I'll leave you with one set of keys and I have the second. If anyone tries to come in without keys, then get your pistol ready."

Rebecca nodded then Gabe pulled the keys from his jacket pocket, set them on the table before he turned, walked across the room and after pulling on his Stetson, snatched his Winchester then left the room, locking the door behind him.

Rebecca then took the keys, slipped them into her dress pocket and continued to eat, glancing at the back door as she did, still not trusting Gabe Owens. Nobody was that nice. Nobody.

Gabe had Dancer saddled in ten minutes and trotted him out of the small barn to run his errands. His first stop would be the Ulrich home. He wanted to let Eli and Sarah know that Rebecca was safe. She may be a seriously annoying person to be around, but she was safely away from the logging camp, and she was a very valuable witness.

Ten minutes later after dismounting and tying off his Morgan, he stepped into the big cutting room and spotted Eli hard at work again. If he hadn't met him before, he'd have a hard time picking him out from the other men.

Eli spotted Gabe, set down his maul then headed towards him.

"Did you find the logging camp?" he asked when he was close.

"I did. You didn't tell me that they were clearing the whole forest. There weren't many trees left standing where they'd been."

"Stupid, isn't it?"

"Greedy more than stupid. I just stopped by to let you know that I took Rebecca out of the logging camp without a problem."

"*Is she all right? How did she look? How did she act*?" he asked excitedly in rapid fire with wide eyes.

"She was a sad sight, Eli. She said that Bob had given her over to Frank Stanford yesterday and he beat her severely. I'm glad I got her out of there as quickly as I did. Aside from the bruising and cuts though, she looks fine. And to answer your unasked question, she didn't appear to be pregnant and didn't have a baby with her either. I brought her to Mike Wheatley's house because I have the only keys and Angela is still out at the logging camp."

"Thank you for getting her out of there, Gabe. I'll tell Sarah that she's safe and staying with you for protection. Do you need anything?"

"I need to get her some clothes and other things. Did she leave any at home before she left?"

"No, she took everything with her."

"Okay. I'll handle that. I've got to make a couple of more stops on my way back to the house, Eli. I'll keep you informed when I can and maybe I'll still be able to convince Rebecca that hating the world is a waste of a life. Except for telling me that Bob and Frank were behind the murders, she hasn't spoken a civil word to me. She just oozes anger and hate.

"I was going to send her to Helena for her protection because once Bob finds her missing then he'll want to shut her up, but she refused that offer too. I'd say that you were a saint among men for putting up with that kind of behavior for so long, but I'll just say that you're a good man and leave it at that."

Eli smiled at his 'saint' comment but said, "I wish there was some way that Rebecca could understand that we all miss her and want her to be happy, but I tend to agree with you that she's just too set in her hate for that to happen."

"There's always hope, Eli. Keep faith."

He shook Gabe's hand and said, "Thank you, Gabe."

Gabe nodded then turned and Eli walked with him out the door. Gabe mounted Dancer while Eli continued on to his house to talk to Sarah. At least he could tell her that Rebecca wasn't pregnant, at least not visibly. How that had happened seemed nothing short of a miracle to him.

After his visit to the lumber yard, Gabe decided to see the sheriff. He needed to find out if he'd heard about Rebecca's disappearance. Gabe was sure that when Bob found out about it, he'd notify the sheriff to have him search the town under some pretense.

Five minutes later, Gabe dismounted, tied Dancer to the jail's hitchrail, crossed the boardwalk and entered the sheriff's office, seeing Deputy Collier behind the desk.

"Deputy, you seem to be chained to that desk. Does anyone else ever do that boring job?"

Rafe Collier grinned and replied, "It seems that way, doesn't it? The other deputy, Billy Cooper, is down with the flu or something. Do you need to see the sheriff, Mister Owens?"

"If he's available. I was going to ask about that report he promised to have done but was sidetracked by Mrs. Wheatley. She let me into the house, so I could look at the crime scene while she told me what had happened."

Before Deputy Collier could say anything else, the sheriff popped out of his office and asked loudly, "What did she say?"

"Oh, good afternoon, Sheriff," Gabe said with a smile.

"Come on into my office and you can tell me her story. I never got to talk to her."

"Okay," Gabe said and then when the sheriff turned to go back into his office, he winked at Deputy Collier, who held back a snicker as he smiled.

Gabe thought he could trust the deputy to at least not interfere. He then walked into the sheriff's private office but left the door open.

"Close the door, would ya?" asked the sheriff.

Gabe closed the door and asked, "Don't trust your deputy?" knowing the answer already.

"No, he's fine, but other folks might come in."

Gabe nodded took a seat then asked, "Did you get your report done?"

"Nope, sorry. Been too busy."

"Well, it doesn't matter, I suppose, now that I've talked to Mrs. Wheatley about what happened that night."

The sheriff asked, "So, what did Mrs. Wheatley tell you."

Gabe leaned forward slightly and said softly, "Between you and me, Sheriff, and this goes no further, she confessed to shooting her husband."

Sheriff Reinhold looked astonished as he asked sharply, "*She did?*"

Gabe nodded and continued, saying, “She was really upset because she said he’d been beating her and even showed me some bruises on her arms and neck. I would have shot the bastard myself if he was still alive when I got here. I never got to tell you, but back in Minnesota, I had asked her to marry me, but she married Mike Wheatley instead before coming out here.”

“Well, that explains why she wanted to see you when she showed up and how she greeted you, too.”

“I think that’s why she told me. She knew I still had a soft spot for her, and I told her that I wasn’t going to arrest her because she killed him in self-defense, and I know that you still can arrest her, but I’d appreciate it if we just let this one slide. The way I look at it, justice was served when she put that bullet through his chest.”

The sheriff leaned back in relief and nodded before saying, “I agree with you, Mister Owens. Are you gonna head back soon?”

“In a couple of days, I think. I’ll wait until the new yard manager arrives and everything is settled down because that’s part of my job. Angela said I could stay in her house while I was here, which makes it easier. Obviously, I don’t need the report anymore, so I’m going to head back and write my own report now.”

Sheriff Reinhold had been so relieved about hearing Gabe swallow Angela’s story that he just sat there like the string-less marionette that he was for a few seconds before looking at Gabe.

“Well, I appreciate your tellin’ me about what happened, Mister Owens.”

Gabe stood then said, “And I appreciate your agreeing that justice was delivered by Mrs. Wheatley.”

The sheriff smiled then Gabe shook his hand, turned, opened the door and walked past Rafe Collier, rolling his eyes as he did and getting a new smile and snicker in the process.

Gabe pulled on his hat before leaving then after he mounted Dancer, he turned west to make two more stops. He’d learned a lot from his short chat with Sheriff Reinhold.

The most critical was that he still wasn’t aware that Rebecca wasn’t in the camp any longer, which meant that Bob Johnson probably didn’t know either, which really shocked him. *Was Frank Stanford really that much afraid of Bob?*

Then he’d confirmed that the sheriff was deeply involved in Mike Wheatley’s murder and coverup, and he had to know he would hang if it ever went to court making him very dangerous and capable of anything. But the good thing was he now believed that Sheriff Jack Reinhold was the only crooked lawman in Missoula, at least as far as Deputy Collier was concerned. He still hadn’t seen the flu-ridden second deputy.

Just a few minutes later, he turned onto Front Street then stopped at Worden & Company General Merchandise. He walked to the women’s clothing section and told the sales clerk that his wife was enroute and needed a lot more clothes and other things that a woman would need that he didn’t have in the house, so he let her choose anything that Rebecca could need. He just gave the young lady her height and weight and was a bit embarrassed when he had to describe her figure. He did specify that she include a nice vest.

After the clerk went to fill his order, he walked to the men’s clothing section just to browse and to really just let his mind wander while he tried to imagine the scene of the murder in the kitchen. He felt as if he was missing something and finally decided that he'd examine the room in greater detail now that he had the time.

Forty-five minutes after entering the store, he hung two large bags on Dancer before mounting to make his final stop, and it had to be the last one for a reason.

He rode down Front Street, stopped at Hartman's Ice House and purchased a block of ice and then had them crush it before pouring the chips into a heavy canvas bag. He slipped it over his saddle horn and then set Dancer to a medium trot to get back to the house before the ice melted.

Gabe pulled up behind the house, stepped down and tied Dancer to the hitchrail, hung the two bags of clothing and other items over his shoulder then took the canvas bag of ice from the saddle horn. He carried them up the steps and put down the wet canvas bag, unlocked the door and then picked it back up and went inside.

Rebecca wasn't in the kitchen which didn't surprise him at all, but he didn't hear her footsteps either which did. She should be checking to see who had just entered the house.

He set the two bags on the floor and carried the bag of ice to the other side of the kitchen and set it in the sink.

With no sounds from Rebecca, he was going to call out to her but didn't want to face retaliation for what she would probably consider rude behavior, so he just left the house and led Dancer to the barn where he stripped him of his tack then brushed him down.

He reentered the house, locked the door and before he hunted for Rebecca, he started his reexamination of the murder scene. First, he looked down at the spot where the pool of blood had been. Mike had to have fallen forward because of the table which meant that the shot had to come from the other side of the room. None of the chairs had been disturbed, so he hadn't been sitting down either, so he probably had just entered the room.

He walked back to the hallway, turned back to face the kitchen and pretended to be Mike Wheatley. Gabe first looked at what was visible in the kitchen from the hallway then slowly entered the kitchen even though Mike would have walked in normally expecting to find Angela. He wanted to watch the view of the room expand as he walked closer.

He took a step, stopped and scanned the room then a second. If it was a planned killing, which Gabe believed it was, then the shooter wouldn't be near the door because Mike would have seen the derringer pointed at him and quickly backed into the hall. The distance from the back doorway to the hall was about twelve feet which, while well within the range of a derringer, would have greatly lessened the likelihood of a killing shot.

He took another step into the kitchen and still believed that Mike would have been able to back out.

That meant the shooter had to have been near the door of the cold room in the opposite corner of the kitchen from the back door. When he turned to look at the cold room door, he was puzzled because if Mike had turned to see his killer, he still could have just dived to the right into the hallway. He would have been able to get away unless he was frozen by what he found.

Gabe walked to the cold room door and then began looking more closely at its heavy wood surface and finally caught a glimpse of a light stain. He stepped back to look at the door from a distance and saw that it was a spray pattern that was almost invisible unless the sunlight was on the door as it was now.

He stepped to the door and slid his finger through edge of the pattern then smelled his finger. It was gunpowder residue. He then put his back to the wall facing the table where he'd just put the two bags. The cold room door was on his left with the hallway four feet beyond the edge of the cold room door as he aimed with his right hand at the entrance to the hallway. Then he did it with his left and felt his stomach flip.

The spray pattern began just halfway along the back of his left hand. Whoever killed Mike was shorter than he was by about six inches and was left-handed. Angela was both.

Angela hadn't been lying when she said she had killed her husband, at least not about the act itself. He was sure she was lying about the circumstances, though. But he couldn't see her just waiting for Mike in the kitchen with the derringer pointed at the hallway, then Mike walking in and allowing himself to be shot.

Bob Johnson had to be in the room and close to Angela, or Mike would have seen him. The only thing that made any sense was if Bob was doing something with Angela in the corner of the kitchen when Bob walked in and was stunned to find them together, and then Angela shot him from behind Bob.

He finally let the murder go for the time being because the ice was melting in the sink, and he thought he'd better find out where Rebecca was. It was possible that she'd run away, which would have been incredibly stupid and while she may have been many things, stupid wasn't one of them.

Gabe walked down the hallway, glancing in each of the empty rooms then climbed the stairs and when he reached the upper landing, he noticed that one of the bedroom doors was closed, but all of the others were open.

He debated about knocking or just going back downstairs but finally decided to knock. The ice wasn't going to last forever.

He rapped on the bedroom door and was just about to leave when he heard Rebecca reply from the other side of the door.

"What?"

"I wanted to make sure you were okay. I brought you some things. They're in the kitchen when you want to come down."

She didn't say anything else, so Gabe just shrugged, grateful she hadn't decided to try out the Bulldog then trotted down the stairs and returned to the kitchen. He restarted the cookstove's fire, so he could make some coffee then took a seat at the table, put his head back and put his palm over his eyes. He needed to think. Maybe there was another scenario that would explain the positioning of the gunpowder spray.

He had to write a preliminary report and get it on the next eastbound train to Minneapolis soon, just in case he came out on the wrong end of the conflict with Bob Johnson. He had the hard evidence of poaching and the perpetrators, and he'd add all the evidence he had about the double homicide and then he'd give the report to Joe Lofton and have him put it on the next passenger train and have it hand delivered to Herb Erikson.

Rebecca was the wild card in all this. She was a perfect witness but her angry demeanor wouldn't win points with a jury. He still doubted very much if it got that far. Her value to him right now was the enormous wealth of information she must have about Bob Johnson and his camp. He wanted as much as he could get, including the layout of the inside of the two houses and the guns that they had. He'd also need to know as much about the men themselves, including the thugs who did the nasty work.

He was so deep in his planning that he didn't hear a barefoot Rebecca enter the kitchen.

After Gabe had gone, she had kicked off her shoes and laid on the bed, falling asleep in just minutes. When she was awakened by his knocking, she had been disoriented for a few seconds and then the full impact of being away from that situation had struck her like a lightning bolt. She felt liberated and free, but she was still far from happy.

She was living in a house with a man she didn't trust mainly because she trusted no one. She had this one torn dress and if he brought her clothes, then she knew what he'd demand of her. But still, being away from the camp put her in a slightly better mood and that slight improvement in her demeanor was crucial.

When she entered the kitchen, she stopped and saw Gabe at the table with his head back, hand over his eyes and the two large cloth bags on the table. Her price for submission, she thought. Then she saw the bag in the sink, wondered why it was there and her curiosity pushed aside her hostility, at least for the moment.

"Excuse me," she said quietly.

Gabe jerked upright as his hand flew from his eyes before he said, "Oh, I'm sorry. I didn't see hear you enter."

She pointed at the sink and asked, "What's in the bag?"

"Ice. I thought it would help."

"With what?" she asked.

He stood, walked to a drawer and took out a towel, spread it on the counter then opened the bag of ice took out a handful and dumped it on the towel. After folding it over the ice, he stepped closer to Rebecca but not too closely and handed it to her.

"Sit down at the table, and press this gently on your swollen eye and lips. It will reduce the swelling and make it numb, so it won't hurt so much."

Rebecca eyed him suspiciously but accepted the towel of ice chips then took a seat at the table. She kept her open eye on him as she slowly put the towel to her face. It hadn't been there for five seconds before she closed her good eye as she felt the cold take away some of the pain.

"How did you know about ice?"

"I thought everyone did. We had a lot of bumps and bruises at the logging camps and we always had a lot of ice around. I'm surprised that you wouldn't know about it. Surely, when you were a girl, you fell down or something and had something cold pressed onto the injury."

"No, I never did. I wasn't clumsy just because I'm tall, you know."

Gabe understood that Rebecca viewed even simple gestures of kindness as a slap in the face, so he didn't reply but walked back to the table and took a seat.

Then she pulled the towel away from her face and looked at Gabe with both eyes before she asked sharply, “What do you want?”

“You have to be more specific than that, ma’am. I want many things, mostly Bob Johnson and Frank Stanford.”

“You bought me two bags of things and this ice to make me feel better. What do you think you’ll get in return? I know what you’re expecting and you’re going to be disappointed.”

“Everything isn’t a barter, ma’am. I bought you the clothes and the ice because you needed them, nothing more.”

“Do you expect me to believe that?”

Gabe let out a long breath and replied, “What you choose to believe or not believe isn’t up to me. Now, Miss Ulrich, if you’ll just stop acting as if you hate and distrust every human being walking the face of the earth, then we can have a normal conversation which is what I need right now. You know things that can help me get my job done. I have a lot of work to do and I’d rather not spend the next few hours defending myself. Is that clear?”

Rebecca looked at him then after a few seconds answered, “Alright, I’ll try.”

“Now the first thing I need to know is what you can tell me about Bob Johnson and Frank Stanford. I got a glimpse of Frank from about eight hundred yards with my field glasses, but I don’t even know what Bob Johnson looks like.”

Rebecca couldn’t see any harm in helping him if he was going to shoot Bob and Frank, so she said, “He’s actually a bit shorter than I am, around five feet seven inches, and I’d guess his weight is around a hundred and sixty pounds. He usually dresses in a dark suit. He's handsome with black hair and brown eyes and has a trimmed moustache. He's well-groomed and acts like a gentleman. Frank Stanford is much taller, about your height but probably weighs two hundred and twenty pounds. You saw him, so that's how he dresses most of the time and he doesn't act like anything other than the brute that he is."

"Is Bob left-handed?"

Rebecca tilted her head slightly and asked, "How did you know if you've never met him?"

"I didn't. I was hoping that he was. I'll explain later if you're interested. Tell me about the others they use for their dirty work."

"There are six of them, and they're all lumberjacks but have special privileges. The ones that they rely on the most are Red O'Rourke and Hack Tanner. They're both bigger than you and Red has red hair but no beard, while Tanner had dark brown hair and wears a full beard. He keeps it long, too. The other four I don't know well, but they all look the same. Jack Finlay, Alex Hall, Pete Swanson and Carl Short are their names. They're all big men."

"Did you hear Bob giving them instructions to do anything?"

"Only to rough up some of the workers that were causing trouble, but Pete Swanson did kill one when he got carried away. Bob didn't seem to care."

"Okay, that's good. How about weapons? Do they have a lot of guns?"

"Bob has a rack with eight repeaters in his office, but he only lets them use them when he thinks it's necessary. Frank and the other six all have pistols that they wear almost like badges to let the others know who's in charge. Bob only carries a derringer in his left jacket pocket."

"Tell me about the two houses. What are they like inside?"

"Bob's house is twice the size of Frank's. There's the big front room, his office then three bedrooms on the left side of the hallway, a bathroom on the right and there's the large kitchen in back."

"Is there a back door?"

"Yes."

"What's Frank's house like?"

"It's much simpler. It has a main room, two bedrooms and a small kitchen, but there's no back door."

"Good. Tell me about Angela."

"What is there to tell? We didn't exactly spend a lot of time chatting. Why should we? When she came to the camp, I knew I was in trouble."

"Do you believe she murdered her husband?"

"I hope so, because I wouldn't mind seeing her hang."

Gabe asked, "Why? Were you that jealous? Do you still love Bob Johnson?"

She laughed as she replied, "Love him? Bob? You have to be joking! I only liked him when I thought he was handsome and a rascal. It sounded exciting and I knew it would hurt my father when I ran off with him. I stopped liking him before the month was out when I realized just how cruel he really was. Now I hate the man more than I thought possible."

"Did he beat you like that?"

"Not this much and not in the face. He was rough and slapped me around some, but not like Frank. This was after one night with Frank and I'm not sure I could have survived another."

Gabe paused while he digested that information. Maybe it hadn't been Mike that had caused all of Angela's bruises after all. They were old, but if Bob had been seeing Angela for a while, maybe he'd made them. But if that was true, then Mike should have seen them, and if he hadn't been beating her, he'd wonder who had.

"Do you think Bob was beating Angela before she came to the logging camp?"

"No. He didn't start hitting me for the first month or so, but that was only because I was there. He'd be nice to her until he could get her to the camp."

"Then if you weren't jealous, why would you hate Angela so much?"

Rebecca rolled her eyes and said, "Don't you understand? Once he started seeing her, I knew it was only a matter of time before he'd give me to Frank. I hated her before I even saw her. Then once I saw her, I knew that even if I wanted to, and I didn't, I knew I couldn't compete with the likes of her."

"Now you've got me confused. Why would you think you couldn't compete with Angela?"

Rebecca snorted and said, “That's a silly question. Have you ever even seen her?”

“No, it's far from a silly question because I've seen a lot more of her than than you or Bob have.”

Rebecca snickered and said, “Be serious. I doubt if you've seen as much of her as Bob has.”

“You'd be surprised, ma'am. It's why I was surprised that you'd say that you couldn't compete with her because, despite your swollen face, I think you're more attractive than Angela.”

Rebecca squinted with her good eye and growled, “You never even met her, have you? You bought those things and now you're saying something like that, so you can get me into your bed, just like Bob. You're no different than he is and probably just as cruel inside.”

Gabe exhaled sharply before he replied, “I never lie, Miss Ulrich. Never. Not only have I spent more time with Angela than anyone except Mike Wheatley, but I've also been intimate with her twice. Do you want to know where she has a mole that isn't visible while she's wearing even a modicum of clothing? I even proposed to her a few years ago in Minneapolis.”

Rebecca yanked the towel from her face and exclaimed, *“What?”*

“I knew Angela in Minneapolis, proposed to her, and then before she gave me an answer, I had to go on a job in Billings. When I returned, she had accepted a proposal from Mike Wheatley. I never understood why because she didn't say, and I never talked to her again after she told me. She moved out here just two weeks after they were married. It was one of the reasons they didn't send me here in the first place to investigate the possible poaching of railroad timber by Bob Johnson."

"Now that's funny," she said without a trace of humor.

"What's funny?"

"You tell me that you only like some women, and you proposed to a harlot like her. She offered herself to Bob Johnson after knowing him for just two weeks. I bet you really don't like women at all."

"Then why would you believe I'm trying to lure you into my bed, Miss Ulrich? You should feel completely safe if you believe that."

Rebecca began to object but had insulted herself into a corner.

Gabe then asked, "And how long did you know Bob before running off with him? Did he even offer to marry you as I had asked Angela?"

Rebecca didn't reply but just sat there and seethed.

Gabe realized that he might have pushed her too far and that was the last thing he wanted to do. He needed her to talk to him.

"Miss Ulrich, I apologize for asking that question. It's just that Angela has always been a touchy subject with me since she accepted Mike's proposal while I was gone. I understand why you would run off with Bob Johnson. I think it was a poor decision but at least I know your motivation. I also believe I understand why Angela did as well, and I think it was a much worse decision because of her misguided notion that he would be better than Mike. Would you like me to explain what happened when I finally met her in the sheriff's office?"

Rebecca's curiosity overrode her fury, so she replied, "Go ahead."

Gabe nodded then said, "When I got here, I was worried when I couldn't find her, and no one seemed to know where she'd gone. I checked with the sheriff, understanding that he was probably owned by Bob Johnson. That is right, isn't it?"

Rebecca just nodded.

"Anyway, I'm guessing that after I left, he trotted out to Bob's camp to let him know that I was here to investigate the death of our station manager."

Rebecca found herself becoming interested in the narrative and interrupted, saying, "He did. That's where I first heard your name. But Bob had a strange reaction when the sheriff told him you were here to investigate the murder. He said he was happy that it was you, and I thought it meant that you could be bribed, so he sent Angela because, well, men can be bribed by things other than money."

"No, he didn't send her to bribe me because even Angela knew that it wouldn't work. At least it wasn't bribery in the normal use of the word. He wanted it to be me because he believed he could send Angela to Missoula to convince me to stop my investigations and return to Minnesota because of our past relationship and hoped I'd be willing to accept whatever she told me as the truth and end my investigation."

"What happened when she found you?"

"It was embarrassing, really. I walked into the sheriff's office and saw her sitting there talking to a deputy. She leapt to her feet, raced across the room and threw herself into my arms, sobbing. From the moment she opened her mouth the lies began.

"First, she acted as if she was horribly afraid but that was downright silly when you think about it. Who was she afraid of? The sheriff? Bob Johnson? Me? Then she asked me to take her to this house and on the way, she said she'd gone to Bears Mouth to hide but that made no sense either. Then once we entered the house, she saw the patch of dried blood, pretended to faint, and I carried her into the bedroom.

"That's where she used all of her very impressive womanly charms to get me to end my investigation. She told me that Mike beat her, which I'm sure was true because the bruises she showed me were all sorts of different ages. It was why I asked you if Bob had beaten her. She even opened her blouse and hiked up her skirts to show me her bruised thighs at least that was the excuse she used. When she thought I was excited enough, she kissed me and asked me to make love to her to rekindle the old passions that we shared."

"And you expect me to believe that you turned her down?" Rebecca asked in disbelief.

"Yes, I turned her down, and trust me, it was extraordinarily difficult. But she still played on my old feelings and told me how she should have married me instead and said that she still loved me. It was hard to describe, but I could almost sense that she wanted me to ask her if she killed her husband, so I did."

"She didn't admit it, did she?" Rebecca asked with raised eyebrows.

"Yes, she did. She began crying and said that she had to kill him because he was coming at her with a knife."

“Did you believe her?”

“About Mike coming at her with a knife? No. Do I believe that she killed him? I’m not sure. Killing someone in cold blood from ten feet away while they’re looking at you is much harder than most people realize. Trust me on that. I don’t believe she has it in her, but I could be wrong. I thought she’d agree to marry me, too.

“But I’d put my money that Bob Johnson was in the kitchen with her and maybe had her in a compromising position when Mike entered the house, saw them and Bob shot him with a Remington derringer while Mike stood gawking. I knew before I talked to her that whoever killed Mike probably used a Remington derringer and not the Colt that the sheriff said had been used.

“Just a few minutes ago, I did a thorough examination of the kitchen and found some gunpowder residue on the cold room door. That’s why I asked about Bob Johnson being left-handed.”

“What difference would that make?” she asked.

Gabe looked at Rebecca then asked, “I’d like to use you to check on that if I may, ma’am. I won’t have to touch you, okay?”

Rebecca was now too caught up in the mystery to care if he did or not and replied, “Okay.”

He stood and walked to the wall near the cold room.

“Miss Ulrich, can you please step over here?”

Rebecca stood set her cold towel on the table and walked to the cold room door.

When she was there Gabe said, "Now, put your back against the wall leaving a three or four-inch gap between your left shoulder and the corner."

She did and stood facing the table and chairs with the hallway entrance to her left just past the cold room door.

Gabe stood facing the cold room door until the gunpowder spray was visible.

"Now, ma'am, if you'll bring your left hand up and point it as if you had a gun in your hand. Aim at the top of the bags I left on the table and pretend you just pulled the trigger."

She pulled her hand up made a fake gun out of her fingers and pulled her fake trigger while Gabe looked at the gunpowder spray. She'd said she was an inch taller than Bob Johnson, so the difference would be negligible in their arm lengths. The beginning of the spray was just three inches from her bent trigger finger.

"Perfect!" Gabe said then added, "Come stand where I am now and look at the cold room door."

She quickly walked to the spot as he stepped away and let her see the spray.

"What am I looking for?" she asked as she examined the door.

"See this pattern of what looks like dust?" he asked as he pointed at the gunpowder.

"Oh! I see it now. What is it?"

"That, Miss Ulrich, is the residue from a pistol shot. There isn't a lot, either. If it had been made by a .44, it would have been much larger. If it had been a .44, I would have discovered a lot of blood splatter on the far wall and a hole where the bullet passed through the wood after killing Mike Wheatley. That's why I was sure it was a Remington derringer, and the small amount of residue confirms it.

"I had you stand there because you said you were an inch taller than Bob Johnson, so it's exactly where it would be if he'd fired the pistol. If he'd been right-handed that residue wouldn't be there at all, either. Now before you object, I'm well aware that Angela is about the same height as Bob and is left-handed, too. All that means is that either one could have pulled the trigger. It really doesn't matter in a court of law, though. Angela's only defense would be is if she was trying to stop Bob, but you and I both know that would be a lie."

Rebecca was surprised that he so calmly said that Angela, a woman he'd wanted to marry was probably a murderer.

She walked back to the table picked up her ice towel, sat down and pressed the soothing pack to her face again.

"What happened after she told you that she'd killed her husband?" she asked.

"She said that she still loved me and even if I arrested her, she was happy to see me again."

"I know you didn't do that. Why did you let her go?"

"After I told her I wouldn't arrest her, she told me what a wonderful man Bob Johnson was and that she would marry him and be happy. I went so far as to tell her that because she vouched for Bob, I'd just end my entire investigation. She was ecstatic then told me she didn't want to stay in the house anymore and drove her buggy back to see Bob.

"I went and told the sheriff that she'd confessed but asked him to let it go because she was acting in self-defense from her abusive husband. He readily agreed, and I left the jail. As to the reason that I went down this path, I'll have to admit to performing my own part in the play. It was really the only choice I had once she started lying. I had to know why she was lying. If I had arrested her and taken her to the sheriff, what do you think would happen?"

Rebecca recognized the issue and simply said, "Oh."

"Yes, exactly. All hell would break loose and I needed time. By releasing Angela and telling her that I was just going to write my report and head back to Minneapolis, I bought more time."

"What will you do when you find her again?"

"A lot depends on what additional evidence I uncover, Miss Ulrich."

Her anger had subsided enough for her to say, "Will you please stop calling me that? My name is Rebecca."

"I know that, but would you rather be called Rebecca or Becky?"

She slowly replied, "That's what they called me at the camp, and I hated it. The next man that calls me Becky will be rolling on the floor and squealing like a little girl."

Gabe sighed, stood then stepped in front of Rebecca, spread his legs apart and his arms wide, then said, "Okay, Rebecca, get it over with."

She stared at him and asked, "What are you talking about?"

"You just told me that you'd deliver a haymaker of a kick into the next man who called you Becky. I actually like Rebecca much better, but now that you put it into my head, it's only a matter of time, probably within the next ten minutes, before I make the mistake and call you Becky.

"It's like anything else that sits in your brain when someone tells you not to do something, or you say it to yourself. It can be something as stupid as 'don't tap your head' or something much worse like 'don't fill that sixth chamber'. The more you tell yourself not to do something, the more likely it will be that you'll do it. So, go ahead, get it done now, so I can talk like a girl when there aren't any men around."

She looked at Gabe as he stood there, looking at the ceiling with his arm spread wide and despite her injuries and distrust, Rebecca laughed.

Gabe brought his eyes and arms back down smiled at her and said, "I imagine laughing doesn't make that face feel any better, ice or no ice."

"No, it hurt, but I'm still glad I laughed. It's been a long time."

"Laughter is a powerful medicine, Rebecca."

He sat back down and said, "Now the other question I have for you is about their relationship."

She asked, "Why do you want to know? Are you jealous?"

"I'll admit that the thought of her in his bed does irritate me, but not as much as it did when she first married Mike Wheatley and I thought I was still in love with her. That really set me off. I had to leave town and run three boxes of .44 cartridges through my Winchester '73 before I calmed down."

"So, what exactly do you want to know? Remember, we didn't talk much."

"After she confessed to murdering Mike Wheatley, she seemed pretty happy to be going back to see Bob. After she'd just done as he asked her to do, what happened when she got back?"

"He met her outside, and she told him that you weren't going to arrest her and that you were dropping the investigation. Then he told me to unharness the buggy and stay away from the house for twenty minutes, so they could be alone. She seemed happy about it."

"Twenty minutes and she was happy about that?" he asked with raised eyebrows then realized that he probably shouldn't have asked.

But Rebecca didn't seem offended which surprised him even more when she replied, "That included time for him to get dressed again, too. Bob Johnson is only concerned with Bob Johnson and that includes when he's using women because that's all it is to him. But that's when Frank asked Bob if he could have me now that he had Angela all the time. I made the mistake of arguing that I wasn't for sale and Frank slapped me to the floor and then dragged me out of the house while Bob laughed."

Gabe exhaled and added, "And Angela just sat there and watched quietly."

"I don't know what she did. I was fighting too hard to keep my balance. Then, when he got me into his house…well, you can imagine."

Gabe said quietly, "Rebecca, I know you won't believe me, but all men aren't that way. Right now, I'd like to put a bullet through both of them, and I'm really disappointed in Angela. I guess I shouldn't be, but I am."

After five seconds of silence, Rebecca said quietly but simply, "Thank you for the ice," as her own icy shell began to crack by the honest conversation.

"You're welcome, Rebecca. And you can call me Gabe if you'd like or maybe Your Imperial Majesty or my personal favorite, Gabe the Omniscient Almighty Terror, or as my subjects call me, The Goat."

Rebecca laughed again and said, "The goat. That's funny."

Gabe smiled at her then said, "I've got to write out my preliminary report. It'll take me about forty minutes or so because it'll be pretty long. Did you want to get changed out of that dress? It looks to be in pretty bad shape."

She nodded as she handed Gabe the towel and said, "Thank you for the ice. It does feel much better already."

"The ice won't be completely melted for another hour, so you can use it again when you come back down."

"I'll do that," she said as she stood, picked up her two bags then looked at Gabe and said, "You're not the horrible bastard I thought you were."

Gabe laughed lightly and said, "That's the nicest compliment I've ever received."

Rebecca smiled then padded out of the kitchen in her bare feet and disappeared down the hallway.

Gabe watched her leave and was glad she was gone. Now that she wasn't Miss Ulrich the Harpy, he began to notice just how handsome she was. He hadn't even come close to fibbing when he had told her that she was more attractive than Angela. Even with her swollen, bruised face, she was a very pretty woman. Why any man would disfigure that face was beyond him. He knew that he'd like to disfigure Frank's face to the point he couldn't be recognized by his mother, assuming he had one.

He left the kitchen and found the still seriously messy office, found some paper, a pen and some ink then sat down and began to write.

The part about the poaching was easy but the rest wasn't. He kept it as detailed and as comprehensive as he could but wrote on the assumption that he wouldn't be able to explain it in detail. That would have to wait for his final report.

As he wrote, Rebecca was upstairs emptying the bags. She found what she expected to find but was initially confused about the vest until she remembered that Gabe had showed her his shoulder holster. It was so she could be armed without anyone knowing.

She began to change and after she removed her torn dress, she removed her undergarments and looked at herself in the mirror. There were big black and blue marks on her back, her thighs, calves and chest. She began to touch them and was surprised how many of them didn't hurt any longer. They were Bob's bruises. But there were almost as many Frank bruises after just one night and they were larger and still very sensitive to the touch. She shuddered at the thought of how bad they would have been if she'd had to stay with him much longer.

She recalled Gabe saying how Angela had showed him her bruises in an effort to lure him into bed, but he had been able to refuse her. *Was it because of the bruises?* She didn't see how any man could have had the control to resist a woman with Angela's many gifts when she offered them freely. For a reason she didn't completely understand, she really wanted to know.

After Gabe finished writing his report, he had the six pages drying on the desk and took another blank sheet for his personal notes. He began writing the names of the six men that Rebecca had given him. She said they all carried pistols, but he forgot to ask her if they used them often. Having one didn't mean the wearer was good with it. It took practice, and Gabe practiced often.

Once the list of men was done, he drew two outlines of the houses then a third map of the structures on the camp. He was just finishing the last map when Rebecca entered the office, not as silently this time because she was wearing shoes.

He looked up and smiled as she asked, "All done with your reports?"

"Yes, ma'am. I even made some maps of the camp and drawings of the houses."

"This room is a disaster," she said as she sat down on the other side of the desk.

"This was how I found it. I'm guessing that either Bob or the sheriff was searching for anything that Bob had filed about the poaching operation. I'll clean it in a little while."

"Thank you for the clothes and other things, Gabe. I thought the vest was a nice touch. Was it so I could wear my shoulder holster without it being seen?"

"It was the only thing that I specified for the order. The sales clerk selected the rest."

"The dresses fit perfectly. How did you get them right?"

"You forget what I do for a living. I'm basically a detective, so I can usually get a pretty good estimate of height and weight after a few seconds. You were easier for me to get that estimate because I had picked you up."

"I didn't forget that. I was really nasty to you, wasn't I?"

"You were past being nasty, Rebecca, and up until an hour ago, you were bordering on being eligible to be burned at the stake in Salem, Massachusetts. You weren't exactly pleasant to have around, but you've made up for it since I wrangled that first laugh out of you."

"It's hard for me to admit that not everyone is bad. You've been more than considerate since you knocked on that door and brought me out of that camp and I should have been appreciative from that moment on, and I apologize for that."

"Apology accepted, Rebecca. Before I forget, did you ever see the six men that Bob uses as his muscle fire their guns? Do they practice very much?"

"In all the time I was there, I don't think I heard more than ten gunshots."

"That's good to know."

Then he picked up the papers and said, "I'm going to straighten the office out. Can you cook better than I can?"

"I didn't want to say anything about lunch but yes, I can cook."

"You surprised me at lunch, Rebecca. At the time, I would have thought you'd throw it back at me once you tasted it."

She smiled as she stood and said, "I was hungry."

As she turned, Gabe laughed and then began to put the office back together.

As Rebecca walked back to the kitchen, she still found it hard to believe that she was so comfortable with Gabe. She'd hadn't even known him for a day, and they were talking about things some very private things and none of it bothered her. She no longer worried about him trying to hurt her but now, she had to concern herself about something that she had never expected to happen. She liked Gabe Owens, but it could go no further.

She opened the cookstove firebox started the fire, closed the door and began to gather foodstuff and cookware to prepare something better than his barely edible lunch.

As Gabe worked, he shifted his mind back to the problems that had been created by Rebecca's departure from the logging camp. He had expected the sheriff to say that she'd been reported missing or find Bob and Frank in town visiting the Ulrich family home, but there had been nothing.

But he had his preliminary report done, and he could send it out on tomorrow's train.

The sun was low in the sky as Gabe and Rebecca sat down at the table to have their dinner, which was a noticeable improvement over Gabe's lunch creation.

"What are you going to do tomorrow, Gabe?" she asked.

"That's a good question because you, ma'am, have created a dilemma."

“A dilemma?”

“Yes, ma’am. When I pulled you out of the camp, I expected to hear pounding hoofbeats behind us minutes later and was preparing all sorts of ways to meet any threats, but when we made it to the road, I was wondering what was taking them so long. Now I’m really confused. I visited your father, and no one had come to the lumber yard or the house looking for you, either. The sheriff didn’t know about it which he should have. How could they not notice that you were gone?”

She thought about it for a few seconds before replying, “Maybe Frank was too ashamed to admit to Bob that I wasn’t there. Frank is a vicious, cruel man, and he’s a lot bigger than Bob, but seems almost afraid of him.”

“Now, that’s an interesting thought. So, you think it’s possible that they don’t know you’re gone?”

“I’m sure Frank knows, but I could understand why he wouldn’t tell Bob.”

“That’s as good an explanation as I could come up with, so if that’s true then after I give my report to Joe over at the station to send to Minneapolis, maybe it’s time that I paid a visit to Bob.”

Rebecca looked horrified as she exclaimed, “You can’t do that! He’ll have you killed!”

“I don’t believe that he really thinks I’ll be leaving anyway, and I’m surprised that Angela did. I thought at least she knew me better than that. I’ll keep an eye out for any shooters when I go in. I have my Winchester ’76, so unless they have one like it, I’ll have the range advantage and probably the accuracy advantage because they don’t shoot much. I’ve been in worse situations.”

"Don't you even worry about what will happen to me if you're shot?"

"More than you probably realize. Besides, you have your family, Rebecca."

"No, I don't. They hate me. As far as they're concerned, I may as well be dead."

"You're lying to yourself, Rebecca, and that's the worst kind of lie. You know that they don't hate you. I saw them all yesterday and I talked to your father again today. Your father loves you very much."

She shook her head violently, her long black tresses flying, as she exclaimed, "He does not! My mother died because of him! I lost her because of him!"

"Those are more lies, Rebecca, and I'm surprised that someone as smart as you would even think that. You know that he wasn't responsible in any way for the loss of your mother. She died during childbirth, didn't she?"

She quickly quieted, closed her eyes and replied, "Yes, she did, and he was the one who made her that way."

"Why did he make her that way, Rebecca?" he asked softly as he looked at her across the table.

She quickly answered, "Because he's a man and he couldn't leave her alone, that's why."

"No, Rebecca. I want you to be honest with yourself and recall how your mother and father were when you were ten or eleven. Don't let your anger cloud your memories. If you do that, you'll have to admit that he made her that way because he loved your mother."

Tears began to flow over her swollen cheek as she softly said, “But he didn’t wait six months before he married my Aunt Sarah. He betrayed my mother and then took her own sister to his bed.”

“And you hate Sarah for that, don’t you?”

“Yes, I hate her. She hates me, too.”

“No, Rebecca, she loves you as much as your father does. I heard it in her voice when I talked to her about you. It’s why I know that they both love you very much even after you’ve treated them as if they were prison guards or worse.”

“She doesn’t love me! Why would she love me?”

“Did you love your mother?”

She sighed and answered, “More than anyone else in the world.”

“Don’t you think Sarah loved her sister just as much?”

Rebecca didn’t reply because she knew the answer, and it would make her house of hate cards fall if she admitted it.

Gabe continued as he said, “Sarah loved her sister, and you were all she had left to remind her of her lost sister, Rebecca. She had to love you with every tiny piece of her heart. She was probably so much like your mother that it was natural that your father and Sarah would love each other, too.

“What would you rather happen, Rebecca? Would you rather that your father spent the rest of his life alone and die by himself with no one to love him in his last days? Would you rather have Sarah be denied the chance to be with her sister’s only child? You’ve wasted all those years hating the very people you should have loved the most. You could have been happy, but you chose the wrong path. You let your anger and hate fill you and it finally took you away to a place that almost killed you. You would have died alone and miserable, Rebecca.

"But now you have a chance to change all that. Just a mile away, your father and Sarah are in their house with your brother, Aaron, and your little sister, Rachel, and they have a hole in their hearts that only you can fill."

Rebecca asked softly, "How do you know all this? You don't even know my family."

"When I met your father, I liked him immediately. Then he took me to your house to meet Sarah and the children. It didn't take long for me to see there was a lot of love in that house and recognize the sadness that was there when I spoke of you. But there was a reason that I could see it, too.

"I was very lucky when I was growing up. I had wonderful parents who loved and laughed all the time and I knew that they loved me. I knew other boys who had a much worse situation. Some had fathers that beat them and others had stepparents who ignored them or disliked them. I saw almost daily the difference it made. You can see it everywhere, each day in our lives. Anger and resentment breeds hate and pain. It doesn't have to be that way, Rebecca, especially not for you."

She used a napkin to dry her eyes, being careful with the swollen eye then barely whispered, "But it's been so long, and I've shamed them by going off with Bob and other things. I can't go back. I can't."

"The only one who feels shame is you, Rebecca. I think the hate was to hide the shame you felt for how you acted. You were a hurt little girl who wanted to blame someone for the loss of her mother. Many people blame God or the devil, but some, like you, have to focus on someone close to hold to account for the tragedy. You blamed your father. But it was no one's fault, Rebecca, and I'm sure that deep down, even when you were twelve, you knew that.

"But once you started down the path of blaming your father, your pride kept you from admitting your mistake. Then he married Sarah, and it reinforced the lie you were telling yourself. But it was all just because a sad girl lost her loving mother and didn't want to believe that it had just happened as it had to many other girls' mothers. I think that your father at least knows why you were so angry, but he never lost his love for you, Rebecca. Never."

"Do you really believe that they'd welcome me back?" she asked quietly.

"Rebecca, when I talked to Sarah and your father, you have no idea how badly they miss you. Sarah said to tell you just how much they all loved you and wanted you to return. Your father even said to tell you he was sorry for driving you away. They are such good people."

"Did you meet Aaron and Rachel, too?" she asked, followed by a sniff.

"Yes, ma'am. While I was in the kitchen having coffee with Eli and Rachel, Aaron walked up to me and said, 'We're Jewish'."

She laughed, sniffed again and exclaimed, "He didn't!"

"Oh, yes, he did. Then he followed that by asking me if I was Jewish then after I said I wasn't, he asked me if I hated Jews."

"Aaron said all that? I can't believe it."

"You should. He's seven and that's what kids do when they're seven. Then I told him he was lucky to be a Jew, and he asked why."

Rebecca's one good eye was sparkling as she asked, "And you said?"

"Because it's a lot easier to spell than Episcopalian, although I should have used Presbyterian which is worse."

Rebecca laughed again then Gabe said, "You know, Rebecca, we really need to eat."

She kept her smile but nodded and they finally began to eat.

Rebecca ate without tasting the food as she thought about everything that Gabe had said to her. She began to recall the fights that she'd had with her family, and it didn't take long to realize that she had instigated every one of them by something she'd said or done.

But even as she mentally reconciled with her family, she'd glance at Gabe and wished she'd met him before she'd so easily gone off with Bob Johnson, and not because of the twenty minutes they'd just spent in deep, personal conversation.

She'd never talked to anyone like him before, but she knew it didn't matter anyway. She was more than just ruined; she was nothing but a whore who didn't get paid. She had even been given away like an old, swaybacked horse. But it was the other horrible things that she'd done that meant she had to keep her emotions in check. Being able to see her family again excited her and being with Gabe was now a comfortable thrill, but that was all it could be.

Besides, he would be returning to Minneapolis in a few days if he survived, and she was glad that he was going because this tiny sliver of happiness wasn't right.

After two minutes of silence Rebecca asked, "Gabe, could you take me home tomorrow?"

Gabe looked up smiled and said, "I'd be honored, Rebecca."

"Could you come with me into the house, at least until I'm comfortable? I don't doubt what you told me, but I know I'll be nervous."

"Whatever you need, Rebecca."

Then despite her desire to push him away, she succumbed to her greater need to feel happy and asked, "After we're finished eating, can we go to the parlor and just talk for a while?"

"I can't think of a better way to spend the evening, Rebecca."

———

After they'd cleaned up, they walked to the parlor and as Gabe lit a lamp, Rebecca took a seat on the couch then took off her shoes to be more comfortable. She was surprised when Gabe sat next to her on the couch and wished he hadn't but found herself pleased at the same time.

"What would you like to talk about, Rebecca?" he asked.

“What exactly does a special agent do?”

“We’re like the sheriffs for the railroad. Back East, they’re called railroad detectives and out West, we’re called special agents, but it’s the same thing. The purpose was to protect railroad property and personnel, but it expanded pretty quickly as the land grants were authorized and the railroads began accumulating more property.

“In most places along the railways out West, we’re the only law around, and the territories and states have granted us legal authority to apply the law. We’re a lot like the U.S. Marshals in that our jurisdiction crosses state boundaries, but we don’t have nearly their legal power.”

“Are you good at it?”

“Just like I told your father when he asked, I’m the best there is. It’s not bragging, Rebecca. It just is.”

“Do you get into many shootouts, like the one you’re planning on doing?”

“More than most, but the reason I’m a special agent at all was because I was on a surveying crew in western Dakota Territory a few years ago and were attacked by a band of Lakota Sioux. When we finally drove them off, there were only three of us left, so I became a special agent.

“Last week, I corralled the Dakota Gang when they tried to rob one of our trains. We had a gunfight and five of the six didn’t make it. But it wasn’t so much that I was a better shot than they were, it’s because I studied the way they pulled off other jobs, learned their weaknesses and took advantage of them. They made the mistake of being consistent.”

“Have you been shot very often?”

“Not once, which bothers me, to be honest. It’s like I’m playing with house money.”

“Do they pay you a lot?”

“I’m the highest paid special agent they have, and I get to keep the reward money on any of the bad guys that I capture or kill, except for the rewards offered by the Northern Pacific, of course. They kind of negotiate that down by giving me a bonus that’s about half of the amount they offered as a reward, but that’s okay. It was never about the money, anyway.”

“Why not?”

Gabe then explained about his father’s business and his being the only child, but when she asked about his childhood, he began talking about the joy of growing up in boy paradise in Brainard where there were summers full of frogs and fish and winters of deep snow.

When he finished, he asked, “How about you, Rebecca? Do you think you can talk to me about your mother and what it was like when you were a girl?”

Rebecca had originally hoped to keep the conversation about him, but when he asked, she found that she not only could talk about her mother but was almost bursting with stories. Stories she’d stored away as securely as any bank kept their gold. For the first time in years, she happily freed them from her mental lock box.

Gabe sat on the couch next to Rebecca watching her still swollen, discolored face as she animatedly talked about her mother as her hands flew to emphasize her verbal outpouring. It was as if a dam had given way and all of those happier memories held back for so long came rushing from her mouth in a torrent. She didn't try to avoid talking about her father either.

Rebecca continued for almost twenty minutes non-stop when she finally slowed down and smiled.

"I'm making a fool of myself, aren't I?"

"Hardly. I think you were amazing. Did you want me to get some water?"

"I can get it," she replied as she quickly bounced off the couch and went tiptoeing out of the parlor.

Gabe just watched her leave and wondered what Eli and Sarah would think of the suddenly happy Rebecca. He still had a hard time reconciling the Rebecca who had been so incredibly angry that morning with tonight's jubilant Rebecca and definitely preferred the one getting the water.

He read so much in her eyes even though one was still barely able to open. There was still some hate behind those now smiling eyes, but he knew it was now reserved for Bob Johnson and Frank Stanford with maybe a little left over for Angela. But Rebecca was so complex that he found her incredibly intriguing. She was like the toughest mystery he'd ever had to unravel but knew that it was one he hoped to have the chance to solve. Rebecca Ulrich was fascinating.

She padded back into the parlor, set two glasses of water on the lace doilies and sat back down.

"I already drank some, but I might need more," she said as she pulled her feet up under her again.

Gabe had just drunk some water and was replacing the glass when he asked, “So, Rebecca, are you still nervous about going to see everyone tomorrow?”

“I am, but it’s a happy nervous,” she replied then asked, “Gabe, can I ask you about Angela?”

“Of course, you can.”

“How long did you know her before you proposed?”

“Not long at all, three or four weeks. I was pretty well smitten but then, I guess other men were too, including Mike Wheatley who had known her longer than I had.”

“I met him a couple of times, and if it doesn’t sound bad, he wasn’t as handsome as you are, and he was, I don’t know, less masculine, too,” she said.

Then she immediately chastised herself for what sounded like flirting. She was going places she knew she shouldn’t but couldn’t help herself. Rebecca wanted to enjoy every moment being with Gabe because there was no possibility of anything more serious.

Gabe then said, “I’ll give you that, which was one of the reasons that I was surprised when Angela married him after I’d proposed. I knew Mike for a couple of years before he and Angela went off to Missoula. His father was a vice president of the railroad, and I’m sure that’s how he got his position as a project manager.”

“Do you think she married him because of the money?”

“No, because my salary was higher than his and even if you counted family wealth, it wasn’t close. What was strange was the assignment to Missoula. I didn’t pay much attention for the first few months after they'd gone because I was too angry, but when I thought about it, it didn't make a lot of sense. Why did Mike take the job? Granted, it was probably more money, but not that much. Maybe he had a falling out with his father. I never looked into it, though."

Rebecca then asked, "You said you only knew her for three weeks, but you said that you were intimate with her twice. How did that happen?"

"Like I said, I was smitten and thought I was in love with her and made my intentions clear about wanting to marry her after just a week. One thing led to another and once we were able to find privacy in a secluded location, well, nature ran its course."

She didn't think it was flirting but just curiosity when she asked, "When I said that Bob had said that he needed twenty minutes of privacy with Angela, you seemed to be surprised and asked if she was happy with just twenty minutes. Did you spend longer than that with her?"

Gabe was surprised that he wasn't even uncomfortable about talking to Rebecca about it and replied, "Much longer. Even our first time, we took over an hour, and it was a difficult thing to do because, well, it was my first, first time. Although, I should have been more accurate when I said that we had been intimate twice because I meant that we had had two occasions where we had been together, but it was really four times. We spent more than three hours together the first time and almost four the second. That's why I was more than just a little surprised that Angela would have been content with only twenty minutes."

Rebecca may not have been uncomfortable talking about it either, but she was definitely unhinged by his reply and sat just staring at him as he answered and for the ten seconds of silence after he finished.

"You're telling the truth, aren't you?" she finally asked quietly.

"I never lie, Rebecca. If you asked Angela, I'm sure she'd tell you the same."

"Are you that way with all of the women you've been with?"

Now, Gabe was decidedly uncomfortable and looked past Rebecca as he ruminated on whether or not he should tell her. He finally decided that he may as well.

"I don't know, Rebecca, because Angela is the only woman I've ever been with."

Rebecca blinked with her good eye and asked, "Is it why you said you only liked some women when I insulted you about not liking women earlier?"

"Yes, ma'am. I have a flaw, a frailty that is highly embarrassing for me to acknowledge, but if you want to know what it is, then I'll tell you. I've never told another human being, not even my parents."

"Then why would you tell me?"

"Because you've changed so much, and I've never talked so personally to anyone outside of my parents before."

"Not even Angela?"

"Not even Angela. In fact, Angela was the one who was the final confirmation of what I had first realized when I was sixteen."

Rebecca just sat and watched his eyes, waiting to hear what he considered so embarrassing that he couldn't tell anyone about, but was incredibly pleased that he would tell her. Even before he spoke the first word, she knew that she was getting too close to him and felt like the town drunk who should have refused that next whiskey but convinced himself that it would be just one more. She was becoming addicted to Gabe Owens and knew she'd have to stop this downward spiral before much longer.

Gabe began describing his problem by saying, "When I was sixteen, I arranged to meet with a girl named Edie Goodnight, and yes, that was her real name. We snuck off to an empty barn and engaged in some serious petting which soon led to much more and she then asked me to satisfy her on a stack of hay. I wanted to oblige her more than you could imagine, but I found that I couldn't go through with it.

"She wasn't very happy with me and I thought she'd go and tell all of my friends, but she didn't. I thought it was because she didn't want to admit that she'd dropped her knickers at all. I convinced myself that I was just being a gentleman. Two days later, one of my friends, Al Hoffman, asked me how I liked 'Easy Edie', and I just grinned after he told me that he'd enjoyed her, too. When Edie found herself with child two months later, every boy in the high school scattered to the winds, obviously fearing her father's shotgun. It made me feel worse, actually.

"Then, less than a year later, I had another offer from an older, married woman, who was very, um, very voluptuous, and still couldn't do it. I put that off as not wanting to be an adulterer, but it kept happening and I didn't know what was wrong with me. I really liked women but couldn't do it. I kept coming up with one excuse or another for my failure.

“Then I met Angela, and as enticing as she was, I was concerned that I wouldn’t be able to even consummate the marriage if she agreed to be my wife. But I thought I was in love with her, and when she asked me, I found I was not only able to satisfy her, but to make love to her twice in just hours. After our second liaison, I figured out what my problem was, and it was slammed home less than two months after she’d gone to Missoula when I couldn’t enjoy the pleasures of Miss Abigail Wilkerson, who was more than willing.”

Gabe looked at Rebecca’s pretty but hurt face and said, “I realized that I could only bed a woman who I loved, or thought I loved. I don’t know why that is, but it’s very real.”

Then he laughed lightly and said, “So, you see, Rebecca, you really had nothing to worry about in the first place.”

Rebecca said softly, barely above a whisper, “I don’t think that it’s a flaw, Gabe. I think it’s romantic in the truest sense of the word.”

“Well, now you know my deepest secret, Rebecca. Don’t go telling the boys down at the train station. It’d be in Minneapolis faster than a telegram.”

“I won’t tell anyone, but please don’t make light of it. It’s too precious.”

Gabe nodded but had a mixture of relief and embarrassment for having told her.

He cleared his throat and said, “Tomorrow morning, I’ll go and rent a buggy, so I can get you to your family’s house. I’ll want you to have a shawl over your head, so no one will see you. I think Bob’s going to be unhappy when he finds out.”

“I think you’re right.”

Gabe pulled out his pocket watch then said, “We’ve talked a long time, Rebecca. It’s almost eleven o’clock. You go upstairs and get some sleep. Don’t worry about getting up early. I’ll put on the coffee and then head out and rent that buggy.”

“I’m really glad that you came and rescued me this morning, Gabe. You rescued me from myself, too.”

Gabe looked at her and said, “You were worth rescuing, Rebecca.”

She smiled then slid her feet to the floor, picked up her shoes then gave him one more smile with her swollen lips, then walked to the stairs and slowly climbed the steps without looking back. But before she reached the top step, she was already regretting the incredible amount of pleasure she had felt in just talking to him and shivered when she imagined how it would feel if she allowed it to go beyond conversation. By the time she reached the door, she suddenly wanted to go home just to be able to focus on someone other than Gabe. This had to stop…now.

Gabe was watching as she disappeared down the upper hallway to her room then stood and knew he could definitely make love to Rebecca if she gave him the chance, but only if she felt the same way.

Frank was lying on his bed with his hands behind his neck, staring at the dark ceiling. That bitch hadn’t returned, not that he really expected she would and tomorrow, he’d have to tell Bob. He’d have to act as if he discovered her missing when he awakened, though. It would still be difficult to admit he’d let her get away, but he knew he had no choice.

But when they found her again, he'd make her wish she'd never set one toe outside of the house.

Two hundred yards south of Frank's house, Angela lay in bed with Bob Johnson. He was already snoring as he always did just after he'd satisfied himself, not caring one bit if she did. She'd been so excited by his early visits, anticipating the hurried undressing and forbidden love in the bed she had shared with Mike that his actual performance hadn't mattered.

But once she had moved to the logging camp, things changed. With Mike gone, she wanted more and received less. At first, she blamed the presence of Becky but now, Becky was gone and being abused by Frank next door. The sight of Frank hitting her and then dragging her out the door still ate at her inside. *Would Bob tire of her and give her to Frank after he'd killed Becky, as he surely would, given what he'd done to her just taking her from the house?*

She glanced at Bob lying beside her, his rasping snore irritating her more with each breath. *What had she ever seen in him? Mike had beaten her for his own pleasure when he was bedding her, but was that any better than this?*

But then she closed her eyes and remembered how she had been so close to having Gabe again. She remembered that kiss and how she had shown him her bruises and a lot more but didn't know why he hadn't taken her offer. She knew he was excited and thought that maybe she should have been a little lustier and less weepy. Maybe Gabe was put off by the bruises and didn't want to hurt her. That must have been it. He was always like that. When they were making love, he always wanted to please her, and he probably thought it would hurt her if he did.

It was the only reason that Angela could believe that could account for his refusal, and it meant that Gabe still loved her after all. If only she'd told him the truth and stayed with him in Missoula, but it was far too late now. She'd confessed to murdering Mike and no matter what she said now, he wouldn't believe her. *Why had she lied for that bastard next to her?*

Bob's snore rattled before he rolled over, and Angela looked at him knowing this was all she would get and just lay there in disgust.

CHAPTER 4

Gabe was the first one up the next morning as he'd set his pocket watch's alarm to wake him. He slipped out of bed and thirty minutes later, was dressed, clean-shaven and had the fire in the cookstove going.

Rebecca smiled at him as she trotted past wearing one of the two new nightdresses that he'd bought for her then left the house to use the privy. Her swelling had gone down noticeably but the discoloration, if anything, was more pronounced.

He had the coffeepot on the stove along with two large pots of water when she returned and looked at the cookstove.

"What are you cooking, Mister Owens?" she asked pleasantly.

"Coffee, and I'm heating some water, so you can take a bath while I'm getting the buggy. I thought you might want to have one before you went home."

"That's very thoughtful. I'd love a bath."

"Don't forget to bring your pistol, ma'am."

She smiled and replied, "No, sir."

"The water for the bath won't be heated for another ten minutes, and I've already filled half of the tub with water, so you can just park yourself on a chair and we can chat some more."

“I’d like that,” she said as she took a seat, breaking the promise she had made to herself before she went to sleep.

“Gabe, do I have to go to Helena?” she asked as Gabe sat down at the table.

“Not if you don’t want to go. Now that you’re going to be able to be with your family, I think you’ll be better protected. I counted six men working in your father’s sawmill, so I think you’ll be safe there.”

“That’s good. I don’t want to leave if I don’t have to. Are you still going to go out to the logging camp today?”

“I don’t know. It depends on what happens when Bob finds out that you’re gone. If he does, I don’t think he’ll bring his thugs into Missoula even with the sheriff backing him up. He’ll probably use the sheriff to search the town by making up some story to justify looking for you. Now, he can’t enter a house without a search warrant, so I’ll talk to your father about that. Does he have a gun at home?”

“Not when I left.”

“Okay. When I go to rent the buggy, I’ll pick up a twelve-gauge shotgun and bring it along. It’ll be more than enough protection.”

“What will you be doing?”

“After I get my preliminary report to Joe, so he can send it to Minneapolis, I’m going to find out what’s going on and still might go out there.”

“Gabe,” she asked, “did you mean it when you said that you thought I was more attractive than Angela?”

"I never lie, Rebecca, and I never pass phony compliments either. Even with your hurt face, and the swelling has down quite a bit, by the way, I could tell that you're prettier than Angela. You're very different women, of course, but you're actually more classically beautiful than she is."

Rebecca practically glowed from the inside out when she heard his description, but now wanted more. She knew she was giving into her addiction but knew that she would only be able to indulge for a couple of more days, so it really didn't matter.

"Do you think my figure matches hers?"

"No, it doesn't, Rebecca."

She was crushed by his honesty, although she should have expected it.

Then he continued, saying, "Your figure is better than Angela's. In fact, having seen hers recently, I'd say yours is much better, and don't forget, I had my arm around your waist."

Rebecca's downward spiral instantly reversed and became the shooting trail that culminated in the explosion of emotional fireworks as a giant smile crossed her lips, painful that it may be.

"Really?" she asked.

"Really. Now, I'm going to pour that hot water into your tub while you go upstairs and get your clothes ready. I imagine there's some womanly soap in the bathroom, so you can clean your better-than-Angela figure while I'm off finding a buggy."

Rebecca nodded happily then stood and trotted out of the room trying to suppress the giggle that she hadn't released since she was twelve but failed. She finally told herself to hell with her promise and she'd enjoy every minute she could before he left.

Gabe watched her leave with almost as big a smile on his face as she wore but had work to do.

After dumping the two almost-boiling pots of water into the tub, he checked the temperature and found it even warmer than he'd expected and as he turned to leave the bathroom, he almost bumped into Rebecca.

"Sorry, ma'am," he said as he stepped aside.

"I'll excuse you this time, sir," she said with a smile as she showed him her Webley.

"Take your time, Rebecca. I'll be back within an hour."

"Thank you again, Gabe," she said before closing the door.

Gabe turned and walked to the kitchen, grabbed his hat and his Winchester then headed for the door. After locking it behind him, he trotted to the small barn and began saddling Dancer.

"*She's gone?*" exclaimed Bob as he sat eating his scrambled eggs and ham as Angela poured his coffee.

"I don't know where she went, Bob. It couldn't be that long, 'cause her bed wasn't that cold when I went into her room."

"You keep her in a separate room?" Bob asked before shoveling in a large forkful of eggs.

"No, I meant her side of the bed. I reached over to grab her, and she just wasn't there."

"Were her shoes gone?"

"Yup, but that's all. She grabbed her dress and shoes and lit out."

"Well, she couldn't have gone far. Let's get the men searching the woods. You and I are going to pay a visit to our friend, the sheriff. He can check out her father's house and lumber yard in case she got that far."

"Okay, Bob," Frank said as he quickly turned and half-walked, half-jogged out of the house in relief.

Bob threw down his fork then stood, grabbed his slice of ham put it his mouth and held it between his teeth as he donned his jacket and hat and left the room.

After he'd gone, Angela sat down and began to finish the eggs and coffee as she digested the news of Becky's escape. She could understand why she'd run after spending a night with Frank and was a bit surprised that she could still walk. Frank was monstrously brutal.

But as she chewed, she wondered if Becky had made it. It was only eight miles to Missoula and if she trotted, she could make it in less than two hours. Angela then began to think about following in her footsteps depending on whether or not they caught Becky. She knew her time window for a possible escape was small because the only one she could run to would be leaving for Minneapolis as soon as that new yard manager arrived.

She began to formulate her own plan as she sipped Bob's untouched coffee, not even bothering to recall that she'd already confessed to murdering her husband to the man she was hoping to find.

Gabe had Dancer trotting down the street headed for Barret Brothers Agricultural Equipment, Carriage and Buggy, Etc. on Front Street. He decided he'd just buy a buggy and a second horse, not wanting to have to explain any bullet holes in the buggy or horse when he returned them. He could have them both shipped back to Minneapolis when he left and wouldn't have to pay for the shipping anyway.

It didn't take long or much negotiation to buy the new buggy and a handsome black mare. She was taller and heavier than Dancer and hoped he wouldn't be intimidated. He tied Dancer to the back of the buggy and soon was driving back to the gun shop.

One of the advantages of working for the railroad was that in addition to the two hundred dollars that he always had with him at the start of a mission, he had six bank drafts on his Minneapolis account which were backed by the Northern Pacific which enabled him to cash them wherever he was with no questions asked even if it was over a thousand dollars. He'd never had to write one even close to that amount, including just now when he bought the buggy and mare, but it was a nice cushion.

He had most of his expenses paid by the railroad anyway, but he still found that he'd need cash when he went to different locations and bought things he wanted.

He pulled the buggy to a stop outside of A.J. Staus to get the shotgun for Eli. He didn't think he'd need it, but if he had to defend his family, a shotgun was the best choice.

Gabe entered the shop and spotted Mister Staus with another customer, so he thought he'd take a few minutes to browse the surprisingly large and diverse selection. There were a lot of older models that he was sure were there just for display, but even they were in excellent operating condition, probably because of the skill of the gunsmith.

He walked all the way to the back then turned up the far aisle and stopped when he saw a rack with long range rifles, most of which were used and probably traded in by departing buffalo hunters. That market had died when the gratuitous slaughter of the huge herds had reduced them to almost nothing. The Easterners and foreigners that used to come to kill the buffalo still showed up but in much fewer numbers to hunt grizzlies and elk.

He picked up one of them and ran his fingers across the steel as A.J. Staus sidled up beside him.

"What do you think of it?" he asked.

"I've never seen a Sharps-Borshadt before and this one's got a Malcolm scope, too."

"It was used by a man from Baltimore, but he never got his trophy bear and was mighty upset. You ever used a Sharps?"

"I've got one at home in Minneapolis, but it shoots the .45-70 cartridge."

"You any good with it?"

"Not as good as I'd like to be, but I've hit eight-inch targets at eight hundred yards. I'd bet with that scope that I'd be able to reach out another four hundred yards."

"With the .50-110 cartridge, you could probably go a mite further to about fifteen hundred yards."

"Do you have any ammunition?"

"I've got four boxes of the .50-110s up front, and a few more of the .50-90s."

"I'll take the four .50-110s and two of the .50-90s. How about a scabbard for this big boy?"

"It's got a special scabbard with it on the shelf right next to the rack," he said as he slid the thick leather scabbard from the shelf.

"I'll take this with me, and I need a twelve-gauge along with a couple of boxes of #4 buckshot shells."

"Let's go up front and we'll take care of it."

Gabe followed him back to the front of the store, admiring the rifle as he walked. As soon as he'd seen it, he'd wanted it, and it wasn't because he expected to need it if he had to go into the logging camp but now that he'd found it, he appreciated the advantage it would give him.

When he arrived at the counter, he gingerly laid the heavy rifle on the counter as Mister Staus set the shotgun on the counter and then stacked the cartridges and shells nearby. He also added the cleaning kit for the big gun.

"You just spent $78.50 of your hard-earned money, Mister Owens."

“I’m impressed that you remembered my name, Mister Staus.”

“Oh, I guessed who you were when you came in the first time. I read about that takedown of the Dakota Gang and figured they’d be sending their best man to investigate. Did you figure out what really happened yet with Mike Wheatley’s murder?”

“Pretty much,” he said as he counted out the cash, “now I’ve just got to make a few arrests, if they decide to give up.”

“They won’t though, will they?” he asked as he took Gabe’s money then began putting the cartridges and cleaning kit into a heavy cloth bag with the scabbard on top.

“Nope. I’m pretty sure it’s going to come down to throwing lead.”

“Well, good luck, Mister Owens, and I hope that long gun gives you an edge.”

Gabe nodded shook his hand, then he took both guns while Mister Staus carried the heavy bag as they exited the shop.

The gunsmith set the ammunition onto the buggy floor while Gabe gently leaned the Sharps-Borshadt against the seat and then put the shotgun on the floor and boarded. He waved to Mister Staus then flicked the reins and headed back to the house.

Bob and Frank were sitting in the sheriff’s private office with the door closed.

“I’ve got all of my men out there searching the woods, and when we go back, we’ll join them. I want you to go and talk to her father and see if you can spot her in the house. You can lean on him to see if he’s lying. If you find her, bring her straight back to the logging camp. Don’t bring her into the jail. You just remember that she’s seen you come out to the house and she probably knows enough to get you hanged.”

Sheriff Reinhold then said, “I have to have a search warrant if I want to look around and they won’t let me in.”

Bob snapped, “You’re the sheriff, for God’s sake! People are afraid of you. What are they going to do, complain to the governor?”

“Okay. Okay. I’ll head over there after I go and saddle my horse.”

“Let us know if you find her or hear anything.”

The sheriff nodded then Bob and Frank stood, Frank opened the door and they left quickly passing Deputy Collier who’d heard most of the conversation quite easily despite the door. It was almost impossible not to.

After he heard Bob and Frank’s horses trot away the sheriff appeared from his office grabbed his hat and without saying a word, walked out the door.

Deputy Collier watched him leave and was already wondering what had happened. *Becky Ulrich had run away from the logging camp?* Now that was interesting, he thought. It had been a black day for him when she’d gone off with Bob Johnson as it had been for many young men in Missoula. Now it seemed that Bob was anxious to get her back and whatever she knew would get the sheriff hanged and probably Bob and Frank, too.

He wished he could go and try to find Becky, but he was on the desk and he had no idea where she could be anyway.

Gabe turned the buggy back into the house's drive, then pulled to as stop at the back of the porch and checked his watch. It was only 9:10, and he was pleased with his efficient use of the morning.

He had barely slid his plain watch into his pocket when he heard a distant train whistle. He knew it wasn't a scheduled train and assumed it was a freight or a coal train which made up most of the railroad traffic, and coal trains probably were sixty percent of all traffic as there was an insatiable demand for coal and coal oil. Back east, they got the coal in West Virginia and Pennsylvania mostly but out here, it came from Wyoming and Montana, although deposits could be found all along the Continental Divide. It was just that the biggest mines were near the tracks and operated by the Union Pacific and Northern Pacific.

He pulled the buggy up to the house then stepped down, untied Dancer and led him into the barn where he unsaddled him, brushed him down and filled his oat bag to let him know he wasn't being replaced and he'd never be made to pull the buggy.

After he was sure Dancer was content, he trotted back to the buggy, opened the bag took out the shotgun shells, set them on the buggy floor then grabbed the Sharps-Borshadt and the bag then walked to the porch. After bounding up the steps, he stopped, set down the heavy bag took his keys out of his pocket and unlocked the door before picking the bag back up and hurriedly entering the house. Once inside, he carefully set his newest toy against the wall and smiled at Rebecca as he set down the bag.

She was sitting at the kitchen table wearing a much nicer solid dark blue dress with a white belt and white accents on the sleeves, and she was wearing her vest. Even with her facial injuries, she looked stunning. And to add to the eye appeal, she smiled at him.

"Did you rent a buggy, Gabe?" she asked as she stood.

"No, ma'am. I bought one and a pretty black mare, too. Come on out and I'll show you."

She stood and walked slowly towards him and asked, "Is that a new rifle?"

"Yes, ma'am. I saw it at the gunsmith when I was buying the shotgun and had to have it. It's a man thing."

She laughed and when she stepped closer, he held out his arm and she quickly took it before they walked out onto the porch then closed and locked the door behind them.

"You didn't ask if I had my Webley," she said as they walked down the porch steps.

"I saw that you were wearing your vest, so I assumed that you had the shoulder holster on underneath."

"I do, but it was a bit of a job getting the thing fitted correctly."

"I imagine that would be true, and it's not because of your shoulders."

She laughed lightly as he held her hand when she stepped into the buggy and sat on the fresh leather.

When he stepped inside, she said, “This is very nice, Gabe.”

“I’m glad you like it, Rebecca” he replied before he snapped the reins and the mare started the conveyance forward.

Rebecca slipped the shawl over her head as the buggy rolled easily along.

Even though they were in the buggy, Gabe still used the back alley to go west. He also noticed that Rebecca was a lot closer than she needed to be and unlike his buggy ride with Angela, it was greatly appreciated.

He could sense her nervous excitement as he turned the buggy west toward the Ulrich home and looked at her. Her swollen eye was looking straight ahead in anticipation, and he wondered if she completely believed him that they would welcome her back. He had no doubts, but she might.

She then turned her face toward him, smiled and took his hand. He smiled back and gave it a light squeeze to reassure her that it would be as he’d promised.

She then turned her head forward again as her family’s home appeared in the distance. Her father may or may not be home, but Rebecca felt she owed Sarah even more of an apology than she owed her father. At least he had spent twelve years with her when she was a normal girl, but Sarah had to endure all of the time since then being treated as if she was a despicable, heartless woman.

Five minutes later, Gabe pulled the buggy to a stop before the Ulrich home, stepped out then walked to the other side and assisted Rebecca’s exit but once on the ground, she froze.

Rebecca's eyes were centered on the door that she had slammed almost a year earlier when she'd stormed out of the house and now prayed that Gabe wasn't wrong. She knew that she'd been so absolutely horrible to everyone in the house for years and now that she was so close, she had serious doubts about their willingness to forgive her.

Gabe could feel the slight tremors in her hand as she threatened to cut off his forearm's circulation.

"It will be all right, Rebecca," he said soothingly before he took a small step forward to get her moving.

She matched his step with a short stride of her own and soon reached the porch steps with her eyes still focused on the ominous door. After they had stepped across the porch, she unintentionally stopped breathing as Gabe's knuckles rapped on the wooden surface as the knocks sounding like cannon fire.

She heard footsteps as her heart was thundering against her ribs then the door opened, and Sarah's eyes met hers.

Rebecca opened her mouth to speak, but nothing came out as she looked at Sarah.

But then Sarah's face split into a welcoming smile before she said, "Rebecca! You've come home!"

Rebecca nodded as she fought back tears but smiled when Sarah opened the door wide to let them inside.

Gabe smiled at Sarah then had to nudge Rebecca through the door before following her over the threshold and taking off his hat.

As he closed the door, Gabe saw Sarah reach with her right hand to Rebecca's damaged face and saw tears begin to flow as she said, "You've been hurt."

Rebecca's voice was shaking as she replied, "I'm all right now, Sarah. I came home to tell you, my father, Aaron and Rachel how sorry I am for being a thankless, hateful person and to ask for your forgiveness."

Sarah's gentle tears turned into a sobbing torrent as she threw her arms around Rebecca and Rebecca began to seriously weep as she embraced Sarah in return, ignoring the pain of the fresh bruises.

Gabe caught sight of Aaron entering the parlor from the hallway with Rachel walking behind him. He waved at Aaron, who grinned and waved back, but both children stayed at the parlor entrance watching, unsure of what they should do.

Gabe was sure that despite the obvious joy that Rebecca was feeling, she had to be enduring a great amount of pain from the hidden injuries that he knew she must have. He doubted if Frank Stanford had stopped after hitting her in the face, but it didn't seem to matter to Rebecca as she and Sarah continued to hold onto each other and simply cry.

The timing couldn't have been better when the door opened and as he turned, he saw Eli who was asking, "Who owns the…"

Eli stopped with the doorknob still in his right hand as Sarah and Rebecca both turned their wet faces back to him.

"Rebecca?" he croaked as he let go of the doorknob but left the door open.

Rebecca released Sarah then turned to her father and said, “Papa,” before she began to cry again, took two steps forward and threw her arms around him.

Eli hugged his daughter and didn’t bother holding back his tears as he began repeating her name while he held her close.

Gabe took advantage of the open door to slip outside onto the porch. He wanted to be sure that no one could interfere with this much-needed reconciliation.

He walked to the buggy, picked up the shotgun, cracked it open and loaded two of the shells before snapping it closed. After picking up the two boxes, he returned to the house, and when Eli spotted him, he left Rebecca and Sarah, his face beaming as he exited the house and closed the door.

“Gabe, how did this happen? How did you do it?”

“We talked, Eli. Nothing more than just long talks about family. I think Rebecca really knew that it was all her own doing and once I cracked that outer shell, the real Rebecca emerged. She’s a very special young lady, Eli.”

“She is and now she’s back. I’ll never be able to thank you enough, Gabe. I came back to the house to check on Sarah because the sheriff showed up at the mill, began looking around and asked me where she was. I guess Bob paid him a visit. I was kind of surprised it took this long.”

“Rebecca explained it to me, and it made sense. She thinks Frank is afraid of Bob and didn’t want to get him mad.”

“I’m not surprised. Bob Johnson is a wicked man.”

“Eli, Rebecca said you don’t have a gun, so I picked up this shotgun and a couple of boxes of shells. I already loaded it, and she is also wearing a pistol under her vest. I've got serious work to do now, and she said she'd rather stay here. I don't think Bob will send any of his thugs into town, but the only one you have to worry about is the sheriff.

"Either way, I'd keep the house locked and the shotgun handy. I'd have some of your workers act as watchmen, too. If you have any problems at all, let me know. If someone breaks into the house, I don't care if it's the sheriff, let him have both barrels. It's within your rights."

"But can't the sheriff come in if he wants to?"

"No, he can't. He has to have a search warrant. If he doesn't, then he's just another criminal, which we know he is anyway."

Gabe handed him the shotgun and boxes of shells then Eli asked, "Gabe, when you find Frank Stanford, make him pay for what he did to our Rebecca."

"Eli, you have no idea the amount of pain that I will inflict on that bastard for what he put Rebecca through."

He nodded then smiled at Gabe and said, "She is pretty, isn't she? Even with what he did to her."

"That's what I told her, but she's much more than pretty, Eli, she's beautiful."

"I think so, too. Let's go back inside."

Eli opened the door and when they entered the parlor, they found Rebecca and Sarah already sitting on the couch chatting and laughing as Aaron and Rachel sat on the floor watching.

The train whistle that Gabe had heard earlier belonged to the fully loaded coal train operated by engineer Wally Drummond. It was now eighteen miles east of Missoula and rolling east at thirty-eight miles an hour and accelerating.

Wally had pushed his locomotive as it had strained to go up an incline but once he crested it and began the long downslope, he had opened the throttle to build up speed and momentum for the next climb on the other side of the Blackfoot River.

Three days earlier, in the black of night, a flash flood had rolled down the Blackfoot and the surging waters had climbed over the banks before settling down. No one had been there to witness the raging river torrent but even if they had, they couldn't have seen below the churning river as the tumbling water sucked supporting sand and rock from around one of the deeply set supporting timbers of the Northern Pacific's trestle bridge. The twenty-seven trains that had passed over the bridge since the flood had all shaken the loose timber, shifting it further each time it was rocked by the heavy vibrations transmitted to the unsteady support timber.

Wally Drummond had made this run so many times before that he could probably do it in his sleep, but when his speeding train began crossing the long trestle bridge that crossed chasm of the Blackfoot River, the weight and vibration pushed the joints and structure of the bridge as they normally did but this time, the critical loosened timber slipped past its design limits, cracked, and then gave way before the locomotive reached the eastern end of the bridge.

Once that critical load carrier was lost, the trusses that were being supported by the now useless timber sagged and then snapped themselves just seconds later. The long wooden bridge initially just leaned hard to one direction then held there for a few heartbeats before the center of the bridge bowed and then crashed into the river.

The loud cacophony of noises produced by the steam engine prevented the men in the cab from hearing the collapsing bridge behind them, but Wally felt the initial jolt and at first thought there was a problem with the locomotive and quickly scanned the dials as his fireman, Joe Lassiter, shouted, "What the hell was that?"

By the time Wally was convinced that his steam engine wasn't the problem even Joe knew what had happened when they felt the train suddenly slow and for an instant pause motionless on the tracks. It was then ripped backwards on the iron rails, screeching mightily in protest as its drive wheels fought in vain to prevent its violent, unintended reversal.

Just fifteen seconds after the initial fracture had been felt, the train plummeted the hundred and twenty feet into the Blackfoot River creating a massive cloud of black dust from the huge amount of coal thrown into the air from the dumping coal cars. When the steam engine's firebox touched the enormous cloud of coal dust, it set off a colossal explosion, vaporizing the remains of the bridge, throwing trees and boulders everywhere and sending an enormous cloud of steam and dirt into the sky.

The river was temporarily dammed by the debris from the bridge and the train as coal, steel, wood, and the accompanying rock slides plugged the flow of water. But the river wasn't stopped long as it found its way past the hissing, mangled pieces of steel and other detritus that was all that remained of the train that had almost made it across.

The shock of the explosion was so enormous that it broke windows in the few buildings in Bears Mouth including the small railway station.

The telegrapher in Bears Mouth immediately tapped out a message to Missoula asking if they'd heard the rumbling, but the lines were down which raised alarms in the small town. This was no natural earthquake. It had been a massive, man-made disaster.

Gabe was listening to Rebecca and Eli talk when he felt the ground shake and then heard the distant rumble that sounded like thunder. He quickly turned, opened the door and trotted out onto the porch looking in the direction of the sound but couldn't see anything past the buildings, trees and mountainous terrain.

He knew that whatever it was, it was catastrophic, so he turned and stuck his head back into the house just as everyone was heading for the door.

"I think we have a problem," he said calmly as he stared to the east.

Eli turned and asked, "Was someone using dynamite?"

"No, I don't think so. It came from the east, so I'm going to run over to the station and see if they know anything."

"Okay," Eli said, "Let us know when you can."

Gabe nodded then trotted back to the buggy, climbed inside and cracked the reins to get the mare moving.

He raced to the railway station and bounded from the buggy just five seconds after pulling it to a stop and saw most of the railroad workers looking in that direction then ran to the water tower and began climbing the ladder up the side to get a better look.

It wasn't until he reached the top of the water tower that he could see the clouds in the distance from the train wreck, and already had a pretty good idea what it was just by its location.

He quickly climbed down, jogged toward the group and spotted Joe Lofton with the other railroad men.

"Joe!"

Joe and the other men all turned to see Gabe trotting toward them.

"Did you see anything, Gabe?" he asked.

"I think we have a disaster on our hands. I heard a steam whistle about forty minutes ago. Was that an eastbound train?"

"Yup, a coal hauler. He was loaded down pretty heavy, too. You figure he derailed?"

"No. If you climb the water tower, you'll see a lot bigger cloud than you'd even see from a derailment. I think we lost the bridge over the Blackfoot."

"Let's go and see if the telegraph to Helena is down," Joe said as he and the others began quickly walking toward the nearby Western Union office.

Gabe caught up with them and as station manager, it was Joe's job to ask, so he let him take the lead.

Joe and Gabe entered the office and Joe asked, “Did you lose the line to Helena?”

Fred Lemon turned and answered, “Yup. What was all that shaking? You blow up somethin’ you shouldn’t have?”

“No, I think we lost a bridge and a coal train. Give me a minute to write out a message.”

Joe quickly wrote down the message and handed it to the operator, who would have to route it through Ventnor then all the way around through Washington until it followed the Union Pacific lines through Wyoming. It would get to Minneapolis and eventually to Helena, but it would take longer and have a higher likelihood of being garbled somewhere along the line. But it would let them know that the bridge was probably down, and a train lost.

After the message had been sent, Joe and Gabe left the office with the other men and stopped on the boardwalk.

Joe said, “It’ll take a while to get there, and there probably isn’t anyone still alive, but I need someone to ride over and at least verify that we lost the bridge.”

Jim Clover volunteered, so everyone returned to the station to prepare for his departure.

As they walked, Gabe said, “Joe, it’ll take them at least a week to get that bridge repaired, so any rail traffic will have to be rerouted through Ainsworth and the Union Pacific lines. When you get an idea when we’ll get another train, let me know. I need to get my preliminary report back to Minneapolis.”

“Did you find out about Mike’s murder?”

"Yes, sir. That and the poaching are all tied together."

"Where are you staying?"

"I'm at Mike's house, but I'll come and see you when I can. Even if they diverted a train right away, it won't be here for three days. By then, I might not even need it."

"Okay, Gabe. Good luck."

"Thanks, Joe. It's a hell of a thing to have happen on your first week as station manager."

"I hope they won't fire me 'cause I let that train go."

"If they do, I'll tell them that I'll be leaving, too. You're a good man, Joe."

"Thanks, Gabe."

Gabe gave a quick wave to Joe as he clambered back into the buggy and was soon rolling back to the Ulrich home already thinking of how this would impact his plans. With the woods probably full of men searching for Rebecca, he wouldn't be able to get into the camp, but he knew he'd have to get into there soon just to get Angela out. He may be misreading her again and she may have pulled the trigger on Mike, but he knew he'd never know what actually happened unless he talked to her and made sure she understood she'd have to tell the truth this time.

That meant he'd have to deal with at least eight shooters, but he doubted if any of them were even within spitting distance of his proficiency, but they didn't have to be either. If Bob issued those Winchesters that Rebecca said he had then that would be a lot of firepower raining down on him. He'd have to start reducing their numbers and was suddenly very glad that he'd bought the Sharps-Borshadt.

He didn't even bother thinking about the sheriff, not because he underestimated him as that was a surefire way to get yourself killed but because he believed the sheriff would only act if Bob told him to do something.

But there were other things he could do that might make things better. He doubted any of the lumberjacks and other workers at the logging camp really wanted to be a part of the criminal world, so he needed to separate them from Bob Johnson. He needed to know who he had to deal with, and he only had the six names, but Rebecca had only given him two descriptions.

He rolled the buggy to a stop and hopped out, tied the reins to the hitchrail then stepped up onto the porch and knocked.

Sarah opened the door, grinned up at him and said, "Welcome back, Gabe. We are all very happy to see you again. Come in, please."

Gabe removed his hat as he entered smiled at Sarah and said, "I'm really glad to see everyone together again, Sarah."

Everyone was in the parlor looking at him, even little Rachel.

"That explosion you felt was probably caused by the collapse of the bridge across the Blackfoot River when a coal train crossed."

"Did the train make it across before it failed?" asked Eli.

"No, I'm sure that it didn't. If a bridge collapses, and I've seen three by the way, but usually right after they were built.

It's impressive, but not that explosive. A fully loaded coal train passed through forty minutes ago, and I'm almost positive it went down with the bridge and all that coal dust in the air ignited which caused that explosion. It was eighteen miles from here, so I can't imagine how bad it was nearby."

Rebecca then asked, "That means trains can't come through, doesn't it?"

"The bridge will take a while to rebuild, and the last eastbound train went through earlier this morning, so trains will be rerouted through Wyoming and Washington, but I don't think they'll be here for a few days. The direct telegraph is out, too. So, we're pretty isolated for a few days."

"What are you going to do about Bob Johnson?" asked Eli.

"I'm not sure how I'll handle him just yet. I need to think this out a bit, but I do know that I have to get Angela out of there if I can. I'm sure with Rebecca out of the camp, he's going to realize soon enough, if he already hasn't, that Angela is as big a threat as Rebecca is."

Rebecca then stood and walked towards him and asked, "Gabe, could I talk to you outside for a minute, please?"

"Yes, ma'am."

Gabe wasn't sure what she wanted but opened the door and once she'd passed by, stepped outside, closing the door behind him.

Rebecca turned and said, "Before I say anything else, Gabe, I want to thank you from the bottom of my heart for what you did. You were so very right about my father, Sarah, and my brother and sister. They all treated me as if I was a sweet, innocent girl, and don't you dare tell me I am."

Gabe smiled then let her continue because he was sure that there was something much more significant coming.

"Gabe, I know you want to protect me, but I think I need to stay here with my family. I have the Webley and my father has the shotgun. Besides, you'll need some time to think about what you'll be doing."

"I already told your father and suggested he have some of his workers stand watch over the house until I'm done. I'll run your things over here as soon as I can, Rebecca."

"That's alright, Sarah has clothes I can borrow, so there's no rush."

"Well, I've got to go. Enjoy your time with your family, Rebecca."

Rebecca looked at him and wanted to have him stay at least for a little while but had to end this now before it became an obsession.

"I will. Stay safe, Gabe."

"Yes, ma'am," he said as he tipped his hat then turned and untied the mare and buggy, climbed inside and drove back to the center of town wondering where the significance of her question had gone.

Rebecca watched him go and wondered if it would be the last time that she saw him. She was already going through Gabe withdrawal, but knew it was for the best. She exhaled sharply then returned to the house.

———

As Gabe drove back to Angela's house, the only lawman in Missoula that he hadn't met, Deputy Billy Cooper was about to throw a relatively stable situation into anarchy when he walked down the boardwalk and entered the office.

He walked through the door, removed his hat and as he was hanging it on his peg Deputy Collier said, "It's about time you got back, Billy. My butt's numb from sitting in this chair so much."

Billy Cooper walked toward the desk and said, "Your butt would be a lot worse if you had the belly problems I had. I had to get out of my place and figured I might as well come here. What's going on?"

Rafe Collier stood to give the chair to Billy as Sheriff Reinhold entered the office after visiting Bob Johnson with his negative report.

"Not much," replied Rafe.

Billy gently lowered himself into the chair and said, "What was that ground shakin?"

"There was a railroad bridge collapse over the Blackfoot and a big explosion to boot. We won't be seeing a train for a while."

Billy grinned and said, "Speakin' of seein' somethin', guess who I saw yesterday? Becky Ulrich! She was ridin' on some feller's horse sidesaddle. Looks like she was beat up pretty good, too."

Before Deputy Collier could shut him up, Sheriff Reinhold turned and asked, "What are you talkin' about, Billy?"

Billy shrugged and said, “Well, I was comin’ out of the privy where I’ve been kinda livin’ lately and I saw this feller with Becky sitting on his horse and I was wonderin’ why she left Bob Johnson’s place.”

Jack Reinhold asked, “Are you sure it was her and she was with him?”

Billy grinned and said, “Becky isn’t the kind of girl you mistake for anyone else, boss.”

“What did the horse look like?”

“Black with white boots on all four legs and kinda short.”

“Did you see where he took her?”

“Nope, but he was ridin’ east down the back alley past my place.”

The sheriff didn’t reply but grabbed his hat and shot out the door to go and saddle his horse to see Bob Johnson again.

Billy looked to Rafe Collier for an answer for the sheriff’s rapid departure and Rafe said, “The man you saw her with is Gabe Owens, the railroad special agent. If I had to put my money on what happened, I’ll bet that he went and got her out of that camp. I don’t know why, but I think all hell’s about to break loose.”

“What can we do about it?”

“For now, we just have to wait, but we have to figure out right now what we do if we have to choose between the sheriff and agent Owens.”

"Why would we have to choose, Rafe? The sheriff's our boss."

"Billy, you've only been on the job for a year. Our boss is only our boss because he's got the sheriff's badge. Where do you think he's going right now? He's on his way to Bob Johnson's logging camp to tell Bob where Becky is."

"He is?" he asked in surprise.

"Of course, he is. Then Bob Johnson and that bastard Frank Stanford will come back into town and that's when we have to make our choice. We can either be deputies and do what the sheriff says or be men and do what's right."

Sheriff Reinhold had been sitting on the porch steps for twenty minutes when he finally spotted a frustrated Bob Johnson riding from the logging road with Frank Stanford, who seemed to angry more than frustrated then stood and waited to give Bob the news.

"Now what," Bob said aloud when he saw the sheriff standing in front of his house.

Either Frank hadn't heard him or knew better than to say anything because he remained silent. The longer the fruitless search had gone on, the more Frank was sure that Bob was blaming him for her escape and felt his best defense was to stay quiet.

When they pulled up to the house before they even dismounted Sheriff Reinhold shouted, "I know where Becky is!"

Both men quickly stepped down and Bob quickly asked, "Where is she?"

"One of my deputies spotted her ridin' with Gabe Owens in town. He was probably takin' her to Mrs. Wheatley's house."

Bob turned to Frank and said, "That's how she escaped. That bastard somehow got her out of there."

Then he turned to the sheriff and said, "You'd better get back on the job, Jack, and be ready for anything that might happen at that house later."

"I'll be ready, Bob," the sheriff replied then mounted his horse and wheeled him away.

"Let's go into the house, Frank. We need to talk to Angela about a few things."

A relieved Frank Stanford said, "Okay, boss," as they tied off their horses.

———

Five minutes later, Bob and Frank had Angela sitting in the main room of Bob's house as they both stood in front of her.

"Did you help Owens to get Becky out of here?" Bob growled.

"No, of course not. Why would I do that?" Angela asked, her heart pounding.

"I don't know what you women think," he answered, "it just seems pretty queer to me that you go and talk to Owens one day, tell me that everything's taken care of and then he shows up here and snatches Becky right out of Frank's house. How else can you explain it?"

"I have no idea. He told me that he wasn't going to do anything, but like I said, he's one of those men who tries to do what he thinks is right, so he probably had second thoughts. He was probably just watching the camp and saw how badly she'd been beaten and wanted to rescue her. Nothing more than that."

Frank snarled, "You're lyin', Angie. You were jealous and wanted Becky out of here, so she couldn't move back in."

Angela looked at Frank disdainfully and said, "You've got to be kidding. I never even talked to her."

Then Bob looked at Angela and said, "Well, you'd better not even think about running, Angela."

Then he turned to Frank and said, "What's important is that we need to get to Becky and soon. Go and get Red and Tanner. I have a job for them."

"Okay, boss," Frank replied then shot a menacing glance at Angela before turning and leaving the house.

After he'd gone Angela just sat staring at Bob knowing her recently made plans for escape were useless now.

Gabe was in the house examining his new Sharps-Borshadt and was impressed with the improvements over his Sharps back in his house in Minneapolis. The hammer assembly had been moved inside, leaving two smooth sides, making it look like an oversized Henry except for the lever.

He'd never used a telescopic sight before either but doubted it would be difficult to use. He thought it was as good a time as any to go out and do some target practice with the big gun, so after he made a quick lunch he took a box of the mammoth cartridges loaded one into the breech then left the house, locking the door behind him.

Gabe had to hang the new scabbard, but when Dancer was saddled and both his Winchester and the Sharps-Borshadt were stowed, he mounted and rode east out of town. He crossed the bridge over the Hells Gate River and kept going for another three miles before he left the road and found an open field where he could get his practice.

It didn't take him long to appreciate the power and accuracy of the rifle. There was a good wind coming out of the northwest, but once he made an adjustment on the scope to compensate, he still was putting rounds through a foot-wide target at twelve hundred yards.

After just six of the .50 caliber slugs had passed through the long barrel, he was satisfied with his new gun he saddled Dancer and put the rifle into its scabbard.

He checked his watch, found it wasn't even three o'clock yet then wound the stem, slid it back into his pocket, mounted Dancer and began the ride back to the house.

———

Red O'Rourke and Hack Tanner were sitting in the large chow hall eating their steak and potatoes. Both were large, well-muscled men who had worked for Bob Johnson since he started and had been tapped by Bob to join the group of men who he knew he could trust to do anything he wanted. He was generous to both men, and they enjoyed the perks of being in the near orbit around the boss.

They were the boys that Frank had trusted to take out Willie, and Bob had been impressed with that job, so rather than spread the wealth, Bob had asked that they be the ones to take care of Becky. The added bonus to the job was that after they killed Owens, they could have their way with her before killing her. They were assured that they would be protected by the sheriff, so they didn't have to worry.

The one weakness in both men was that they had rarely used pistols to do their dirty work. They used blades because most of their jobs involved either other lumberjacks or some troublesome locals. They both carried Colt '73s but didn't expect to be using them for tonight's job. They were simply more comfortable with knives and believed that a quiet killing was better anyway.

As they ate, they studied the hand-drawn map of the house where Owens and Becky were staying. As they planned on breaking into the house, they spent a lot of time passing bawdy comments about what they would do to Becky after slicing up Owens.

Bob had told them they'd probably be in the first bedroom near the parlor because it had the largest bed in the house which was where he'd bedded Angela. None of them, not even Angela, believed Gabe and Becky were sleeping in two different rooms, much less two different houses. Angela should have known better.

Gabe reached the house, rode Dancer into the small barn down, unsaddled his Morgan, brushed him down and patted the mare on the flank before he grabbed his Winchester and Sharps-Borshadt, left the barn and walked to the house.

When he opened the back door, he stepped inside, and his left heel slipped almost dumping him on the threshold and making him drop his guns.

After the required oath, he looked down and saw a folded sheet of paper. He leaned his rifles against the wall then reached down, picked it up, closed the door and opened it.

His eyebrows rose when he read:

Mister Owens:

The sheriff knows that Becky is in the house. He told Bob Johnson. Plan accordingly.

There was no signature, but he was sure it was from Deputy Collier, but it really didn't matter who was author was because now, as the letter suggested, he had to plan accordingly.

He hadn't expected Bob to send his thugs into Missoula during the day but that didn't mean he wouldn't send them into the house at night, especially now that he knew that Rebecca was already with him. Bob couldn't afford to let them both live now and just hoped that they wouldn't send anyone to the Ulrich home but didn't think it was likely for a few reasons. Bob was probably well aware of Rebecca's determination not to return to her father's home and now that Bob knew she was with him, he probably thought he was treating Rebecca just as he would. Men like Bob and Frank couldn't imagine a man treating a woman any other way.

He convinced himself that Bob would be sending men to the house to kill him tonight, and he wasn't about to let them leave alive.

———

Two hours later, Gabe had finished eating and cleaned up. The sun would be setting soon, and he expected he'd be having visitors later, but still lit some lamps. It would have looked odd to anyone watching if the house had stayed dark. He hoped that if anyone was watching the house, they weren't there when he and Rebecca had gone to her family's home. He didn't think so because he'd been scanning for observers.

Once the house was ready, he began setting up for his defense. He didn't think either Bob or Frank would be showing up but hoped that they would. That would effectively end this case.

This would be a pistol fight, so he had the Webley and the Remington fully loaded and laying on the kitchen table. He couldn't imagine that his intended assassins would be bringing sharp steel to do the job.

He'd already decided not to lock the back door, just the front. It was more likely that they'd enter that way, and if they broke in the front door before they even tried the back door then they were too stupid to live anyway.

Then he ran some cord across the kitchen floor about four inches above the surface connecting one end to the cookstove and the other to the decorative hinge on the cold room door. Once he was satisfied that it was taut enough, he looked around the room and decided there was nothing else that he could do to prepare.

Two hours later, he began turning out the lamps until the house was completely dark. He walked to the kitchen then sat in the far corner from the door and slid his finger across his Remington and then the Webley on the table before him. He had the Webley on the right rather than the left because of the double action. It was only a fraction of a second difference, but he wanted that tiny bit of time in case he needed more than two shots. He knew he'd have enough audible warning before they walked through the door, and once they were in the house, they could be legally shot. In this case, he wasn't particularly worried about the legal nuances anyway.

Angela knew when she climbed into bed that night that Bob had sent two of his men to kill Gabe and Becky. And to make sure that she didn't go and warn Gabe, Bob had locked her in the center bedroom with a leather strap around the door knob but only after enjoying her despite her passive participation.

Bob was going to stay awake until the men returned, but by eleven o'clock, he decided that he wouldn't waste the night trying to stay awake. They wouldn't get back until almost four o'clock anyway, so he went into a different bedroom and went to sleep.

Red O'Rourke and Hack Tanner set out from the camp just after midnight. The ride into Missoula would take them more than an hour at night, and they'd already come up with a plan that couldn't fail. Bob had told them that the doors would probably be locked, but the kitchen window could be opened and was big enough for them to sneak into the house.

Once inside, Red would take the lead and listen for snoring or any other sounds but if they didn't find any, they'd inspect each of the downstairs bedrooms as silently as possible. They knew that after one o'clock, it was highly unlikely that either of them would be awake especially after their expected exertions from coupling. Bob had used that word and they'd both thought it was hilarious and now used it exclusively to describe the act of lovemaking.

Owens would be the first to go of course, and both of them would use their big blades to make sure that he didn't get a chance to even raise a finger to stop them. Then they'd have Becky all to themselves. Neither had seen her with her bruised and swollen face, but it wouldn't have mattered anyway.

So, as they rode, they talked about Becky and by the time they were riding into town, they were getting more excited about the job when what they needed was to be cool and detached in order to have even a small chance of being successful.

———

Gabe was so sure that Bob would send at least two assassins that he'd overloaded on coffee to make sure he would stay awake, even if it meant having to delay his attempt to get Angela free of the camp. So, he had a chamber pot on the floor nearby rather than having to make the frequent trips outside he knew would result from the excessive coffee intake.

But as he waited, a new plan to get Angela free of the camp began to blossom in his mind. The killers that rode to the house would be expected back at the camp about an hour after doing the job. If they arrived early enough, he'd be able to ride their horses back to the camp to get Angela out of Bob's house. He thanked his lucky stars Rebecca had told him about the house's layout which was already firmly planted in his mind. If the back door wasn't locked, he could just sneak in just as the men who might already be on the way to slip into the kitchen to kill him. Everything would depend on the arrival of the assassins if there were any. There was always the chance that Bob was going to delay trying to kill him and Becky, but just didn't believe Bob could take the chance of letting Rebecca live that long.

He had just finished using the chamber pot when he heard the first noises. They weren't loud but just muffled hoofbeats about thirty yards away and then they stopped. He didn't know how many were there, but it sounded like two horses.

He slowly took both pistols in his hands and cocked the Remington with his left thumb, but not bothering to cock the Bulldog. He then rested both hands on the table rather than hold them and let his forearm muscles stiffen.

Then he just listened. There was a half moon, so there was some light coming in through the big window and it illuminated the kitchen enough for him to see the cord strung across the floor but wasn't sure if they'd see it.

He had been listening for over a minute without hearing a twig break when he finally picked up the very soft creak from one of the back-porch steps. He was impressed with how silent the killers were as he knew they had to be on the porch by now. Maybe he should be more impressed with the skills of the carpenters who had built the house.

Gabe rotated the two pistols until they were both level and pointed at the door when he saw the doorknob begin to turn and then heard a hushed snicker on the other side of the door when the assassins were surprised to find it unlocked. He knew he was buried deep in the shadows and couldn't be seen as he waited for them to enter.

The door swung open slowly as the first assassin listened for any telltale squeak, but no sounds crept from the hinges and the door kept silently arcing across the kitchen floor as moonlight flooded the room. He suddenly saw the moonlight illuminate the cord that was supposed to be his first line of defense and now saw it as an alarm for the killers and he cursed himself for coming up with the idea, but it was way too late now.

But Red O'Rourke and Hack Tanner weren't looking down. Their eyes were focused on the hallway just three feet from Gabe's face. They left the door open as they stepped into the room and Gabe saw their knives flashing in the light and couldn't believe it. *They weren't using pistols!*

He knew he could legally kill them both but as he'd told Rebecca, shooting a man at ten feet when you were looking at his face wasn't easy, even for Gabe.

"Drop the knives!" he shouted as he pointed one barrel at each large target.

Both men were startled out of their wits by the sudden challenge and rather than drop their knives, thought they had the advantage when he shouted and Red, the first to regain his composure, quickly drew his knife back to hurl it at the voice while Tanner decided to take two long strides and plunge his knife into Gabe.

Gabe saw Red's blade come up and fired the Webley at the immediate threat and then fired the Remington at the second man and at ten feet, missed when Tanner suddenly moved forward.

The Webley's .44 ripped through Red's chest and unlike the .41 caliber shot that had penetrated Mike's chest in this very room just a week earlier, the more powerful .44 drilled through his chest without slowing down very much and after exiting, blew through the outside wall and finally stopped when it struck the wall of the small barn but missed the two horses.

Tanner was shocked by the two large flames and accompanying roars from the pistols so close to his face, but then knew instantly he only had a heartbeat to act and took one lunging step as his right toe slid under the cord. Then the cord bowed when it caught the instep of his heavy lumberjack boot and his two hundred and twenty pounds worked against him as he began to plummet face first into the kitchen floor.

Gabe had already moved the Webley's front sight four inches to the right to stop the fast-moving killer and had just fired when Tanner began his tumble. The bullet left the Bulldog's muzzle at over nine hundred feet per second, traveled the forty-nine inches and penetrated Tanner's skull just behind the frontal bone. It then ripped through his brain and crashed through his skull's thick occipital bone before wedging into the floor near the far wall. He never felt his nose crumple on the varnished floor.

After the three gunshots' echoes left the house the room was eerily quiet. There was no groaning and no breathing from the two men on the floor. Gabe stood, put his Remington into his holster and then slipped the Webley home. Gabe thought that this was as close to murder as he ever hoped to get.

He suspected that the sheriff would be here soon just as he had been handily available when Mike Wheatley had been shot, so the first thing he did was to cut the cord and then toss it into a waste basket. He then walked into his bedroom, removed his gunbelt and shoulder holster and hung them over his bedpost then pulled off his boots and tossed them near his bed. He then pulled up the quilts and blankets, mussed up his light brown hair and walked quickly back to the kitchen.

He was going to light a lamp but hesitated. *Would the sheriff enter the house if he saw the light?* Then he realized that the sheriff would have had to wait until the assassins left the house before he arrived. If he knew they were going to use knives then the gunshots should have told him they had failed.

But there was enough light for him to do some cleanup. First, he picked up their heavy blades. They were both enormous knives, each one a foot long and a good three inches wide. He felt a chill run up his spine just by looking at them knowing the damaged they'd do. He set them on the counter then rolled the body that was closest to his shooting position, the one who'd tripped on the cord. He was a real mess with a clean bullet hole almost in the center of his forehead, but the back of his skull near the bottom had been blown open when the tumbling bullet had exploded out the back. He took a towel and wrapped it around his demolished skull then rolled him over, stripped his gunbelt from his body and set it on the table.

He then took two long strides to the second would-be killer, and saw his open eyes staring blankly ahead as he lay half propped against the open door. Gabe closed Red's eyes then took his gunbelt off and put it on the kitchen table with the first one. He then looked at both bodies, noting that their dress and boots identified them as lumberjacks.

After waiting for the sheriff for ten more minutes, he finally just walked back to the bedroom, pulled on his boots, belted on his Remington and his shoulder holster then put on his light jacket, hiding his Webley again. He then returned to the kitchen, slid the first body out onto the back porch and then walked back inside to retrieve the towel-wrapped body.

When both men were on the porch, he pulled out his pocket watch and turned it so he could see the face in the moonlight. It was just before two o'clock. There was time to go and get Angela.

CHAPTER 5

He returned to the kitchen, lit a lamp and after pumping some water into a bucket, he quickly cleaned up as much of the brain tissue, bone and blood that he could in five minutes. He then walked outside dumped the water into the alley and returned to the kitchen. He grabbed his hat, blew out the lamp then picked up his chamber pot and walked back to the porch, emptied it and set it on the porch. Then looked around at the lit windows from nearby houses.

Gabe wanted to get moving, so he shouted, “The intruders are dead! Could someone help me, please?”

He was surprised that the first one to answer his summons was an elderly woman from across the alley who trotted up to him in her nightdress.

“What happened? Was it another murder?” she asked excitedly.

Gabe wanted to laugh when he thought that need for gossip must outweigh the need for safety when you get old enough.

“No, ma’am. My name is Gabe Owens. I’m a special agent with the Northern Pacific. I believe these two men came here to kill me tonight but failed. When someone else arrives, can you tell them to let the sheriff know?”

“Won’t you be here, young man?”

“No, ma’am. I’m going to go and pay a visit to the man who sent them, but don’t tell that to the sheriff. That’ll be our secret, but when I come back later this morning, be sure and stop by and I'll tell you what happened."

She smiled and said, "It'll be our secret, Mister Owens. And you can rest assured that I'll be over later. My name is Mildred, Mildred Honeysuckle."

"Well, it's a pleasure to meet you, Mildred. Call me Gabe."

She nodded and said, "You know, Gabe if I was twenty years younger," then she paused for a heartbeat and said, "Oh, hell, if I was fifty years younger, I'd be visiting you at night."

Gabe grinned and said, "And I'd be anxiously awaiting your visit, Mildred."

She giggled as Gabe tipped his hat then strode quickly down the alley to where their two horses were tied off on a shrub.

He mounted the tan gelding and took the reins of the gray gelding and set off down the alley wondering where the sheriff was.

The sheriff was in his house, six blocks away, still asleep. Unlike Mike Wheatley's murder which had happened early in the evening, this one wouldn't happen until the wee hours of the morning and he figured that he'd have plenty of time to 'discover' the bodies after a good night's sleep.

He knew that the two men that Bob was sending were knife killers, so there wouldn't be any loud noises to awaken the neighbors anyway.

Gabe had tied the gray gelding's reins to his saddle and was pleased to find that both horses had Winchester '73s in their scabbards. As he rode, he reloaded his Webley and Remington. He'd already made up his mind that if he could somehow get Angela out of there without any noise, that it would be the best thing to do. He may have cut down Bob's manpower by killing the assassins, but he didn't want to get into a gunfight at night with an unknown number of shooters. He didn't know what he'd do if he had to separate Angela from Bob's arms, though. He might lose his temper and that would be bad. The thought of finding her in his bed was bad enough.

If possible, he'd get Bob out of there too, but knew he could only do it if Bob was unconscious. He finally decided to stop trying to plan ahead for something like this. He'd have to go whichever way the wind blew.

There was also the very real possibility Angela would scream for help. He knew he couldn't shoot her, *but could he even silence her with a tap on the head?*

This would be a much touchier rescue than Rebecca's had been if it was a rescue at all.

As he passed the darkened Ulrich house, he smiled when he thought of Rebecca sleeping peacefully with her family around her for the first time in a long while. Even if he died in the next few days, he was glad he'd come to Missoula for that reason alone. He may not rescue Angela, but he knew that he'd rescued Rebecca and not just from Bob Johnson's logging camp. He was annoyed that he didn't see any of the expected sawmill watchers outside, so he'd have to ask Eli about it when it was daytime.

He made better time than Red O'Rourke and Hack Tanner had in their ride into Missoula because he knew he was running out of time. The predawn would be around quarter of five this morning, and he only had an hour and a half left when he finally slowed as the logging camp appeared before him.

There were no lights and no smoke coming from any of the chimneys or pipes, so he walked the horses around the left side of the big clearing, the moonlit shadows of the tree stumps giving the landscape a bizarre, alien appearance.

He kept his eyes on the big house which was on the southernmost end of all of the structures, which was handy for him.

As he walked the horses a hundred yards or so from the house, he wondered if Bob was setting him up as he'd waited on his assassins. Maybe Bob was sitting in the kitchen right now with his derringer cocked and pointed at his back door, but the odds were remote at best.

Gabe turned the horses toward the back of the house and when he was fifty yards out, stepped down and tied off the horse on one of the stumps that had a small branch sticking out from its bark.

He walked slowly toward the back of the house. Unlike the front, it didn't have any stairs at all because the slope met the back of the house. He didn't pull either pistol, but kept his eyes focused on the door in the moonlight. There was a porch that was only three or four inches above the ground and hoped the builders were as good as the ones who had built Mike's house.

He reached the porch, carefully placed one of his size twelve boots on the wood and slowly lowered his weight, not hearing any noise at all. Then he took two more slow steps, reached the door, put his hand on the doorknob and slowly rotated it expecting it to hold fast, but it turned easily. But that didn't mean much if there was a deadbolt, so when he pulled back, he was almost stunned when the door slowly opened. Again, the nagging thought that Bob was sitting there with his derringer popped into his mind as he set his foot inside the threshold and held his breath.

He left the door open and let his eyes adjust to the diminished light that filtered through the small window. He stood there for a good thirty seconds, finally remembered to breathe then took one long step inside then another step, then another.

Each step was carefully placed as he reached the other end of the kitchen and found himself looking down a surprisingly long hallway. There were three doors on the right side but weren't evenly spaced. Rebecca had said they were the bedrooms and all of them had their doors closed. One of them had Bob Johnson and Angela inside, but which one?

He took two steps down the hallway and as his hand reached for the first doorknob, he suddenly stopped and looked closer at the next door down the hallway. He hadn't seen it before because of the low light, but now that it was visible, he noticed the door had a leather strap running all the way to the next doorknob, holding it closed.

He forgot about the door he was about to open and sidestepped carefully to the second door eight feet away. Once he stood in front of the door, he recognized the strap as a makeshift lock to keep someone inside. He was relieved when he realized that Angela was probably being kept inside against her will and Bob had to be in the only room that wasn't strapped closed. Either she had tried to escape, or Bob expected her make a break soon. Whatever the reason, it meant she didn't want to stay there and should want him to take her out of there.

He pulled his pocket knife, opened the blade and quickly cut through the strap making sure to hold onto the leather so it didn't fall to the floor.

After he'd severed the leather, he slipped the strap into his jacket pocket then folded his pocket knife, dropped it into his pants pocket turned the knob and slipped inside, leaving the door open.

It was even darker in the room as there wasn't a window, so he had to wait for his eyes to pick up what tiny amount of light was available then he spotted a head and was grateful that Angela was a blonde.

He stepped slowly to the bed, knelt close to her face and did something that he hoped would just wake her without any noise. He gently put his finger on her cheek and as he slid it across, he whispered, "Angela, it's Gabe."

Angela felt his touch and when she heard him say her name and then his, she smiled. It was such a wonderful dream.

Then when she felt his fingers trace across her face again and whisper her name a second time, she opened her eyes and saw a shadow and the bare contours of a face just inches from her eyes, a contour that she recalled from even closer encounters.

She finally whispered, "Gabe."

"Angela, do you want to come with me?" he asked.

She didn't answer but slipped her feet off the bed and sat up. She was wearing a nightdress, but her jacket and other clothes were in Bob's room. She was barefoot too, but would have to stay that way.

Gabe stood and took her hand as he stepped out of the door, carefully closing it behind them. Angela's bare feet made no noise at all as they left the hallway and entered the kitchen.

They soon exited the kitchen and Gabe stopped her on the porch then slowly closed the door, but before they left the porch, Angela turned to Gabe and pointed to her bare feet.

Gabe nodded then slipped his arms behind her as she put her arms around his neck, and he stepped off the porch then began walking to the horses. He couldn't believe that he'd gotten away with it again. Bob must feel pretty secure inside his logging camp.

When they reached the horses, Gabe set her down, then removed his jacket and held it out to her.

Angela slipped her arms through his large jacket and then pulled her nightdress up to her hips, slipped her foot into the stirrup and sat in the saddle.

Once Angela was on board, Gabe untied the reins from her horse and handed them to her before mounting and without saying a word, set the tan gelding off at a walk taking a wide, curving path to the logging road, letting Angela catch up to him.

He kept watching the house to his left, waiting for lights to come on as their horses plodded along and didn't even glance at Angela.

Angela was still euphoric about Gabe's daring rescue, having already given up all hope of escaping after watching how Bob and Frank had reacted to Becky's escape. It was when she thought of Becky's escape that she began to look at Gabe, wondered if they had slept together and the idea triggered a surge of jealousy then began to think about where he would be taking her.

They reached the logging road and soon the camp was lost behind the trees and Gabe looked over at Angela and asked, "How are you, Angela? I couldn't tell in the dark."

"I'm fine now. Bob was furious when Frank told him that Becky was missing. How did you get her out of Frank's house?"

"Would you believe I walked up to the door, knocked, and asked if she wanted to leave?"

"You're kidding? You didn't!" she exclaimed in a loud whisper.

"Yes, ma'am. I did. I was watching the camp from the trees, watched Frank leave to go to Bob's house then just walked down there."

"Why did you even think of rescuing Becky? Did you know what had happened to her?"

"Not until I saw her face. I'll make Frank pay for that when I get him. The reason was simply that I met and liked her family, and I said if I had a chance to get her out of the camp, I'd try."

"Where is she?"

"Right now, she's with her family. I need to protect her just as I need to protect you. Both of you know a lot about what

Bob Johnson and Frank Stanford did and Bob knows that your testimony can get him hanged. I was going to send Rebecca to Helena until the trial, but that's not possible anymore because of the collapse of the Blackfoot River bridge."

"Where are we going?"

"Your house. I left the two bodies on the back porch, but the sheriff hasn't shown up yet. Now that you're safe, I hope he does. I'll throw him in jail and let Deputy Collier take over."

"You can do that?"

"Maybe not legally, but I'll work out the legalities later. Now, Angela, you have some serious explaining to do. Since I first found you at the sheriff's office, you've been telling me nothing but lies and don't compound the problem by lying again. I want to know exactly what happened in the kitchen when Mike returned home and walked in."

Angela wasn't at all surprised that he knew she'd been lying and wasn't about to lie again anyway.

"Bob found out about Willie Bernstadt talking to Mike, and I'll admit that I was the one who told him."

"Did you know about the timber poaching?"

"Yes, because Mike told me."

"Did Mike give you those bruises?"

"Yes, I didn't lie about that."

"I didn't think you did. Keep going."

"After I told Bob about Willie, he came to the house the next day just before Mike came home and pulled me into the corner of the kitchen, near the cold room and began undressing me. I'll admit that I was excited and began to help. Then we heard the door open and Mike shouted my name, but Bob covered my mouth and then stopped me from trying to cover myself.

"I heard Mike's footsteps coming down the hall and wanted to scream, but I was scared to death. Bob took out his derringer and held it level, facing the hallway. When Mike showed up, he saw us together stopped and began to say something when Bob shot him in the chest. I was shocked."

"But you didn't pull Bob's arm down, either."

"No, I'm ashamed of that. After Bob checked to make sure that Mike was dead, he told me to go and get my clothes and he was taking me to the logging camp. Then he reminded me that I was just as guilty of killing Mike as he was. He was right, wasn't he?"

"Yes, and no. It depends on the prosecutor. Okay, that matches what I had already suspected, it was just a question of who pulled the trigger. You and Bob are both around the same size and both left-handed, so it could have been either of you, although I was pretty sure it was Bob. Now tell me about that farce you played to try to get me to stop my investigation. You had to know it wouldn't work."

"I wasn't sure, but Bob kept telling me how I'd hang if I didn't at least try, and I have to admit I believed that he loved me, so I did it voluntarily and thought he'd be pleased with me when I returned."

"Why didn't you just tell me the truth, Angela?"

"I was still afraid you'd arrest me. Why did you say you wouldn't?"

"Because I knew you were lying, and I needed the time. I had to get Rebecca to safety, but then the bridge collapsed and we're pretty isolated for a few days, so she's still in Missoula."

"Did you have her in my house with you?"

"Since I pulled her out of the logging camp yesterday morning until I dropped her off at her father's house late this morning, and no, we slept on different floors before you ask. You should know me better than that, too."

"You're right. I should have known better to think you'd do something like that."

"Now, I'm going to have to keep you safe, Angela. Bob and Frank will want to kill you and Rebecca, too. You both know too much. You both have it in your power to get them both hanged."

"What are you going to do about me, Gabe?" she asked.

"I don't know, Angela. I really don't. You've made horrible mistakes almost from the time I met you. I never understood why you accepted Mike's proposal and rejected mine while I was in Billings. It devastated me, Angela. Why did you do it?"

"I wasn't happy about it at all either, Gabe. You have to believe me. It's just that, well, I thought I was pregnant with Mike's baby and he'd been asking me to marry him for months. I missed my monthly just before I met you and thought it was just a fluke, but then I missed my second, and you left, so I accepted his proposal and told him I was carrying his child."

Gabe wasn't shocked by her explanation, but he was a bit nauseous when he realized that Angela had been having them both in her bed at the same time.

"Why did he take the job in Missoula?"

"To get away from you. He knew that you'd proposed and suspected that we had been together, so he asked his father to get him a job away from Minneapolis, so we came here."

"What happened to the baby?"

"I had a miscarriage after four months and never conceived again."

They reached the main road and turned east in the moonlight as the sky began to lighten with the predawn.

"Angela, you always could have talked to me, even then."

"I know that now, but it's too late. Isn't it?"

"Yes, Angela, it's too late."

"You don't love me anymore, do you?"

"Surprisingly, I do, but not the kind of love you mean. I have a soft spot for you, Angela because despite all of your mistakes, I still think you're a naïve and innocent young woman."

Angela looked at Gabe and asked, "You aren't serious, are you?"

Gabe looked back and said, "I most certainly am. When I examined all the things that you've done wrong, it was always because you were either afraid or uncertain. That's why I was almost sure that you hadn't shot Mike, despite his beating you.

By the way, if he was still alive and I'd seen those bruises, I would have beaten him until he'd never walk right again, and I don't care if his papa is a vice president."

Angela smiled and said, "Thank you for saying that, Gabe."

"I can't imagine what I'm going to do to Frank Stanford for what he did to Rebecca. You haven't seen her face, have you?"

"No, but I saw her get slapped and dragged out of the house. It made me sick."

"She probably has more bruises than you do after just one night with that bastard."

When they turned toward a sleeping Missoula, Angela said, "All of my clothes are back in Bob's house."

"He must have quite a collection now. I bought some dresses and things for Rebecca and she left them in her room in your house after I left her with her family. I'll bring all of your clothes and hers back from the camp when I finish with Bob and Frank."

"Are you that sure of yourself that you can to it?"

Gabe turned looked at her and said, "I'm the best there is."

Angela replied, "In more ways than one, Gabe."

He understood her reference but just looked forward again at the dark town as they passed the Ulrich house. There were no lights on yet, but no watchmen either. If he didn't have Angela with him, he would have just turned and ridden over there and stood watch himself.

As they approached the house, Gabe did a quick scan and didn't see anything moving, so he pulled the two horses to a halt in front of the house, pulled out one set of keys from his pants pocket and handed them to Angela.

"Go in the front door and go upstairs to the first bedroom on the right. That's the one Rebecca used. Get dressed and then come back downstairs, but don't go into the kitchen yet. I have to make sure there's nothing I missed when I was cleaning up in the dark."

"Okay," she said as she accepted the keys then dismounted and scurried up the front steps, crossed the porch, unlocked and opened the front door and disappeared inside.

He then began walking the two geldings to the back of the house and as he approached the small barn, he glanced at the back porch and saw the two bodies. It was only with the added light that he was able to see the orange hair of Red O'Rourke. He guessed that the other one was Hack Tanner, judging by his huge beard. They may not have been Bob and Frank, but they were the next two on the pecking order.

As he stepped down, he shook his head and said aloud, "Knives."

He began unsaddling the horses and when he finished ten minutes later, he led them to the trough and after a couple of minutes, brought them to the side of the barn, hitched them to the hitchrail and then walked into the barn to gather some hay for them.

When he was finished with the horses, he finally walked past the two bodies, took a good look at them both then turned, unlocked the door with his second set of keys and went inside. He didn't see Angela there which almost surprised him because it would have been a bad idea for her to walk into the kitchen then discover some missed skull fragment after he'd warned her not to go into the room. She seemed to always follow the wrong path.

But she hadn't this time, so after tossing his hat onto the table, he lit a lamp then picked up the wet cloth he'd used for his quick cleaning earlier, soaked it with water, and wrung it out. He then picked up the lamp and slowly examined the only places where missed pieces of Tanner's skull could be, found some and just picked them up with his fingers. He missed a few places where blood had splattered, but after another ten minutes, deemed the kitchen safe enough for Angela to enter.

Before he let her in though, he picked up his Sharps-Borshadt, opened the pantry door, and put it inside. He didn't want the sheriff to know he had the long-range rifle. He probably didn't know that his '76 was any different than a '73, either. The sheriff had done nothing to impress him so far.

Gabe started a fire in the cookstove then filled the coffeepot with water before he shouted, "Angela, it's okay to come in now."

When he hadn't received a reply or heard footsteps, he thought she might have run back out the front door after getting dressed. So, he headed for the hallway then stopped when he heard her footsteps as she came down the staircase quickly reversed direction and returned to the kitchen.

He took a seat at the table when she entered the room and ran her eyes over the kitchen for any signs of the shootings.

Angela then exhaled stepped over to the table and sat across from Gabe.

“Now, what do we do?” she asked.

“Angela,” he replied, “I’m going to take a big chance and trust you with my life.”

Angela was startled and asked, “How?”

Gabe pulled his Webley from his exposed shoulder holster and set it on the table.

“This is a Webley Bulldog. If you need to use it, just point it and pull the trigger. You don’t have to cock the hammer. I’m going to go into the bedroom and lay down for as much sleep as I can get. I expect the sheriff to show up shortly and when you hear someone pounding on the door, wake me up.”

“Why do I need the pistol?”

“In case the first one through the door isn’t the sheriff.”

She looked at the Webley then wrapped her fingers around the grip. She’s never held a pistol before, but it seemed simple enough.

“Okay,” she said.

“If you want some coffee, I just put on a pot of water. I’ve had too much already.”

Gabe then stood walked down the hallway and entered the bedroom. He didn’t remove his boots or his gunbelt but just stretched out, put his head on the pillow and closed his eyes.

Angela had followed him into the bedroom, the same place where he had taken her when she had pretended to faint and sat on the edge of the bed with the Webley on her lap.

"Gabe," she said softly, "if it means anything to you, I really wished that I had met you before I was with Mike. I guess the worst decision I ever made, and you know I've made a lot, was that I had already decided to marry him before I met you because he was a man of substance. I would have married you even if you were a lumberjack."

Without opening his eyes Gabe replied, "I was a lumberjack for a while, you know."

Then after a short pause he said, "Speaking of timber, do you know what's really stupid about what Bob Johnson is doing?"

"Everything that he's doing is stupid and most of what I did was stupid too, for that matter."

"What you did was based on fear, but I don't understand why Bob Johnson murdered Wille and Mike."

"He was worried about going to jail for poaching all the timber, wasn't he?"

"That's why I thought it was so stupid. If he was caught poaching timber, the most likely outcome would be that we'd tell him to stop and pay for the trees he'd already cut, and they'd probably take about half of what he made by selling them. The government would make noise about prosecuting him and sending him to prison, but they never follow through with anything this far away from Washington.

"What I'm saying is that he should have known that. If you're going to get into a criminal activity or anything else, you should know in advance what you can profit from it, and what the costs and risks are. Too many criminals never look at it as a business, and I guess Bob never bothered to find out what happened to poachers in the past ten years."

"He could have taken his money and walked away?"

"Most likely. Once he went past simple poaching and entered the world of murder, he put the noose around his neck. Now, I'm going to have to go out there and tighten it."

Angela then stood and sat on a chair still watching Gabe but listening for the sheriff's arrival.

Once Gabe finished talking, he drifted off to sleep in less than a minute.

Sheriff Reinhold was up at six-thirty that morning, slid out of bed and hurriedly dressed. He had a crime scene to investigate but would have to visit the office first.

But he wasn't the first one to arrive at the jail. Deputy Rafe Collier showed up just before seven o'clock and found a note hung from a nail on the door jamb that had been placed there for that purpose.

He pulled the note from Mildred Honeysuckle then quickly turned and remounted his horse and began riding to the Wheatley house.

Gabe had managed more than two hours' sleep when Angela heard boots pound onto the front porch and then a rapid series of knocks.

She jumped to her feet, began shaking Gabe and said, "Gabe! Gabe! The sheriff's here!"

Gabe's eyes flew open, but he lay there for a few seconds before he swung his feet around, stood and as he rubbed his eyes, he said, "Stay here and close the door."

Then he walked out the room, heard the knocking at the front door then quickly began walking toward the parlor, releasing his hammer loop as he did.

He unlocked the door and was surprised to see Deputy Collier standing there rather than the sheriff.

“Mister Owens, I have a note from Mildred Honeysuckle that says you have two bodies here.”

“Come in, Deputy, and call me Gabe.”

He removed his hat and stepped inside then Gabe closed the door behind him.

“Did you leave me a note telling me to plan accordingly?”

“Yes, sir. I figured you and Becky might be in some danger once Johnson found out she was here, and I’m Rafe, by the way.”

“Follow me, Rafe,” he said and once they began walking down the hallway, he began explaining.

“I was waiting in the kitchen with two pistols. They came in around one o’clock and had these big knives in their hands. I shouted for them to drop their knives, but they chose to try and kill me anyway. I thought it was stupid enough to bring knives to a gunfight, but to then believe that I was just sitting in the dark playing solitaire was far beyond that level of stupidity. Anyway, I’ve got their bodies on the back porch.”

Angela had heard Gabe talking and knew he wasn’t talking to the sheriff which puzzled her. *Who was with him?*

They reached the kitchen and Gabe showed Deputy Collier where he was sitting and then took the cord from the wastebasket, showed how he'd strung the cord to trip anyone who came in that way if he missed his shots. He showed him the sink where he'd put their knives and gunbelts and the deputy whistled at the size of the blades.

After Gabe unlocked and opened the back door, Deputy Collier had his first glimpse of Red O'Rourke's and Hack Tanner's bodies.

"I recognize both of them. I had to toss the redhead into jail a few times for getting into drunken fights in one of the saloons. The sheriff always let him go the next morning."

"Speaking of the sheriff, when do you think he'll come by?"

"Pretty soon, I'd imagine. What are you going to do now?"

"I'm going to head out to the logging camp shortly and have a chat with Bob Johnson, but I doubt if it will come to just exchanging words."

"I meant about Sheriff Reinhold."

"Let's go back inside and I'll explain it to you and Angela Wheatley."

"She's here?" he asked in surprise.

"I went and got her out of Bob's house early this morning after those two tried to kill me and Rebecca. I knew that Bob would probably kill her once he got rid of Rebecca and me."

"Is Becky here, too?"

"No, she's with her family. I'll need to stop by there on the way to the logging camp. Bob will be finding out soon enough that Angela is missing, and I'll need someone to protect her while I'm gone."

"Did she kill her husband?"

"No. I asked her that this morning on the ride here, and I believe her when she told me that Bob had pulled the trigger. She was in the room though, and could have prevented it, but probably would have been killed for her trouble. Bob had one more shot left in that Remington."

Gabe then reentered the house and shouted, "Angela, it's okay. Come into the kitchen."

As he walked to the sink to take out the two gunbelts with their mammoth sheathes and knives the bedroom door opened and Angela strolled out, stopped then saw Deputy Collier and understood that Gabe must trust him, so she continued into the kitchen holding the Webley in her hand.

Gabe had the two gunbelts over his shoulder when she entered the kitchen then said, "Angela, you know Deputy Collier, don't you?"

"Yes, I've seen him a few times and met him at the jail when you arrived."

"Rafe, before the sheriff arrives, I'll explain what I want to do. When he gets here, I'm going to disarm him and take him back to your office and lock him in a cell. He's going to be charged with accessory to murder, malfeasance, accepting bribes and probably a few more crimes. I'll need you to guard Angela. If you want to do it at the jail or here is up to you. After I stick him in the cell, I'm going to ride out to the logging camp. Is your other deputy still laid up?"

"No. That's how the sheriff found out that you had Becky with you. Billy Cooper spotted you and inadvertently told the sheriff, who then ran off to tell Bob Johnson."

"Can I trust him?"

"He's fairly new to the job, but he's a good kid."

"Okay, I'll trust him to do his job," he said as he turned and looked at the cookstove.

"It looks like I boiled away the water for coffee, so I'll get some more going."

Angela then stood and said, "This is my kitchen, Gabe. I'll make you and Deputy Collier some breakfast while we wait for the sheriff."

"Call me Rafe, ma'am," Deputy Collier said as he smiled.

"Please call me Angela," Angela replied as she smiled in return.

Then she realized she was still holding Gabe's Bulldog and held it out to him. After he took the pistol and replaced it in its holster, she started cooking.

Gabe then returned to the bedroom, left both gunbelts on the dresser then donned his light jacket.

Bob Johnson slid his feet to the floor, yawned and stretched before he stood and twisted to unkink his back then slipped on his boots and left the bedroom. He didn't pay any attention to Angela's room as he hurried through the kitchen and out the back door. After he'd emptied his bladder from the back porch, he glanced around at the camp saw men in the distance already leaving the chow hall to go to work with their assorted axes and saws then turned and walked back inside. Time to let Angela out and have her make his breakfast.

He walked down the hallway and when he reached the second door, he momentarily forgot that he'd used a leather strap to keep her inside then opened the door and saw the empty room.

"Son of a bitch!" he swore as he quickly left the room, trotted across the big front room and out the front door.

He knew she couldn't have escaped without help and he thought that Frank must have decided to use her now that Becky was gone. The idea was without any logic whatsoever, but he couldn't imagine anything else.

Bob reached Frank's house a minute later and just burst through the front door as he shouted, "Angie! Frank?"

With no response, he thought Frank had taken her away and his anger exploded into full-blown fury as he turned to leave the house.

He was passing the threshold when he spotted Frank casually walking toward the house.

"*Where did you put her, Frank?*" Bob angrily asked as he stepped onto the ground.

Frank had just spotted his boss and was confused by the question believing he was asking about Becky.

"She's back? I thought she was with Owens."

Bob stormed up to Frank glared at him and asked, “What the hell are you talking about? Where is Angie?”

Frank looked at Bob with a blank expression and asked, “Angie? Is Angie gone, too?”

Bob saw his confused look and knew instantly that it hadn’t been Frank who had freed her.

“Yeah, she’s gone. I’m sorry I yelled at you. I figured somebody cut her out of there and I thought you took her, but it had to be Owens.”

“But Red and Tanner went out last night to kill him. How could he be alive and then come here and take Angie?”

“They didn’t return, did they?”

Frank then realized they were missing and said, “You really think Owens came here and got Angie?”

“Who else could have done it? She told me before that he was the best agent they had and now I believe it. Okay, Frank, I don’t like the way this is going at all. Let’s pull up stakes and get the hell out of here. I’ve got the money in the house. First, I want you to tell Jack, Alex, Pete and Carl to come to my house. Once you’ve done that, go and saddle a couple of horses and we’ll ride into town and get the next train out of here.”

“Boss, you forgot the sheriff said that the bridge blew up and there ain’t any trains comin’ through.”

Bob’s jaw muscles bulged as he ground his teeth before he snapped, “Damn it! You’re right. Alright, we’ll ride out of here and head west. We’ll have to ride to Ventnor and wait there for a couple of days until the trains start coming from the west end. Get a pack horse saddled, too. Load it with food and supplies for three or four days."

Frank was more than happy to be leaving Missoula, so he said, "I'll send the boys to see you, Bob," then turned and trotted away.

Bob watched him go and then turned around himself and headed back to his house. If Owens had killed Red and Tanner already then he knew the odds of the other four stopping him were almost nil, and he wasn't about to risk getting in a gunfight with him either. Frank was incredibly loyal, but he was only marginally better with a gun than he was.

He walked up the steps to his porch and went through the open door leaving it that way for the four men he'd summoned. They might get lucky, but he really just wanted them to delay Owens, certain that he would be arriving soon.

He entered his office but didn't take out the money yet because he didn't want the four goons who he was probably be sending to their deaths to see the cash. There were a lot of greenbacks in his safe. The last time he'd checked, there was more than sixty-two thousand dollars in there. When you don't have to pay for the trees you're cutting down, it makes for a big profit margin.

Bob took down two of the remaining six Winchester '73s he had on the wall and carried them to his side of the desk, leaned them against the wall and took a seat, expecting the men to show up soon. There was no point in giving them extra ammunition. He didn't believe any of them would get off more than three shots.

Five minutes later Jack Finlay, Alex Hall, Pete Swanson and Carl Short all walked past the threshold, removed their assorted hats then crossed the main room floor heading for the office.

Once inside, Bob smiled at them and said, “Boys, we have a problem. That railroad agent came in here this morning and snuck Angie right out of here while I was sleeping. Now he’s got Becky and Angie and they’re probably telling him everything. I’m sure he’ll be coming this way soon, and I know that you can stop him. I’m not as good as any of you with guns, but what I’m going to do is give you each a Winchester to make the odds in your favor. Four Winchesters would put up a wall of lead that will turn him into a messy target. Go ahead and pick out a repeater.”

They all grinned, turned and each man took a Winchester from the rack then looked back to Bob.

Pete Swanson then asked, “Can we have a box of cartridges too, boss?”

Bob was about to tell them that they were too good to need any more ammunition but decided to give them each a box of cartridges. It was cheap insurance.

“Go ahead. The spare ammunition is in the drawer under the gun rack.”

Pete nodded then turned, opened the drawer and handed each of the other men a box of .44s before taking one for himself and closing the drawer leaving just two more boxes.

“What I’ll want you to do is one of you watch the logging road then the other three spread out about a hundred yards apart. Once you see him, wait for him to get within range and open fire. When the others hear the first shot, you all converge on the shooter and help him if he needs it.”

“Okay, boss. It sounds like a good plan,” Jack Finlay said, unsure of what ‘converge’ meant. He’d ask Pete once they left the house.

“Good luck, boys. And there’s a hundred-dollar bonus for the man that buries the first shot into him. The others get fifty.”

That created grins on all their faces before they nodded, turned and quickly left the room already arguing about who would be collecting the hundred dollars.

After they’d gone, Bob murmured, “Idiots”, then walked around the desk, removed the last two boxes of Winchester cartridges set them onto the desktop then walked to the safe, dropped to his heels and began to spin the dials.

Sheriff Reinhold had arrived at the office and found Deputy Cooper at the desk when he entered.

“Where’s Rafe?” he asked.

“Beats me, boss. I unlocked the office this mornin’ and put on the coffee. It’ll be ready in a few minutes.”

“I’ll have some when I come back. Hank Logan stopped me on the way and said he heard something suspicious over at the Wheatley house, so I’m going to go and check on it.”

“Want me to come along, boss?”

“No. You stay here in case anything else happens.”

“Yes, sir.”

The sheriff turned around and left the office and as he mounted his gelding, he wondered where Rafe Collier was. As long as he could remember, unless he was out on a job, he'd be the first one into the office and have coffee already made before anyone else showed up.

He finally shrugged it off as he rode along the cobbled street. There was no rush as all he expected to find was a house with two brutally stabbed bodies. He was a bit squeamish with the thought, though. It was bad enough to see a man stabbed with those huge blades that Red and Tanner carried, but to see such a beautiful young woman cut open was already making his stomach recoil, and he wished he hadn't eaten breakfast.

He pulled his horse to a stop in front of the house, knowing it would be locked but had to make a pretense of not knowing what was inside in case anyone was looking. The streets were already busy, but he didn't notice that there were women's faces in some of the windows. Mildred Honeysuckle had not only passed along the word that there had been killings again in the Wheatley house but had also suggested that the sheriff was involved. She always liked to embellish rumors and she had never liked the man. She simply had no idea how accurate her added bit of gossip was.

Sheriff Reinhold calmly climbed the steps to the porch approached the door and knocked loudly then stood waiting, knowing the door wouldn't open. After ten seconds, he raised his hand to knock again when the door swung wide quickly, startling him.

He was even more surprised when he found himself facing Gabe Owens with a cocked pistol in his hand.

"Uh…Uh…Mister Owens! You startled me!" he stammered.

"I'm sure I did. Come inside, Mister Reinhold."

The sheriff didn't object to Gabe's failure to address him as sheriff, not with a pistol in his hand and stepped inside.

Gabe closed the door behind him and then the sheriff was shocked again when he saw Angela sitting in the parlor. *And she was sitting on the setee with his own deputy!*

Gabe then walked behind him took the Colt from his holster and said, "Jack Reinhold, you are under arrest for accessory to murder. I'm going to escort you to your jail, and you'll remain there until you are removed from your office and face trial."

He then said, "You can't do this! You don't have the authority! I'm the sheriff of this county."

"You might be right about the legalities, Jack, but let's face it, you don't care very much about legalities, do you? Mrs. Wheatley has told me and Deputy Collier of your involvement and coverup of the murder of her husband and as of this moment, he is the acting sheriff of Missoula County."

Gabe then ripped the badge from Jack Reinhold's chest and tossed it to Rafe Collier, who caught it.

Jack Reinhold then pointed at Angela and shouted, "She killed her husband! You even said so yourself! You can't believe a word she says!"

"I'm going by the evidence I collected in the kitchen, Jack. What she told us matched the signs of the murder that were still there because you were too damned lazy to clean it up. You're going to hang, Jack."

The ousted sheriff glared at his deputy and snarled, "I'll get you for this, Collier."

Rafe rose and replied, “I’m ashamed for having put up with your shenanigans, Jack. I should have stopped you years ago. All I can do now is make amends for my failure to follow what was right and not what was expedient.”

Gabe then walked the ex-sheriff to a chair and pushed him into the seat. He then handed Jack’s Colt to Rafe Collier and said, “Keep an eye on him while I get ready to take him to the jail.”

“Okay, Gabe,” Rafe said as he accepted the pistol.

Gabe then walked quickly down the hall and through the kitchen, pulled on his hat, retrieved his Sharps-Borshadt and his Winchester ‘76 then left the house. Once he reached the barn, he saddled Dancer, slid his two rifles into their scabbards then mounted him and walked him around to the front of the house, dismounted and tied him off next to Reinhold’s gelding.

He then walked into the house and said, “Let’s go, Jack.”

Reinhold noticed that Gabe’s pistol was still in his holster and thought he’d have a chance so he rapidly stood then took two quick steps toward Gabe.

Gabe then pulled his Remington in a blur and the sheriff froze. The display was just Gabe’s way of letting the ex-sheriff know that he would be dead if he tried anything, and it served that purpose.

Jack Reinhold then walked past Gabe who said over his shoulder, “I should be back in a few hours.”

“Good luck, Gabe,” Rafe said as Gabe followed Jack Reinhold out the door.

Once they were outside, Rafe set Jack's pistol on the table walked to the front door and locked it.

Gabe mounted Dancer at the same time that Jack Reinhold stepped into the saddle and they both wheeled their mounts to head to the jail as sixteen female eyes of assorted shades watched eagerly from nearby windows and all of the watchers with a newfound respect for Mildred Honeysuckle.

Five minutes later, Gabe led Jack into his own jail and met Deputy Billy Cooper for the first time.

"Deputy Cooper, I'm Northern Pacific special agent Gabe Owens and I've arrested Jack Reinhold for accessory to murder. Deputy Collier is back at the Wheatley house guarding Angela Wheatley. She's a prime witness to the murder of her husband and has knowledge of other crimes committed by Bob Johnson. I want Mister Reinhold held in a cell until either I or Sheriff Collier returns to begin legal proceeding against him. Is that understood?"

Billy hopped up from behind his desk and replied, "Yes, sir," as he reached for the ring of keys.

Gabe escorted Jack Reinhold to the cells as Deputy Cooper unlocked the first cell and swung the door open. Once the ex-sheriff was inside, Gabe slammed the iron door closed with a loud clang.

"I'm going to go to the logging camp and arrest Bob Johnson and Frank Stanford. There are four other men that need to be arrested as well, but they may have to wait."

"Yes, sir," Billy replied as he returned to his desk.

Gabe nodded then turned and walked out of the jail, mounted Dancer and headed west. He should have taken the cell keys with him.

Neither Gabe nor Rafe realized that because it was Gabe bringing the sheriff to his jail, they had inadvertently provided him with the means to make his escape.

Inside his cell, Jack Reinhold sat on the cot and knew that he would surely be hanged, just from the testimony of the two women and knew had to get free before Owens or Collier returned, so as he sat, his attention focused on Deputy Billy Cooper.

———

Just a few minutes after leaving the sheriff's office, Gabe arrived at the Ulrich home and pulled Dancer to a stop, dismounted and tied him off.

He hopped onto the porch and knocked loudly, knowing it probably wasn't necessary.

The door remained closed, but he could hear noises on the other side, so he shouted, "It's me, Gabe!"

The door then immediately swung wide and a relieved Eli Ulrich said, "Sorry, Gabe, we thought the sheriff might be coming back."

"He won't be going anywhere. He's in one of his own jail cells. Could I come in for a couple of minutes? I need to talk to everyone."

"Oh, I'm sorry, Gabe. Come on in," Eli said as he lowered his shotgun.

Gabe stepped inside removed his hat and noticed the empty parlor with satisfaction. That was smart.

"Everyone is in the kitchen," Eli said as they began walking across the parlor.

When they reached the kitchen, he spotted Rebecca sitting with her little sister on her lap and Gabe smiled at the sight. He was awed by the remarkable level of comfort she already had with her family and gave Sarah as much credit as Rebecca for the change.

He then said, "Last night, Bob Johnson sent two assassins to the house to kill me and Rebecca. I'd been warned by Deputy Rafe Collier when I found a note saying that the sheriff had told Bob that I had Rebecca at the house. By the time I found out, it was too late for me to come here and warn you, but I was pretty sure that he wouldn't have suspected that you were here anyway, Rebecca."

"How did he find out?" Rebecca asked.

"Rafe Collier said that the other deputy, Billy Cooper, inadvertently mentioned that he'd seen you with me when we returned from the camp, but I guess he was out sick and didn't know about the rest until he walked into the jail and said he'd seen us together."

"Oh."

"By the way, Eli, when I was riding by your house this morning, I didn't see anyone watching. What happened?"

Eli grimaced and replied, "I didn't want them to risk themselves, Gabe. I stayed in the parlor with the shotgun thinking it would be enough."

"They wouldn't be at very much risk, Eli. Anyway, the two killers came in through the back door around one o'clock this morning. I had left it open, which should have set off an alarm that I was expecting them, but this pair were as dumb as rocks. They came in with these huge knives in their hands. I told them to drop the knives, but they decided to make a fight of it. After I dragged their bodies out onto the porch, I took their horses and rode out to the logging camp and took Angela out of Bob's house."

Rebecca exclaimed, "*How did you do that? Did you kill him?*"

"No, I didn't even see him. I still haven't. I got there, and the house was quiet, so I just walked in the back door expecting to find them together, but I guess Bob was concerned that Angela might realize what danger she was in and follow your example and run off. He'd put her in a windowless bedroom next to the one he was using and had a long leather strap securing the knob to keep her from escaping. I just cut the strap and snuck into her room and walked out the back door with her. I'm sure he knows she's gone now, and he'll be waiting for me."

"Where is she now?" Rebecca asked.

"She's in her house being guarded by Rafe Collier. I don't think that Bob, Frank or the other four will come into Missoula now. They're probably setting up for my arrival knowing that I have to come there sooner or later. They can hold out there for a month and with the bridge collapse, I can't get any help."

Eli said, "I'll come with you, Gabe."

"I appreciate it, Eli, but I can handle this. I have a new long-range rifle, my Winchester '76, and I'm expecting them to be ready for me. I'll be all right."

Eli nodded, knowing that he was probably right. He hadn't fired a rifle in quite some time now.

Gabe smiled at Rebecca then said, "I'm very happy to see you with your family again, Rebecca."

"I'm happy too, Gabe."

He then gave them a short salute, turned and walked quickly down the hallway passed through the parlor and soon mounted Dancer to head to the logging camp. As he rode away, he glanced back at the house and was disappointed not to see Rebecca on the porch but then looked ahead as he set Dancer to a medium trot.

Rebecca had remained at the table with Rachel on her lap wanting desperately to go out to the porch and say goodbye to Gabe, but knew she had to stop. She had her family back now.

Gabe already had a plan of sorts, but it was a flexible plan which was the best kind of preparation. First, with only six possible shooters, and he expected it would only be the remaining four thugs, they couldn't cover the entire forest that made up the eight square miles that hadn't been touched by the axe yet. He knew that the crews were working the government section on the north side of the logging road, so once he reached the main road five minutes after leaving the Ulriches, he continued to ride after he passed the logging road.

He finally turned when he'd ridden another three minutes, knowing he was near the edge of the row of land grant sections which ended in the government section that was being harvested illegally.

Dancer entered the tall pines and Gabe didn't even bother pulling his Winchester but kept his eyes moving as he rode his Morgan deeper into the forest and up the incline. If any of the shooters was this far away from the logging road, he'd be shocked, and it could take the form of a .44.

The next sound he picked up wasn't the report of a Winchester but the cracking and subsequent crash of a tall pine at his eleven o'clock which he estimated was a half a mile away, so he angled that way.

The nearest shooter, Carl Short, was almost two hundred yards to his left when he changed Dancer's direction.

———

As Gabe was drawing nearer to the logging crews, Bob Johnson and Frank Stanford were already on the main road that ran beside the tracks and were on their way west. The next town was Thompson's Falls twenty-two miles away, but it was little more than a watering station for the trains. Bob hoped that, as they rode toward Ventnor, they might spot a train heading for Missoula. They wouldn't board it, but they knew it would be returning soon because it couldn't go any further and they'd be able to get tickets at the next station when it was on its way back.

———

Gabe soon heard the sound of axes just ahead, dismounted and took his Winchester out of his scabbard. He made sure his badge was displayed on his jacket as he tied off Dancer to a nearby pine branch then began to stride toward the men swinging the axes.

He spotted the large work crew less than a minute later and quickly identified the man in charge. He ignored the stares of the men who saw him, but kept his eyes focused on the leader.

The crew chief, Dave Horowitz, noticed that some of the men had stopped work and were looking away, so he turned to see what had attracted their attention and spotted Gabe, saw the badge on his chest and knew that he was trouble.

Gabe stepped close to him and asked, "Are you the crew boss?"

"Yeah. Who are you?"

"Gabe Owens. What's yours?"

"Dave. Dave Horowitz."

"Dave, I'm sure that you know that you're poaching on government land, but I'm not concerned about that at the moment. In fact, I'll tell you right now that if you get all of your men to stop cutting trees right now, I won't even mess with you and can probably make sure you'll all still have jobs within a few days."

Dave asked suspiciously, "Why would you do that?"

"Before I worked for NP, I did damn near anything you can think of at a logging camp except cook. I know it's a hard and dangerous job and you don't get paid what you should. I know you're only doing what Bob Johnson told you to do and you needed the work. Bob Johnson and Frank Stanford are both guilty of murder, which is an entirely different thing.

"If they'd stuck to just poaching, Bob would have paid a fine and still had a lot of money, but they went too far to protect themselves. What I'm asking you to do is to tell everyone, including the baker, blacksmith and everyone else to head to the chow hall, have some coffee and enjoy a break. I don't want to shoot anybody by mistake. I already killed two of them."

"Which two?"

"I killed Red O'Rourke and Hack Tanner this morning when Bob sent them into Missoula to kill me and Rebecca Ulrich."

"Becky's with you?" he asked with wide eyes.

"No, she's with her family and Angela is in her house under protection. I want to have only targets out there right now, so if you can gather your crew and then pass the word to the others, I'd appreciate it."

Dave looked at Gabe then nodded and said, "Okay, Mister Owens. I'll get 'em movin' into the chow hall. And thanks for saving Becky for me. I think I'll head over and see Eli when I get a chance."

Gabe was a bit thrown off by his last statement, but said, "Thanks, Dave," before turning and heading back to Dancer.

Dave then called his crew together which wasn't difficult as they'd all been staring at the two-man conference and wondered what had been said.

Gabe soon reached Dancer untied him and mounted, keeping his Winchester in his hand. As he trotted away, Dave's apparent claim to Rebecca left him confused and disheartened. She hadn't mentioned his name at all, but he'd said he was going to see Eli and he had a feeling there was a lot behind that short statement. His name sounded Jewish too, so that probably meant there was even more meaning to his apparent familiarity with Rebecca.

But he had to focus on the serious work ahead as he cut directly across the edge of the trees, hoping he would come up behind the shooters who would be expecting for him.

Jack Finlay, Alex Hall, Pete Swanson and Carl Short were all behind pine trunks waiting for Gabe Owens. Each had positioned himself leaving at least a narrow view of the logging road but only Jack had the clear view down the length of the road as he was behind a tree that was only twelve feet away from the road's edge.

Alex Hall was about a hundred yards to his right and Pete was another hundred yards away. Carl was on the other side of the road about a hundred and fifty yards inside the trees. He also had the worst view of the road, just a small gap. If Gabe Owens rode past, he'd see him for less than a second, so he kept his attention riveted on that gap. For some reason, each of them believed that Gabe would take the road and not ride through the trees. It wouldn't have made any difference anyway, as Gabe was already behind them.

———

As Gabe was executing his plan, Jack Reinhold was making his attempted jail break.

He knew that Billy Cooper wasn't dishonest, but he also knew that Billy was still young, naïve and also hero-worshipped him which was one of the reasons that he'd hired Billy. He was counting on his ability to convince Billy that Owens was not only wrong, but crooked and had to be stopped. And only he, the duly elected Sheriff of Missoula County, could stop him.

"Billy, you gotta listen to me. I walked into that Wheatley house to find out what happened, and Owens opened the door and had his cocked pistol on me. Do you know what else I saw?"

Billy didn't turn around because he didn't want to look at the sheriff. This was all so sudden and confusing to him.

"I saw Rafe Collier's body on the floor. He didn't know that I spotted it either, but I saw Dan's boots just past the sofa where he'd slid the body. Remember how Rafe needed to get new boots and we were always kiddin' him about that hole in his right one?"

Bill suddenly turned around looked at Jack and asked, "He killed Rafe? Why would he do that?"

"I think it was because Rafe figured out that he was coverin' for Mrs. Wheatley for murderin' her husband and was gonna arrest him and her."

"But what about Becky? He saved Becky, didn't he?"

"Is that what you think? I thought you saw the bruises on her face. Where do you think she got 'em? He went out to the logging camp and got her out of there by hittin' her and draggin' her away. He needed to get her outta there to keep her from testifyin' against Mrs. Wheatley. Don't you know that he was her boyfriend before she came here with Wheatley?"

"Nobody told me."

"Well, it's true. Now he's gonna go and kill Bob and Frank, pretendin' that they were the ones who killed Wheatley, but it was her and he knows it."

It all made sense to Billy despite what Rafe Collier had told him. Gabe Owens arrives, gets Becky, beats her into submission then goes and gets his girlfriend. Now he has to make sure no one else is alive that might get her hanged.

Jack Reinhold could see the confusion and then the belief in Billy's eyes and his hope for a possible escape flared.

"Billy, you gotta let me out of here. We've got to go and arrest Mrs. Wheatley. He's probably got Becky Ulrich tied up in some room too, and we need to save her."

That did the trick. Billy was one of the many young men smitten by Rebecca, so he quickly stood walked to the far wall, removed the key ring then headed to the cell and unlocked it.

"Thanks, Billy. You're a good man," Jack Reinhold said as he followed Billy out into the office.

He pulled a Winchester down from the rack and as Billy reached for his hat, he quickly worked the lever, ejecting the cartridge that was in the breech and pointed it at his deputy.

The moment he heard the loud Winchester cycling a new cartridge into its breech, Billy knew he'd made a terrible mistake.

Jack stepped forward and yanked the Colt from Billy's holster and dropped it into his own.

"Get in the cell, Billy," he said, and Billy began to walk.

He felt like crying as he passed through the cell door but never had the chance when Jack Reinhold smashed the Winchester's barrel onto his skull, dropping him like a sack of potatoes to the cell floor.

He then quickly slid Billy into the cell then turned, left the cell and slammed it closed not even bothering to see if Billy was still breathing. He took a breath then calmly walked out the door, closed and locked it behind him before he headed for the livery to get his horse, not having any idea where he would go next. But he was free now and that was all that mattered at the moment.

———

Gabe had dismounted and was on foot as he walked through the trees. All of the workers were well behind him and he expected that Bob and Frank were still in Bob's house with Winchesters in case he made it past their guards, but they were already six miles west as Gabe walked away from the logging camp, searching for the ones who were waiting to kill him.

The first one he spotted was Carl Short when he caught a glimpse of his red flannel shirt in the gap between pine trunks. He was less than a hundred feet away, but Gabe wanted to get closer hoping to be able to put him noiselessly out of commission. If he surrendered which would be the smart thing for him to do, Gabe had some of the cord he'd strung across the bedroom floor in his pocket. He still had the leather strap that Bob had used to keep Angela in her room, too. He slowly pulled the hammer back on his Winchester as he closed in on Carl.

He kept walking slowly toward his target and after ten more steps, had him fully in sight and just sixty feet away had his cocked Winchester level and his sights on Carl's back as he kept placing one foot in front of the other.

Gabe was just forty feet away when his right foot stepped on a small branch, sending an alerting crack to Carl Short.

Carl whipped around then saw the Winchester pointed at him as Gabe said in a normal voice, "Drop it!"

Carl did drop but not the Winchester. He quickly fell to the pine needle covered ground and was bringing his Winchester into a firing position when Gabe squeezed the trigger of his '76.

Carl never even had a chance to pull the hammer back on his repeater before the powerful .50 caliber bullet slammed into his fourth thoracic vertebra right between his shoulder blades, blew through his spine then his aortic arch, pulverizing any tissue it touched before it punched into the ground beneath him, burying itself nine inches into the dirt, the small explosion actually popping Carl's torso a couple of inches into the air before it dropped back down.

Carl's head dropped to the ground as Gabe then cycled in a fresh round and trotted quickly to his right, away from his large cloud of gunsmoke expecting the other shooters to arrive soon.

The other three heard the shot and as they had been told, all rapidly converged on the gunfire, expecting that Carl would be the one collecting the hundred dollars.

Gabe was slowly moving toward the logging road when he spotted Jack Finlay as he passed between trees about fifty yards away. He then turned back and tried to catch sight of him and soon caught another glimpse. He was almost to the first man's body, and he knew that he'd have to get him soon.

Jack got a glimpse of Carl's body on the ground and ran toward him as he was being tracked by Gabe who was now just forty yards away.

Jack trotted closer to the body and didn't lean down to check if he was breathing as there was no point, not with that much damage and quickly brought his Winchester to the ready position then began swinging it in a wide arc as he sought out Carl's killer.

Gabe knew he didn't have much time, but still stepped out from behind a thick trunk and shouted, "Drop the rifle!"

Jack quickly turned his Winchester to the shout and fired as soon as he saw Gabe, his muzzle still having another ten degrees to go.

Gabe fired and the big bullet rocketed from his Winchester, crossed the hundred and thirteen feet between the pines and drilled into Jack's chest as he continued to rotate. The bullet crushed two ribs on his left side before slipping between his heart and his sternum, ripping both as it continued through him and then exited his right lung, taking out two more ribs before nicking his right bicep and slamming into a nearby tree.

Jack's rotation continued his angular momentum spinning him into the ground as his smoking Winchester then fell against a nearby tree trunk and remained standing as if waiting for someone to remember to pick it up.

Gabe then turned and began jogging back toward the logging road where the last shooter had been. If there had been another one on the opposite side, he'd either already run or had just stayed put, but he was betting the other two were on the other side of the road.

Alex Hall had slowed his headlong rush to get to the other side of the road after the second shot. He didn't think Jack took either of those shots and began to walk then finally stopped and waited for Pete to show up.

Pete Swanson had slowed only because he was out of breath and was now walking quickly to the site of the shootings. He almost missed Alex who was another twenty yards further down the logging road, but Alex spotted him and waved him over.

Pete changed direction and quickly reached Alex and asked, “What do you think happened?”

“I figure that Owens got Jack and Carl.”

“Are you sure?”

“No, but we gotta play it safe and figure he did.”

“How do you want to do it?” Pete asked.

“Look, we got two repeaters and four eyes, so we should spot him first. Those shots came from the other side of the road, so we’ll go in that direction. You walk on my left side, have your rifle cocked like I will. You cover that side and I’ll cover the right. We’ll have a lot more area covered. If you see anything moving fire and I’ll start firing as soon as you do. We’ll keep firing as we walk towards him and keep his head down. We’ll get him, Pete and we’ll split that extra hundred, so we’ll each have seventy-five dollars.”

Pete grinned, not understanding the math then nodded and said, “Sounds good, Alex. Let’s start moving.”

Al started to slowly step forward as he kept his head moving back and forth like a mongoose watching a cobra, while Pete did the same just three feet to his left. After fifteen steps, they could see the thinning trees ahead as they moved closer to the logging road.

Gabe had reached the logging road and taken a knee to listen for a minute. There could be four more men out there, but he was reasonably sure there were only two. It was also possible that after the shots, the remaining pair had hightailed it back to the camp. But just like hunting game, hunting men required patience and silence. Unlike the ones who were trying to kill him, he would wait until his targets came to him.

Pete and Alex then continued their lockstep walk toward the logging road and finally left the trees. Both then scanned the road, but Pete didn't spot Gabe just forty yards away as he was still on one knee on the other side of the thick pine trunk.

Gabe hadn't heard anything, but his peripheral vision picked up the motion to his left and he quickly stood.

By then Pete and Alex had shifted their focus to the front as they stepped out into the road. They had taken just a single stride when Pete caught a flash of movement to his left and turned his head and his Winchester at the same time.

Gabe already had him in his sights as he shouted, "Drop it!"

But Pete already had his Winchester close to firing position and cocked. He wasn't about to do any such thing as Alex began to bring his repeater to bear.

Gabe squeezed the trigger unleashing the fury of the .50 caliber round as the big cloud of gunsmoke erupted from the muzzle and the deeper report of the '76 echoed down the road.

Pete fired, but almost simultaneously, Gabe's larger round punched into his chest, ripped through ribs and lungs and then exited before slamming into Alex's left side and penetrating just three inches and lodging in his heart.

Pete's .44 buzzed a good six feet over Gabe's head as he watched both men collapse to the ground. Neither man moved as he began trotting toward them, not believing for a moment that the second man was dead. The '76 was powerful, but even he didn't think the .50-95 Express had that much penetrating power. He should have, as it had been designed to bring down big game from buffalo to grizzlies. Hitting a man's chest at twenty yards wouldn't have come close to removing all of its kinetic energy even after it had passed through the width of the chest.

He discovered that fact when he reached the two bodies, noticed the absence of breathing and then stood over them for a few seconds. He finally dragged the first body off the logging road and into the trees then returned and did it to the second one. He didn't want Bob and Frank to know that their guards were gone.

Gabe then spent another fifteen minutes collecting their weapons. By the time he reached Dancer, he had four gunbelts over his shoulders, four Winchester '73s in the crook of his left arm, and four boxes of .44 cartridges in his pockets. When he reached his gelding, he put the ammunition and gunbelts into his saddlebags then slid all four Winchesters into his bedroll. It was a tight fit and after sliding his '76 back into its scabbard the protruding repeaters made mounting awkward, but he managed to get into his seat and then turned Dancer toward the logging road to go and find Bob and Frank.

He expected to find them in Bob's house, but they could be anywhere in the camp, so he'd keep his options open.

Jack Reinhold was indecisive after leaving the jail, wondering where he could go. He couldn't go back to the house, so the first place he went was to the Missoula National Bank. The one thing he knew was that he'd need money wherever he went.

After almost cleaning out his bank account, leaving his wife, Millie, with only two hundred dollars, he mounted his horse, trotted out of town, and headed out to tell Bob what had happened. Then he'd pick up a packhorse and supplies there before riding west which was the only practical way out now.

He left the town and thought he heard a rifle report in the distance but after another two minutes, dismissed his concerns. It was probably just a hunter.

———

Gabe had turned onto the logging road and soon crested the rise at the end of the road and the camp came into view. He spotted Bob's house about eight hundred yards ahead and then glanced at Frank's house a couple of hundred yards to his right. Neither house had smoke coming from its cookstove pipe, which didn't mean anything. He expected at least one of them was watching him from behind one of the windows and thought about putting his Sharps-Borshadt to use but pushed that notion aside.

He wanted to see Bob Johnson face-to-face, and he really wanted to meet Frank Stanford fist-to-face. So, he just set Dancer to a trot straight toward the front of the house, pulling his '76 from its scabbard as he focused on the windows. He'd take a quick glance every few seconds at Frank's house, but it would have been out of range anyway, so he concentrated on Bob's.

When he got within a hundred yards, Gabe began to get a bit more nervous about his approach and started a jolting zigzag toward the front of the house. It's what made Dancer such a special mount. Just a tap on his shoulders and he'd instantly respond and shift in that direction.

He was within fifty yards and could see into the windows but saw no movement and began to suspect they weren't in the front room at all.

Gabe slowed Dancer when he was just twenty yards away from the high porch then swung his leg around the Winchesters' barrels and stepped down. He led Dancer to the hitchrail, keeping his eyes on the windows but still not seeing any movement.

He tied off his Morgan then shifted the Winchester to his left hand, pulled his Remington and began to slowly ascend the stairs. He reached the doorway, leaned his Winchester against the door jamb, took in a deep breath as he cocked the hammer then quickly opened the door and stopped, expecting gunfire to start slamming into the door's wood where they thought he would be.

But it was quiet, so he reached down, picked up his Winchester and entered the house slowly. Once in the main room, he listened but heard nothing then began to slide to his right toward the office door.

He glanced inside found it empty then walked into the room, and when he saw the open safe door, he knew Bob had run.

He then left the office and made a quick search of the house to be sure then trotted back to the front of the house, pulled the four Winchesters from the bedroll and brought them back inside. He didn't bother putting them on the gun rack, but just laid them on the couch and then left the house, closing the door behind him.

He mounted Dancer much more easily with the Winchesters gone and wheeled him to Frank's house to make sure it was empty as well. It was possible that Bob had run without Frank or maybe he'd killed Frank to keep him quiet.

It only took a quick check to confirm that Frank and Bob had both skedaddled then remounted and rode Dancer to the chow hall to talk to the workers.

He dismounted outside the large building then after tying off Dancer, walked through the heavy doors as the loud chatter suddenly subsided when he walked into the room and sixty-one sets of eyes looked at him.

"Gentleman," he said in a loud voice, "I'm Northern Pacific Special Agent Gabe Owens. I was sent here to investigate the murder of our station manager, Mike Wheatley and the poaching of company-owned timber. I discovered that the murder was committed by Bob Johnson, so I came here to arrest him, but it seems that Bob and Frank Stanford have fled, probably riding west. As I told Dave Horowitz, none of you need to worry about any kind of prosecution or losing a job. I'll take care of that when I return. Now, do any of you know where Bob and Frank went?"

The cook stood and said, "Frank came and got some food and then loaded it on a packhorse. I don't know where they were going, though."

"That's okay. I can find them, but knowing they took a packhorse helps. I've got to get going. Just don't take down any more trees. You can work the ones that are already down, though."

He didn't wait for a response but turned quickly and left the hall, hearing the conversations take on a new life as he passed over the threshold.

Gabe was in the saddle and heading for the logging road when a rider appeared over the crest. He wasn't sure at almost a thousand yards, but swore he was dressed like Sheriff Reinhold. The man must have recognized Dancer because he suddenly wheeled his horse around and raced back down the logging road.

That confirmed Gabe's guess and he set Dancer to a fast trot in pursuit. Even though it was only eight miles to town, he knew that the sheriff's horse would never make it at that pace.

By the time he entered the logging road, the sheriff was already a mile away, but his horse was laboring. He kept glancing behind him but the curve in the road limited him to less than two hundred yards, and he thought that somehow, Owens had cut the gap and was just around the corner even though he actually had a considerable lead.

As Gabe chased, he wondered how the hell the sheriff had escaped. He knew that Rafe Collier hadn't let him go, so it must have been the other deputy and he cursed himself for not taking the jail keys with him.

Jack Reinhold's gelding was exhausted, and his speed had dropped off to a slow trot. Jack kept looking behind him waiting to hear the sound of pounding hooves or the crack of a Winchester. *Where was Owens?*

Gabe was gaining on the ex-sheriff now and was less than eight hundred yards back, but like the sheriff, his view ahead was limited to two hundred yards. The advantage was that two hundred yards was at the far end of a Winchester '73's range. It could put a .44 that far out, but it would lose a lot of its punch by then. He knew he had an advantage with his '76, not to mention the Sharps-Borshadt.

Jack Reinhold finally realized he had no chance if he stayed on horseback, so he slowed his horse and then walked him into the trees. He dismounted, pulled his Winchester and trotted back toward the road. When he was at the tree line, he hid behind a thick trunk cocked the repeater's hammer then watched down the logging road and waited for Owens to arrive.

Gabe kept Dancer to a fast trot as he kept his eyes on the road ahead, expecting to see Jack Reinhold on his tired horse soon, but never even saw the ex-sheriff hiding in the trees two hundred and twenty yards away.

But then he was startled when the sheriff's horse suddenly just walked from the trees and trotted away down the logging road, He quickly yanked Dancer to a sudden stop just as Jack Reinhold's Winchester spat out a .44.

Gabe felt the slug punch into his gut almost dead center but had to ignore it as he brought his '76 level and fired quickly where he'd seen the muzzle flash. His first shot exploded into the tree that the sheriff was using for cover then he nudged Dancer forward with his knees as he fired every few seconds at the tree to keep the sheriff behind it.

Jack Reinhold had his back pressed to the thick bark of the tall pine as the .50 caliber bullets began to chip away both sides of the trunk. He knew he couldn't stay where he was, so he decided he'd run straight away from the tree and keep it behind him to act as a shield.

He levered in a new round then began to run, but his chosen direction was in line with where Gabe had taken his first shot. Since then, he'd ridden another sixty yards closer, changing the angle.

Gabe saw him suddenly appear and was ready for the sprinting escape and just had to move his sights another half an inch to the right before he squeezed the trigger. The rifle popped into his shoulder and less than a half a second later, the heavy, grooved bullet slammed into the left upper back of the sheriff, spinning him around and sending his Winchester flying through the air. He hit the ground and began squirming as he screeched in pain.

Gabe set Dancer to a trot and slid his Winchester into its scabbard as he approached the ex-sheriff. He pulled his Remington, dismounted then approached Jack Reinhold as blood soaked his jacket and he alternated between swearing and asking the Almighty for His help.

When he reached him, Gabe holstered his pistol then bent down, pulled the Colt from Jack Reinhold's holster and tossed it aside.

"You should've stayed in jail, Jack," Gabe said.

"You killed me, you bastard!" the sheriff screamed.

"Well, you put a bullet…" Gabe began then stopped and looked down at his gut. *Where was the blood?*

The answer was that his blood was exactly where it was supposed to be. When he looked down, then opened his jacket and stared at his gunbelt, he saw a .44 wedged in the thick steel buckle.

"I'll be damned," Gabe said softly before letting go of his jacket, covering the extraordinary memento.

He was going to show Jack Reinhold how close he'd been to staying alive when he looked down and knew that he wouldn't be able to see anything again.

Gabe then picked up his pistol and Winchester and left his body where it was. It was still visible from the road, but not on the road. He'd send the mortician to pick up the five bodies after he picked up the two from Angela's house.

He never did get a chance to ask how he got out of jail either, so he'd have to stop at the sheriff's office to find out what Billy Cooper had done.

But right now, he needed to head back to Missoula and prepare to chase down Bob Johnson and Frank Stanford before they got too far ahead. He imagined that they were a good ten miles away by now.

As he rode down the access road, he spotted the sheriff's horse and took him in tow as he headed for Missoula at a slow trot. This part of the job was done, but there was one act still left in this play before he could drop the curtain on Bob Johnson.

CHAPTER 6

Bob Johnson and Frank Stanford were a little more than ten miles away, but soon took a break to let their horses rest.

"What are we gonna do when we get to Thompson's Falls, Bob?" Frank asked.

"Get something to eat, feed the horses and have their shoes checked. Then we keep going. We can't stop at a town that small. Besides, Owens probably will send telegrams once he knows we're gone."

"Why don't we cut the lines?" Frank asked.

Bob grinned at him and said, "Now that's a good idea."

Frank grinned back after hearing his praise.

The telegraph lines ran parallel to the rail lines, so less than ten minutes later, Frank used his Winchester, targeting the glass insulators. It only took three shots before the line snapped and fell to the ground, effectively isolating Missoula for at least a day and by then, they'd be another fifty miles west.

In an ironic sense of timing, just twelve minutes after Frank had cut the telegraph connection to the west, the line across the Blackfoot that had been severed by the bridge collapse was restored as Northern Pacific work crews continued working on the destroyed bridge.

In the Wheatley house, Angela felt uncomfortable having Rafe Collier in the house after Gabe had gone. She knew that the deputy was aware she was present at her husband's murder and that she'd run off with Bob Johnson. Then she didn't like the way he looked at her, either. There was only one man that she wanted to look at her that way, and he was off trying to stop Bob and Frank. She wanted him to much more than look at her, but after he turned her down earlier, she wasn't sure how that could ever happen again.

Rafe Collier had walked out onto the front porch and stopped a passerby and had him send the mortician to come and collect the two bodies on the back porch before returning to the house and while he may have been looking at Angela, he was trying not to be too obvious about it. He had admired Mrs. Wheatley for quite some time, although he knew she hadn't seen him at all. She was a hard woman to ignore.

Now he was sitting at the table with her sharing lunch in awkward silence.

Gabe had passed the turn to the Ulrich house to continue to the nearby railroad station and its nearby Western Union office to send a telegram down the line to the western stations advising them of the possible arrival of Bob and Frank. He wouldn't be able to provide much detail, but a lawman or another agent if one was on their route they needed to know.

He turned into the station, crossing over the tracks leading Jack's horse. He stepped down and tied off Dancer before spotting Jim Clover and needed to talk to Jim anyway to ask about the bridge collapse, so he headed that way.

When he was thirty feet away, he shouted, "Jim!"

The stock manager turned saw Gabe and walked to meet him.

"Gabe, where have you been?"

"Chasing bad guys. Was it as bad as we expected, Jim?"

"Probably worse. The whole eastern side collapsed into the gorge. You could barely see the train at the bottom."

"Is the river dammed up?"

"Nope, it found its way around it, but there's a waterfall down there now. The work crews are already there workin' and Joe just told me the telegraph to Helena is back up already."

"That's some good news. I've got to send a telegram back to Herb and then send one west. Bob Johnson and his toady, Frank Stanford, made a break west out of the logging camp."

"You gonna chase 'em down, Gabe?"

"Yes, sir. After I send the telegrams, I have to go and talk to Deputy Collier before I leave."

"Good luck, Gabe," Jim said.

"I'm going to need it, Jim," Gabe replied as he turned and trotted back to the Western Union office.

He entered the small office and saw three people already in line waiting to send messages. He quickly took two sheets and began to write out his telegrams. By the time he finished, the three that had been queuing to send messages had paid their fees and gone.

He then walked to the desk and said, “I need these two messages sent priority, and I just wanted to let you know while I was here that Sheriff Reinhold is dead and Bob Johnson and Frank Stanford are on the run. Do you understand why I’m telling you this?”

The telegrapher looked at his menacing eyes and nodded without saying anything.

“Tell the other telegrapher what I just told you. If I ever hear that either of you so much as alter one letter of a message again, I will personally return and hook your privates up to that big battery, flip the switch and walk away.”

The telegrapher swallowed then nodded before Gabe said, “Bill the Northern Pacific for the messages.”

The telegrapher glanced at the first message and squeaked, “The…the line to Ventnor is down.”

Gabe wasn’t surprised at the news but just grunted, turned and left the office.

Once outside, he walked quickly to the station manager’s office, entered and found Joe Lofton writing furiously. He looked up, saw Gabe and put down his pencil.

“Gabe, things have been going crazy since you left.”

“They were that way before I got here, Joe. I don’t have much time, but I wanted to let you know that I just sent a wire to Herb Erikson letting him know that Mike was murdered by Bob Johnson and that he and Frank Stanford are on the run heading west. I’m going to go after them now. Could you do me a favor and send someone to the mortician and have him go about four miles up the logging road? Tell him to take a wagon because there are five bodies up there, including Sheriff Reinhold's."

"I'll send someone over there, Jake. You didn't take a hit?"

"Not really, but look at this," he said as he opened his jacket and showed him the .44 buried into his belt buckle.

"Holy Cow! Gabe, who put that in there?"

"The sheriff did from about two hundred yards. Any closer and it would have punched through. I've got to go, Joe," he said after dropping his jacket closed, doing a crisp about face and leaving the office.

He then rode directly into Missoula wishing he could stop and see Rebecca on the way, but thought he'd be able to stop by on his way out of Missoula to begin the chase.

When he reached the town, he stopped at the sheriff's office first, found the door locked then peered through the window and saw Deputy Cooper lying in the first cell. He then walked back to the door, stepped back and crashed his shoulder into the door splintering the lock and slamming the door open.

He stepped quickly to the cell, found it locked then noticed the large key ring on the floor, scooped it up, unlocked the cell door and rushed over to the deputy who was laying on the cot.

As he reached to feel his chest for a heartbeat, the deputy rolled over looked vaguely at him and asked, "Who are you?"

"Gabe Owens. Can I guess that the sheriff talked you into letting him out and then paid you back by hitting you in the head?"

"Yeah…I'm such an idiot. I shoulda listened to Rafe."

"We're all fools when we're young, and you're no exception. You just learned a harder lesson than most of us. I've got to go and see Rafe, and I'll send him back here. If it makes you feel any better, the sheriff took a shot at me and he's lying dead out near the logging road."

Deputy Cooper closed his eyes and said, "Good."

Gabe then stood, left the deputy lying on the cot and quickly left the office. When he exited the doorway, several citizens were nearby watching him.

He looked at them and said, "I'm special agent Gabe Owens. Earlier today, I arrested Sheriff Reinhold for accessory to the murder of Mike Wheatley and left him in the cell under guard. He escaped after hitting Deputy Cooper on the head and then we engaged in a gunfight near Bob Johnson's logging camp. You're going to need a new sheriff."

He then untied Jack Reinhold's horse from Dancer, tied him off to hitchrail, mounted Dancer and headed for Angela's house. He was moving as quickly as he could, knowing that Bob and Frank were moving away from Missoula with each passing minute.

Gabe turned Dancer into the drive and straight to the small barn. He quickly dismounted, tied off Dancer and bounded up the stairs to the back door took out his second set of keys, unlocked the door and walked inside finding Angela and Rafe sitting at the table drinking coffee.

"Gabe!" Angela exclaimed, but remained seated.

"Hello, Angela," he replied then turned to Deputy Collier and told him quickly what had happened after he left and that the bodies would be picked up by the mortician.

"I should have known he might talk Billy into letting him out."

"He learned the hard way, Rafe. He's probably going to be goofy for a few days. I left Reinhold's horse in front of the jail, so you can head back and help Billy then get someone to fix the door."

"Okay. I'll take care of it. When are you leaving?"

"As soon as I switch horses. I can't expect Dancer to make a long ride after I've already put him through so much. I'm going to take the two geldings that those two knife wielders left here. I need to make up time and distance."

"Good luck, Gabe," he said as he took his hat from the table, smiled at Angela and said, "Ma'am," then walked down the hallway leaving through the front door.

"Are you going to leave me alone now?" Angela asked.

"You're safe now, Angela. I have to go."

"Will you come back?"

Gabe grinned and replied, "I sure as hell hope so."

Angela smiled at him and said, "So, do I."

Gabe then said, "Angela, could you make me some sandwiches or something that I can eat on the way while I switch saddles and prepare to ride?"

She stood, smiled again and said, "I'll have everything ready in ten minutes."

"Thank you, Angela," he replied then turned and left the kitchen.

Once in the small barn, he quickly moved the saddle and the Winchester scabbard to the gray gelding and then put another saddle and the Sharps-Borshadt's scabbard on the tan horse. He adjusted the second saddle's stirrups to match his then took both canteens and walked to the outside pump and filled them both before returning to the barn.

He was just finishing when Angela trotted out of the house, and as Gabe watched her walk quickly to the barn and didn't wonder why he'd been smitten so quickly all those years ago.

"This should keep you going for a few days, Gabe," she said as she held out the big cloth bag.

He took the bag, smiled at her and said, "You take care, Angela. Just relax and take care of yourself. When I come back, I'll see if I can't remember to stop by Bob's house and pick up your clothes."

"Don't worry about it, I'll probably go shopping while you're gone."

"Well, enjoy your shopping then," he said as he mounted the gray gelding.

"Stay safe, Gabe," she said as she gazed up at him.

"I usually do, Angela," he replied as he turned the gelding and walked him out of the barn with the tan gelding trailing behind.

He turned west and set the two horses off at a slow trot and soon left Missoula behind as he headed for the Ulrich home.

His stomach was already rumbling when he pulled up in front of the house and dismounted and felt a bit guilty for wasting the time to stop to see Rebecca, but not that guilty.

Gabe rapped on the door, then when it opened just fifteen seconds later, he smiled as he said, “Good afternoon, Mister Ulrich. May I please enter?”

Aaron grinned at him and said, “Okay,” before he turned and walked into the house leaving the door open.

Gabe walked inside, closed the door and followed Aaron who was disappearing down the hallway. He removed his hat and walked down the hall then as he entered the kitchen was amused when he found everyone sitting in almost exactly the same positions as they’d been when he left, even with Rachel sitting on Rebecca’s lap.

Eli stood and asked, “Gabe, what happened?”

Gabe began with his arrest of the sheriff, and five minutes later, concluded the narrative, leaving out the dangerous parts, but obviously not well enough.

“Did you get shot at all, Gabe?” asked Eli.

“Not exactly, but the sheriff did get a lucky hit from two hundred yards.”

“What does ‘not exactly’ mean?” asked Rebecca.

Gabe opened his jacket, exposing his belt buckle and Eli just stared with wide eyes as he said, “I’ve never seen anything like that before.”

“Neither have I, but it’s better there than other places. Anyway, I wanted to let you know that everyone is safe now, and Eli, I told the crews out at the camp that they wouldn't have to wait very long for a new job. What I'm going to do is tell, not ask, that the NP sell you those sections of their land on both sides of that logging road for a very low price. That's four sections, plus the half-section that they already began harvesting. Right now, there is enough cut timber to keep them busy for a few days until I return. Will you be able to handle that?"

Eli grinned as he replied, "I really appreciate that, Gabe. Some of those boys were mine to start."

"Can I guess that one was named Dave Horowitz?"

"How'd you know that?"

"He said he was coming to see you and thanked me for saving Becky."

Eli nodded and said, "Two years ago he asked if he could marry Rebecca and I gave him my blessing, but you can imagine what happened. That's when he left and went to work for Bob Johnson."

Gabe paused, finally understood Dave Horowitz's comment then said, "Well, I've got to get going. It's going to be a long chase and every minute I delay they're going to be harder to catch. They're probably a good twenty miles ahead by now."

He then turned and walked down the hallway crossed through the parlor, opened the door and left the house. He mounted the gray gelding, made a point of adjusting his gear, hoping that Rebecca would walk through the door, but after another minute, knew she wasn't coming and turned the gray gelding west and set him off at a medium trot with the tan gelding trying to keep up.

Rebecca was sitting with Rachel on her lap and a new worry arrived. Not about Gabe's brush with death or that he might get hurt because she truly believed that he was more than just the best in his business, he seemed to be blessed. She was worried because he had said that Dave Horowitz would be coming to visit.

As Gabe had just been told, after her father had given him permission to court her, she had rejected him, if for no other reason than it had hurt her father. She'd never liked him much either but now, she suspected the subject of his giving Dave his blessing would be resurrected.

She felt she owed her father so much for how shabbily she had treated him for eight years that she couldn't tell him no. Besides, Dave might know what none of the others did and if he wanted to marry her, she almost had no choice. She probably deserved that fate, too.

———

After Gabe crossed the tracks and began riding west, he finally believed he understood why Rebecca had stayed in the house and what she was trying to tell him but had been interrupted. He didn't know much about Judaism but knew that most religions placed strict rules about marrying outside of their faith. It got pretty silly at times, even among different sects of the same religion.

After Eli had told him that he'd given his blessing to a marriage between Rebecca and Dave, he understood why she had to stay in the house. He'd already lost his chance with Rebecca before he even had a real opportunity.

But he had to forget about that now. He had a job to finish.

———

The sun was setting in his face as Gabe pulled the geldings over to the side of the road and let them drink and graze while he opened the saddlebags, removed the bag and pulled out a butcher paper-wrapped sandwich then took down a canteen. He'd skipped lunch because he needed to make up the gap and ridden the two geldings fifteen miles since leaving Missoula. He had picked up the fresh tracks of three horses just three miles past the logging road, and then checked the horses' droppings and estimated that he was still a good twenty miles behind them when he stopped.

He took big bites out of the thick ham sandwich which was already a bit dry, but it was still tasty because Angela had lathered some mustard sauce on the ham and made up for the dryness by drinking a lot of water. When he finished, he appreciated the tangy aftertaste left by the mustard sauce as he mounted the gray gelding and started moving again.

He felt he could make up distance at night when they stopped to rest, but the longer he rode, the more he began to drift, and knew he had to get some sleep himself. He'd only had the nap to satisfy his mind and body's demand for rest and he knew it would be dangerous to go into a gunfight without being alert.

So, he pulled over to the road by one of the many tributaries of the Missoula River, stepped down, and unsaddled both horses. Once the horses were stripped and his rifles nearby, he set one of his two bedrolls on the ground and sat down to eat. He had a canteen nearby as he pulled out another sandwich, unwrapped the butcher paper and peeked at the inside, was satisfied that it was ham and mustard again, then took a big bite and sat chewing as he looked at the stars overhead. He knew that he might not catch up with them tomorrow, but hopefully the day after.

Gabe took another long drink of water after finishing the sandwich and briefly thought about eating another, but decided he'd hold back because he might need them tomorrow.

He removed his gunbelt and shoulder holster then lay on his bedroll and continued to stare at the Milky Way that filled the sky over his head. But he really wasn't studying the stars, he was thinking about Rebecca. *He'd only known her for two days, for heaven's sake!* And not only wasn't he Jewish, he wasn't even a very good Christian. But as he thought about Rebecca, he suddenly laughed when he realized that he may have to stay celibate for the rest of his life, knowing he'd never find her equal again.

———

Seventeen miles west, Bob Johnson and Frank Stanford were sitting before a campfire, having already eaten a hot supper and were having coffee.

"Do you figure he's behind us, Bob?"

"I'd be surprised if he wasn't unless he took a hit when he went looking for us. With four of them, it would be possible. In fact, with most men, I'd give him a low chance of surviving a trip into the camp, but I'm not sure about Owens. If he got Red and Tanner, he might have gotten all four of them but even if he did, he wouldn't have left Missoula for at least six hours after we did. If he's back there, he's a good thirty miles away and he'd be hard pressed to catch up to us. We'll reach Ventnor in two days and should be able to catch a train out of there."

"Where are we goin'?"

"I figure we can head to Oregon and then maybe down to San Francisco. What do you think?"

"San Francisco sound good."

"Okay, then San Francisco it is."

Frank grinned and took a long drink of coffee. Bob was pretty smart to get out of there when they did.

Gabe had been so tired when he stopped that he set his pocket watch's alarm and it was the chiming from his pocket watch that awakened him early the next morning. It was the last week of July, but it was chilly when he slid out of the bedroll, answered nature's call and started his preparations to return to the chase.

Thirty-six minutes later, he was mounting the tan gelding and had his Winchester with him as he led the gray gelding out of the campsite and took to the road at a medium trot. He hadn't had his breakfast yet, so as he rode, he reached back and pulled out another sandwich and as he opened the butcher paper, he saw writing inside. He almost didn't want to read it because he suspected that it might be something that would cause more trouble, but he knew he'd be curious about it if he just tossed it aside, so he unfolded the paper, took out the sandwich then folded it again and stuffed it in the bag.

He ate the even drier sandwich and kept the canteen handy as he finished his breakfast. There were three sandwiches remaining, and he gave up hope of anything other than ham, but he couldn't blame Angela because he had given her such a very short time to prepare them.

He took a break two hours later, changed horses and then continued his ride. He didn't know how far back he was because he hadn't caught up with their fresh tracks yet.

———

Believing they had at least thirty miles when they stopped, and that Owens might not even be back there, Bob and Frank finally left their campsite when Gabe was just eleven miles behind and because they were trailing a pack horse, they kept their pace to a slow trot.

———

When Gabe spotted the turnoff to their camp for the night, he followed and stayed in the saddle long enough to look at the remnants of their campfire before he turned the gray gelding back to the road and less than two hundred yards later, spotted the first droppings and stepped down, kicked them over and knew he was a lot closer than he expected to be.

He quickly remounted and set off with renewed expectation of being able to catch up with them later today, if not early tomorrow. They'd passed by Thompson's Falls without slowing down, and the next water stop for trains was Clark's Falls, which would be interesting because the road took a sudden left turn away from the railroad which had to cross the Missoula River just on the other side of Clark's Falls. There was another tall trestle for the railroad, but the roadway had to follow the downslope away from the water stop for two miles, before it was low enough to cross at a ford. After the ford, the road gradually returned to the other side of the Missoula River to resume its parallel course with the tracks.

If he continued to gain on the pair, he'd catch up with them either before or after they crossed the ford. Either way, he knew he'd finally put his Sharps-Borshadt to good use.

———

Bob and Frank stopped for lunch around one o'clock but didn't take long despite their continued confidence in the distance between them and Gabe. When they remounted that gap was just eight miles.

Gabe had finished his fourth sandwich then succumbed to curiosity and pulled out the note from Angela. When he read it, it did nothing to satisfy that curiosity because all it said was:

My Dearest Gabriel: Destiny. Love Always, Angela

"Destiny?" he asked aloud as he stared at the brown sheet of paper in his hand.

He flipped it over wondering if she had written more on the other side but found nothing. He pushed it back into the bag, took out another sandwich, checked the paper, found nothing but blank paper and after rewrapping it and putting it back examined the last one. Again, there was nothing. Now, he knew he'd have to see her again just to ask what she meant by the cryptic note. *And why had she addressed him as Gabriel?*

As he continued to close the gap, he began to worry that he was getting too confident. He had been overconfident when he'd gone after the sheriff and had gotten away with a bullet in his buckle rather than in something softer that couldn't be replaced as easily.

Rebecca had said that neither man practiced much, but that didn't mean they couldn't set up an ambush and catch him in a crossfire. Compared to the plains of Dakota, this section of the Northern Pacific's domain was almost nothing but continuous ambush sites on both sides of the road. The only thing he had to prevent an ambush was the good trail left by the three horses. He could see that trail from sixty yards away but that was still well within the effective range of a '73.

He began trying to dial down his confidence without eroding it too much.

As the sun reached late afternoon, just before he pulled off the road for a break, he suddenly heard the crack of a Winchester ahead and flinched, expecting a .44 to go buzzing past his head. But it had been too far away, so he continued riding rather than stop. Ten seconds later, he heard a second report echo from the west. It was difficult to estimate the distance, but it had to be no more than two miles away. *But who was shooting and what was the target?* It surely wasn't him.

Dave Horowitz stepped onto the porch, removed his hat and knocked on the door.

Thirty seconds later, Eli opened the door, smiled and said, "Good morning, Dave. I was expecting to see you. Come in, Rebecca is in the parlor."

Dave walked into the parlor, saw Rebecca sitting on the couch with Rachel then smiled and said, "Hello, Becky."

Rebecca didn't smile but said, "Hello, Dave," even as her stomach flipped, and she refrained from doing what she had told Gabe she would do to the next man who called her Becky.

"I'm really happy to see that you're back with your family. You look as pretty as ever."

"Thank you."

"Do you wanna go for a walk with me?"

Rebecca sighed, set Rachel on the floor then stood and said, "Alright."

Dave took her hand, smiled back at Eli, opened the door, then he and Rebecca left the house.

After they'd gone, Eli turned to Sarah, grinned and said, "Things are looking up for Rebecca. I didn't think Dave would be back."

Sarah replied, "Neither did I."

She didn't add that she hoped that he hadn't returned because she hadn't liked the man when Eli had first given him his blessing either. Dave had always been on his best behavior when he was around Eli, but she could see through his façade.

But she felt it was Eli's prerogative to choose her prospective husband because she was his daughter.

Once they began their walk, Dave said, "It looks like I'm gonna be your husband, Rebecca. You know that; don't you?"

"I know."

"You don't sound very happy about it."

"I'm not."

“Well, that’s just too bad. You just be nice to me and I’ll forget all about what Fannie told me.”

Rebecca felt nauseated as she walked beside Dave, her hand tightly in his grasp.

———

“It only took me two shots this time,” Frank said as he grinned back at Bob as the telegraph wire twirled to the ground.

Bob said, “You’re getting to be a regular sharpshooter, Frank.”

Ten minutes earlier, Bob figured that by now, they’d be fixing the telegraph line they’d broken yesterday, and it was time to keep them guessing.

They then continued riding west, passing Clark’s Falls ten minutes later.

———

Gabe came up on the downed telegraph line fifteen minutes after they’d gone and understood who had taken the shots and their intent. It also gave him a very exact estimate at the gap at around two miles, so he picked up the pace. His only issue now was that the sun was low in the sky and would be in his eyes when he caught up to Bob and Frank. He wanted to get them today. Besides, he was almost out of sandwiches.

After he passed Clark’s Falls, he followed the road when it made it’s hard left and began his descent to the ford across the Missoula River which was on his right side as he led the gray gelding down the slope. The river carved a gorge in the rock that was about forty feet wide up near Clark’s Ford, but at the bottom of the slope a couple of miles ahead, the river and earth seemed to come to a compromise for some geological reason and the ford was only four feet deep but wider, about sixty feet across. He imagined that they were close to crossing the ford as he kept the tan gelding at a medium trot and kept his eyes trained for the ford but couldn't see it yet because of the trees and rocks that blocked his view.

Suddenly, the ford and two riders popped into view about a mile ahead. They were trailing a pack horse and hadn't seen him. The Sharps-Borshadt was on the gray, but he didn't think he'd need the distance yet. He might be able to catch them while they were in the river crossing the ford but either way, he wanted them to see him soon, so he picked up the pace to a fast trot, taking advantage of the downslope.

———

Neither of them had checked their backtrail for hours because no one should be there, but Frank just wanted to see the gap that the Missoula River had carved through the rocks behind them and turned in the saddle.

"Jesus!" he shouted when he spotted the rider behind them.

Bob whipped his head around, saw Gabe and asked, "Is that him?"

"I don't know."

"Well, we have to believe it's him. Do we have enough time to cross the river?"

"I don't think so. Where do we go?"

Bob looked ahead again and said, "Straight ahead, after the road turns to the ford, the slope rises again and there's a ridge we can reach pretty quickly. Let's get that pack horse moving!"

Gabe had seen them turn to look at him and even heard Frank's shout. He was still more than eight hundred yards behind them and slowed the tan gelding and watched as they sped their mounts forward then surprised him when they passed the ford and began climbing the rise on the other side.

He then looked where they were headed and spotted their goal. About a half mile on the other side of the ford, they could turn off the slope, follow a switchback and reach a ridge that looked down on the slope. If they stayed there, the only way he could get them would be to ride up the slope as they just lay prone on the edge and kept him under their Winchesters. It was a perfect defensive position if all he had was a Winchester '73 and the more he looked at it, it would be hard to get them with the '76 either.

Gabe knew that they were sure they'd be able to outlast him because they had that pack horse of supplies. There were two of them too, so in a few hours, the sun would set and he'd either have to leave or they could sneak down and shoot him at a time of their choosing.

Gabe had to agree it was a great defensive position, but even that position had a fatal flaw. The ridge that they chose as their shooting platform was only about twenty feet deep. If they stayed there, the only way out was either to come back down the slope or make the forty-foot drop into the Missoula River. What added to their predicament, which they didn't know yet, was that he could stand outside the range of their Winchesters and pick them off with his Sharps-Borshadt.

His only issue was one of altitude and shooting angle. They'd be up on that ridge, and if he went all the way down to the ford, he wouldn't be able to even see them if they were kneeling or sitting on the ridge. He could shoot their horses, but the idea of doing that made him queasy.

He pulled the tan gelding to a stop as they continued to climb the slope then watched them hook around to the left and then make another sharp right just a minute later and reached the shelf of rock. From where he was now, he already lost sight of everything below their saddle horns but kept them in sight as they dismounted and pulled their Winchesters. The shorter man, Bob Johnson, stood watching him with the repeater leaning against his shoulder while Frank tied off their horses on some scrub brush.

Gabe leaned back in his saddle and almost smiled. He couldn't see Bob Johnson's face, but was about nine hundred yards away from him and decided he'd give them a warning. He'd never even heard Bob's voice.

So, he nudged the tan gelding forward at a slow trot, knowing that the sun had a limited time left in the sky and he didn't have a lot of light to waste. He passed the ford and when he was about six hundred yards away from their position and could see them both from the waist up, standing with their repeaters over their shoulders looking down at him, he pulled the gelding to a stop.

He took a deep breath and shouted, "My name is Gabe Owens. I'm a special agent for the Northern Pacific Railroad and I'm here to arrest Bob Johnson for the murder of Mike Wheatley and Frank Stanford for accessory to murder. Come down and surrender or I'll have to open fire!"

Then after a few seconds, he finally heard Bob Johnson's voice and was surprised at its smooth, melodious tone as he almost sang his reply.

"Why do you think we'd surrender, Owens? If you want us, come and get us, but you'd better make it quick. You probably already know that, don't you?"

"I do, and that's why I'm giving you this chance. You're better off taking a shot with a jury than trying to get into a gunfight with me."

He heard Bob laugh and then yell back, "I don't think we have to worry."

"We'll see," Gabe shouted before turning his tan gelding and leading the gray back past the ford and began climbing the slope.

Frank turned to Bob with a puzzled look and asked, "You think he's leavin'?"

Bob had no idea what he was doing either and replied, "I haven't got a clue. I thought he'd dismount and come charging up the slope zigzagging. It's the only way he could get in range, and then he wouldn't be able to fire at us until he reached our level and made the first turn on the switchback. He'd never make it that far either, no matter how much he zigged or zagged."

Gabe was sure that he'd confused the hell out of them with his apparent departure. He didn't even turn around but kept estimated the range as he walked the geldings up the slope.

He was almost twelve hundred yards away when he stopped and turned the horse to look at the ridge. He could see both of them clear down to their boots, so even if they both dropped, he'd still be able to get hits. He could probably get closer but was running out of time. He dismounted then walked the horses to the side of the road, hitched the tan gelding, walked back to the gray, slid the Sharps-Borshadt from its scabbard, then opened the saddlebag and pulled out a box of the .50-110 cartridges and slipped it into his pocket.

———

Twelve hundred and thirteen yards away, Frank and Bob were mesmerized watching Gabe, still wondering what he was doing. At this range, they couldn't see the telescopic sight on the rifle, much less distinguish the size of the weapon he was preparing to use. As far as they could tell, he was taking out a Winchester '73 like the one they each held.

"Is he crazy, Bob?" Frank asked as he stared.

"I have no idea," Bob answered truthfully.

———

Gabe figured he'd get one free shot with the Sharps-Borshadt. They'd see the smoke and probably have a good laugh until the heavy bullet arrived, so had to make that first shot count. After the first one, anyone on the ridge would be able to watch what he was doing then as soon as smoke erupted from the muzzle, they'd have more than three seconds before the bullet reached them three quarters of a mile away. If his target had guts enough to stand there watching, he'd be impossible to hit.

He set up in the center of the road, assuming a kneeling position. With the downslope, it wasn't comfortable, but it was the only position he felt stable enough for a shot of this distance. Two of his practice shots east of Missoula were over a thousand yards and there was a lot more wind. Now the wind was almost completely calm as he prepared for the critical first shot. After removing the lens caps, he looked down at the scope, made sure that he had reset the windage adjustment, saw that he'd returned it to center then cocked the hammer of the long gun.

Now, he had to choose his target. For more than one reason, he chose Bob Johnson. He was guilty of murder, had given Rebecca to Frank, took advantage of Angela, and was responsible for a lot more pain. He didn't think Bob would be feeling as much pain as he had earned if he took the hit, though.

Frank, on the other hand, he wanted to be alive to experience the pain and was the major factor in his decision to shoot Bob Johnson.

———

"He's gonna shoot from way back there?" asked Frank just as a big cloud of gunsmoke poured from the muzzle.

Bob suddenly realized the truth and started to shout, "Maybe he's got a …" when a massive blow smashed him in the right upper chest, spinning him in a half circle before he stumbled twice and fell backwards, screaming as he plummeted from the ridge, the shriek ending suddenly when he struck the water.

Frank was horrified and ran to the edge of the ridge and looked down to the swiftly flowing river and spotted Bob's bloody body floating quickly downstream, face down in the water.

He whipped his head back to Gabe and shouted, "You bastard!"

He was so enraged with the murder of his friend and hero, that he just ran past the horses with his Winchester and raced for the downslope to get a shot at Gabe.

———

After he'd seen Bob Johnson fall through the scope, Gabe shifted it quickly to Frank as he pulled another cartridge from his pocket then before he could even open the breech, he saw Frank shout something and then make his angry sprint past the horses.

Gabe quickly stood then walked to the gray, slid the Sharps-Borshadt into its scabbard, pulled his Winchester from the tan's scabbard and began walking down the slope toward the ford to meet Frank.

Frank made the second turn and began to trot down the grade toward the ford when he spotted Gabe walking toward him and slowed down. His Winchester was cocked and after shooting those wires, he was confident in his marksmanship. He owed it to Bob to kill the man who'd cowardly shot him from more than a thousand yards.

He was still furious as he kept walking with his eyes fixed on the railroad agent, now only four hundred yards away. A quarter of a mile was all that separated him from his revenge. After he killed Owens, he'd try and find Bob's body downriver and give him a proper burial, but he'd leave Owens out in the open and let the critters eat him.

Gabe cocked the hammer of his Winchester but kept the muzzle pointed down as he watched Frank. He still had only seen Frank through his field glasses at range, so as they closed the gap, Gabe was getting a better look and finally saw a face that was pretty much what he expected.

They were a hundred yards apart when Frank brought his Winchester level and then stopped.

Gabe saw him stop and halted himself, but kept his Winchester pointed at the ground. He was going to give Frank a free shot. Why he decided to do that wasn't clear to him, but he could dwell on it later…if there was a later.

Frank wasn't even the least bit curious why Owens wasn't aiming yet. He didn't care if he did anything other than just die. He took careful aim at Owens face and then saw him looking right at him and hesitated. *Why didn't he fire?*

Frank blinked then remembered Bob's scream and pulled his trigger. He felt the rifle's butt punch his shoulder and the gunsmoke cloud expanded in front of him and he knew his .44 was on its way to kill Gabe Owens.

Gabe saw the muzzle flash and gunsmoke and almost immediately felt a tug on his Stetson when the bullet cut through the right rim of the hat. He then pulled it from his head, tossed it aside, brought his Winchester level then took three seconds to aim, and as Frank was levering in a second round, he fired.

Frank saw him fire and just a fraction of a second later screamed in pain when the .50 caliber all but ripped his right foot off when it drilled through his boot and shattered his ankle. He fell to the ground screeching from an agonizing pain he hadn't even believed was possible.

Gabe began walking as soon as he made the shot, the big bullet hitting exactly where he had aimed his Winchester. He kept his eyes on Frank as he strode down the road, but not expecting him to do anything but scream.

When he was close enough, he reached over, picked up the Winchester '73, tossed it aside then ripped Frank's Colt from his holster, stuck it in his waist then turned and started walking back to the geldings.

"You bastard! Come back here!" Frank yelled as Gabe continued to walk back to the two geldings.

Gabe reached the horses, slid the Winchester into the gray's bedroll then put the Colt in the saddlebags, untied the tan gelding and stepped into the saddle. He then turned the horse back to the ford and headed back to where Frank continued to shriek.

Frank saw him riding back and shouted, "It's about time, you son of a bitch!"

Gabe rode the gelding to Frank then right past him without even looking down and then continued to ride up the slope to their ridge.

Frank was in anguish from the pain in his leg and when Gabe rode past, he began to swear at him using every curse he had ever heard.

Gabe rode up the slope, around the switchback then reached their horses He unhitched them, extended the trail rope from their pack horse and then led all four horses back down from the shallow ridge. He was soon headed for Frank who was still cursing at him as he drew near with all five horses.

Gabe reached Frank, pulled the gelding to a stop and dismounted then walked over to Frank, pulled the leather strap that Bob had used to lock Angela in her room then sat on his heels and began to wrap it tightly around Frank's leg above his boot.

"That'll stop the bleeding," Gabe said then returned to the horses and untied the gelding with the longer stirrups that he assumed was Frank's and led him to where Frank glared at him.

Gabe then stood next to Frank and with no warning smashed his right fist into Frank's face, crushing his cheekbone.

As Frank wailed with the added pain Gabe said, "Her name is Rebecca, not Becky."

Gabe then hoisted the blubbering Frank to his good foot and after almost two minutes managed to get him into his saddle then turned and walked back to the tan gelding.

Frank was having a hard time staying in the saddle, but snarled at Gabe, "You are a cold-hearted bastard!"

Then he suddenly turned his horse to his left and trotted him into the ford as Gabe had expected him to do. But then Frank did something he could never had anticipated when he walked his horse into the river and when he was just ten feet into the Missoula River, he shouted, "Bob!" then flopped into the water and was swept quickly downstream not even attempting to swim.

Gabe just watched in disbelief as Frank disappeared from sight as his horse turned and trotted back to join the others.

Gabe shook his head, reattached the gelding then mounted and began to climb the slope to return to Clark's Falls, still in disbelief of what he'd seen and just when he couldn't imagine this trip getting any stranger.

It was almost sunset when Gabe passed Clark's Falls and continued riding east. He could have stopped and sent a telegram or had something to eat, but he didn't want to see or talk to anyone. It was almost ten o'clock that night when he finally pulled over and dismounted then unsaddled all of five horses and let them graze before he took one of Angela's sandwiches but didn't bother with a campfire.

He knew he should clean the guns, but he'd do that in the morning. Right now, he just wanted to sleep.

So, after finishing the next to the last sandwich and guzzling the necessary water, he spread out his bedroll, laid down and closed his eyes without even bothering to remove his Remington or his Webley.

Thirty-eight miles to the east, Rebecca lay awake in her bed with her eyes closed. She was now engaged to be married. Her father had assented to the marriage and they'd even set a date for the wedding. It was almost enough to make her rebel again, but she knew she wouldn't make the same mistake again. Gabe had taught her that, and she almost wished he hadn't.

She was now reaping what she had sown. All of her hate had rebounded to create the hell she was going to live in for the rest of her life.

Angela was lying in the same bed where she'd exposed her bruises to Gabe a few short days ago. Like Rebecca, she had no doubt he'd return after catching Bob and Frank. She had only written the note when as she was making his sandwiches, she had the epiphany and knew he would come back to her and this time, when she had him in this bed, he'd make love to her as he had those two glorious occasions back in Minneapolis.

As she drifted off to sleep, she fantasized about having Gabe as her husband because it was their destiny.

CHAPTER 7

Gabe slept longer than he had expected, and the sun was already well into the sky when he opened his eyes and slid from the bedroll far enough to sit up. He pulled his pocket watch, found it was already 7:18 then wound it slipped it back into his pocket and finished extricating himself. He took care of his morning needs, washed and shaved in the nearby stream, then found the last sandwich was pretty dried up, so he just pulled the ham from between the bread slices, tossed the bread away and polished off the ham in a few big bites.

He crumpled up the wrapping, threw it into the stream and said, "Destiny," still not having a clue why Angela had written it.

He began saddling the horses, but when he was hanging Bob's saddlebags, he recalled the open safe in Bob's office. He dropped the saddlebags to the ground and flipped one open and wasn't surprised to find money inside, but he was taken aback by the numbers of bills. He began removing the cash from the leather pouch and when he finished, he was amazed there was over thirty thousand dollars. But he shouldn't have been as he didn't have to pay for much of the timber he was cutting. He sighed, began putting the currency back into the saddlebag and almost put it back on the horse when he decided to see what was in the other side, expecting to find clothing and ammunition, but was beyond stunned when he found more cash, and it appeared to be about the same amount. He didn't bother counting the money but needed to get going, so he tossed the saddlebag onto Bob's horse and made sure it was securely tied down.

He was riding the gray gelding as he reached the road and set off at a slow trot.

The money presented an unusual dilemma for Gabe. He didn't need or want the money, but he knew that if he gave it to the railroad, they'd thank him and just deposit it into their company account. Bob hadn't married either Rebecca or Angela, so legally they weren't entitled to the money either.

It took him over an hour to come up with his answer, so he was able to push that question aside then focus on the real problem that awaited him when he returned to Missoula, or maybe he should he think of it as two separate problems, and both were female.

Angela's note, as vague as it was, seemed to suggest that she expected him to stay with her or to bring her back to Minneapolis with him. Why she thought that way was as big a question as use of the word 'destiny' in the note.

Rebecca was a much more complex conundrum. It all revolved around his ignorance not only of Judaism, but of Eli's level of commitment to his faith and his promise to Dave Horowitz. He could never deny her the happiness that she seemed to have rediscovered in being with her family and for all he knew, she loved Dave Horowitz but was too embarrassed to tell him.

Dave, on the other hand, seemed to believe that Rebecca was all but his wife. He couldn't imagine how he could have worked in that logging camp knowing she was in Bob Johnson's house all that time and not try to get her free. She must have known he was there, so why didn't she seek him out and ask him to take her away? There were so many things about her situation that were confusing to him.

But he remembered all too well how he'd felt after losing Angela to Mike Wheatley and knew he'd feel much worse if he lost Rebecca to Dave Horowitz.

As he sat on the gelding's saddle, he smiled wryly and said aloud, "It's just my destiny, I guess, but I'll have a few more miles to go before I find out what it will be."

It was late afternoon and just four miles out of Missoula when he heard a sound that he hadn't expected to hear for another two days when a train whistle sounded behind him. The first of the rerouted trains had arrived. He then realized that he'd been gone for three days, so the train wasn't that early at all.

Gabe was almost to the logging road when the locomotive rolled past with its bell ringing as it approached the station. He knew it would have to be turned around, coaled and watered before leaving and he guessed it wouldn't be leaving until the morning because there wasn't a replacement crew at Missoula.

He glanced to his right and waved back at some of the passengers who were waving at him then smiled when he saw the wavers were young boys.

He continued at the same pace and after another ten minutes, passed the train as it sat at the platform disgorging its passengers and cargo. He crossed the tracks in front of the locomotive and headed for the stock corral where he spotted Jim Clover unloading a horse from the stock car.

Gabe rode the geldings to the corral, opened the gate and walked them all inside before closing the gate and dismounting. He untied Bob's saddlebags, hung them over his shoulder then waited for Jim as he handed the reins to the horse's owner.

Jim turned as the man led his horse out the gate on the passenger side of the large corral and waved to Gabe then walked his way.

“I guess you got those bad boys,” Jim said.

“I did. Jim, I’m going to leave the horses here for a while. I need to go and talk to Joe.”

“No problem. How hard was it?”

“Not hard, just really different.”

Jim glanced at the train and then said, “The new yard manager is supposed to be on that train.”

Gabe nodded and asked, “When is it supposed to leave?”

“At 6:40 in the morning. It’ll head to Ainsworth then hook onto the Union Pacific tracks and head all the way back to Omaha before it heads north to Minneapolis. It’s gonna be a hell of a long trip.”

“Still beats covered wagons, Jim,” Gabe said as he tapped Jim on the shoulder and headed for the offices.

When he walked into the station manager’s office, Joe Lofton looked up and grinned.

“Gabe, you sure are a sight for sore eyes. I’ve got some news for you if you want to take a seat.”

“Good or bad?” he asked as he sat down.

“I haven’t got a clue,” he said as he pulled three sheets of paper from his desk and handed them to Gabe.

"These came for you while you were out chasing down those two. You got them both, didn't you?"

"Yes, sir," he replied automatically as he began reading the telegrams.

The first two were from Herb Erikson. The top one was nothing more than an acknowledgement of his telegram about finding the poaching and the murderers of both Mike and Willie and he was chasing down Mike's murderer.

The second was a summons to return as soon as possible on the train that would be arriving with the new yard manager but didn't say why.

The last one was from the Northern Pacific president, thanking him for stopping the Dakota Gang, but nothing beyond that.

He folded the telegrams, slipped them into his pocket and said, "I don't have much time here, do I, Joe?"

"Nope. How can I help, Gabe?"

"I could ask you to delay the train's departure for a day, but that wouldn't be right. I'll just have to get things done quicker than I thought."

"Well, then I reckon that you'd better get going."

Gabe stood and just nodded before turning and quickly leaving the office then walked taking long strides to the corral. He had a lot to do in about fourteen hours, and hopefully that would include getting some sleep.

His first stop had to be Angela's house. Dancer was still there as was some of his clothes and he could clear up the

Angela question while he was at it. Then, he had to stop at the sheriff's office before his last and most difficult stop at the Ulrich home.

He'd already decided to leave the buggy and the black mare with Rebecca. The others he'd turn over to Deputy Collier and wondered if he'd been given the job of sheriff yet.

He turned his herd into the Wheatley house drive shortly after four o'clock and walked the horses to the small barn where he caught sight of Dancer as he stood next to the black mare. The Morgan turned his eyes to the sound of the horses and Gabe felt better just at the sight of him. He dismounted and tied off the gray gelding, entered the barn and rubbed Dancer on his neck.

"Good to see you again, Dancer. I hope you enjoyed your respite. We're going on a long train ride tomorrow morning, but your new friend here will be coming with you for at least part of the way."

He then turned to head for the house and spotted Angela waiting on the back porch with a big smile. Gabe exhaled and then started walking suddenly realizing his dire need of a bath.

"Welcome home, Gabe," Angela said, still with a broad smile on her face.

Angela was a very handsome woman, Gabe thought as he ascended the steps, the saddlebags full of cash over his shoulder.

She took his hand and said, "I'm sure that you're hungry. Let me get something for you while you tell me what happened."

Gabe entered the kitchen as she led him to the table then pulled out a chair for him as if he wasn't able to handle it himself but sat down.

Angela began lighting a fire in the cookstove as she asked, “So, what happened, Gabe?”

“Um, I chased them for a day and a half and caught up with them at the ford across the Missoula River outside of Clark's Falls. We exchanged gunfire and they're both dead, so I rode back.”

“And that's all?”

“Pretty much. When I returned, I stopped by the station because the first of the rerouted train arrived and I was given three telegrams, one of which directed me to return to Minneapolis on that train, so I'll be leaving early tomorrow morning.”

Angela turned quickly and exclaimed, “*You're leaving?*”

“I have to, Angela.”

“But what about our destiny. Can't you see it? Don't you understand? It was there all the time and I only realized it when I was making your sandwiches.”

“I was going to ask about that when I read your note because I didn't understand it at all.”

“Destiny, Gabe. It's our destiny to be together, and it even included Mike. Don't you see?”

Gabe shook his head and said, “I must be awfully dense because I don't even have an inkling of what you mean.”

Angela looked at him and with her left hand closed, she extended her index finger and touched it with her right index finger and said, “Angela.”

Then she extended the middle finger, touched it and said, “Michael.”

Finally, she opened her ring finger and pressed it with her right index finger and said, “Gabriel.”

Then she held had the fingers spread apart as she held them in front of her and slowly brought them together and said, “Angela, Michael and Gabriel. See? It’s our destiny to be linked together forever, Gabe. Before we were even born, it was written in our future.”

Gabe said, “Angela, that would be fine, but my name isn’t Gabriel. It’s Gabe. I was named after my father’s brother, who was Gabriel, but they didn’t want it to be exactly the same, so on my birth certificate it says, Gabe Andrew Owens. I’m sorry.”

Angela stared at Gabe and slowly lowered her fingers. It had all seemed so clear to her. Gabriel was supposed to be with her after Michael was gone.

Then Gabe said, “Angela, you do know that Deputy Collier’s first name is Rafe, don’t you? That’s short for Raphael.”

Angela blinked and asked, “It is?”

“Yes, ma’am. I have to stop by the sheriff’s office and write a report about what happened because it was still in Missoula County. Would you like me to have Rafe come by and make sure you’re safe?”

Angela tried to remember Deputy Collier and after a few seconds, she said, “If you really have to leave, I think I’d feel safer if he did.”

“I’ll do that. Don’t worry about feeding me, Angela. I’ll get something when I’m finished running around. I’ll need to get my clothes out of the bedroom. Did you get your shopping done?”

Angela was still picturing Rafe Collier in her mind then snapped out of her reverie and replied, ‘Oh…yes. I did. I have all of Becky’s things packed in a travel bag in the room she used, too.”

“That was very thoughtful. I’ll go upstairs and get them and pack my things as well.” Gabe said as he stood and smiled at the distracted Angela.

He walked into the room he’d used and quickly removed his things from the dresser. It wasn’t much, but he carried them out of the room and up the stairs to the room Rebecca used. He saw the travel bag, but he also saw the bags he’d brought to the house when he’d bought the clothes for her that first day. He picked up one bag, folded it and put it in the second, then put his clothes in the bag, closed the drawstring then picked it up and then the travel bag, left the room and quickly trotted down the steps.

He reached the kitchen and Angela seemed to have recovered when he walked into the room.

She smiled at him and asked, “Will I ever see you again, Gabe?”

“One can never understand our true destinies, Angela,” Gabe replied as he smiled.

She laughed lightly then put her hands around his neck and kissed him softly before stepping back.

"Be happy, Angela," Gabe said then turned and walked out the door.

Angela followed, but stopped on the back porch and watched as he began moving saddles.

She spotted movement out of the corner of her eye and turned to find that busybody, Mildred Honeysuckle striding toward Gabe. She glared at the old biddy as she approached the barn and was surprised when Gabe saw her and smiled.

"Why, hello, Mildred. Come to ask about the ending to the story?" he asked as he continued to unsaddle the tan gelding.

"You promised, Mister Owens."

"I did, and if you don't mind, I'll continue moving things around. I have to be on the train by early in the morning."

"More trouble?" she asked.

"Probably just for me, but I'll handle it."

"I'm sure you will. Now, tell me what happened."

Gabe began his narrative as he moved his saddles and gear to Dancer, tied him to the buggy and then harnessed the mare, putting the money saddlebags in the buggy with Rebecca's travel bag. He didn't leave much out of the story other than his feelings for Rebecca and the dilemma she posed.

"Well, Mildred, I'll be leaving now, and I hope that you find the pleasure in telling that tale."

"Before you go, can I see that belt buckle?" she asked in anticipation.

"Of course, ma'am," he answered as he opened his coat and she stared wide-eyed at the tail end of the .44 embedded in the steel.

"That's the most amazing thing I've ever seen, and I've seen some pretty extraordinary things over my eighty-one years."

"Why, Mrs. Honeysuckle, you lied to me!" he exclaimed as he looked at her.

She looked at him with a puzzled expression and asked, "I did?"

"Yes, ma'am. You told me if you were fifty years younger that you'd chase after me. I think you were right the first time when you said twenty years."

She giggled and slapped him on the side before she stepped over and kissed him on the cheek.

"Thank you, Mister Owens. You've made this old lady very happy."

Gabe stepped into the buggy and said, "Stay happy, Mildred."

She smiled and waved at Gabe as he turned the buggy down the drive then waved at Angela, who waved back as tears slid across her cheeks. He may have been a Gabe, but she knew he would always be her Gabriel.

Gabe pulled in front of the sheriff's office five minutes later, stepped out of the buggy, detached all of the spare horses, tied them at the hitchrail and walked inside, noting that the damage he'd caused when he'd smashed in the door had been repaired already.

Rafe Collier was sitting at the desk when he entered and stood before Gabe made it to the desk.

"How's Billy doing?" Gabe asked as he sat down.

"He still has headaches and he's woozy, but the doc says he'll be okay in a week or so. Oh, and just so you know, Mrs. Reinhold arrived and said her husband had emptied their bank account, and when we checked his saddlebags, we found her money, so what happened after you left?"

"If you'll give me some paper and a pencil, I'll write out my statement while I tell you."

As Rafe pulled open a drawer, Gabe asked, "So, are you the sheriff now?"

"The acting sheriff, but I've been told that it'll become permanent within a week. Did you get Johnson and Stanford?"

Gabe began writing and said, "I caught up with them just this side of the Missoula River ford near Clark's Falls."

He continued his story as he wrote the details down on the paper. He left out the money that was sitting in the saddlebags in the buggy out front because to him, the county had no claims on it at all. They would probably argue the point, but he wasn't about to give them the opportunity.

He told him there were some horses outside with Winchesters in their scabbards and Colts in their saddlebags he could have, which brightened his day. Then Gabe figured he'd make it even better.

When he finished, he slid his report over to Acting Sheriff Collier and asked, “Is Rafe short for Rafael or Ralph?”

“It's spelled Ralph, but everyone always pronounced it Rafe. Why?”

He briefly explained the whole destiny idea that Angela had told him, and he followed closely.

When Gabe finished, Rafe asked, “So, if I'm Raphael, she'll probably be interested?”

“Oh, I don't think interested is nearly what she will be. Just don't let anyone even think of calling you Ralph.”

“I think I'll go and see Judge Bannister tomorrow and get my name legally changed.”

Gabe laughed then stood and shook Rafe's hand as he said, “Good luck, Raphael.”

He then turned left the jail and boarded the buggy. He drove off with only Dancer trailing then turned west toward the Ulrich house, still unsure of what he would do or say when he got there.

He had just made the turn when he spotted Rafe trot out of the sheriff's office, climb onto the tan gelding and trailing the other horses, he quickly rode in the direction of the Wheatley house. At least that problem seemed to be solved.

It was five minutes later when he pulled up in front of the Ulrich home, climbed out of the buggy, took the money saddlebags out and hung them over his shoulder. He then picked up Rebecca's travel bag, walked to Dancer, set the travel bag down and rummaged around in the cloth bag and pulled the second, folded bag from the bottom and slipped it into his jacket pocket. Once he was satisfied that he hadn't forgotten anything, he trotted onto the porch and knocked on the door.

The door opened a few seconds later and was met by a smiling Eli.

"Gabe! Come in! Come in!"

Gabe smiled, pulled off his hat and entered the house as Eli closed the door.

The rest of the family was sitting in the parlor, and his stomach dropped when he saw Rebecca sitting on the couch with Dave Horowitz.

When Dave saw Gabe was looking their way, he put his arm possessively around Rebecca's shoulder then grinned and said, "Me and Becky are gonna be hitched next week, and I have you to thank for makin' that happen."

Gabe took six seconds to recover before he turned to Rebecca and said, "Congratulations, Rebecca. I'm happy for you."

Rebecca nodded and said softly, "Thank you, Gabe."

Eli said, "Come over and have a seat while you tell us what happened."

Gabe nodded and was directed to an empty chair that had just been vacated by Aaron. He sat down and set the travel bag and saddlebags at his feet.

Sarah asked, “If you’re here, can we assume that Mister Johnson and Mister Stanford are no longer with us?”

“Yes, ma’am. I chased them to the Missoula River and caught up with them there. I won’t go into details, but neither will ever hurt anyone again.”

“Would you give me the details in private?” Eli asked.

“I would. In fact, I need to talk to you about that offer about the timber on the Northern Pacific land, too.”

“I suspected that you wouldn’t be able to follow through with the offer, and that’s quite all right.”

“No, no. That’s not it at all, it’s just that the circumstances have changed a bit. I have to tell you now because I’ve been ordered back to Minneapolis and I’ll be leaving early tomorrow morning. My boss wants to talk to me as soon as possible.”

“Do you think he has another job for you already? Even after all you’ve been through?” asked Sarah.

“Maybe. I’m not sure because he didn’t specify why he wanted me back so quickly.”

Rebecca asked, “Did you see Angela?”

“I did. She had already packed your clothes that you’d left. They’re in the travel bag. She went shopping after I was gone, so she didn’t need anything. I also brought the black mare and buggy. I’ll leave them with you.”

“Is she going back to Minneapolis?” Rebecca asked softly.

“No, she’s staying here for a very strange reason. Before I left, she packed some sandwiches in a bag while I saddled the horses. When I got on the trail, I found she'd written a note on a sheet of the butcher paper that said it was our destiny to be together. I had no idea why she would think that but when I returned, she explained how she believed that her destiny was intertwined with mine and her husband because of our names: Angela, Michael and Gabriel."

Eli raised his eyebrows and said, "I hadn't noticed that, but that's a pretty odd coincidence."

"It would be if my name was Gabriel, but it's not. It's Gabe. So, I mentioned that she might want to talk to Acting Sheriff Rafe Collier because his name was Raphael."

"Now that is odd," Eli said.

Gabe then smiled and said, "He told me that he was going to have his name legally changed from his current Ralph to Raphael before he rode over to her house."

Eli and Sarah laughed as Rebecca just sat embarrassed to have Dave's arm still holding her close.

Eli then said, "Gabe, did you want to go and have some coffee in the kitchen while you tell me the details?"

"That's fine," Gabe replied as he stood, picked up his saddlebags and smiled at Rebecca who was looking at him with sad eyes before following Eli down hallway to the kitchen.

After arriving in the kitchen, Eli filled two coffee cups before he and Gabe took seats at the table.

"So, what are the gory details that you couldn't talk about in front of the women and children?"

Gabe explained how he'd shot Bob Johnson from twelve hundred yards without warning other than telling them both he was going to do it, which sounded bizarre when he said it. Then he began talking about his extraordinary confrontation with Frank Stanford.

"I shot him in the ankle, knowing that the pain would be excruciating, so he could experience what he had inflicted on Rebecca. Then, while he was on the ground, I hit him hard in the face for the same reason. He had to feel pain, Eli. Shooting him and letting him die quickly wasn't justice. Rebecca's perfect face was marred by that bastard, and even though she'll still be as beautiful as ever, he needed to be punished for what he did.

"But the strangest thing was that after I stopped his bleeding, I got him on his horse and knew he'd make a break for it. I didn't care because he had no money and no weapons, but it was a chance. He rode his horse into the river but instead of continuing across, he suddenly shouted Bob's name and dove in. I'm not sure if he drowned himself to be with Bob or to end the pain, maybe both. I've never seen anything like that, and I hope I never do again."

Eli nodded then asked, "What did you want to tell me about the NP property?"

"Now I'll tell you about the property," he said as he picked up the saddlebags and set them on the table.

"When I get back to Minneapolis, I'll negotiate a price for you. I'll even get you another six sections in the adjoining strips. Now one of those sections is more than half stripped courtesy of Bob Johnson, but I know you won't be doing that, so that's a good selling point when I talk to them. They usually get five dollars an acre for heavily timbered property, which comes to over three thousand dollars a section. I can probably get that price knocked down to three dollars an acre, so each section would cost less than two thousand dollars. So, for all ten sections, I think I can get a package deal for say, eighteen thousand dollars, including the half-cut section. Add another five thousand for Bob Johnson's logging camp then toss in another two thousand for the workers' pay for a couple of months to round it up to twenty-five thousand. How does that sound?"

Eli had followed the numbers and said, "It's a great deal, but I don't have half that much money, and that would drain my account."

Gabe opened one of the saddlebag's flaps and dumped the contents onto the table, sending bundles of currency across the surface and onto the floor as Eli's eyes bulged.

"Where did you get that?" he asked, totally flustered at the sight.

"Bob Johnson had been stripping the forests for six years and stealing timber that wasn't his and I don't want to see that happen anymore. You're a good man, Eli, and I know you'll be able to supply the railroad with ties at a fair price without turning those forests into a desert. I'll leave this money with you, so you can make the purchase and fix up that logging camp and turn it into a first-class operation. If I turned it all back to the railroad, they'd just shake my hand and put it into their bank account. It's not all theirs anyway."

"I can't take all this, Gabe."

"Sure, you can. I'll deliver the other half to the railroad and they'll be tickled pink. That's one of the reasons that I know they'll give you a good price on the land."

Eli, despite his guilt about accepting the cash knew that Gabe was right. If he didn't take it, it would disappear and not help anyone but the bankers.

"Okay, Gabe. I'll do as you ask."

Gabe smiled and began to stack the cash as Eli picked up the bundles that had fallen to the floor. Once it was all on the table, he pulled the folded bag from his pocket, opened the mouth and began swiping the bills into the bag. When they were all inside, he tightened the drawstrings and handed the bag to Eli.

"If your banker asks about the money, just tell him it was compensation from the Northern Pacific for having your business almost ruined."

"Charlie wouldn't care if I robbed the National Bank in Helena, as long as it was real, and it was going into his bank."

Gabe nodded and said, "Eli, there's more than thirty thousand dollars in that bag. Would you use some of it to build a nice house for Rebecca and Dave?"

"Of course, I will. Will you be joining us for supper?"

"No, I don't think so. I really enjoy spending time with your family, but I think that I'll just make Rebecca uncomfortable being around when she's with her fiancé, and I wouldn't like to do that. Rebecca is special."

Eli looked at Gabe nodded and said, "She is, and she's even more so since she's returned."

Gabe nodded then stood, hung the unbalanced saddlebags over his shoulder again, picked up his hat and began walking down the hallway.

When he reached the parlor, Sarah looked at him and wondered what Eli had told him because he looked as if he'd been to a funeral.

"Well, I'll be heading back to the train station to handle some problems," then he looked at Rebecca and said, "Be happy, Rebecca."

Rebecca thought she'd fall apart as she looked into his eyes but just nodded. She had to let him go.

He granted himself another five seconds sharing the look then turned, opened the door and walked out of the house. After he closed the door behind him, he exhaled sharply, scanned the late afternoon landscape then stepped down from the porch, hung the cash saddlebag on Dancer and tied them down securely and mounted. He wheeled Dancer to the east and set him off at a slow trot.

Eli was still standing in the parlor, ready to explode with the wonderful news that Gabe had just told him.

"Did you and Gabe have an argument about the timber?" Sarah asked.

"No," Eli replied slowly, "It was just the opposite, Sarah. I have some amazing news. Gabe found all of Bob Johnson's money in his saddlebags. He left half of it with me, so I could buy ten sections of timber to harvest and the logging camp."

Sarah's mouth dropped and then she asked, "Why did he do that? Is it even legal?"

"He's taking the other half of the money back to the railroad and then negotiate a price on the land. He said because the money wasn't the county's, he thought that I would be able to provide work for the crews. I can make Dave the foreman too, and that would give him and Rebecca a nice income. And that's not all, either.

Sarah asked, "What else could there possibly be?"

Eli smiled as he looked at Dave and Rebecca who were sitting on the couch again and said, "Gabe said to use some of the money to build a nice house for Rebecca and Dave. Isn't that wonderful, Rebecca?"

Rebecca smiled weakly and said, "Wonderful."

Dave was grinning as he hugged Rebecca and said, "Becky, we're going to have a good life."

Sarah looked at Rebecca's face and noted the striking similarity to Gabe's forlorn expression when he entered the parlor. She was sitting next to her fiancé, had just been told that she was going to have a new house, and she had the same morose expression. She wanted to have a long, private talk with Rebecca when she had a chance.

Gabe had regained his composure despite his internal misery as he stepped down outside the train station. Dancer was now encumbered with his clothing bag, two sets of saddlebags, and two rifles. He looked like a small, but handsome, pack horse.

He walked into Joe's station manager's office and plopped down in the chair as Joe looked at him.

"All done, Gabe?" he asked.

"Done is a good word to describe it, Joe. Do you have any more wires for me?"

"Nope. But I did get some news that you might find interesting. The new yard manager, a feller by the name of Henry Caruthers, showed up a little while ago and told me that Jimmy Norquist and Jack Wheeler, you know, the engineer and fireman that you named when you caught the Dakota Gang? Well, when they got back and were arrested, they went and started telling the boss that you told them to stop the train and that you killed all of the gang because you were afraid they'd talk."

Gabe smiled and asked, "So, they obviously didn't know yet that one of the gang members survived and fingered them both, did he?"

Joe grinned and replied, "I guess not, because after the boss let them ramble on and on about how you set them all up, he tells them about Jensen being alive and that took the wind out of their sails."

"What happened to them?"

"Would you believe they're in the same prison with Jensen? He's doing his ten years and they each got fifteen, but knowing the crowd that Jensen hung around with, I don't figure they'll make it for their full sentence."

"How's Caruthers? I've only met him a couple of times."

"He's okay. We need to rough up his smooth edges a bit to fit in, though."

Gabe laughed then said, "I'm going to go and get a room at for the night and I'll be back around six o'clock."

"See you in the morning, Gabe," Joe said as Gabe stood, gave him a wave and headed for the door.

He mounted Dancer and soon left the station behind as he headed for the hotel. Oddly enough, even with the loss of Rebecca, he had no desire to return to Angela's house, knowing she would probably boot Rafe out of the house if he showed up. He headed for Rodger's House on Front Street.

He arrived at the hotel's livery, left Dancer and took his two sets of saddlebags and his cloth bag of clothes into the hotel, then ten minutes later was in his room and disarmed.

Gabe decided he'd finally take that long overdue bath, so before he left the room, he slid the saddlebags with the money under the bed and headed down the hallway.

After he'd returned and dressed, including his Webley, but not his Remington, he was reminded of his failure to send anything of nutritional value to his stomach for too long. So he donned his light jacket and left his room, locking the door behind him then headed for the International Restaurant just a block away on Front Street.

As he walked along the boardwalk, he passed a bakery and saw some enticing pastries in the window and was seriously tempted to just buy some and return to his room but decided someone in his gut would file a formal protest with whomever was in charge down there.

He entered the nice restaurant, found a table and soon gave his order to the waitress and began sipping the coffee she'd set on the table. Gabe scanned the other diners, knowing he was the only one eating alone, when his eyes reached the far corner, and he spotted the back of a blonde head and the left side of Rafe Collier. He was smiling as she spoke, so it appeared she had altered her view of her destiny after all.

Gabe made note of his lack of even the tiniest bit of jealousy as he watched the couple for a minute but hoped that Rebecca didn't walk through the door on Dave's arm. That would cause a totally different reaction.

His meal was served ten minutes later, and he ate more quickly than usual, even though he should have spent more time savoring the best steak he'd had in months. He glanced at Rafe and Angela periodically to make sure they were still there then finished eating, left payment and a large tip before taking his hat and leaving the restaurant. He may not have been jealous, but he thought if they saw him, they'd feel uncomfortable.

As he walked past the bakery, he thought of that word, uncomfortable. The feeling that it described was the reason he'd never really talked to Rebecca about how he felt about her, or even talked to Eli about his promise to Dave Horowitz. He didn't want to make them uncomfortable, and now he was going to pay the price for it. But he had noticed how uncomfortable Rebecca had been with Dave and finally just assumed it was because he was there and let it go.

He reached his room, went inside and verified the saddlebags were still under the bed. He slid them out and then balanced the load of cash, doing an exact accounting of the money they contained as he shifted the stacks and coming up with a grand total of $31,245.00. That was still an enormous amount of money, so the Northern Pacific should be generous in its pricing of the land for Eli.

After setting up his clothes for tomorrow's trip, he set his pocket watch alarm for four-thirty, stripped and stretched out on the bed.

Trying to avoid any thoughts of Rebecca, he concentrated on the telegrams from Herb Erikson then pulled them out to reread the one that said he needed to return as soon as possible. It wasn't like Herb to have him return to Minneapolis if there was a job that needed to be done because he'd just send him to the trouble spot with basic information. He couldn't think of anything the big bosses at the NP would want to see him about either. The only job he'd done recently was the Dakota Gang, and they had been pleased with that outcome. It couldn't be anything personal because his parents would have wired him directly.

Gabe finally just gave up trying to read Herb's mind and switched to calculating the length and time that he'd be on a train in his return to Minneapolis. It was going to be a very long trip but acknowledged that it would still be much faster than covered wagons. As soon as he thought about covered wagons, he almost smacked himself in the head. He was so wrapped up in railroads, he forgot the obvious other choice for making his return trip.

He could get there much faster if he just rode east out of Missoula then south and crossed the Blackfoot River at the ferry. He'd be able to ride to Helena in just a day and take the train from there. It would save him two days on the journey. He might not even have to go as far as Helena if he caught up with one of the returning supply trains that were probably on the other side of the Blackfoot with equipment, men and timbers necessary for rebuilding the bridge. If he did, then he'd get back even sooner as it wouldn't have to stop as often as passenger trains.

He slid under the blankets, leaving his early alarm. He'd swing by and tell Joe he'd catch a train in Helena then head out. It would be a better way to clear his mind, too.

———

Rebecca was still sitting in the parlor with Dave, who had barely left her side since arriving. He was excited about getting a new house and being made the foreman and never seemed to notice that he was doing all the talking. The rest of the family had emptied the room an hour ago giving the couple some privacy.

But then she turned looked at him and asked, "Why didn't you take me out of there, Dave? It would have been much easier for you to do it because you'd know when Bob and Frank were gone."

"Don't ask so many questions. Just be grateful that I'm marryin' you."

Rebecca knew what he meant, too. He knew what had happened in the logging camp and probably saw her as only marginally better than the camp whores he used. But she was now a whore who could give him a better future than he could have expected.

Dave smiled then leaned over and kissed Rebecca then let his hands wander as she sat placidly on the couch while memories of Bob Johnson floated in her mind as she felt like an extension of the couch.

Two miles away, Rafe Collier kissed Angela good night, then bounced off the porch mounted his horse and returned to his room at Wood's Boarding House and hoped he wouldn't be staying there much longer.

CHAPTER 8

Gabe's pocket alarm had done its job and by five-thirty, he was riding out of the hotel's livery and heading for the railroad station as the sun was just lifting above the eastern horizon casting long shadows to the west. He glanced down and saw his and Dancer's shadow spread a good forty feet along the cobbled street in front of him as he rode west along Stevens Street which took him directly to the station in the distance, his shadow almost like an enormous, dark compass needle.

He reached the station, hitched Dancer then dismounted and walked inside. Joe wasn't there yet, so he took out a pencil and sheet of paper and wrote a quick note telling him he'd be riding to Helena then picking up the train there. He left the paper on the desk turned left the office and mounted Dancer.

He didn't have any supplies though, and remembered the pack horse that he'd unloaded at Angela's and thought about going there but decided against it. Instead he turned east back down Stevens Street, thinking he'd just stop at the bakery on Front Street before crossing the Hells Gate bridge and riding east.

Gabe didn't go overboard at the bakery, but bought six apple bear claws, and four rolls then stopped two doors down and bought some cooked sausages at the butcher shop. After the food was stuffed into his non-money saddlebags, Gabe rode out of Missoula even as he heard the train whistle a couple of miles away announcing its departure for Washington on its long, looping journey back to Minnesota.

He soon crossed the bridge and rode east.

Rebecca was standing with her arms folded on the porch of their home watching the train rolling past knowing that it was taking Gabe back to Minneapolis and probably out of her life forever. She listened to the plaintive whistle hating the sound as it shrieked in the morning air then closed her eyes and let tears flow across her face. After a minute, she wiped her face with her handkerchief, turned and walked back through the open door then after pulling it closed, returned to the kitchen to have breakfast with her family.

She hadn't been able to talk to any of them after they left her with Dave because he didn't leave until well after midnight and promised to be back in the morning. Her life was changing again, and it wasn't for the better, but she shouldn't have expected it to be anything more than she deserved.

Gabe had followed the road until it turned into little more than a used set of wagon tracks. Since the arrival of the railroad just two years earlier, traffic on the road had dropped off to a trickle. Those that did travel overland took the much better, but much longer northern road that used passes rather than river crossings.

It was around ten o'clock when he reached the ferry and wondered if it was even in use anymore. The rope was there, and the barge was even on this side of the river, but he didn't see anyone as he rode Dancer closer to the Blackfoot River. It was noticeably higher now, probably courtesy of the jam caused by the bridge collapse another three miles downriver. The new bank was just four feet from the shack that had been used by the ferry operator.

He reached the shack and shouted, “Hello! Anyone there?”

No one replied, so he dismounted and led Dancer to the shack. On the front door, someone had scrawled:

USE THE FERRY IF YOU WANT
LEAVE TEN CENTS INSIDE

Gabe grinned. It had become a self-service ferry. He reached into his pocket, found a quarter and opened the door, leaving the coin on an empty table wondering if anyone ever paid or even used the ferry at all anymore.

He then led Dancer onto the barge, felt it rocking in the water as his gelding stepped aboard and began to reconsider his decision not to take the train or at least the longer road, but it was too late now.

He tied off Dancer to the side railing then pulled on his gloves, grabbed the rope and began to pull. The barge was stuck on the mud of the bank, so it took a good amount of strain to break it free, but once it popped free, the barge lurched, and Gabe began to use a fast hand-over-hand motion pulling the barge across the hundred-yard wide river. The barge wallowed in the water as it bucked the fast-moving current and Gabe glanced up and saw the whites of Dancer’s eyes as he felt the floor beneath him roll and yaw.

“Just a minute more!” he shouted to his equine friend as he worked the rope.

It probably only took three or four minutes to cross the Blackfoot, but it seemed a lot longer before the bow slid onto the opposite bank. Or was it the stern? Either way, Gabe wasted no time in untying Dancer and leading him onto solid ground. The Morgan gelding was only too happy to be away from that contraption and after Gabe was in the saddle, he was skittish for the first half mile as the road began to turn left and climb away from the river.

When they reached the tracks, Gabe turned west to see how they were progressing and maybe find a supply train. Five minutes later, he smiled when he saw the back end of a train and then six empty flat cars. The locomotive wasn't fired up, so if it was leaving, it wasn't going to be in the next hour.

He spotted a group of men ahead and singled out the group of engineers who were directing the rebuilding effort as they studied drawings on a crude table. He could hear the construction in the distance and was curious about the progress.

Gabe dismounted and led Dancer to the table as one of the engineers turned and saw him.

"Didn't expect to see you out here, Gabe," he said as he smiled.

"I did expect to see you and your friends out here, Bill. How's it going?"

He glanced back at the chasm then looked back at Gabe and said, "Better than I expected when we first saw the damage. That must have been a pretty impressive explosion."

"I was almost twenty miles away when it shook the ground and sounded like thunder."

"When the rock face collapsed on the eastern side, it actually made reconstruction easier because we had a sloping rock face to start building our supports. We should have it all done in another four days."

"When is your supply train heading back to Helena?"

"In a couple of hours. You need a ride?"

"Yup. My boss wants me back in Minneapolis."

"You're in luck then. The train is going to turn around in Helena and head back to Minneapolis. A second supply train is coming this afternoon."

"That'll help."

"We've been hearing all sorts of rumblings about Mike Wheatley's murder in Missoula. I assume that's why you were here."

"It was. That and some timber poaching operation that was the root of all of it."

"Can you fill us in while they fire up the locomotive?"

"You boys get me some coffee and I'll share my pastry with you and tell the tale."

"Well, let's head over to the fire and have some coffee," Bill replied before he turned and walked with the other three engineers to a small, almost-dead fire with a cooking grate and a coffeepot on top.

Gabe led Dancer nearby, hitched him to a bush then pulled the bag of bear claws from his saddlebag and took a seat on one of the stumps surrounding the fire.

As they had their coffee and pastry, Gabe told them the basics of the story that left out Rebecca completely and Angela as much as possible. Of course, that meant he had to show them the .44 in his belt buckle and as engineers, they were more interested in the range and energy expended by the bullet. One of them began talking about tensile strength of the steel and even the other engineers shushed him.

The steam engine was being fed its coal and building steam pressure when Gabe finally shook hands with the engineers then turned back to the supply train, found an empty stock car, pulled out the ramp and led Dancer inside. After tying him off into one of the stalls, he pulled the ramp back into the car, hopped down and trotted to the front of the train and climbed aboard the locomotive.

The engineer, Ernie Flannery, turned and said, “Gabe? How did you get here?”

“I crossed the Blackfoot on a ferry. Ernie, I’ll be riding in the stock car with my horse. They want me back in Minneapolis and Bill Evans said that you were heading that way.”

“That’s where we’re goin’. We have to pick up a load in Helena though, so we’ll be there for a few hours. We need to get my noisy girl here serviced, too. After that, it’ll be a straight shot. You should be there late tomorrow night.”

“That’s a lot sooner than I expected. If I’d taken that rerouted train, I wouldn’t be there for four more days.”

“I’ll be rollin’ out of here in about forty minutes.”

“You’ll probably be happier driving forward after you get turned around in Helena, too.”

Ernie laughed and said, “You got that right. I’m havin’ to depend on signals from old Ben Kuiper back in the caboose. With his eyesight, we’ll be lucky if we don’t run into a herd of buffalo.”

“If there were any left,” Gabe said before he hopped down.

The fireman watched him leave and turned to Ernie and asked, “Who was that?”

Ernie spun a wheel to open a valve as he replied, “That, Sam, was Special Agent Gabe Owens.”

“The feller that took out the Dakota Gang all by himself?” he asked as he looked at the receding man.

“Yup. He’s the best there is.”

“Seems kinda young, don’t he?”

“Not to me,” Ernie said as Sam threw a shovelful of coal past him into the firebox.

Thirty-six minute later, the train lurched and began its backward trip to Helena.

Gabe felt the motion as he sat on an empty crate near Dancer with his Sharps-Borshadt across his lap. He was giving it a more thorough cleaning than the quick onceover he’d done on the trail. He oiled where it needed oiling and then wiped it clean before sliding it back into its scabbard. He’d unsaddled Dancer while he waited for the train to leave, knowing that even this much shorter ride would be a day and a half if there were no mechanical failures or track problems, which were common.

He pulled out his Winchester to brought it back into top condition too. When that was done, he decided to clean his two pistols as well even though neither had been fired. After finishing the Remington, he pulled the Webley out of his shoulder holster and smiled when he looked at the pistol when he recalled that his other Bulldog was with Rebecca. She may never wear it under the vest he’d bought for her but knowing she had it meant there was still some connection between them however tenuous it may be.

Dave had kept his promise and arrived at the Ulrich house that morning and found Sarah with Rachel and Aaron, but no Rebecca.

“Where’s Becky?” he asked Sarah.

“She went with Eli to the bank, so he could deposit the cash that Gabe gave him.”

“When’s she comin’ back?”

“I have no idea, but I would think they’ll be here for lunch, unless my husband splurges and buys lunch for her in town to celebrate his good fortune.”

“Why did he give Eli all that money? Nobody does that unless they want somethin’.”

“I think you’re very wrong, Dave. Gabe gave it to him because he knew that Eli would do the right thing for the workers and those trees. Gabe is an extraordinary man. He risked his life to save Rebecca, even though Eli had told him how difficult she was. Then after just one day with him, he talked her into coming back to us. And when she did, she not only asked Eli to forgive her, she confessed how poorly she had treated me and begged my forgiveness as well. I can’t begin to tell you how astonished we all were with that change, and it was all because of Gabe.”

“Are you sure it wasn’t ‘cause Bob gave her to Frank?”

"No, it wasn't. It was all because of Gabe. She told me that."

"She stayed with him all night?"

Sarah stared at him and said, "You didn't seem to care that she spent a whole year with Bob Johnson, and now you're worried that she spent a night with Gabe Owens?"

"Well, Bob's dead and Owens ain't."

Sarah gritted her teeth and said, "Gabe never even touched Rebecca out of respect."

"Maybe he just doesn't like girls. We got a few of 'em at the camp."

Sarah finally asked, "Are you going to wait or leave?"

"I'll wait. Can I get some coffee?"

"In the kitchen," Sarah replied, wishing she had been able to talk to Rebecca.

The train's stopover in Helena lasted exactly three hours and eleven minutes as they turned it facing east in the roundhouse then serviced the locomotive and the trucks of the rolling stock as it was being loaded with cargo bound for Minneapolis. Gabe took the opportunity to have a full lunch, leaving the rolls and sausages for later. He did buy a big sack of oats for Dancer and picked up a small bag of apples, too.

Ernie had the train hurtling east by four o'clock as Dancer enjoyed his bag of oats and Gabe stood in the stock car's open door watching Montana Territory pass before his eyes.

By sunset, Gabe had fashioned a sleeping compartment of sorts out of one of the stalls, mucked out the car, and had given the first of the apples to Dancer.

He closed the stock car's sliding door then sat down and had his first sausage after slicing the roll with his knife and laying the sausage inside. He wished he had picked up some mustard sauce in Helena, but it was still pretty tasty.

The train made stops for water three times and coaled once before he slid into his bedroll and let the monotonous clacking of the steel wheels as they passed over the rail gaps and the swaying motion of the car lull him to sleep.

He was awakened by the sounds of screeching wheels as Ernie threw the locomotive's drive wheels into reverse to bring the train to a stop at Glendale to fill the water tanks and the coal car.

Gabe slid out of the bedroll, checked the time then pulled on his boots, donned his shoulder holster, his gunbelt and jacket before pulling on his abused hat and sliding the car's door open. The sky was gray and there was the threat of rain as he hopped down then trotted to the privy behind the train station, not wanting to offend any residents or travelers.

He knew that they'd only be there for forty minutes or so, so he just walked up front to find Ernie, unsure if he was still there or another crew had replaced him when they'd stopped in Billings.

When he got to the locomotive, he discovered that the crew had been swapped out and talked to the new engineer and fireman for a few minutes to let them know he was there, then returned to the stock car and gave Dancer another apple and had one himself.

An hour later, they were leaving Montana Territory as they crossed the border into Dakota Territory. The train seemed to be making better time than he'd expected and figured he might make it back to his house in Minneapolis before nine o'clock that night.

———

Gabe was able to get a full meal in Bismarck when the train not only took on coal but had its routine greasing and oiling done as well.

As the sun was going down, the train raced into Minnesota and Gabe knew he'd be passing through Brainard in a few hours. The train would stop for water and coal, and he was tempted to run over and see his parents but didn't believe he'd be able to talk to them about everything that had happened, especially about Rebecca. His mother would be able to read him too easily and he wanted more time to be able to get far enough past Rebecca, so he could mask his feelings.

So, he stayed in the stock car as it rolled into Brainard and then twenty minutes later, it began its southern leg heading for Minneapolis.

At 9:17 PM, the tired train rolled into the expansive Northern Pacific yards in Minneapolis and finally slowed to a hissing, exhausted stop at the unloading ramps near the warehouses.

Gabe had saddled Dancer and didn't have to lower the ramp but just slid the door open and led him across the gap onto the nearby ramp and then down to the level ground. He mounted his Morgan and walked him around the warehouses, stepping carefully over the multiple lines of tracks in the yard and finally reached the streets of Minneapolis and headed for his house.

He reached his home ten minutes later, dismounted, led Dancer into his barn, put him into his stall and began unsaddling him. After brushing him down, he gave him the last of the apples then patted him on the neck and loaded himself down with saddlebags over both shoulders and rifles in both hands as he headed for his back door.

He leaned his Winchester against the wall near the doorway, unlocked the door and swung it wide before picking up his repeater and entering his kitchen. He set his rifles against the wall, closed the door and then dropped the saddlebags on the floor.

Gabe then stood there in his almost black, deathly silent kitchen and felt incredibly alone and didn't know why. He'd been places where there hadn't been another human being for fifty miles around and hadn't felt this isolated even understanding that there were probably hundreds of people within a mile.

He shook off the feeling then walked over and lit his kitchen lamp. He then picked up the two saddlebags and moved them into his bedroom before returning to the kitchen for his rifles.

Gabe finally slid under his quilts just before midnight still wondering why Herb had summoned him back to Minneapolis.

The next morning, Gabe mounted Dancer, leaving both rifles at his house. Dancer was only carrying him and the money saddlebags as he headed for the company's offices in the bright sunshine. His mind had been sliding into thoughts about what Rebecca would be doing since he'd awakened, and it was beginning to annoy him. He had to let it go. She was marrying Dave Horowitz and that was that.

He reined in Dancer at the office, pulled the saddlebags free and hung them over his shoulder before walking into the building and heading for Herb's office. He reached the outer office and walked inside, spotted Herb's secretary who looked up from some papers then just waved him in.

Gabe opened the office door, stepped inside and closed it behind him.

"Well, you sure got back here faster than I figured you would," Herb said as he looked at him.

"I crossed the Blackfoot using a ferry and caught a supply train back rather than taking the rerouted train."

"That was smart. Have a seat, Gabe."

Gabe set the saddlebags on the floor took off his hat and sat down.

"Well, Herb, you've got me wondering what this is all about. You didn't put much in the telegram."

"I know. I'll tell you in a minute after you tell me about the job."

"Well, the basics are that I discovered that nothing we had been told was true. Mike had been shot with a derringer at close range in his kitchen by Bob Johnson, who had been running the poaching operation northwest of Missoula. He had ordered his foreman to have Willie killed and they dropped a tree on him. I stopped the poaching, chased the Bob Johnson and his foreman down about fifty miles west of Missoula, had a gunfight of sorts, and the two men responsible floated down the river. Now, tell me why you needed me back here so quickly."

"There's a lot more to it than that, isn't there?" Herb asked.

"There is, but you're not going to get it until you tell me what you want."

"Okay. You win. I've been promoted, Gabe. I'm going to be a vice president and they want you to take over my job."

The offer didn't require a lot of thought as Gabe quickly replied, "I'm not going to do your job, Herb. I like doing what I do, and I can't sit in an office and tell others to do it."

"I told them you probably wouldn't take it, but you need to know the other side, too. It pays more, and you'd be able to stay here and start a family, Gabe. It's about time, isn't it?"

"You know I don't worry about the money, Herb, and I don't think I'll be starting a family either. Not now and maybe not ever."

Herb looked at Gabe and asked, "Why would you say that? Did you find Angela in Missoula?"

"Yes, I did, but she's fine now. I'll give you the complete story if you stop offering me your job."

"That sounds like a fair deal. Go ahead."

Gabe then started his extended narrative, not skipping anything, not even Rebecca because it would all have to be part of his official report anyway.

The first time Herb stopped his story was when Gabe told him about his confrontation with the sheriff and had to show him the belt buckle, which elicited the expected awe.

The second time was after he explained about the money and the arrangement he made with Eli Ulrich.

Hebe looked wide-eyed down at the saddlebags and said, "There's thirty thousand dollars in those?"

"A little more, but yes."

"And you're planning on giving it to the railroad?"

"Yup. I don't know how much of the money Bob Johnson made poaching timber from the railroad's land, but I'm sure it wasn't more than fifteen thousand dollars. The rest was mostly from his own land and some of the government's land. I want that land harvested like my father's contracted land is harvested, not turned into a damned desert. Eli will do that and I'm sure he'll provide the railroad with ties at a good price, too."

"I'll tell you what, Gabe, let's go and talk to the boss right now and see what he says. Personally, I wouldn't have given them more than they lost but then, that's not you; is it?"

Gabe laughed and said, "Are you implying that I'm a dim bulb, Herb?"

Herb stood smiled and said, "Maybe."

Gabe picked up his hat and Herb asked, "What happened to your hat?"

Gabe glanced at his gray Stetson and replied, "Oh, that. I forgot about that, but that's where Frank's shot arrived before I hit him in the ankle with my Winchester."

Herb rolled his eyes and said, "Let's go."

Gabe wasn't surprised when, after meeting with the president and accepting his praise and gratitude, he was sent to the office of the vice president of finance and handed over the entire amount. But what did surprise him was that rather than negotiating for the ten sections that he'd promised Eli, the president had given him a memo to take to the railroad's land office management department and simply transferred the timber rights for the ten sections to Eli Ulrich. The land itself would still be owned by the Northern Pacific, but Eli could harvest the trees on the land. It was a pretty good solution for the railroad, and he was sure Eli wouldn't object, either.

He left the land management office and returned to Herb's office about an hour after he left.

"Well?" Herb asked as Gabe sat down.

Gabe told him about the transactions and Herb said, "I still think you should have kept the money, but at least you got the timber contracts. Now, tell me about Rebecca. She's obviously the reason for that sulky 'never having a family' comment."

"She is, but she's getting married this week, and there's that whole Jewish thing in the way, too."

"I didn't think you'd care about something like that."

"I don't, but she does, and her father does, but I have to let it go, Herb. Do you have any jobs that can keep me busy?"

"I always have jobs, Gabe, and I have one that came up while you were in Missoula. If it hadn't been for the whole promotion issue, I would have sent you there directly because you were so close."

"What is it?"

"Do you remember Stan Harriman?"

"Sure. He was an agent that we lost in an attempted train robbery in Pierre about, what, two years ago now?"

"That's the man. Well, it turns out we didn't lose him. One of the bodies they found looked like him and was identified by the sheriff as being Stan, but it wasn't. It was one of the robbers who just looked like him. We only found out that it wasn't Stan when he resurfaced in Oregon last week. And guess what he was doing?"

"Don't tell me he's robbing trains?"

"Among other things, but he knew a lot more about our operations and the only reason we knew it was him was that he bragged about it to the brakeman as he held him under his gun while the rest of his men robbed the passengers. He doesn't limit himself to Northern Pacific trains but has been working his way east across Oregon and we guess he'll be reaching Ainsworth soon. The way he robs the trains is a lot like the Dakota Gang, too."

"I talked to Bill Evans while the crews were restoring the Blackfoot bridge and he said he'll have it done in four days, and that was two days ago. So, I'll take the train west then wait in Helena until the bridge is done, which should be soon."

"I appreciate it, Gabe."

"Can you give me what you have on Stan while I write my report?"

"Sure," Herb said as he stood and walked to his file cabinet.

Gabe was wondering if there was some train robbery college that he didn't know about. Train robberies just weren't that common, and now he'd be going after another gang that seemed to think it was a good idea. As he read the report, it was just as Herb had just mentioned. There were amazing similarities in the way Stan's group mimicked the Dakota Gang.

Gabe was back in his house two hours later and was making his plans for the trip back west. Compared to the Dakota Gang, Stan Harriman's bunch seemed downright friendly. They'd wait when the train stopped at one of the small watering stations, board the locomotive, put the engineer and fireman under a gun, tie them up then take what they could from the passengers and if they had the time, would empty the express car. They would cut the telegraph lines at the station, disable the locomotive's steam engine then mount their horses and ride away. They'd never even shot anyone, although that could have been because none of the victims had given them cause to pull a trigger yet.

He had a good description of Stan Harriman and tried to match it to his own memory with the only difference being the full beard that he was reported to wear now.

Gabe sat back and tried to concentrate on the job but kept recalling Dave Horowitz's line about marrying Rebecca next week. Rebecca Ulrich could already be Rebecca Horowitz by now, and his stomach recoiled at the thought. He almost wished he hadn't helped her to get past her anger and hate, but knew that no matter what the outcome, she was still happier now.

In Missoula, Eli and Sarah were planning for Rebecca's wedding. A visiting rabbi would perform the ceremony on Tuesday, July 29th at ten o'clock in the morning.

Rebecca and Dave were out marking off the spot for their new house that would be built in the lot next to Eli's home. They'd visit Danforth and Otto, the builders, that afternoon and Dave was already excited to be going to Sweeney's to pick out all their furniture tomorrow. Eli had put no limit on how much they could spend, and Dave was planning on taking advantage of his generosity at the builder and the furniture store.

Rebecca just walked along as Dave excitedly pointed out where the new barn would go and how big the kitchen would be and then, when no one was looking, he kissed her and told her how big their new bed would be, too.

After they finished exploring the site of their new home, Dave harnessed the black mare to their new buggy and held her hand as he helped her into the fresh leather seats. Once he had them rolling toward Missoula, Rebecca ran her fingers across the red leather and fought back her tears as she remembered how happy she had been when she was sitting exactly where she was now, and Gabe was driving.

They passed by the sheriff's office a minute later on their way to Danforth and Otto. Inside, Angela was sitting on the desk as newly appointed Sheriff Raphael Collier wrote a report.

"Are you going to visit again this evening, Raphael?" Angela asked.

Rafe set down his pencil smiled and replied, "Would you like me to visit, Angela?"

"I'd like you to do more than visit, Sheriff," she said as she smiled down at him.

"Then I'll be happy to oblige, ma'am," Rafe replied as he looked into her blue eyes.

They stayed gazing into each other's eyes for a few seconds before Angela said, "Well, I'll head back to my house. I know you have to keep everyone safe now."

"Especially you, Angela."

She slid off his desk walked around the desk, kissed him passionately then stood, smiled at him once more and left the sheriff's office, leaving a very anxious Sheriff Collier.

———

Gabe climbed aboard the train for Helena at 7:15 in the morning on Monday, the 28th of July. Dancer was in the stock car, and his saddle and two rifles were stored with him as Gabe settled into a passenger seat in the first-class car. He still had his damaged hat but had left his bullet belt buckle at the house and was wearing a replacement.

He knew that the train could be stopping in Missoula as early as Wednesday afternoon, but that depended on the progress they were making on the Blackfoot bridge. He had already decided that he'd just leave the timber rights paperwork with Joe to deliver to Eli as the train would only be stopping in Missoula for forty minutes. He didn't think he could bear meeting Mrs. Dave Horowitz.

The wedding preparations were complete, the plans for the house were in place and the furniture either purchased or ordered. Rabbi Roth had arrived and was staying at the Occidental Hotel.

Sarah had never had an opportunity to talk to Rebecca alone as Dave always seemed to be hovering nearby and it bothered her immensely. She had mentioned Rebecca's glum demeanor to Eli and he just assigned it to expected nervousness about the upcoming nuptials.

Later that afternoon, Dave took Rebecca for a long buggy ride, crossed the bridge east out of town and finally turned the buggy off the road and rolled another quarter of a mile until he stopped behind some boulders. Rebecca knew why he'd chosen the secluded spot and knew that there was no purpose in resisting. She was just going to get what she deserved.

He pulled her close, kissed her and let his hand slide to her left breast then said, "Becky, it's time you gave me what you gave Bob and Frank."

Becky left his hand where it was but didn't say or do anything which seemed to irritate Dave thinking she was going to refuse him.

Dave's eyes darkened as he said, "You're gettin' all high and mighty for a woman who spread her legs for any man who wanted you. You went runnin' to Bob instead of lettin' me have you then you let Frank take you and then you probably couldn't wait 'til you got that Gabe in your bed,either. So, you'd better show me some lovin'."

Rebecca glared at him and said, "You know nothing! Gabe never even touched me. He treated me with respect and love. You're just like Bob."

Dave then ripped the front of her dress open and as she brought her hand down to stop him, he grabbed her wrist and snarled, "No, Becky. Bob was a sissy. He wore those fancy suits and was a little man, and I'm a real man. Now if you want to fight me, you can. But remember that I'm gonna be your husband tomorrow and you may as well give in now, or do I talk to your papa about Fannie?"

Rebecca knew that he was right and that after the wedding, he could beat her if he chose. She realized Dave was closer to Frank than Bob and couldn't bear the thought of more pain.

She said, "Alright," as Dave smiled released her wrist and pulled her from the buggy.

Rebecca was on her back in the tall grass five minutes later and after a few slaps was having to be more active and enthusiastic to satisfy Dave's lust.

This was her new life.

Gabe was on the train between Mandan in Dakota Territory and Glendale in Montana Territory when Rebecca Ulrich was married to Dave Horowitz. Eli was smiling with Sarah by his side as the ceremony concluded.

Sarah was watching Rebecca closely and knew that there was something very wrong. Rebecca was putting on a brave front but her eyes told a completely different story. *Why had she agreed to marry that man?*

The bridge repair was completed late Wednesday afternoon and the supply train that had brought the last of the beams, rails and ties crossed over the new construction with no one else on board except the engineer, who wasn't even getting a bonus for making the run across the untested structure. Once he reached the other side, the engineer relaxed, gave three long blasts of the whistle then reversed the wheels to cross back over.

Once the train returned and their equipment loaded all of the workers and engineers happily boarded the train with most of the workers just sitting on the flatbeds as it began rolling back to Helena.

The Northern Pacific's main line was now open again and telegrams were soon being sent to all stations alerting them of the completed repair.

Gabe was in Helena when the supply train rolled backwards down the line and didn't need to be told of the success of the completed bridge when he saw all of the workers on the flatbed cars.

After the supply train pulled onto a siding, the normally scheduled train was finally able to continue its journey but would be held until morning because the replacement crew wasn't there, and the engineer needed some sleep. Most of the passengers didn't complain as they didn't think the bridge would be repaired this soon anyway. Some groused, but they were usually the ones who complained if it was too sunny, too.

So, it wasn't until very early the next morning before the train began rolling west again.

Gabe was sitting his upholstered first-class seat watching the mountainous terrain roll past as the train climbed one of the numerous grades the Northern Pacific had prepared when they were building the railroad. Soon the train was speeding down the other side which made up for the slow climb.

He pulled his pocket watch and wondered how much longer it would be before they crossed the new trestle bridge. This was the first fully loaded train to cross the bridge, but he wasn't really worried.

He moved to the left side though because he wanted to be able to see the ferry that he and Dancer had used a few days earlier.

It was sunrise when they crossed the new bridge, but no one noticed. Gabe wasn't able to spot the ferry, but he knew they were about forty minutes out of Missoula. It was such an odd sensation, wanting so much to see Rebecca and wanting just as much not to see her. She was probably happily making dinner for her new husband who had already consummated their marriage.

He shook his head to toss the vision from his imagination and tried to think about Stan Harriman.

There was good reason for Gabe to have spent some time thinking about Stan Harriman. He and his four men had left Ainsworth two days earlier, stopped at Ventnor and had continued on to Clark's Falls. Stan had heard about the downed bridge, estimated how long it would take to repair and thought that the first passenger train coming west would be packed with potential victims. He picked Clark's Falls as their boarding location because he'd been there before and liked its setting with the hard curve right after the water tower. The town itself was almost nothing, which is what he preferred to use.

They arrived in Clark's Falls just as word went around town saying that the bridge had been repaired and the first westbound train would be coming through at ten-thirty.

The other four were still in camp, and Stan was the only one in Clark's Falls because five armed men would be noticed. When they spotted the train coming down the track, they'd make themselves known.

———

The train was slowing as it pulled into Missoula, and Gabe stood on the passenger car's platform then as soon as the station's wooden platform arrived, he hopped onto the surface, slowed down and heading for the station manager's office. There were a fairly good number of passengers waiting to board the train, and he wasn't surprised.

He entered the office, Joe looked up, grinned and said, "Gabe!"

Gabe grinned back and said, "How are you doing, Joe?"

"Good. Good. What brings you back here so soon? I thought you were going to Minneapolis?"

"I got there, and Herb sent me back. I'm heading for Ainsworth. Could you do me a favor?"

"Sure. What do you need?"

Gabe pulled out Eli's timber authorization papers, handed it to Joe and said, "Can you give that to Eli Ulrich? His house is only about a half a mile from here."

"Hell, Gabe, why don't you run over there? The train isn't going anywhere for forty-five minutes."

Gabe was about to argue the point, but something made him change his mind and he said, "You're right. Don't let that thing go without me, though. You're the station manager now."

Joe laughed and said, "Don't remind me."

Gabe slipped the papers back into his jacket pocket as he turned and left the office.

He walked west and then cut to his right slightly as he headed for Eli's home. He figured it was safe because Rebecca probably wasn't there anyway but didn't want to think where she probably was.

Four hundred yards from the house, he could see the construction work already beginning on Rebecca's new home and was a bit surprised to see how large it was. He guessed that she was planning on having a lot of children.

He reached the house three minutes later, stepped onto the porch and knocked on the door.

It swung open and he stopped breathing when his eyes told him Rebecca Horowitz was standing two feet in front of him.

Neither could talk for ten seconds before Gabe said, "Oh. Good morning, Rebecca."

"Why are you here, Gabe?" she asked quietly, disguising her pounding heart.

"I have some papers for your father. Is Eli in?"

“No, he’s at the office,” she replied which began another ten seconds of silence.

“Oh. I guess I should go there, then,” Gabe said without moving.

“I guess so,” she replied as they just stared into each other’s eyes.

Then Gabe took a deep breath and said, “I’ll be going now.”

Rebecca nodded, but both remained anchored in place.

Gabe managed a smile and said, “You remember my flaw?”

“Yes,” she whispered.

“Well, I know that it will keep me celibate for the rest of my life now.”

Then he finally tore his eyes from hers, wheeled about and began walking quickly to the sawmill as Rebecca just watched him leave knowing what he had just told her, and it made everything about her life even worse.

She watched until he disappeared into her father’s buildings then turned slowly, reentered the house, closed the door, then leaned back until her back was against the door and began to cry.

Sarah was in the parlor and had watched her but even though she hadn’t been able to see Gabe, finally understood Rebecca’s sad countenance. She didn’t know what Gabe’s fault was, or why it would keep him celibate, but with both Dave and Eli at the sawmill, she finally thought this would be a good time to talk to Rebecca.

She stood, walked to the door where Rebecca still leaned with her eyes closed, sobbing, and put her hand on Rebecca's shoulder.

"Rebecca, can you tell me?" she asked softly.

Rebecca opened her eyes and replied, "Sarah, I've made so many mistakes in my life and this one may be the worst."

Sarah hooked her arm through Rebecca's and guided her to the sofa where they both sat down to talk.

———

Gabe sat in Eli's office and tried not to slam his fist into Dave Horowitz's smiling face. It wasn't his fault that this had all happened, but he sure as hell didn't like the man. As long as he made Rebecca happy, he could live with it, but seeing him grinning like a Cheshire cat irritated him something fierce. He had barely entered the office and received Eli's surprised greeting when Dave announced that he and Becky were now married and would soon be moving into their new house and implied they were already busy trying to have children to fill it.

Gabe finally was able to get down to business when he slid the papers across the desk to Eli and said, "The railroad didn't sell you the land after all. It's still theirs, but what these papers do is to give you the right to harvest the timber on those ten sections. They did it that way, so they can sell the land later or mine it if there's any coal under the ground."

"So, I don't have to pay them for it?" asked Eli with wide eyes.

"No, sir. The president of the railroad was so pleased with the money I gave back to them that he just wrote a memo telling the land manager to give you the timber."

Dave whooped and began bouncing around the office then stopped grinned at his father-in-law and said, "Eli, you're rich!"

Eli ignored Dave, looked at Gabe then said, "You've got to take the money back, Gabe."

"And do what with it, Eli? Look, buy the logging camp, fix it up then get some better equipment. Improve your sawmill," then he paused and said, "And buy Sarah anything she wants."

Eli smiled and said, "She would really like a sewing machine."

Gabe smiled back and said, "There you have it. I've got a train to catch."

"You can't stay for at least a day and catch the train tomorrow now that the schedule is back to normal?"

"No, I really can't. I'm chasing down another gang of train robbers, and this one is led by an ex-agent of the Northern Pacific."

Eli nodded then said, "I know that Rebecca really misses you."

"I just talked to her. I'm glad to see her face's coloring is returning to normal," then without looking at Dave, he added, "I shot Frank Stanford's foot off then punched him in the face for what he did to Rebecca. Lord only knows what I'd do to another man who hurts her."

Dave was going to say something, but Eli was there, so he held back.

"She's married now, so she'll be all right," Eli said.

Gabe stood and said, "I'm glad to hear that, Eli," then turned and quickly left the offices without saying a word to Dave.

After he'd gone, Eli said, "Let's go to the house and I'll tell Sarah the good news."

Dave smiled and said, "Okay, Eli."

Gabe trotted away from the sawmill and made a hard turn to head straight for the station. He didn't think Dave Horowitz would hurt Rebecca, but the man just put him in a foul mood, and not just because he'd married Rebecca. His reaction to learning about Eli's good fortune had sounded all wrong.

He reached the station, stopped by and told Joe he was back then headed to the stock car to see Dancer.

After he climbed inside the car, he decided that he'd stay with his horse and weapons as he had when he rode backwards to Helena on the supply train. Dancer had companions now as other passengers' horses had been loaded aboard.

He stood in the doorway looking at Missoula in the distance and wondered how Rafe and Angela were doing.

Sarah hadn't talked to Rebecca nearly long enough when she heard bootsteps on the front porch and knew that Eli and Dave had returned.

Rebecca had dried her eyes and had only gotten to the story about the buggy ride east of town the day before the wedding when the door opened and hadn't talked at all about her time in the logging camp.

Eli saw Sarah and Rebecca sitting on the couch and said with a smile, "Sarah, you're not going to believe this, but Gabe just stopped by and said the railroad gave me the rights to the timber on more than six thousand acres and I don't have to pay for it at all. That means I'll be able to make a lot of improvements on the sawmill and logging camp."

Sarah was stunned as she asked, "So, all of the money is ours?"

Eli nodded and said, "I tried to give it back, but he said that I could use it to make everything better, and I will. And that includes buying my perfect wife a sewing machine."

Sarah grinned and said, "Really? I can get a sewing machine of my own?"

"I should have bought you one years ago, sweetheart. And maybe we should buy one for Rebecca, too. She may be needing it to make baby clothes soon."

As he smiled at his daughter, Rebecca blanched at the thought and even Eli noticed.

"Is something wrong, Rebecca?"

"No, Papa, I'm all right. I'm happy for you."

Sarah came down from her sewing machine ecstasy and said, "Well, why don't you menfolk go back to work while we ladies discuss the glories of sewing machines, unless you'd like to stay and listen about needles and bobbins."

Eli took one more look at Rebecca then said, “You and Rebecca talk about sewing while Dave and I will go back to the office and start thinking about the improvements we can make in the camp and the sawmill. We can start cutting timber again too, Dave, but not the way that Bob Johnson did.”

“Okay, Eli,” Dave said as he smacked Eli on the back before they left the house.

Gabe was standing in the doorway of the stock car when the train pulled out of Missoula and began slowly accelerating west. After it cleared the station, he watched the new house’s construction in the distance and was certain that the size was Dave’s idea and not Rebecca’s as he just seemed to be impressed with money. But mostly, he thought about the time he had just spent living in Rebecca’s eyes. He realized that she was probably just as unhappy about the marriage as he was. But unlike Rebecca, he had totally misunderstood the reason she had agreed to the marriage.

Once the last remnants of Missoula were hidden by trees, he closed the stock car door and sat down with his back leaning against the door as the train swayed and clacked its way westward.

Stan Harriman was already in Clark’s Falls and so was his number two man, Rex Clark. He’d found it uproariously funny when Stan had told them they’d be using Clark’s Falls for their next job. He’d laughed until Jimmy Roland had pointed out the second half of the town’s name and that he might be taking one himself. The other two members of the group, Larry Lowenstein and Dan Chapman both thought Jimmy’s comment was even funnier.

Now they just needed for the train to arrive.

———

Sarah felt terrible after listening to Rebecca, wishing she could have asked before the wedding and put a stop to it.

"Why did you marry him, Rebecca? You love Gabe and he obviously loves you, so why did you do it?"

Rebecca, despite telling Sarah many things hadn't told her the full reason because she was so ashamed. Instead she professed the secondary reason.

"I didn't want to hurt father anymore, Sarah. I was so mean to him for so long and he had promised Dave that I'd marry him. Besides, Gabe is a Gentile."

"Oh, Rebecca, we should have had this talk so much sooner. Your father didn't care about having given Dave his blessing two years ago. He thought you were happy to be marrying him for your own reasons. If you had told him that you didn't want to marry him, he wouldn't have been angry. As to Gabe being a Gentile, let me ask you this. How many Jewish single men of marrying age do you know?"

"Just one," Rebecca replied.

"Yes, exactly. We're not that strict about such things, Rebecca. You've been so distant from your father for so long, you never even noticed. If you had told him that you loved Gabe Owens, he'd be dancing in the street, and I'd be out there with him."

Rebecca closed her eyes and said, "It doesn't matter now. Does it? It's too late."

"Yes, Rebecca, it's too late," she replied then asked, "How bad has he been since that day he took you on that buggy ride?"

"Not so bad because he's had to be quiet even when we stayed in the hotel, but he's told me that once we move into our house, things will be different."

"Are you afraid of him, Rebecca?" she asked.

Rebecca bit her lower lip and then opened her vest, revealing her shoulder holster and Webley.

Sarah's eyes grew wide when she saw the pistol then asked, "Have you ever used it before?"

"No, and I don't know if I ever could."

"I hope you never have to pull that thing, Rebecca," Sarah said as Rebecca buttoned her vest.

———

Gabe was sitting in the stock car with his Winchester on his lap as it slowed to enter Clark's Falls. He wasn't paying any particular attention. It was just another watering stop.

But there was no water gushing into the engine's water tanks as the fireman, who normally handled the operation, had his wrists being bound while another man tied the ankles of the engineer. It was a fast job and soon, Dan Chapman, who had tied the fireman, bounded from the locomotive and stood with the other three while Stan Harriman shut down the engine then used the heavy wrench to smash the main steam control valve and dropped down next to him.

"Okay, boys, let's get going," Stan said.

There were three passenger cars. Stan always took the first-class car which usually had fewer passengers, more rewards and fewer risks than the two other cars.

Rex Clark and Jimmy Roland took the middle car and Larry Lowenstein and Dan Chapman would take the last car. Once they were done, if Stan thought they had time, they'd move onto the express car before making their escape. In this case, they'd take the road south, cross the ford and return to Ventnor. By the time anyone noticed the delay, they should all be back in their hotel rooms, or maybe having a beer while they played poker.

They were making their way through the passenger cars, when Gabe began to wonder what the holdup was, not realizing that was exactly what was causing the delay…a holdup. A stop like Clark's Falls should take maybe ten minutes and it had already been twice that. Sometimes there were mechanical issues that needed to be resolved, so he wasn't concerned yet.

Stan decided that it was quiet enough to take the express car, so while Jimmy Roland and Larry Lowenstein kept an eye on the passenger cars from outside, Stan, Stan, Rex and Dan Chapman headed for the express car.

"Open up!" shouted Stan, "I know you're in there. Don't make me use this dynamite. I'd rather just let you live past today."

The expressman doubted if he had dynamite, but wasn't brave enough to find out, so he unlocked the door and slid it open.

Gabe had heard the shout and instantly knew what was happening and was surprised that they were this far east. Maybe it wasn't Harriman at all, but regardless of who was robbing the train, he didn't want to get into a gunfight so close to the train, so while the gang was emptying out the contents of the express car, he began quickly saddling Dancer.

As he tightened his cinches, he wondered if they would be making their escape following the same route that Bob and Frank had taken just a few days ago. This time, he wasn't going to let them get up to that ridge. He wouldn't need the Sharps-Borshadt's range, but he did like the added range of the '76.

There was the possibility that at least some of them would give up because they hadn't committed any hanging offenses yet, but he doubted it. Five to one odds were too good for most gamblers to throw away. If he took out one or two then maybe the others would throw down their guns. He didn't even give the likelihood of his own death a second thought until he remembered the belt buckle .44, and wondered if he was losing his magic.

Dancer was ready,so he backed him out of his stall and led him to the edge of the stock car. He slowly slid the door open a foot, so he could listen to what was happening outside.

Just a hundred and twenty feet away, Dan Chapman had led their horses to the open doors of the express car and had all of the passengers' cash and valuables in the saddlebags as they watched Stan and Rex fill the larger, canvas mail bag with cash from the safe. It was a good haul as Stan had promised it would be.

Stan saluted the tightly bound expressman and said, "Thank you for your business, sir," then tossed the heavy canvas bag to Rex Clark who had already stepped down from the car.

Stan then hopped down, mounted and the gang wheeled to the west and rode past the passenger cars as some of them gawked out the window watching their possessions ride away.

Gabe heard the hoofbeats then quickly slid the stock car door open, lowered the stored ramp to the ground, led Dancer to the ground, mounted and then set off after the bandits who were already in rifle range as he circled around behind the caboose.

As the gang cleared the locomotive, Stan and the others all looked to their right for the signs of anyone coming out of the small town, knowing that it was highly unlikely. Once they knew that no one was there, they pressed on westward along the road and as they approached the Missoula River, turned left down to the ford.

Gabe was only a hundred and fifty yards behind when they made the turn and knew they hadn't seen him yet, but the odds were they that they'd spot him soon enough when he would be at their eight o'clock position instead of directly behind them. He had his Winchester in his hands as Dancer still gained ground, moving at a fast trot.

But none of them saw Gabe and he was soon directly behind them again. Now that he was sure that none of the passengers could be hit by a stray bullet, he let them maintain the hundred and fifty yards of separation and cocked his Winchester's hammer, aimed at some rocks to the left of the front rider and fired then quickly levered in a new cartridge.

The loud report behind them startled each rider as the bullet ricocheted loudly off the granite to their left, but they didn't all react at exactly the same moment, so the horses began jostling each other as they all turned in the saddle to see who had taken the shot, but some also quickly began pulling their own Winchesters.

Gabe slowed Dancer to a walk and shouted, “I’m Special Agent Gabe Owens! Throw down your guns! You won’t hang yet, and it’s not worth dying for some trinkets!”

Stan laughed and shouted back, “Trinkets? Is that what you call it, Gabe? Oh, that’s right, your pappy had all that money, so it’s not important to you, is it?”

Gabe had his identity now and shouted back, “Stan, you know you’re going to die if you try and fight. You’re smarter than that. You haven’t killed anyone.”

“Not yet, but you’re going to be the first, Gabe. I’m not spending twenty years behind those bars, and we’ve got five Winchesters to your one. You’re good, but you’re not that good.”

“No, Stan. I’m the best there is, and you know it. It’s your last chance. Throw down the guns.”

In a normal speaking voice, Stan said, “Shoot the bastard.”

Gabe saw the all five of the Winchesters muzzles rise to pint at him, and quickly fired at Stan then nudged Dance to his right.

Stan took the .50 caliber just to the right of the center of his chest and rolled over the back of his horse hitting the ground making his Winchester fire when his finger jerked back the trigger.

The other four men fired at the same time and all missed when Dancer made his sidestep.

Jimmy Roland felt Gabe’s next shot as hit a little high as it punched through his neck just above the shoulders, severing his spinal cord as the bullet crashed through his cervical spine.

Jimmy just slipped off the right side and fell straight down, landing on the top of his head, which would have killed him if he wasn't already dead.

Gabe levered in a third round as Rex Clark, Larry Lowenstein and Dan Chapman fired their second shots while Dancer took a sudden jog to left making all of their .44s spin wide to Gabe's right.

Gabe's '76 blasted another cloud of gunsmoke after its fifty caliber bullet spun out of the muzzle and a fraction of a second later buried itself in Rex Clark's chest, disintegrating his sternum before turning the well-defined organs in his chest into a mass of useless tissue.

Gabe nudged Dancer to the left again as he cycled his Winchester while Larry Lowenstein and Dan Chapman began to rapidly fire their rifles without really aiming anymore as it didn't seem to matter with that damned bouncing horse.

After he fired his fourth shot at Larry, he felt one of their bullets hit his left forearm, and unlike before with the belt buckle, this one hit tissue and he felt blood beginning to slide across his skin.

But Larry didn't feel anything when Gabe's fifty caliber slug slammed into this right eye then exploded out the back.

Dan Chapman felt, more than saw Larry fall and he knew he was alone now and about to die, but he knew he had a chance if he only put a little more distance between him and Owens, so he fired one more shot and was counting on the huge cloud of gunsmoke to prevent Owens from being able to hit him and wheeled his horse around after taking the shot.

Gabe couldn't let him get away, not after they had tried to kill him, so he steadied Dancer then held his shot leading

Chapman as he cleared the gunsmoke, then squeezed his trigger.

His Winchester slammed into his shoulder and less than a half a second later, the bullet found its home when it entered Dan's chest on the lower left, cut a groove in the bottom of his heart then exited his chest.

Gabe watched as he just fell from his horse, bounced and then rolled twice before stopping. He slid his hot Winchester back into its scabbard pulled back his sleeve and looked at the gash in his arm. It could have been worse.

Rather than do all of the cleanup now because none of them were going anywhere, Gabe wheeled Dancer around to return to the train, reaching it five minutes later.

He stopped at the locomotive, dismounted, climbed aboard and saw the two bound men.

"Did you get 'em, Gabe?" asked Earl Nesbitt, the engineer.

"Yes, sir. They're all lying dead in the road down to the ford," Gabe replied as he took out his pocket knife and began cutting their ropes.

"That bastard broke the valve wheel off," Earl said as he rubbed his wrists.

"How long will it take you to fix it?"

"Oh, about twenty minutes or so. He didn't break the valve, so it's not too bad."

After he'd cut the fireman free, Gabe said, "I have to get this patched up back in Missoula, so what I'm going to do is to wrap it, then go back down and get their horses. I'll leave all of the saddlebags with their loot with the conductor, but I'll bring their horses back with me."

"You might want to check and see if there's a doctor on the train, Gabe. If he's there, he'll be in the first-class car."

"That's a good idea, Earl. I'll do that."

Gabe stepped back down and led Dancer past the coal car and then climbed the platform to the first-class car and opened the door.

Once inside, he said, "I'm Gabe Owens, a special agent for the railroad, the men that robbed you are all dead and lying in the road and your property will be returned to you shortly while the engineer fixes the damage to his locomotive. Is there a doctor in the car?"

No one answered, so Gabe began to turn when a woman's voice said, "I'm a midwife, so I can probably fix that wound."

Gabe turned back around and said, "I'd appreciate that, ma'am. I have a sewing kit in my saddlebag along with some grain alcohol just for such an occasion."

She stood and walked down the aisle and when she was near, she said, "Let's get this done, so you can get my brooch back."

Gabe smiled and said, "Yes, ma'am."

The repair job on Gabe's arm took less time than the one on the locomotive and when she finished, he asked, "What's your name, ma'am?"

"Becky Ahearn."

“Is that short for Rebecca?”

“No, it’s just Becky.”

“Well, thank you, Becky. I’ll go and get your brooch and the other things now.”

“And thank you for stopping them, Mister Owens. We all watched from the car and couldn’t believe you weren’t killed.”

“Neither do I, Becky,” he said as he tipped his hat, mounted Dancer and rode back toward the ford.

He made a trail rope and led all five horses back to the train ten minutes later, removed the saddlebags and the large canvas bag and gave them to the expressman and conductor.

Gabe had just mounted again when the whistle sounded, Earl waved from the locomotive and the train began to move. He waved to the passengers as they passed and found Becky Ahearn waving and gave her a grateful smile.

Soon the train was out of sight, so he led the five horses down the road to the five bodies, stripped them of their guns, and checked their pockets, only finding some loose cash. He thought about dumping their bodies into the Missoula River, but instead, rode up the long incline then rode into Clark’s Falls. He found a small general store, entered and arranged to have the five bodies buried somewhere. He then gave all of the gunbelt and Winchester laden horses to the proprietor as payment for the burial. Then he stopped at the privy-sized telegraph office and sent a message to Herb with the basics of the incident and that he’d be on his way back soon.

It was early afternoon when he started back on Dancer. He was wearing a new shirt and had enough food to last the trip, including the cold fried chicken he was eating as he rode out of town heading east.

He knew he wouldn't reach Missoula tonight, but would probably get there by midmorning tomorrow. He could have waited for the eastbound train, but wanted to spend the privacy he would only find on the ride.

After they'd been dismissed by the ladies and returned to the sawmill, Eli said he wanted to ride to the logging camp and talk to the men and let them know what was going to happen and asked Dave to join him, as he knew most of them. He wanted to inspect the camp as well, so he could figure out what improvements it needed.

But Dave told Eli that he wasn't well liked by some of the other crew leaders and he'd be a lot better off meeting with them himself. Eli thought he was probably right, so after saddling his horse, he rode off to the camp, leaving Dave in the office.

Dave had been frustrated because when they were in the house, having Eli and Sarah in the next room was stifling. Rebecca had refused his suggestion that they take another buggy ride too, but now with Eli gone, he could just have Sarah go off shopping or something for a while. He didn't care what the kids heard either, he just wanted to have unrestricted access to his wife.

Once he was sure that Eli was gone, he left the sawmill office and walked quickly to the house, passing the workers who were building the larger house nearby.

He entered the house, closed the door and saw Rebecca still talking to Sarah in the parlor.

"What are you doing home so soon, Dave?" Rebecca asked.

He didn't answer, but said, "Sarah, why don't you just go outside and watch the builders for a while or maybe take a buggy ride. I'd like some private time with Becky."

"No, Dave, I'll stay here. I need to talk to Rebecca," Sarah replied fully aware of what he wanted to do in his private time.

Dave glared at Sarah and said, "Now, listen, Sarah. Right now, I'm the man of the house 'cause Eli is off at the loggin' camp, and I'm tellin' you to just go outside and do whatever you want for a half an hour. I want to be alone with my wife, so you just haul your behind outside."

Sarah was mortified, then stood and said, "I beg your pardon? This is my house, and Aaron is closer to being the man of the house than you are. Now go back to the sawmill and leave us alone!"

Dave pointed at Sarah and snarled, "I'm warnin' you, Sarah. You'd better know your place. Now get out!"

Sarah then made the mistake of getting too close when she took two steps toward him and snapped, "No, Dave. You leave. Now."

Dave then brushed Sarah aside like the lightweight she was then she stumbled to her left, tripped over the center table and fell to the floor on the other side.

Aaron saw his mother hurt on the floor, jumped up and raced at Dave while Rachel began to cry and ran to her fallen mother. Dave stepped aside as Aaron flew at him, caught the boy with one big hand as he passed and just threw him into the far wall. Aaron slammed into the wall, fell to the ground and began to cry as Dave turned toward Rebecca and then stopped and stared at her with his eyes wide open.

"Don't you come near me, you bastard!" Rebecca shouted as she pointed her Webley at him.

"Put that damned pistol down, Becky. You're only makin' things worse."

"Get out right now, or I swear I'll shoot you, Dave!" she yelled as the muzzle of the pistol began to shake.

Dave laughed and said, "You ain't gonna shoot anybody, Becky. You're gonna drop that gun and we're gonna go into the bedroom and this time, it's gonna be like the buggy ride."

"No, I'm not going, Dave. I made a lot of mistakes over my life, and the worst was marrying you. Now get out of the house!"

Dave was far from calming down and he surely wasn't going to leave. His blood was boiling for more than one reason as he reached for the pistol, knowing it wasn't even cocked and he could see how nervous she was as the barrel danced in her hand. *Stupid woman.*

Rebecca saw his big hand trying to grab the Bulldog from her hand and took a step back, but it wasn't enough as his hand closed around the short barrel even as she was still moving backward. Her finger then tightened on the trigger, the hammer arced away and then snapped back. The firing pin slapped against the .44 rimfire cartridge and the powder inside ignited.

Dave was stunned as he saw the hammer start to move by itself, but even as it registered in his mind, the muzzle erupted in smoke and flame, and he felt the burn of the .44 leaving the pistol followed by the sudden pain as it sliced across the inside of his elbow and then the jolt as it slammed into the right side of his chest. After destroying two ribs, the bullet cut through his right lung's middle lobe, and then because he was twisted as he tried to take the pistol, the fast-moving projectile continued through his thoracic spine before exiting his body and punching into the far wall of the house.

Dave's eyes were wide with shock as the intense pain took him and he lost all feeling from the waist down, collapsed to the floor and felt his blood pooling under him before he coughed once then gurgled and died.

Rebecca stood frozen in place with the smoking revolver still in her hand, not believing what she had done. Sarah quickly got to her feet as Rachel clung to her mother's legs. Aaron was still sobbing as he lay against the far wall.

Sarah then reached over and slowly pried the gun away from Rebecca's hand and said, "Rebecca, are you all right?"

"I killed him, Sarah," she said softly as her eyes remained wide open just staring ahead.

"No, Rebecca, he killed himself. He grabbed the gun and pulled it. It just went off."

"But I killed him. I took out the gun."

Sarah was trying to get a handle on all this and knew it would be impossible with Rebecca in the same room with Dave's body. First, she set the pistol on the table, pulled Rachel into her arms then walked over to Aaron.

"Aaron, I need you to grow up really fast right now," she said as she bent over her son.

Aaron sniffed, sat up rubbed his eyes then stood and said, “Okay, Mama.”

Sarah pulled Rachel next to Aaron and said, “Take Rachel into the kitchen for a little while. You can each have a cookie. Okay?”

“Okay, Mama,” Aaron said as he walked with Rachel out of the parlor while his sister kept looking back at her mother.

Once they were out of the room, Sarah walked over to Rebecca, put her arm around her shoulders and said, “Let’s go outside, Rebecca.”

Rebecca nodded and let Sarah steer her around the body and out the front door. Once they reached the porch, Sarah closed the door and saw some of the construction workers looking at her, so she waved them over.

Two men approached, and Sarah said, “There’s been a terrible accident in the house. Could one of you please harness the black mare to the buggy and bring it around?”

“Yes, ma’am,” the taller of the two replied and jogged to the barn in back.

The second man asked, “Is there anything else I can do, ma’am?”

“No. But thank you for your help.”

He tipped his cap and said, “You’re welcome, ma’am,” then returned to the job.

The buggy arrived five minutes later, and the man stepped out and assisted Rebecca into the seat. Sarah then climbed in, took the reins and drove around to the back of the house.

Once there, she stopped then quickly exited the buggy and soon returned carrying Rachel with Aaron walking beside her.

Just eighteen minutes after Dave had died in the parlor, Sarah pulled the buggy up to the sheriff's office and stepped out, took Rachel and let Aaron climb out. She then let Aaron take control of Rachel before going to the other side and helping Rebecca out of the buggy.

Sarah led them all to the sheriff's office, opened the door and let Aaron enter first with Rachel then guided Rebecca inside.

Angela turned and was startled to see Rebecca almost statue-like as she was being led to the desk. She slipped off the desktop and stepped aside as Sarah then gently sat Rebecca in the chair before the desk.

Rafe Collier asked, "Mrs. Ulrich, how can I help you?"

"There's been a terrible accident at the house. Rebecca's husband is dead. He was threatening us and Rebecca pulled a pistol and told him to leave. He grabbed it and it went off."

Rafe stood and said, "Where is the gun now?"

"In the parlor with the body."

"Okay," he said, then turned to Angela and asked, "Can you stay here with Becky and the children, Angela? I'll go back with Mrs. Ulrich and take a look."

"Alright, Raphael. You go ahead," Angela replied.

Rafe grabbed his hat and Sarah said, "I have a buggy out front."

"Good. That will save us time."

They left the office and Angela looked at Rebecca who was still just looking ahead with her eyes wide open but apparently not seeing anything.

Angela wondered why Rebecca was so affected by what had happened because she had been there while Mike had been intentionally murdered, yet she hadn't fallen apart at all.

"Rebecca, this is Angela. What happened?"

Rebecca blinked turned her head slightly to look at Angela and said, "I killed him. I had the pistol in my hand, and I killed Dave."

"It was an accident, Rebecca. Sarah said so."

"I wanted to kill him. He hurt me almost as bad as Frank. I couldn't live my life that way."

"But you don't mean that, Rebecca. You didn't pull the gun and just shoot him. Sarah said he grabbed the pistol."

"It doesn't matter. Don't you understand? I wanted him dead. I probably hoped he would try and take it from me, so I could shoot him."

Angela slowly shook her head and said, "If he was hurting you, Rebecca, he deserved that bullet, just like my husband did."

Rebecca, her shock subsiding, said, "But you didn't kill your husband, did you, Angela? Bob did."

“It’s the same thing. I was there when he pulled the trigger. I could have stopped him, but I didn’t. I let him shoot Mike because he beat me too much.”

“I was married for a few days, but you were married much longer than that. How did you last so long?”

“Maybe it was because it wasn’t so bad. I saw what Frank did to you and I was horrified and that was only after one day. You said he hurt you almost as bad as Frank, and if Mike had been that bad, I wouldn’t have put up with it that long either.”

Rebecca looked at Angela and asked, “What’s wrong with us, Angela? Mike, Bob, Dave? Are they all like this?”

Angela then smiled and said, “You’re forgetting Gabe, Rebecca.”

“No, I’ll never forget Gabe. I love him too much to ever forget him. What I meant was it was if we were almost destined to make the same bad mistakes over and over again.”

“I made my first one when I married Mike and didn’t marry Gabe. Then I made a second one when I let Bob into my life, but now I have Raphael, and he’ll be good to me, Rebecca. You went off with Bob then married Dave. Gabe will come back for you.”

“It doesn’t matter now. They’re going to hang me for killing Dave.”

“No, they won’t, Rebecca. Raphael is a good man. You’ll be all right.”

Rebecca wasn't so sure, but said, "I hope so," even if she wasn't sure she wanted her to be right. She knew she was guilty of murder.

Rafe looked at the Dave's body as Sarah watched. He could see gunpowder burns, the path of the .44 as it nicked the elbow before entering his chest, and the angle of the exit wound showed that he was definitely turned when she fired. Everything backed Sarah's story.

He stood turned to her and said, "Mrs. Ulrich, everything I see here confirms what you told me. So, let's go back to the office and you can write your statement."

"Can Rebecca come home with me?"

"Not yet. I have to go and talk to the prosecutor, Mister Williams and then, after I get his okay, she can go home with you."

"Thank you, Sheriff," Sarah said with a feeling of relief as they left the house and boarded the buggy.

The mortician was removing Dave's body from the house as Rafe was sitting in Jerome Williams' office.

"It's a clear-cut case of self-defense, Mister Williams," Rafe said after the prosecutor finished reading Sarah's statement.

Jerome looked at Rafe and said, "I don't think anything of the sort, Deputy."

"I'm the sheriff now, Mister Williams. I looked at the body, and the evidence was clear that Mister Horowitz was trying to take the pistol from his wife's hand, and it went off accidentally."

"Accidentally? How do you know that? Besides, what was she doing with a .44 anyway? I know you've been seeing Angela Wheatley and there was another case that caused me some grave concerns. No, Sheriff, I believe this is far from an open and shut case of self-defense. Do you have the murder weapon?"

Rafe couldn't believe what he was hearing, but nodded then took the pistol from a cloth bag and set it on his desk. It was in the shoulder holster that he'd taken from Rebecca.

"A shoulder holster? This woman shoots her husband with a .44 she had concealed in a shoulder holster and you expect me to believe she wasn't planning on killing him?"

"Yes, sir, I expect you to believe it because I do."

"Then perhaps you shouldn't be the sheriff, Mister Collier. You seem to be too easily swayed by sultry eyes and soft curves. I'm going to charge Mrs. Horowitz with second degree murder."

Rafe stared disbelievingly at the prosecutor until Mister Williams said, "You're dismissed, Deputy."

Rafe didn't argue but stood, turned and left this office, intentionally leaving the door open.

Five minutes later, he walked into the jail and saw five sets of eyes all looking at him, expecting him to say that Rebecca could go home.

He removed his hat swallowed then looked at Rebecca and said, “I’m sorry, Mrs. Horowitz, but the prosecutor is going to charge you with second-degree murder. I’m going to have to put you in a cell.”

Sarah and Angela both leapt to their feet and Sarah was the first to shout, “*What?*”

Rafe threw up his hands and said, “I’m sorry. I argued with him, but he seemed determined to prosecute,” then he turned to Angela and said, “He even mentioned that we’re seeing each other and said he had problems believing the facts in your case, too. I have no idea why he’s so insistent about prosecuting.”

After Rafe had gone, Jerome Williams looked at the pistol and shoulder holster.

“Women,” he murmured, “they think they can get away with murder. That blonde bitch did, but not this one. No sir, not this one.”

He reread Sarah’s statement, snorted and tossed in onto his desk. They murdered and then they lied for each other just like his brother’s wife had. She claimed he was going to kill her, and she stabbed him with his own knife. Bitch.

Eli rode back to the house in a great mood. The men were practically jumping up and down before he left. He told them to take the next few days off and be ready to start work on Monday. None of them would lose a penny in salary and he’d be making the logging camp more livable, give them better equipment, and they’d no longer be stripping the forest.

He passed his sawmill and began to run through improvements in that operation too, then smiled when he saw the new house going up. The workers were making good progress. It was a lot bigger than he had thought necessary, but with Gabe's largesse, it really didn't matter. He just wanted Rebecca to be happy.

He rode his horse into the barn, stepped down and began to unsaddle the gelding when he caught sight of Sarah trotting his way after leaving the house. He smiled then the corners of his mouth began to sag as he saw her face.

"What's wrong, Sarah?"

Gabe pulled up for the night about sixteen miles short of Missoula. He could have ridden through, but he knew that Dancer was getting tired and he wasn't doing so well, either.

He dismounted and unsaddled his Morgan friend, led him to the stream to quench his thirst then let him graze while he made his cold camp.

After cleaning his Winchester, he took a look at his arm. His freshly sewn gunshot wound was swollen and deep red, but it could have been much worse. Two train robberies in the same month and both wound up with five dead outlaws.

When he got back to Minneapolis, he'd have to ask Herb why Stan had gone bad in the first place. Maybe he'd gone bad before he had disappeared but had been operating on the inside. It wouldn't have been the first time. Early in his career as a special agent, he'd been approached twice by outlaws offering him some quick money for his help, but it didn't take long for the word to get around that he couldn't be bought. He wondered if there was a criminal telegraph system to pass along information to other outlaws.

The idea made him laugh out loud.

“Don’t touch that black wire, mister. That’s the Outlaw Western Union line.”

He amused himself with a few more witticisms about the concept before he got tired of the jokes.

As he lay on his bedroll just looking at the half moon, he hoped that August would be better than July had been. The most men he’d ever shot in a gunfight before this month was two, and he’d killed sixteen men in July then he had to do a count again, thinking he’d missed some.

There were the five in the Dakota Gang shootout, the two in Angela’s house, the four near the logging road, the sheriff, then the five today. He was off by one. Then he realized he’d forgotten the two that had caused most of them, Bob Johnson and Frank Stanford. Make that nineteen. *Good God*! He’d killed nineteen men and all he had to show for it was a .44 in his belt buckle and his arm wound that would be just a scar in a few weeks. Maybe he had Gabriel as a guardian angel because the odds surely hadn’t been on his side.

He kept thinking about anything but Rebecca. He had to. But as he had told her when she had threatened him if he called her Becky, once you tell yourself not to do something, you are almost guaranteed to do it. He smiled and let the good memories of Rebecca take him into a deep slumber.

———

Rebecca was lying on her cot in the cell. No one was in the jail with her. Her father had come by to see her, and she had tried not to cry, but the thought that she might hang or go to prison for years made her break down when she saw him. He tried to tell her that he'd make sure that it never happened, but she felt a sense of doom hanging over her. She'd earned all the bad things that were happening to her. She made one bad decision after another and hurt everyone around her. She didn't regret shooting Dave because not only was he going to hurt her, he had hurt Sarah and Aaron too, but she regretted everything else. Everything except for Gabe.

She had her eyes closed and let those last few seconds with him on the porch fill her mind. When he had looked into her eyes and told her that he was going to be celibate for the rest of his life, she knew that it wasn't some silly promise. It was his way of telling her that he loved her and would never love another. She wished she could feel guilty about that, but it was the only thing she had now and knew she didn't even deserve that. Besides, it didn't matter how she felt. Even if she wasn't found guilty by a jury, she'd found herself guilty already, and that was a bigger condemnation.

Nonetheless, with that one memory dominating her thoughts, she slowly drifted off to sleep.

CHAPTER 9

Gabe didn't bother waking early the next morning because he was in no rush to get to Missoula. When he got there, he'd go to the sheriff's office, tell Rafe what had happened, write his report and then get the next train back to Minneapolis.

But as he was saddling Dancer, he wondered if he'd been too hasty in turning down the job offer. When he'd found it difficult to calculate how many men he'd killed in July, he thought that maybe it was time to get out of the business of running around and trying to stop bad guys. He had a house in Minneapolis, his parents lived a few hours away in Brainard, and he wouldn't have to spend all that time on trains and horseback. He then recalled his thoughts after he'd taken his first gunshot and had doubts about his immortality.

Once he took the road heading east, he began to seriously think about taking the job assuming it would still be available and could telegraph Herb from Missoula. At least he could be sure of the accuracy of the message that the man behind the keys tapped out. He thought the man was ready to let his bladder go when he'd warned him.

He wasn't in a bad frame of mind as he had Dancer moving at a medium trot into the bright sun as he dropped his head down so the brim of his hat would block the sun's rays and reminded himself to buy a new hat when he got to Missoula.

When the first buildings in Missoula appeared after the trees cleared his vision, Gabe checked his watch and found it was only 9:20 and debated about going to the sheriff's office first or having a big breakfast. If it had been 8:20, it would have been no contest, but he decided it was too late for breakfast and he'd go and talk to Rafe and then have lunch.

So, after passing the sawmill, he turned toward Missoula, saw the construction workers already putting up the roof and was amazed at the progress they had made. He didn't think he'd been gone that long.

He reached the cobblestones and pulled Dancer to a stop in front of the sheriff's office, tied him off and bounced onto the boardwalk and opened the door. He took one step inside and stopped cold when he saw Rafe at the desk, but what had frozen him in place was seeing Rebecca behind him in the cell.

Rafe stood quickly and said, "Gabe! Thank God you're here!"

Rebecca was already standing and couldn't find her voice as her heart was pounding and her breathing was fast and shallow. She was ecstatic, ashamed, guilty and frightened all at once.

"What the hell is Rebecca doing behind bars, Rafe?" he all but shouted as he closed the door loudly behind him.

Rebecca just stared at him as Rafe replied, "She shot and killed her husband when he was threatening her. I told the prosecutor it was a clear case of self-defense, but he didn't see it that way. He's charging her with second-degree murder."

He handed Gabe Sarah's statement, which Gabe read quickly before handing it back, stalked to the cell and managed to refrain from his urge to rip the bars down then said, “It'll be all right, Rebecca. I promise.”

Rebecca was lost in her jumble of emotions and just nodded.

Gabe smiled at her before he said, “I'll go and talk to the prosecutor right now,” then stepped back and added, “I'll be back in a few minutes.”

Rafe had heard what he'd told Rebecca and said, “Gabe, I don't think that it's too wise for you to go and see him. He's hell bent on prosecution. Becky's father said he'd get the best lawyer in the territory.”

Gabe replied, “She's not going to need a lawyer, Rafe, and her name is Rebecca.”

He then turned and left the jail, closing the door much more civilly than he had when he'd entered.

After he'd gone, Rafe stared at the closed door and said, “I hope he doesn't shoot Jerome Williams.”

Gabe entered the county office building and found the office of the county prosecutor on the directory: County Prosecutor Jerome Williams, room 121.

He walked down the hallway on the left, found room 121, entered the outer office and met the gaze of Mister Williams' clerk, Tom Anderson.

“May I help you?”

“I’m going to see the prosecutor,” Gabe said as he headed for the door.

“Wait! I’ll check and see if he can see you,” Tom said.

“I didn’t ask,” Gabe said as he opened the door walked into the room and closed the door behind him.

“Who do you think you are, barging in like this?” Jerome asked as he stood behind his desk.

Gabe sat down and said, “My name is Gabe Owens.”

The prosecutor’s demeanor shifted rapidly as he took his seat and said, “So, you’re the man who killed the sheriff. I always thought he was crooked.”

“He was, and he paid the price for it.”

“Is that why you’re here? About the sheriff?”

“No, it’s about your decision to prosecute Rebecca Ulrich. Now, I’ve investigated a lot of crimes, Mister Williams. I figured out that it was Bob Johnson who had murdered Mike Wheatley even after your sheriff threw lies and false clues at me to cover it up.”

“So, what’s your point, Mister Owens?” the prosecutor asked.

“My point, Mister Williams, is that you have decided to prosecute an innocent woman for second-degree murder and that doesn’t set well with me.”

“Are you threatening me, Mister Owens?”

“No, I’m not. I’m telling you to open your eyes and look at the evidence. Rebecca didn’t murder that bastard husband of hers. I read the statement of the only adult witness. Dave Horowitz had thrown Sarah Ulrich across a table and then tossed a seven-year-old boy across the room into a wall. Rebecca was not only terrified for her life, but her family's as well."

"She had drawn a pistol, Mister Owens. Not just a derringer, mind you. She had drawn a .44 caliber death-dealing pistol and had every intention of using it."

"How do you know what her intention was? Were you there? Did you witness it? If it was her intention, why would she wait until he reached for the pistol? Why not shoot him after he'd tossed her stepmother across the room?"

"I didn't have to be there, and I resent your insinuation that I'm not competent enough to understand the facts of the case. It's you who don't understand, Mister Owens."

"That pistol wouldn't have gone off if the idiot didn't try and grab it from her hand. All he had to do was leave the house and he'd still be alive to beat her later."

"Oh, is that it? You think all husbands are wife-beaters and deserve to be shot?"

"No, I don't. But I know that Mike Wheatley beat his wife and deserved it. By the way, he wasn't shot with a death-dealing .44, but with a derringer from ten feet."

"I don't care if he beat her every night! No woman can shoot her husband and get away with it again. Not like Angela Wheatley and not like my brother's wife! Never!"

Gabe raised his eyebrows before he said, "So, that's what this is all about, isn't it? You don't even care if Rebecca is innocent or not. You're prosecuting your sister-in-law, not Rebecca."

"No, I'm prosecuting Mrs. Horowitz, and you can't do anything to stop it. It's my decision not yours."

"Well, then, Mister Prosecuting Attorney, I guess you're going to have to charge me with accessory to murder."

"*What?*" he exclaimed.

"You are going to have to charge me with accessory to murder, because I supplied Mrs. Horowitz with that pistol."

"You're just saying that, but even if you aren't, don't tempt me."

Gabe opened his jacket and showed the prosecutor his Webley.

"I had two Bulldogs and gave one, complete with a shoulder harness to Rebecca as protection when she was afraid of Bob Johnson or Frank Stanford arriving to kill her while I was out doing my investigations. Does it look familiar?"

"You're giving me little choice but to charge you as well."

"You go right ahead, Mister Williams. You charge me with accessory to murder and I'll just wire the governor of the territory and let him know what you're doing. You see, Jerome, if you don't mind me calling you by your Christian name, I'm rather a famous sort, although I don't like to brag.

"But with that fame comes a certain level of access to powerful people. Political people. People who like to keep the railroad on their side. Now correct me if I'm wrong, but isn't your job an elected position and this is 1884, so there's an election coming up in a few months, isn't there? How much are you willing to sacrifice to satisfy your personal crusade, Jerome? Your job? Your reputation? All of it will be gone if you insist on trying to prosecute Rebecca.

"Now just for a minute, set aside your frustration and anger and just look at the cold facts of the case. If you'll do that, Mister Williams, you'll drop the charges against Mrs. Horowitz."

Jerome was still unhappy with the thought of letting another murdering woman walk, but it wasn't Owens' suggestion that he examine the evidence, or even his demand that he charge him with accessory to murder that made him change his mind. It was the very real threat that he'd made about losing the election and his job. The thought of being a regular attorney instead of the feared and powerful county prosecutor was unacceptable.

Without saying a word, he pulled a sheet of paper out of his desk, picked up a pen, dipped it into his inkwell and wrote note to Sheriff Collier that charges against Rebecca Horowitz had been dropped.

He blew on the paper and slid it across the desk.

Gabe read the order stood then said, "May I have my pistol back?"

Wordlessly, Jerome opened his bottom drawer took out the shoulder holster and Webley and just tossed it onto his desktop.

Gabe didn't gloat because it served no purpose. He just picked up the pistol, hung it over his shoulder then with the order in his left hand he opened the door walked past the clerk and out the office door.

He stepped out onto the boardwalk, took a deep breath, smiled then turned right and headed for the sheriff's office.

When he took the corner, he spotted a familiar buggy parked in front of the jail and guessed that Eli and Sarah were inside, which meant that Aaron and Rachel were there as well, too. He reached Dancer then opened a saddlebag, dropped the Webley inside and headed for the sheriff's office.

When he opened the door, in addition to the expected Ulrich clan, he found Angela sitting on the desk. Everyone looked at him as he walked to the desk and handed the paper to Rafe.

"Sheriff, I believe you have a prisoner who needs to be released."

Rafe couldn't believe what he was reading but broke into a big grin, stood and said, "Rebecca, you are free to go. There are no charges pending."

Gabe hadn't even noticed that the door was open but soon saw Rebecca trot out of the cell and rush to Sarah and hug her.

Eli walked over to Gabe and asked, "How did you do that, Gabe?"

"I'll tell you all when we get back to your house, Eli. But I've got to stay and talk to the sheriff for a little while."

"Why?"

"I have to make a report to the sheriff about an attempted train robbery near Clark's Falls."

Rafe heard Gabe's answer to Eli and asked, "Gabe, what happened?"

"I was sent by the NP to find a gang that was robbing trains in Oregon, but they moved east, and I caught up with them outside of Clark's Falls. I got all five of them almost exactly where I caught up with Bob Johnson and Frank Stanford. I'll write a statement for you tomorrow, but all of the bodies were handled by the good folks in town."

"*Five more?*" he asked.

"I know. It's wearing me down, so if it's all right with you, I'm going to return with everyone to the house and spend some time explaining things to them. I'll stop by in the morning and spend some time with you."

"Okay, Gabe. I can live with that."

Gabe grinned and said, "You don't have any choice, Raphael. I own you."

Rafe knew exactly what he meant when he glanced at Angela then said, "I know."

Gabe turned to look at Rebecca, but she was still talking to Sarah who seemed to be arguing with her in a low voice that he couldn't hear.

When they finally stopped talking, Gabe expected to see a relieved and cheerful Rebecca but if anything, she was more subdued when he'd gone to visit the prosecutor. Not only that, she didn't even look in his direction which was much more of a surprise. She seemed to trying to avoid even looking at him.

Sarah plucked Rachel from the floor as Eli opened the door and the Ulrich family plus one left the jail.

Once they were all on the boardwalk, Eli said, “We hadn’t planned on bringing Rebecca home, so the buggy might be too crowded.”

Gabe was about to offer to make a bedroll pillow for Rebecca when she said, “Papa, it’s alright. I’ll just walk home. I need time to think.”

“Alright,” Eli replied believing that she and Gabe needed to talk.

Eli smiled at his daughter turned and helped Sarah into the buggy then handed her Rachel while Aaron jumped inside. After he boarded, he took the reins and the buggy rolled away. After it reached the next intersection, he took a right turn heading west and the buggy soon disappeared.

Gabe walked to Dancer untied his reins then looked at Rebecca who had already turned and begun walking following the path of the buggy. Her arms were folded as she walked along the center of the boardwalk meaning that Gabe couldn’t get closer than four feet as he led Dancer alongside even if he walked with her.

Despite her obvious preference that she be left alone, Gabe had to know why she had suddenly seemed almost afraid of him.

He used his long strides to catch up to her and soon was as close as he could get as he had to stay in the street with Dancer.

“What’s wrong, Rebecca? I thought you’d be happy to be out of jail, but you seem to be avoiding me as if I had consumption or something,” he asked after he’d caught up to her.

She kept her eyes ahead as she said, “Thank you, but I think that I should be alone now.”

“For how long?”

“Forever.”

They continued to walk until they turned at the intersection.

Gabe then asked, “Why?”

She didn’t look at him as she said, “It’s not important. You should leave.”

“Is that what you really want, Rebecca?”

“Just go.”

Gabe knew there was no chance of talking her out of her deep pit of self-pity, so he decided on a different approach.

“Okay, Rebecca,” he said then turned, stepped up on Dancer wheeled him back east and trotted away.

Rebecca turned suddenly just in time to see Dancer’s black tail disappear around the corner. What she had said and what she wanted were totally different, and she expected him to at least argue with her. She wasn’t going to change her mind but still, his sudden departure rattled her.

She stood watching the corner, hoping she would soon see Dancer’s face, but after a full minute, she knew he wasn’t coming back then slowly turned west again and let her tears begin to slide across her face as she began to walk the mile to her house. For once, she knew she was making the right decision and it was breaking her heart.

Other pedestrians glanced at her as she walked by, but none said a word as she stepped slowly along, passing the shops and storefronts.

She reached the next intersection and almost stepped off into the path of a freight wagon because of her blurred vision, then hopped back to safety standing near Choquette's Drug Store. The wagon passed and she took a deep breath, put her foot forward when she heard a familiar voice close to her right side.

"That's a long walk, Rebecca. Can I give you a ride?"

She quickly brushed her tears away and turned to see Gabe smiling at her just four feet away.

Gabe held out his hand as she looked at him then said a rushed, "No," turned and hurriedly crossed the street, leaving Gabe standing there like a mannequin.

He had to trot back the twenty feet to retrieve Dancer then once he had the reins in his hand, he jogged after her as she scurried down the boardwalk heading for the family home.

By the time he reached her, she was almost at the next intersection and when he finally was close enough to talk, she had to slow down for traffic.

"What is going on, Rebecca? Won't you even talk to me? Haven't I even earned an answer?"

Rebecca stepped down onto the last of the cobblestoned streets and Gabe thought she was about to say something when her mouth opened then it snapped close again as she picked up her skirts and walked faster.

Gabe kept up the pace and said, “Rebecca, the eastbound train will be arriving in an hour and a half. Do you really want me to get on that train?”

She walked for another hundred feet, keeping her face looking west before finally giving him her soul-crushing answer.

“Yes.”

Gabe just slowed then stopped as he watched Rebecca continue rushing along the boardwalk. She stepped off the end of the boardwalk thirty seconds later and began walking quickly along the dirt street. He could see the Ulrich home another three hundred yards away and simply couldn’t come up with any way to stop her short of shooting her.

For some reason, she’d slipped into a morose almost indifferent mood and he didn’t have a clue why she was suddenly trying to get rid of him.

He mounted Dancer and stayed in the saddle, watching Rebecca as she distanced herself from him. From almost the moment she had walked out of the jail cell, she had been trying to ignore him. *Was it because she felt she should be punished for killing Dave?*

He sat on Dancer for almost five minutes until he watched Rebecca disappear into the house. He thought about going into the house and forcing the issue but believed it would probably cause a scene with Eli and Sarah, and didn’t want to put them in that position.

So, once she was in the house, he turned Dancer around and headed for the sheriff’s office to do his report. When he arrived, Rafe was locking the door as he and Angela were obviously going to an early lunch.

"I decided to write the report now while it was fresh in my mind."

Rafe just tossed him the keys and said, "Just leave the keys in the desk. Nobody will break in over the next hour."

Neither asked why he was back so soon, which was good because he had no way of explaining Rebecca to them or himself for that matter.

He unlocked the door went inside and was soon writing his statement. He finished it just ten minutes later because he didn't dwell on the details like his gunshot wound. He left his statement on the desk then opened the desk drawer and dropped in the keys.

After mounting Dancer, he set him to a slow trot and turned toward the train station. He took a slight detour toward the Ulrich home in case Rebecca had changed her mind but was almost certain she wouldn't. He remembered thinking how complex she was and had hoped to be able to solve the mystery of Rebecca but knew he'd never have the chance now and maybe the complexity of Rebecca was beyond solution.

When he arrived at the station, he dismounted next to the Western Union office and sent his telegram to Herb telling him about the demise of the Stan Harriman gang and he'd changed his mind about the job, and he'd take if it was still available.

He pulled out his pocket watch saw that the eastbound train should be arriving in another forty minutes then after dropping it back into his pocket, he returned to Dancer and led him to the stock corral.

“Howdy, Gabe,” Jim Clover asked when he approached, “You leavin’?”

“Yes, sir. I’ll be heading back to Minneapolis,” he replied as he opened the gate and led Dancer inside.

Jim pulled a tag out of his jacket pocket and scribbled Dancer’s destination on it with a stubby pencil then tied it onto his bridle as Gabe removed his saddlebags.

“I hear you had another gunfight out at Clark’s Falls.”

“Hopefully my last. It’s getting so I can’t even keep track of them anymore.”

Jim noticed Gabe’s glum expression and said, “Well, don’t let it get to ya. You did a good job, Gabe.”

Gabe nodded as he handed the reins to Jim, tipped his hat and headed for the station manager’s office then changed his mind and walked to one of the benches on the platform and sat down, setting his saddlebags on the wooden platform.

After a few minutes, he suddenly remembered he’d never gotten all of Rebecca’s clothes out of Bob Johnsons’ house and thought maybe he could use that as an excuse to try and talk to her again but the finality of her last response put the stop to that idea.

For the next half an hour, he’d glance west, hoping to see a buggy heading this way but saw nothing until he spotted a black cloud on the horizon then heard the lonely steam whistle as the locomotive made its first announcement of its pending arrival.

He stood picked up his saddlebags and hung them over his left shoulder as he walked to the opposite edge of the platform and looked down the tracks as the eastbound train rounded the distant curve.

Five minutes later, the locomotive rolled past, hissing and clanging its bell as if no one knew it was there. Normally, he'd wait for the disembarking passengers to get off the train but this time as soon as the first-class passenger car had slowed to a walk, he leapt onto the steel platform and stepped up then opened the door and entered. There were eight passengers and two were already getting out of their seats, probably to use the rest facilities while the train took on water and coal.

He swung into the second row and took a seat then dropped his saddlebags on the floor in front of him. As he sat with his right shoulder against the window, he looked out at the large forests that began less than fifty yards on the other side of the rails and imagined the men already cutting the trees on Eli's newly authorized sections. At least that part of the job had worked out.

He then bent over opened the saddlebags and took out his spare Webley, the one Rebecca had used to shoot Dave. He really should clean the gun but decided it could wait. But he rotated the cylinder and removed the spent brass from the killing shot and held it in his hand as he returned the Webley to the saddlebag.

Gabe rolled the innocuous brass cylinder between his thumb and index finger, examining the metal and knowing what damage it had done to Rebecca. He assumed it was her guilt for killing him that had made her send him away and knew that she had done nothing wrong, but what he believed didn't matter. He had never heard the full story just what he'd read in Sarah's statement.

The train suddenly lurched forward breaking him out of his reverie and he turned to look down the aisle not really expecting to see Rebecca so when he didn't, his mood shouldn't have changed but it did. There was a crushing finality to seeing the open, carpeted aisle.

He turned forward again with the empty brass still in his hand. He closed his hand with the cartridge inside finally removed his old, soon-to-be-replaced hat and closed his eyes. All of his investigative skills were then focused on what could have possibly happened between the meaningful parting before he took the westbound train to find Stan's gang and his return to Missoula.

He knew that she wasn't happy about marrying Dave Horowitz, and he could understand why. *But why had she married him in the first place?* Gabe was pretty sure he was Jewish, which would have explained Eli giving him his blessing to marry Rebecca, so that was probably it. *Was that why she had to send him away? Was it because he was a Gentile?*

He just hadn't seen that in Eli, but he could understand why that might be a possible reason. He didn't doubt that she loved him as much as he loved her, but something was making her push him away.

The train was up to speed as it headed for the new trestle bridge, and Gabe was still running through any other reasons for her behavior. If she'd been just ashamed of what she had been doing for the past year with Bob Johnson, she wouldn't have married Dave Horowitz. *Would she?*

He returned to the complexity of Rebecca. He'd only really spent that one full day with her when she made that remarkable change. It was that new Rebecca, the one who could talk to him about anything, who had captured his heart. Since he'd returned from Minneapolis, she had almost assumed another personality. *What had driven her back into a shell?*

She wasn't angry or hateful again, but despondent and hopeless. He wasn't sure if he, or anyone else could free her from this personal prison, especially if she wouldn't talk to him. All he could hope was that Sarah would be able to help her.

The train crossed the new trestle bridge and forty-five minutes later the train began slowing as it rolled into Helena.

Gabe had made no more progress in the Rebecca question and decided he'd go and have something to eat while he could as the train would be there for forty minutes as it was serviced, and a new crew boarded.

He picked up his saddlebags joined the queue of passengers who were taking advantage of the long stopover and soon exited the car. He stepped out onto the platform and quickly began walking. He wasn't going to use the hotel restaurant which would be packed with diners, but there was a nice café just around the corner which should be less crowded.

He had almost turned the corner onto the boardwalk, when he glanced back at the train and froze as he looked at the tall, black-haired young woman standing on the platform with a travel bag in her hand.

Rebecca was just looking at him fifty feet away and he could see how fast she was breathing as her eyes held him in place.

Gabe turned and began slowly walking back across the platform until he was close to her and could see the worry in her eyes as if she expected him to slap her or something even worse.

Gabe removed his saddlebags dropped them to the wooden surface then took one more step toward Rebecca and put his arms around her and just held her. She didn't say anything, but he heard her travel bag hit the platform before her arms wrapped around him and he felt her beginning to shake.

He put his hand on top of her head again and said, "I was going to get something to eat. Would you care to join me, Rebecca?"

He felt her nod under his hand so he stepped back, picked up his saddlebags and after hanging them over his shoulder, he snatched her travel bag from the platform then with his free hand took Rebecca's hand and they began to walk to the café.

Neither spoke as Rebecca took out a handkerchief and dabbed at her eyes but Gabe could feel that her hand was no longer shaking.

They turned onto the boardwalk and five minutes later were sitting at a table. Gabe ordered two specials, baked chicken with gravy and mashed potatoes, because it was fast. The café, like the hotel restaurant, had the train schedule posted and prepared for the rush that would arrive soon after the train pulled in.

After Rebecca had poured some cream into her coffee, she finally was able to look at Gabe.

"Is there someplace we can go, so I can talk to you in private?"

"I'll kick the brakeman out of the caboose, and we can talk on the train. Is that alright?"

She nodded then said, "I have so much to explain, don't I?"

"Yes, you do, but can you tell me how you got on the train without me seeing you? I was watching until I got on board."

The waitress brought them their chicken then left before Rebecca said, "Sarah drove me to the station, and I bought my ticket with some of the money my father gave me. I just got on the train and it left five minutes later. I didn't know if you were even on the train until I saw a man loading Dancer onto the stock car as we pulled up to the station."

Gabe had been wolfing down his food as he'd listened to her answer then said, "You must have arrived when I was already on board. What made you change your mind?"

Rebecca was chewing some chicken then swallowed and replied, "Sarah."

Gabe then just nodded and knew there would be plenty of time to talk on the long train ride. He'd hoped that he would finally make some headway in his understanding of the mystery named Rebecca.

Thirty minutes later after Orville Piedmont generously allowed the heavily armed special agent to take over the caboose, Gabe sat on one of the bunks with Rebecca sitting on the opposite bunk. He'd removed his hat and his guns as he looked at her still deeply concerned face.

"So," he asked, "Sarah told you to come after me?"

She nodded and said, "When I returned without you, she asked where you were, and I told her you were catching your train. One thing led to another, and she finally said that of all the mistakes I'd made in my life this one was the worst. My father agreed with her, but I said I couldn't go anyway. My father then told me that if I didn't, he'd put me to work at the logging camp."

Gabe was honestly shocked Eli could say anything like that, and asked, "He was going to turn you into a working girl?"

"No, I don't think so. He just wanted to let me know how mad he was, but I suppose he knew that was how I saw myself anyway. It was Sarah who finally convinced me to leave, but I was still afraid. I didn't want you to hate me."

"Why would I hate you, Rebecca? Is it because you married Dave?"

"No. I married him because I had no choice."

"Because he was Jewish?"

"No. That was why my father had given him his blessing two years ago, but not why I married him. I had to, because…because he knew about me and said he would tell my father."

"Rebecca, your father knew what had happened at the logging camp and there was nothing that Dave could have told him that should have forced you to marry him."

Rebecca dropped her eyes to caboose's floor and said, "No, he didn't know. Neither did Sarah. I can't tell them because they would revile me which is what I deserved, and I couldn't bear it after having just returned to them."

"What could be so horrible, Rebecca?" Gabe asked quietly, "Are you going to tell me, or are you too afraid?"

“That’s why I came. I made up my mind that I have to take the chance, or I’d regret it for the rest of my life. I’ll understand if you put me on the next train back to Missoula.”

Gabe stood then stood and turned then sat next to Rebecca and put his arm over her shoulder. She didn’t react but kept her hands on her lap as she continued to stare at the floor while the caboose rocked.

For almost three minutes, Rebecca remained silent, reticent to disclose her shameful secret she had tried to push into the dark corners of her mind.

Finally, she began wringing her hands, saying in a low voice, “After I’d been with Bob for three months, I missed my monthly and suspected I might be pregnant, but I’d missed them before, so I wasn’t that worried. Then when I missed my second, I thought it was true but still held back the news because he was already showing his bad side.

”Finally, I told him when he noticed my breasts were larger. Even though he hadn’t treated me well, I thought he might treat me better after I told him I was having his child. But instead, he began to treat me much more roughly when he took me. When my tummy began to swell, he acted as if I was disgusting, went into Missoula and found Angela and then…”

Rebecca paused, and Gabe could feel her beginning to shiver as he saw her first tears drop to the dusty floorboards.

“…and then, then he sent one of the camp whores who said she knew what to do about my condition. I knew what she was going to do, and I didn’t stop her. I…I…I let her kill my baby!” she finally blurted out and began to seriously weep.

"I…I didn't run or even fight after I knew what she was going to do. I let her kill my baby! *What kind of monster am I?*" she shouted as her balled up fists pounded her knees.

Gabe didn't say anything because he didn't think she was finished but just held her close. He couldn't imagine how terrible that loss must have been. He knew many women lost their children and had a difficult time recovering, but this had to be much, much worse. As much as she blamed herself, Gabe blamed Bob Johnson even more and wished he hadn't been so kind to him when he killed him.

She didn't continue for almost a minute, probably waiting for his revulsion and condemnation, but when she felt his arm still holding onto her, she began again in a quivering voice.

"Then just four days later, Bob was on top of me again. It hurt so much, but he didn't care. I was even more afraid of getting pregnant again than the pain then he began seeing Angela more, so I became more of a maid and cook than a bedmate. I hated him and everyone even more after that, but I saved most of my hate for myself because I deserved it."

When she paused for a few seconds, Gabe asked softly, "Rebecca, if you had fought what the woman was doing to you, and even tried to run to save your baby, what would have happened? Do you think Bob would just watch you run away?"

Rebecca had been so deep into her guilt for allowing it to happen that she had never even given a thought to the alternatives.

She thought about what Gabe had said for a while, but still wasn't finished as she wanted to complete her confession.

"When Angela came to the camp, and as bad as I thought things were, I became even more terrified about being given to

Frank, because I know what an animal he was. When he dragged me to his house, he proved to me that he was even worse than I expected."

She took in a deep breath and Gabe felt her shuddering subside.

"Then you came and took me away from there. You changed me, Gabe. You made me feel human again. For that one incredible day, I forgot about what had happened to me in that camp and what I had done. I felt myself falling in love with you but knew it couldn't happen.

"Then you left, and Dave arrived and told me he knew what I had done, and he'd tell my father and Sarah unless I married him. I was thrust right back into the life I had before, even though I was now home with my father, Sarah and the children. I was convinced that this was what I deserved for letting them kill my baby. Dave was almost as bad as Frank, and I thought it was the life that I was meant for being so hateful for so long.

"But then when I saw Dave hurt Sarah and then Aaron, I knew I had to stop him and pulled the gun. I wanted to shoot him, Gabe. I saw Bob in his face when I held that pistol pointed at him. Bob gave me my baby and then took it away. I wanted him dead!"

Gabe then said quietly, "But you didn't, Rebecca. He killed himself with his own ignorance. He wouldn't have grabbed that pistol if the hammer was back, but he didn't know it would go off if he tried to pull it out of your hand anyway. He murdered himself."

"It doesn't matter how he died. I wanted to kill him, and I had let my baby die. Why don't you see that? Why aren't you disgusted with me as much as I am?"

Gabe didn't reply but put his fingers on her chin and tilted it up and turned her face toward him. He kissed her softly on her lips and then kissed her wet but still discolored cheek.

"You're hurt much more inside than those bruises you have all over your body, Rebecca. If it takes the rest of my life, I'll make those hurts go away."

Tears were still dripping from her face as she asked, "But why?"

"You know why, Rebecca. I told you before, but not in so many words. I love you."

Hearing him tell her that he loved her sent her into an emotional train wreck that rivaled the one that had demolished the Blackfoot River bridge. Rebecca shook, cried from relief and joy, but more from the catharsis of telling the one horrible secret that she had kept bottled inside. Part of her wanted so much to believe that it was all in her past now, but there was that other part; the shame and the guilt that was still tugging at her heart.

When she was able to talk again, she asked, "Gabe, could we lie down?"

Gabe didn't reply but stood and let Rebecca lay down on the bunk before he laid down next to her. He slid his arm under her shoulder and she rolled against his side until her head was on his shoulder and her left arm was holding onto his chest while his right arm held her close and her left knee was bent on his thigh.

"Gabe, is there anything that you can tell me to make my demons go away? Can you talk to me like you did that first day and drove away my hate and anger? Could you do that for me now?"

Gabe kissed the top of her hair and said, “No, Rebecca. I don’t think there are any words that can make them disappear. Time will make them less sharp and then I’ll do as much as I can to keep them as far away as I can by making you happy. Whenever you start to feel them creeping back, then talk to me and we’ll push them away.”

“Do you think I’ll ever be a happy person, Gabe?” she asked quietly.

“Yes, I do. We’ll get married, you’ll have our babies and be the happy woman that I saw for those wonderful hours we spent together in Angela’s house.”

Gabe was surprised when she began to cry again, so he asked, “What did I say to get you upset? Don’t you want to get married?”

She whispered, “I want that more than anything I’ve ever wanted in my life, but what if I’m pregnant already? Three different men have taken me in the last two weeks. What if I’m pregnant by one of them? I won’t know for another week.”

Gabe looked down into her eyes and said, “Then, Miss Ulrich, the best solution would be for you to end my celibate ways, so if you are pregnant, there will be just as much chance that it will be our baby.”

Rebecca asked, “You’d be willing to do that?”

Gabe didn’t reply, but rolled over to face her, then kissed her passionately.

Rebecca felt a chill run up her spine as she slipped her hands behind his neck and added her own passion.

Gabe showed his willingness as he began to kiss her on her neck and then let his fingers touch her, aware that she may still be sore from the abuse she had been subjected to by Dave and Frank.

Rebecca felt the sharp stabs of pain when Gabe touched some spots, but didn't care because most of the time, his magic fingers excited her. She almost forgot to participate as she let him make her feel like a loved woman, not a piece of furniture.

It was only after he had her dress unbuttoned that she finally was so aroused that she became a full participant in the act of love.

The caboose was swaying and bouncing as they continued to explore each other, and soon all of their clothing was on the floor of the car, and Rebecca knew that soon, she would be the only woman that Gabe would ever love.

But even as she found herself so incredibly ready, Gabe persisted in driving her even closer to the edge of madness with his kisses and touches.

Gabe found so many bruises and welts on Rebecca's perfect body that it was difficult to find spots that were free from the marks of the beatings she had undergone, and it was the sympathy for those injuries and the background anger for the men that had caused them, that actually kept him from fulfilling Rebecca's almost constant demands that he take her.

Finally, Rebecca grabbed his face, kissed him roughly, then told him that his twenty minutes were up an hour ago, and made him understand that she would tolerate no more delays.

By then, Gabe's attention was completely on Rebecca, so he didn't need any added incentive.

So, as the train rolled along toward Bozeman, anyone standing near the tracks as the train passed would have heard loud screams from the caboose that drowned out the loud passing of the steel wheels on the steel rails, but no one was there except a gray squirrel who didn't care.

By the time the train pulled out of Bozeman, Gabe and Rebecca were still in the caboose and were still lying naked and sweaty on the bunk. Gabe had quickly hopped out of the cot to lock the caboose door before it stopped, so even as it had slowed to pull into the station, he had the opportunity to prove to Rebecca he hadn't exaggerated what he had told her that first night in Angela's house.

As she lay on Gabe's chest, Rebecca didn't undergo as dramatic a change as she had before. This time, it was a quieter realization that she had a future after all. She was going to marry Gabe, have his children and may already have one growing inside her. Every day of her life from now on would be filled with love and understanding.

Rebecca slid her hand across Gabe's chest and said simply, "Thank you, Gabe."

CHAPTER 10

Gabe and Rebecca were married in Brainard, Minnesota four days later. His parents were at the wedding and were ecstatic with Rebecca, even after he'd told them about everything that had happened to her but not divulging the one secret that he knew belonged only to her.

She had her monthly three days later which, despite Gabe's assurance that it didn't matter was a source of great relief to her.

He accepted the job of chief of security and he and Rebecca moved into his house in Minneapolis. He gave her carte blanche to make any changes, and she did.

On October 18th, they boarded a westbound train for Missoula to see her family. They'd sent telegrams and letters, but Rebecca wanted to see Sarah most of all. It had been Sarah who had convinced her to chase after Gabe, and Rebecca wanted her to see how happy she was because letters didn't do it justice.

———

When they stepped down on the platform, Gabe and Rebecca were greeted by the family and Eli showed them the new carriage he'd bought to transport the family even in the cold weather, which had already arrived.

When they were back at the house, Rebecca and Sarah went off to the kitchen to cook trailing Rachel, while Eli and

Gabe sat in the parlor and Aaron sat nearby as a member of the menfolk.

"How's the timber going, Eli?"

"Good. Good," he replied then glanced back at the kitchen and asked in a low voice, "Gabe, did Rebecca tell you about something that happened to her at the logging camp that involved the skills of one of the working girls?"

Gabe glanced at Aaron then replied, "Yes. She told me, Eli. It hurt her horribly and it was the reason she didn't want to see me when I left. Don't be too harsh in your judgement."

"No, I won't. I only asked because the woman who'd done it threatened to start telling the other men and wants me to give her a thousand dollars. She told Dave and he promised her five hundred dollars to keep it quiet until he married Rebecca. Then when he died, she waited to try and get double the money out of me. I don't know if I should give it to her. She said that she'll leave and go to Helena after I pay her, but what's to stop her from telling another girl or one of the men? I don't know how to deal with this kind of thing."

Gabe took in a deep breath then replied, "I do. What's her name?"

"Fannie."

"Okay, how long before dinner?"

"About an hour and a half."

"Okay, that's enough time. I'll take a quick ride out there and have a chat with Fannie."

"You aren't going to shoot her, are you?"

“No, sir. I’ll just have a talk with her.”

“Okay. Good luck,” he said as he and Gabe both stood.

Aaron stood as well then Eli walked closer to Gabe and whispered, “Don’t tell Rebecca yet, but she’s going to have another brother or sister in six months.”

Gabe grinned slapped Eli on the shoulder and said in a conspiratorial voice, “It’ll be our secret. At least until Sarah tells Rebecca.”

Eli was grinning in return when a feminine squeal sounded from the kitchen.

Gabe grabbed his hat and said, “I think the secret’s out.”

He gave Eli a wave then shook Aaron’s hand before leaving the house.

Forty-five minutes later, he was riding a tan gelding into the logging camp and could already see many of the improvements Eli had made as he rode past Bob’s house and wondered if it still had Rebecca’s and Angela’s clothes inside. He wasn’t about to bring them back with him as he was sure that Rebecca would just as soon burn them. Besides, she already had a very impressive wardrobe as she spent quite a bit of time exploring the many shops and stores in Minneapolis. He never denied her anything as many of the purchases were for his benefit.

He wasn’t exactly sure where the whore house was on the camp but it didn’t take a master detective to find it and soon dismounted and tied the gelding to the hitching post.

He hadn't set one foot on the porch when one of the girls popped out of the door, and 'popped out' was an apt description of her arrival.

"Well, hello," she said, "I haven't seen you before? Are you new here?"

"Yes and no, ma'am. I need to talk to Fannie."

"Are you sure? She's a bit busy right now, but I'd be more than happy to provide you with some entertainment."

"I appreciate the offer, ma'am, but I need to talk to Fannie."

"Talk?", she asked as she backed into the front room and Gabe entered.

"Talk," he replied, then asked, "where is she?"

"I told you, she's busy."

"Maybe I should have introduced myself, ma'am. My name is Gabe Owens."

"Oh!" she replied then began trying to cover up what had popped out.

"She's in the first room on the left."

Gabe tipped his hat, then walked into the hallway, heard moaning from the room then just yanked open the door and the man who was the source of the moaning, whipped his head to look at Gabe and was about to object when he found himself looking down the barrel of a Remington revolver.

"You can come back and visit Fannie in a few minutes, mister. I need to talk to her."

The man scrambled to pull up his britches with his right hand as he pulled on his hat, grabbed his heavy boots and waddled out of the room.

Fannie was glaring at Gabe as her naked breasts still heaved from her heavy breathing. She made no effort to cover up as Gabe closed the door and holstered his pistol.

He pulled a straight-backed chair near the bed and sat down.

“Who the hell are you to come in here and interrupt me?”

“The name is Gabe Owens.”

Fannie may not have been overly concerned with her semi-nakedness, but she instantly knew why he was there. Everyone in the camp knew that he had married Eli Ulrich’s daughter and taken her away to Minneapolis, but she didn’t think he or Rebecca would be coming back.

Gabe could see the shock in her eyes and knew this wouldn’t be a difficult discussion.

“Now, Fannie, Eli told me that you’re trying to blackmail him by threatening to start spreading the story about what you did to my wife a few months ago. Don’t go trying to lie about it either. What I want you to do is to remember the roughest time you’ve ever had with one of your customers. It was probably with Dave Horowitz now that I think about it. Was he as bad as Frank Stanford, Fannie?”

She may have been worried but she wasn’t about to be intimidated or at least she didn’t believe she could be.

“No, Frank was worse. He broke my hand once. Dave was almost as bad, but I’m a tough whore and I can deal with it.

You can't scare me, Owens. I heard all about how you didn't even take advantage of that old girlfriend of yours. You aren't gonna lay a hand on me, and you know it."

"No, Fannie. You're right. I won't lay a hand on you, but I don't have to. You see, Fannie, I'm the head of security for the Northern Pacific Railroad now. I have eighteen agents working for me, and I'll be honest with you, I have two that I'm getting ready to fire because they're too thuggish. One of them, named Stan Harriman, beat up a whore down in Glendale so badly that she had to quit the business because she was so hideous. Do you want me to describe her injuries?"

Fannie absent-mindedly ran her fingers across her cheek and croaked, "No."

"Now I'd just as soon let you do your work and stay being the pretty, well-endowed young woman you are, but if I find out that you so much as say my wife's name to anyone then you'll be visited by Stan in a few days, and don't think you can run either. You see, most of the men that cut down the trees around here seem to believe I did them all a favor by killing Bob Johnson and Frank Stanford. By the way, did you know that I shot Bob from twelve hundred yards? Anyway, Fannie, do you understand what I'm telling you?"

She nodded but kept her terrified eyes on Gabe's calm face with his cold eyes boring into her.

"Good. Then I'll let you go back to work," he said as he stood took one more appreciative glance at Fannie then turned opened the door and left the room.

As he left the hallway there were four other women watching him.

“Good afternoon, ladies,” he said with a smile before he tipped his hat and left the bordello.

After he’d gone, Fannie stood then had to change anyway and would have to change her mattress too. It had that acrid smell of urine which would surely kill the mood of her next client.

Gabe returned to the house an hour later after unsaddling the gelding. As soon as he entered, he caught Eli’s eye then winked and took off his hat.

Rebecca heard him enter and trotted down the hallway saw Gabe and broke into her usual welcoming smile.

“Did you hear the news? Sarah is going to have a baby!”

He smiled back as he walked to his wife pulled her into his arms kissed her then said, “Yes, ma’am. I heard your squeal of delight as I was leaving.”

They turned to go to the kitchen, arms tight around their waists as they followed Eli and Aaron down the hall.

“Where did you go? Eli said you were looking into a problem he had.”

“I was. I rode out to the logging camp and took care of it. What’s for dinner? It smells really good.”

“We’re having brisket and Sarah added a sweet and sour sauce that you’ll really enjoy, too.”

They entered the kitchen and Gabe released Rebecca long enough to hug Sarah and congratulate her on the surprising news.

Then for the first time that he recall he heard Rachel's voice as she said loudly, "My mama is gonna be a mama!"

Sarah beamed at Rachel and said, "Yes, I am."

It was a joyful meal and Rebecca told her family how wonderful it was in Minneapolis and how perfect her marriage was. Gabe went to the office in the morning and came home in the evening. No one shot at him and he didn't have to shoot at anyone else either.

It wasn't until the cleanup before Eli could get Gabe alone to ask him about his meeting. Gabe didn't hold back anything, including the impressive view he had of Fannie as she sat on the bed although he did add that the bed itself suffered from his visit just not in the usual fashion.

"So, you think she'll really leave me alone and still keep quiet?"

"I don't doubt it for a second. Her choices were either that she keeps enjoying the relatively safe and profitable job she has now, or she gabs and has to worry about being paid a visit by a special agent. He's dead of course but not too many people in this part of the country knew his name. I just needed a name off the top of my head when I was threatening her. You tell a pretty woman that she's going to be disfigured, it's about the same as telling a man he's going to be castrated. As long as they believe it then they'll behave themselves."

"Thanks, Gabe. She had me worried because she felt she was safe now because I'm not like Bob Johnson or Frank Stanford."

"Who is? There aren't nearly as many of them as there are of us, Eli."

"Sometimes, I wonder, Gabe."

After the dinner dishes were all cleaned and put away the family adjourned to the main room where they had coffee and continued their dinner conversation.

Rebecca suspected that Gabe's ride out to the logging camp to solve a problem for her father involved her and couldn't wait to get him alone in their bed to ask him. The new house was completed and up until now had only been used a couple of times by Eli and Sarah. They preferred living in their old house but would probably move into the newer construction soon because of its better insulation.

"Are you going to see Angela tomorrow?" asked Sarah.

"Are they living in her house now?" Gabe asked.

"Oh, yes. She married the sheriff just eight days after you left. I guess she realized she couldn't compete with our Rebecca," Sarah replied as she smiled at Rebecca.

Gabe glanced at his wife and said, "No woman ever could come close. No offense, Sarah."

"Oh, trust me, I'm not offended one bit."

Then Gabe turned and looked at Rebecca and slowly shook his right index finger, "But there was one woman who would be close, now that I think about it. She came close to winning my heart."

Rebecca was surprised because the only other woman he'd mentioned that had been close was Angela.

"Who is she? Does she live in Minneapolis?" Rebecca asked.

“No, she lives in Missoula. You probably even met her. She’s even told me that she wanted me in her bed.”

“She did?” asked an astonished Rebecca.

“Yes, and maybe I’ll introduce you tomorrow when we go and see Angela. Her name is Mildred Honeysuckle and she’s quite a woman.”

“*Mildred?*” Sarah asked before she burst out laughing accompanied by a similar reaction from Eli.

Rebecca had no idea why they were laughing until she looked at her husband’s face and he said, “She’s eight-one and a busybody of the first order.”

Rebecca began to laugh then leaned over and kissed Gabe before asking, “Can you tell us the story of how you met Miss Honeysuckle?”

Gabe spent another ten minutes describing his two meetings with the octogenarian gossip and Rebecca knew she’d have to meet her tomorrow.

An hour later, Gabe and Rebecca took their bags and left the small house to walk to the bigger house next door then didn’t waste any time as Gabe had her in his arms ten seconds after the door closed.

They didn’t bother lighting any lamps as they made love on the thick carpet in the parlor and when they finished less than an hour later, they discovered their short sightedness in not lighting fires in any of the six heat stoves or the two fireplaces in the house.

So, while Rebecca tiptoed with her travel bag into the bedroom to put on one of her flannel nightdresses and get under the blankets, Gabe trotted around the house in his birthday suit, lighting three of the heat stoves. He then grabbed his travel bag and scooted into the bedroom, dropped his bag on the floor, threw back the blankets and quilts and hopped into bed.

Rebecca shrieked and shouted, “Your feet are freezing!”

Gabe laughed and pulled her close but not for her heat and said, “You should feel the rest of me.”

She snuggled in closer and said, “Maybe I will in a few minutes, but not until you tell me why you had to go out to the logging camp. It was because of what happened to me, wasn’t it?”

“Yes, it was. I had to go and visit Fannie.”

Rebecca felt her stomach flip as she asked, “Why?”

“Eli told me that she was blackmailing him and threatening to tell people about taking your baby. She wanted a thousand dollars, but he was rightfully concerned that giving her the money wouldn’t necessarily keep her from doing it anyway.”

“So, my father knew?”

“Yes, and I’m sure that Sarah knew too, but you didn’t see any difference in the way they treated you, did you?”

“No, I didn’t. They really are good people, Gabe.”

“They are and so are you, my love.”

“So, what happened when you found her.”

Gabe then proceeded to tell Rebecca exactly what he had told Eli not glossing over any details including the display that he appreciated when talking to her. When he finished, Rebecca knew that Fannie wouldn't dare to say a word.

But he really hadn't told all of the story until he could feel her relax and knew that she had no worries about Fannie or anyone else.

"I did leave out one thing, Rebecca?"

She just rolled slightly closer and looked into his eyes as he told her.

Rebecca erupted in laughter as she hugged Gabe then exclaimed, "*She peed on herself?* How perfect!"

Gabe then slid her onto his chest until he could look into her laughing eyes.

"Now, Mrs. Owens, I expect you to keep your promise and feel the rest of me, because I intend to feel all of you."

Rebecca kissed him and kept her promise.

The next day, there was snow on the ground as Gabe bundled Rebecca into the buggy and set the black mare away from the nice, warm house and headed for Missoula.

They rolled into the drive of what was now the Collier home and Gabe pulled the buggy to a stop near the back porch and then trotted around the front, slipping and sliding in his haste to help Rebecca from the buggy then once she was walking, they supported each other in the wet snow as they stepped up onto the porch.

Before Gabe could knock, the door flew open and Angela smiled and said, “Get in here where it’s warm.”

They both entered stomped the snow from their boots and then began removing hats, scarves and coats.

“You know, it’s not even that cold yet,” Gabe said.

“Maybe not, but that damp air sure makes it seem cold,” Rebecca said as she draped her scarf over a peg.

“So, welcome back,” Angela said as she poured coffee into three cups.

“Where’s Rafe? He knew we were coming, didn’t he?” asked Gabe.

“He’ll be back in a few minutes, I think. The new deputy arrested the mayor’s son for saying something inappropriate to a young lady, and he’s smoothing ruffled feathers.”

Gabe took a cup and handed it to Rebecca before saying, “Horrors! Hang the young bastard!”

Angela and Rebecca laughed as they all took seats at the table.

“How have you been Rebecca? Enjoying Minneapolis?”

“I’m fine and I love the city.”

“I’m actually happy here, now. With those two unnamed bastards dead, things are much more peaceful.”

“I thought they might be. Did you hear the news? Sarah is going to be a mother again!”

Angela smiled and replied, “Now how’s that for a coincidence? I’m expecting too, and Rafe is delighted.”

“Well, congratulations to you both, Angela,” Gabe said then stood and took one step outside the table and kissed her on the cheek.

“And just to let you know, he confessed to me that he was born Ralph and it was you who convinced him to say it was Raphael.”

“Well, you have to admit, Angela, the whole destiny idea you came up with was pretty spooky.”

“I’ll admit it now that I’m not so obsessed with you. I was looking for any excuse to win you back, and I should have known I was going to lose to Rebecca. But let me ask you, is your name really just Gabe, or was that part of the whole Gabriel-Raphael scheme.”

“No, that really is my name. I can always show you on our marriage license.”

Rebecca smiled at him and was about to say something when the front door opened and closed as Angela shouted, “Rafe, Gabe and Rebecca are in here.”

Rafe arrived a few seconds later pulled off his hat and shook hands with Gabe before he began removing his jacket and Gabe congratulated him on his pending fatherhood.

Once Rafe was there the conversation commenced touching all of the changes that had happened in their lives since Gabe and Rebecca had gone to Minneapolis.

Most of it had been passed with a succession of letters between Angela and Rebecca, who had become almost like sisters after having shared the same horrible experiences at the logging camp and been both rescued by the tall man at the table. They had also shared him in a way that no other woman would ever be able to claim and even as they all chatted at the table, Angela would occasionally glance at Gabe and recall those two incredible nights. She loved Rafe, and he pleased her in the bedroom, but she shivered when she remembered her times with Gabe.

Rebecca never got to meet Mrs. Honeysuckle because after Gabe asked about her, Rafe told them she'd died just three weeks earlier when Mildred had been listening behind a door that was suddenly opened and knocked her off the porch. Gabe thought it was a suitable way for her to pass to the great beyond and was sure she was regaling her fellow spirits with the story of how she'd left the mortal life.

It was almost two hours later when Gabe helped his bundled wife back into the buggy. The snow was melted but the ground was still slippery with mud as he pulled away from the house and soon reached the wet, cobbled street.

Once they were underway, Rebecca asked, "Gabe, do you think that Rafe is the father of Angela's baby?"

"I'm not sure, and if he's as good a man as I think he is, he'll never question the possibility it could be either Bob's or Mike's. As long as they're happy, that's all that matters."

"That's what I think, too," she said, then added, "I hope that Angela can be as happy as I am, but I'm not sure if that's possible."

Rebecca was huddled close to Gabe under the blanket as they rolled along and was completely content with her life. She'd finally come to terms with what she had done and failed to do in the past year, just as Gabe had told her she would.

Time and his love had pushed her demons far enough away that she knew that they'd never return. That, and something else; the secret she hadn't told him yet.

And as the buggy rolled west, Rebecca took Gabe's free hand and placed it softly on her stomach. Gabe kept his eyes to the west as he straightened his fingers and let it rest there, knowing that their child was sleeping inside his loving wife.

EPILOGUE

Late the following spring, as life began to return to the cold north, it started to arrive in the three homes.

Angela's baby was delivered first, when she had a boy on April 27th and named him Ralph James. He had Angela's blonde hair and blue eyes, and even though he would most likely lose the blonde hair, Gabe imagined it was a relief to blue-eyed Rafe.

Sarah had her daughter, Esther Ruth on May 9th, and Eli sent photographs of mother and daughter to Minneapolis.

But before they arrived, Rebecca gave birth to a baby boy. The name presented a bit of a problem even before he was born because Gabe had wanted to name his son, if he ever had one, Michael. But after Mike Wheatley, he had to drop that one. Then the problem arose when he and Rebecca had been going through names and he discovered that almost all of them were names of men he'd either shot or arrested, including his father's.

The finally decided that they'd name him Eli George after both fathers, and he had to explain to his father, who was there when his son arrived why he took second billing. His father had laughed and accepted the decision graciously.

After his parents had returned to Brainard, Gabe was able to spend some time alone with Rebecca and their son.

They were in the nursery that Rebecca had converted from one of the three bedrooms and she was sitting in a softly upholstered chair with the baby suckling at her left breast.

Gabe sat on the chair beside her and just looked at her calm, smiling face as she gazed down at her baby. He didn't want to spoil this moment of complete contentment and tranquility, so he just watched his wife and son in silence.

Rebecca finally tore her eyes away from the miracle on her chest and looked into her husband's eyes and asked softly, "Gabe, could I have another, please?"

BOOK LIST

1	Rock Creek	12/26/2016
2	North of Denton	01/02/2017
3	Fort Selden	01/07/2017
4	Scotts Bluff	01/14/2017
5	South of Denver	01/22/2017
6	Miles City	01/28/2017
7	Hopewell	02/04/2017
8	Nueva Luz	02/12/2017
9	The Witch of Dakota	02/19/2017
10	Baker City	03/13/2017
11	The Gun Smith	03/21/2017
12	Gus	03/24/2017
13	Wilmore	04/06/2017
14	Mister Thor	04/20/2017
15	Nora	04/26/2017
16	Max	05/09/2017
17	Hunting Pearl	05/14/2017
18	Bessie	05/25/2017
19	The Last Four	05/29/2017
20	Zack	06/12/2017

21	Finding Bucky	06/21/2017
22	The Debt	06/30/2017
23	The Scalawags	07/11/2017
24	The Stampede	08/23/2019
25	The Wake of the Bertrand	07/31/2017
26	Cole	08/09/2017
27	Luke	09/05/2017
28	The Eclipse	09/21/2017
29	A.J. Smith	10/03/2017
30	Slow John	11/05/2017
31	The Second Star	11/15/2017
32	Tate	12/03/2017
33	Virgil's Herd	12/14/2017
34	Marsh's Valley	01/01/2018
35	Alex Paine	01/18/2018
36	Ben Gray	02/05/2018
37	War Adams	03/05/2018
38	Mac's Cabin	03/21/2018
39	Will Scott	04/13/2018
40	Sheriff Joe	04/22/2018
41	Chance	05/17/2018
42	Doc Holt	06/17/2018
43	Ted Shepard	07/16/2018
44	Haven	07/30/2018
45	Sam's County	08/19/2018
46	Matt Dunne	09/07/2018
47	Conn Jackson	10/06/2018
48	Gabe Owens	10/27/2018
49	Abandoned	11/18/2018
50	Retribution	12/21/2018
51	Inevitable	02/04/2019
52	Scandal in Topeka	03/18/2019
53	Return to Hardeman County	04/10/2019
54	Deception	06/02.2019
55	The Silver Widows	06/27/2019
56	Hitch	08/22/2018
57	Dylan's Journey	10/10/2019

58	Bryn's War	11/05/2019
59	Huw's Legacy	11/30/2019
60	Lynn's Search	12/24/2019
61	Bethan's Choice	02/12/2020
62	Rhody Jones	03/11/2020
63	Alwen's Dream	06/14/2020
64	The Nothing Man	06/30/2020
65	Cy Page	07/19/2020
66	Tabby Hayes	09/04/2020
67	Dylan's Memories	09/20/2020
68	Letter for Gene	09/09/2020
69	Grip Taylor	10/10/2020
70	Garrett's Duty	11/09/2020
71	East of the Cascades	12/02/2020
72	The Iron Wolfe	12/23/2020
73	Wade Rivers	01/09/2021
74	Ghost Train	01/27/2021
75	The Inheritance	02/26/2021
76	Cap Tyler	03/26/2021
77	The Photographer	04/10/2021
78	Jake	05/06/2021
79	Riding Shotgun	06/03/2021
80	The Saloon Lawyer	07/04/2021

Made in the USA
Las Vegas, NV
22 October 2022